The Judas Code

The Judas Code

by

DEREK LAMBERT

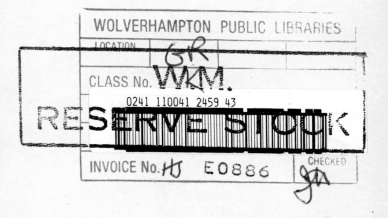

HAMISH HAMILTON
London

First published in Great Britain 1983
by Hamish Hamilton Ltd
Garden House 57-59 Long Acre London WC2E 9JZ

British Library Cataloguing in Publication Data

Lambert, Derek
  The Judas code.
  I. Title
  823'.914[F]   PR6062.A/

  ISBN 0-241-11004-1

Typeset by Saildean Phototypesetters Ltd
Printed and bound in Great Britain by
Richard Clay (The Chaucer Press) Ltd, Bungay, Suffolk

For Len and Dorothy Wellfare

Author's Note

It should not be forgotten that this is a novel. But nor should it be forgotten that it concerns an established and bewildering fact: that, despite all the evidence, Joseph Stalin refused to believe that Hitler intended to invade the Soviet Union in June 1941. If he had heeded the warnings – and there were many – two tyrannies might have remained relatively unscathed and the world today might have been a very different place. With such a momentous fact as the pivot of a novel it soon becomes easy to believe that the accompanying material is also true. Who knows, perhaps it is.

And what of Stalin? How was he reacting to the fact that almost the entire German army was on his doorstep? Incredibly, he appeared to ignore it. Was he the victim of some kind of hysteria that deprived him of the ability to act? Or were there other powerful reasons for not acting – reasons known only to him? – Russia Besieged by Nicholas Bethell and the editors of Time-Life Books

Despite all the indications that war with Germany was approaching neither the Soviet people nor the Red Army were expecting the German attack when it came … History of World War II, editor-in-chief A.J.P. Taylor

Never had a state been better informed than Russia about the aggressive intent of another … But never had an army been so ill-prepared to meet the initial onslaught of its enemy than the Red Army on June 22, 1941. The History of World War II, by Lt. Col. E. Bauer

It is almost inconceivable but nevertheless true that the men in the Kremlin, for all the reputation they had of being suspicious, crafty and hard-headed, and despite all the evidence and all the warnings that stared them in the face, did not realise right up to the last moment that they were to be hit, and with a force which would almost destroy their nation. – The Rise and Fall of the Third Reich, by William L. Shirer

Acknowledgements

My thanks for their invaluable help to Miss Jose Shercliffe, distinguished Lisbon correspondent of *The Times* for many years, and to Diamantino Fernandes da Silva, who appears in this narrative as telephone operator at the Hotel Avenida Palace during World War II and was at the time of writing head porter there. Any mistakes in background material are exclusively my property and not theirs.

Encoding

My advertisement in the personal columns of *The Times* read: 'Would anyone with the key to the Judas Code please contact me.' The response was prompt: at nine a.m. on the day of publication a man called at my London home and threatened to kill me.

The threat wasn't immediate but as soon as I saw him on the doorstep smiling and tapping a copy of the newspaper with one finger I sensed menace.

He was in his sixties with wings of silver hair just touching his ears and what looked like the scar from a bullet wound on his right cheek; he wore a light navy blue topcoat with a velvet collar and carried a furled umbrella; the elegance and the legacy of violence combined to give the impression of a commando who had retired to the City.

'Your request interested me', he said. 'May I come in?'

Wishing that I hadn't unlocked the ground-floor door by remote control and allowed him to reach my apartment on the top floor of the old block near Broadcasting House, I said: 'It is rather early. Perhaps—'

'Nine o'clock? You look pretty wide awake, Mr. Lamont, and I won't take up much of your time.' He took a step forward.

'Before we go any further, Mr. ...'

'Chambers.'

'Do you mind telling me how you found out where I live? I only gave a telephone number ...'

'It's not so difficult to obtain an address from a telephone number. If you know how to go about it, that is.'

'And my name?'

'The same source. Now if you would be good enough ...'

'To step aside? I don't think I would, Mr. Chambers. Perhaps you would be good enough to telephone me to make an appointment.'

'Aren't you being a little formal for someone as obviously enterprising as yourself?' He tucked *The Times* beneath his arm on his umbrella side.

'I've always been a stickler for protocol.'

'Really? You surprise me. I had heard quite the opposite.' His voice frosted. 'Let me in, Mr. Lamont.'

3

'Get stuffed,' I said, terminating my brief relationship with protocol.

He, too, abandoned niceties. He levelled a Browning 9mm automatic at my chest and said: 'Don't try slamming the door. It's only in Hollywood that wood panels stop bullets. Now turn round and go inside.' The door clicked snugly behind me. 'That's better,' he said as we entered the living-room. 'Now sit down in that easy chair beside the fireplace.'

I sat down, feeling slightly absurd in my red silk dressing gown, rumpled blue pyjamas and leather slippers savaged by a friend's dog, and waited. Chambers sat opposite me and appraised the room – the books scattered across the worn carpet, bottle of Black Label and its partner, an empty glass, punished leather sofa, windows looking across the rooftops to the pale green trees of Regent's Park. In short, fading elegance; in fact, the workshop of an author who commuted to a house in Surrey where his wife and children lived.

Having completed his inventory, Chambers waved the gun and said: 'Do I really have to go on pointing this at you? I know I'm much older than you. Forty-five aren't you?' – I was forty-four – 'But I think I'd get the better of you in physical combat, and I'm not just being conceited.'

He could well have been right. Anyway I told him to put down his gun and tell me what he wanted. There was always the possibility that I might be able to surprise him later.

He stood up and slipped off the topcoat. Underneath he wore a charcoal grey pin-stripe with a waistcoat and a gold watch-chain with a seal fob looped across it. He slipped the Browning inside the jacket without spoiling its shape and sat down again. 'And now,' he said pleasantly, 'tell me why you want to know about the Judas Code,' one finger straying to his cheek; the bullet must have taken a lot of bone with it because the scar was almost a furrow.

'You must have guessed that – I'm writing a book.'

'The Judas Code ... a good title. Why did you choose it?'

'I didn't: it was unavoidable. Kept cropping up while I was researching a book about the last war. I wanted to know why Stalin ignored all the warnings that Germany intended to invade Russia in 1941.'

'That's simple. The warnings came from Churchill and Roosevelt and other interested parties and he interpreted them

4

as mischief-making. Most accounts of World War II have made that quite clear.'

'But it doesn't wash, does it? He also ignored warnings from his own spies. Richard Sorge in Tokyo, for instance. And the evidence before his own generals' eyes – the build-up of the German army on his borders.'

'And why are you, a novelist, so anxious to put the record straight?'

'Three reasons. One, because I abhor flawed logic. Any history student who suggested in an exam that Uncle Joe misread Hitler's intentions just because he thought the Allies were deceiving him would deserve to get C minus.

'Two, because if Stalin had got it right then you'd have to re-draw today's maps of the world. If, for instance, Germany and Russia had persevered with their unholy alliance, if their armies hadn't bled each other for more than three years, then Britain might be a Nazi or a Soviet satellite.'

Chambers took a silver cigarette case from the inside pocket of his jacket, on the other side from the Browning. He didn't offer it to me – perhaps he even knew I'd given up smoking – and selected a cigarette. He lit it with a gold Dunhill lighter and inhaled with pleasure. A true smoker, not a chain-smoker. 'And the third?'

'Because it's my guess that the real reasons behind Stalin's apparent stupidity will make a better story than any novel I've written.'

'I see.' He blew a jet of smoke into a shaft of dusty sunlight. 'Yes, I can see that.' His voice had assumed an introspective quality and I wondered if I could jump him. I had never been an athlete, let alone a fighter, but I was big enough and fairly fit. He said crisply: 'Don't try it,' followed by: 'But you haven't explained about the Judas Code.'

'Why don't you explain it? It seems to have worried the hell out of you.'

'Because I have the gun,' slipping his hand inside his jacket.

I told him.

To try and plug the gap in appraisals of World War II caused by Stalin's apparent aberration I had travelled all over Europe winkling out people who might once have had access to secret information that could explain it. Spies in other words; among them former members of Britain's XX Committee, various branches of America's OSS, Germany's RSHA VI (foreign intelligence) and *Abwehr* and the Soviet Union's two European espionage organisations known as the Red Orchestra and the Lucy Ring.

Predictably, most of the agents denied that they had ever been spies. Who wants to admit to a furtive past if he is currently a burgormaster or the chairman of a bank? But a few, mostly the very old whose cloaks of secrecy were now in tatters, did agree that the history books should be rewritten. Watching their reactions to my questions was like peering into coffins and seeing corpses momentarily resuscitated. From each coffin came a dusty whisper: 'The Judas Code.' No more. Ageing reflexes belatedly recognised indiscretion, coffin lids snapped back into place.

Chambers seemed to relax, relieved, I guessed, that I appeared to know nothing more. 'If I were you,' he said, 'I should forget all about it.' He crossed his legs, revealing black silk socks.

'Why? It was important enough to bring you round here like a dog after a bitch on heat.'

'There are some secrets that are best left undisturbed. For everyone's sake.'

'You would have to be more explicit than that to convince me.'

He was about to reply when the phone on the coffee table between us rang, as intrusive as a fire alarm. I reached for the receiver but Chambers beat me to it.

He gave the telephone number, paused and said: 'Yes, I inserted the advertisement. Can you help me?'

As I tried to snatch the receiver Chambers backed away and, with a pickpocket's agility, plucked the Browning from his pocket and aimed the barrel between my eyes.

' ... Yes, my name is Lamont. Can we meet somewhere? ... Very well, midday ... Yes, I'll explain then ... Thank you for calling ...'

'So where are *we* meeting?' I asked as he sat down again.

'You are not meeting anyone.'

'Are you in the habit of impersonating people?'

'Not recently. In the past, well yes, it has been known.' He handled the gun with love, then asked: 'Do you have a price?'

'They say everyone does.'

'What's yours?'

'A niche at the top of the best-seller list.'

'Alas the one bribe I can't offer you because if *The Judas*

6

Code achieved that distinction it would negate everything I have set out to achieve.'

'Which is?'

'To persuade you to abandon your inquiries.'

'And why would you want to do that?'

'I can't tell you that. Would £10,000 persuade you that I had good reasons?'

I shook my head.

'Twenty thousand?'

'I'm going to write the book.'

He stubbed out his cigarette fastidiously, making sure he didn't soil his fingers with tar, and stared at me without speaking. In the hall the grandfather clock chimed 9. 30; a pigeon on the windowsill pecked at the glass; I became aware of the hum of the traffic far below.

Finally he said: 'If you continue to follow this up I shall kill you.'

He took a gold hunter from his waistcoat pocket and consulted it as though shortly he had another appointment to threaten someone with death.

'I'm going to call the police,' I said.

'Please do so,' he said. 'But have the courtesy to wait till I've gone.' He stood up, walked to the window and gazed at the dignified streets below. 'You have a wife and three children, I believe?'

'You keep them out of this!'

'Don't worry, I won't touch them. But they're very fond of you, aren't they? Would it be fair to deprive your wife of a husband, your children of a father? Because, please believe me, Mr Lamont, I mean what I say. Try and crack the Judas Code and you're a dead man.'

Throat pulsing, the pigeon backed away along the window-sill.

Perhaps I should have said: 'I don't scare that easily,' but it wouldn't have been the truth. Instead I said: 'All right, you've had your say, now get out.'

He shrugged, buttoned his overcoat, walked to the door, said: 'Please be sensible,' and was gone.

I considered calling the police but even if they traced my visitor – I doubted whether his name was Chambers but he couldn't escape the scar – he would merely deny everything.

As I was making a cup of instant coffee in the kitchen the phone rang again.

A man's voice: 'If you want to meet Judas go to the lion house at the Zoo at eleven this morning. Be carrying a copy of—'

'*The Times?*'

'The *Telegraph*. And appear to be making some notes.' Click as he cut the connection.

So I had more than an hour. I shaved and dressed in a blue lightweight and took the antiquated lift to the ground floor where the porter, Mr. Atkins – I had never known his first name – had stood guard ever since I had come to the musty old block ten years ago. He was as permanent as the stone horsemen on the portals and just as worn.

'Good morning, Mr. Atkins.'

'Good morning, Mr. Lamont. Fair to middling this morning.'

I don't think he ever left the hallway because the weather was 'fair to middling' even if a blizzard was raging outside.

I walked up Portland Place towards Regent's Park. An April shower had washed the street, the sun was warm, pretty girls had blossomed overnight. A chic woman in grey waited patiently while her poodle watered a lamp-post; a man in a bowler-hat carrying a briefcase danced down a flight of steps; a nun smiled shyly from beneath her halo; an airliner chalked a white line across the blue sky.

Faced by all this, Chambers' lingering menace dissolved; the gun probably hadn't been loaded anyway.

I crossed Marylebone Road and the Outer Circle, Nash terraces behind me benign in the sunlight, and walked down the Broad Walk between the chestnut trees.

Nursemaids were abroad with prams and for a moment I imagined them steering them towards clandestine meetings with red-coated soldiers.

And that scar—he had probably fallen on to the railings at school.

Inside the lion house my mood changed. The big cats hopelessly padding up and down their cages, their prison smelling like sour beer. I displayed the *Telegraph*, took out a notebook and began to make notes. *Lions watching the spectators brought there for their delectation ...*

The young man in the fawn raincoat said: 'I'm afraid you

8

won't meet Judas here.' His voice and dress were irrefutably English but there was a Slavonic cast to his features; he had grey, questing eyes and was, I guessed, in his late twenties. 'You see you've been followed.'

My earlier optimism was routed. A lion bared yellow teeth behind its bars; captivity tightened around me.

'Who are you?'

'That doesn't matter. Just an intermediary. We had to do it this way otherwise ... ' He shrugged. ' ... you would never have got your story.'

'How did you know I wanted a story?'

Without answering, he took my arm. 'Let's get out of here, I can't stand jails. But before you go take a look at the man in the sports jacket with the patched elbows looking at the tigers.'

Casually I glanced towards the tiger cage. The man in question seemed absorbed with the occupant; he was squat, balding, powerfully built, about the same age as Chambers.

We left the cats dreaming about wide open spaces and returned to the sunlight.

'And now,' he said as we walked past a polar bear sunning itself beside its pool, 'I have another assignation for you. But first you'll have to shake off your tail and make sure that he hasn't got a back-up.'

I stopped and gazed at the bear, glancing at the same time to my right. The man in the sports jacket was standing about seventy-five yards away consulting a hardbook.

We walked on. 'One more word of advice,' he said, 'don't use your telephone on Judas business – it's bound to be bugged. That wasn't you who answered the phone the first time, was it?'

'It was a man who says his name is Chambers.'

'We thought as much. It was he who hired the private detective who's following us.'

'Do you mind telling me what this is all about?'

'I can't; Judas can.'

'And when am I going to meet Judas?'

'Soon. But, first of all, do you mind telling me just how you intend to use any information you might get hold of?'

'Write a book. You seemed to know that.'

'We've known about you for a long time, Mr. Lamont. Ever since you started making inquiries. We've checked you out and you seem to be an author of integrity ...'

'Don't forget I write novels. In my particular field it pays to be sensational.'

'At least you're being honest. That's what I want to establish – before you meet Judas – that your book will be honest.'

'I can give you this assurance: I want to write a book that puts the record straight about the second world war. Our civilisation is shaky enough without being saddled with false premises. There was, for instance, no way Britain could have stood alone in 1940-41 unless something occurred behind the scenes that we know nothing about. The Battle of Britain was a famous victory but it wasn't sufficient to deter Hitler from calling off the invasion. There was something more behind that decision, just as there was something more behind Stalin's refusal to believe that Germany was going to attack Russia. Stalin, after all, was a very wily Georgian ...'

'And you'll stick to the truth? If, that is, you believe what you're told?'

'As I said, I'm a novelist. I may use the fictional form to mould the facts into a digestible composition. But, yes, I'll stick to what I learn. If and when I learn it.'

A flock of schoolchildren shepherded by a harassed woman in brogues passed by, watched from aloft by a giraffe. I turned, ostensibly to watch the children, and spotted the man in the sports jacket.

The young man seemed to accept my assurance. He glanced at his wristwatch. 'I wonder,' he said, slowing down as though he was about to break away, 'if you realise just what you're getting into.'

'When you're forced into your own flat at gunpoint you get the general idea.'

'He wasn't play-acting, you know.'

'The gun didn't look like a prop.'

'Well, so long as you understand ...'

I said impatiently: 'Where can I meet Judas, for God's sake?'

'It's 11.30 now. At Madame Tussaud's in one hour.'

'Where at Madame Tussaud's?'

'Beside the figure of Winston Churchill.' Where else? his tone seemed to say. 'Good luck, I'll take care of our friend. But it will only be a temporary measure, so take care.'

He turned abruptly and hurried away – straight into the man in the sports jacket. The man fell. I raced past a line of cages and, while the two men untangled themselves, took refuge in Lord Snowdon's aviary, watched incuriously by a blue and red parrot. There was no sign of the man in the sports jacket.

I emerged cautiously from the aviary and, leaving the jungle squawks behind, made my way to the zoo's exit. At Camden Town I took an underground train to King's Cross on the Northern Line and changed on to the Circle Line, alighting at Baker Street.

At 12.25 I entered Madame Tussaud's Waxwork Exhibition and made my way into the Grand Hall on the ground floor. Churchill, hands clasping the lapels of his suit, chin thrust out belligerently above his bow tie, seemed about to speak. To offer, perhaps, nothing but 'blood, toil, tears and sweat'.

It was exactly 12.30. The voice behind me said: 'He could tell the story much better than I can. But I'm afraid you'll have to put up with me.'

I turned and came face to face with Judas.

Part One

Chapter One

July 11, 1938. A wondrous Sunday in Moscow with memories of winter past and prospects of winter to come melted by the sun. The golden cupolas of the Kremlin floated in a cloudless sky, crowds queued for *kvas* and icecream and in Gorky Park the air smelled of carnations.

In a forest behind a river beach thirty miles outside the city a blond young man who would one day be asked to take part in the most awesome conspiracy of modern times was courting a black-haired beauty named Anna Petrovna.

If anyone had hinted about his future role to Viktor Golovin he would have dismissed them as a madman. And abruptly at that because it was his nineteenth birthday and he hoped to celebrate it by making love for the first time in his life.

It was a daunting prospect. In the first place he feared his inexperience might be ridiculed; in the second, being a serious young man – his solemn demeanour made the laughter that occasionally transfigured his features into an explosion – he believed that the act of love should involve more than casual pleasure. It should, he reasoned, be a seal of permanency. But did he truly desire permanency with Anna Petrovna? And if he didn't wasn't he betraying his beliefs?

Standing under a silver birch where coins of light shifted restlessly on the thin grass he bent and kissed her on the lips and gazed into her eyes, seeking answers. She stared boldly back and gave none. He slipped his arm round her waist and they walked deeper into the forest.

The trouble was that although he loved her there were aspects of her character that angered him. Not only was she supremely self-confident, as any girl desired by half the male students at Moscow University was entitled to be, but she was politically assertive, and dangerously so. She believed that Joseph Stalin had made a travesty of Marxist-Leninism and

15

she wasn't afraid to say so. But surely love should transcend such considerations.

He glanced down at her; she was small but voluptuously shaped with full breasts that he had caressed for the first time two nights ago, and there was a trace of the gypsy in her, an impression heightened today by her red skirt and white blouse. She was three months older than him and unquestionably far more experienced.

She smiled at him and said: 'You're looking very serious, Viktor Golovin. Let's sit down for a while and I'll see if I can make you smile.'

She tickled his lips with a blade of grass as he lay back, hands behind his head, and tried not to smile. He could feel the warmth of her body and see the swell of her breasts.

Finally he grinned.

'That smile,' she said, 'is your key.'

'To what?'

'To anything you want.'

She unbuttoned his white, open-neck shirt 'to let the fresh air get to you', and he wondered if her previous words were an invitation and whether he should accept in view of his misgivings about her character, but when she kissed him ... such a knowing kiss ... and when he felt the pressure of her thighs on his and heard her sigh his principles fled.

He lost his virginity with surprising ease. None of the fumbling and misdirected endeavour that he had feared. And, at the time, such was his need that it didn't occur to him that his accomplishment owed not a little to her expertise.

She helped him with his clothes. She lay back, skirt hitched to her hips, legs spread, breasts free. She touched him, stroked him, guided him. And when he was inside her, marvelling that at last it had happened, wondering at the oiled ease of it all, she regulated their movements. 'Gently ... stop a moment ... harder, faster ... now, now ... '

For a while they didn't speak. Then, when he had taken a bottle of Narzan mineral water from his knapsack and they were sipping it from cardboard cups, she said: 'It was the first time for you, wasn't it?'

As though it implied retarded development. But he had refused to conform with the sexual boasting of the students obsessed with masculinity. If they were to be believed they coupled every night, fuelled on lethal quantities of vodka.

'Yes,' he said, 'it was. Should I be ashamed?'

'Ashamed? Why should you be ashamed? You're young.'

So was she and for a moment the obvious question about her experience hovered between them; but he knew the answer and then, in her way, she answered it: 'At our age a girl is much older than a boy.' She stroked his hair. 'You're very attractive, Viktor, you're not … not so obvious as the others.'

'You mean I'm insignificant?'

'Far from it. You're tall and you're slim and your eyes always seem to be searching for the truth. I think you're going to have terrible trouble with your conscience in the future.'

He grinned at her. 'I didn't just now.'

'It's a pity that politically you're such a conformist.'

Here we go, he thought and said: 'What's so wrong with that? I'm only conforming to communism, the beliefs that have rescued our country from tyranny.'

'Rescued it? Twenty years ago perhaps. But now we've got a tyranny far worse than anything the Tsars ever dreamed up.'

'Watch that tongue of yours, Anna, or it will lead you to Siberia.'

Triumphantly she exclaimed: 'You see, you're proving my point. What sort of a country is it when you can't say what you believe?'

'A better country than Germany,' Viktor said quickly, annoyed with himself for having given her ammunition. 'At least it's not a crime here for a Jew to observe the Sabbath.'

'Anyone with a weak argument always resorts to comparisons.' She stood up and smoothed her skirt. 'You must have heard about the purges …'

Of course he'd heard the stories. But he didn't believe them. Iconoclasm was a permanent resident of student society. He preferred to believe the evidence around him that Lenin, and now Stalin, had helped Mother Russia to rise from her knees and given her self-respect. Not that he believed that the Revolution had been quite as heroic as the historians would have you believe – that was for children and none the worse because of it; but he did believe in equality. He knew older people who had once lived on potato skins, black bread and tea.

'They say he's quite mad you know.' She began to walk back towards the beach.

'Who's mad?' picking up his knapsack and following her.

'Joseph Vissarionovich Djugashvili, better known as Stalin.'

17

'They also say that genius is akin to madness.'

'A psychopath.'

'One of those words created to disguise our ignorance of the human condition.'

How pompous we students can be, he reflected.

Through the birch trees he could see a glint of water and, faintly, he could hear the babble from the beach and the tattoo of ping-pong balls on the tables beside the sand.

'I wonder,' Anna said, 'just what it would take to convince you.' She kicked a heap of old brown leaves and her red skirt swirled. 'Blood?'

'Why do you talk treason all the time? Why can't you enjoy the benefits the system has brought us?'

'It has certainly brought you benefits, Viktor Golovin.'

'And what's that supposed to mean?'

But he knew. For an orphan he had enjoyed a protected upbringing; and for no apparent reason his foster parents seemed to have rather more than their share of communal benefits. An apartment near the University on the crest of the Lenin Hills, a small dacha in the village of Peredelkino where the writers lived. Not bad for a librarian and his wife.

'Your privileges are your cross.'

Would she always be like this after making love? 'I've been lucky, I admit.'

'It must be difficult to hold forth about equality when you've had such luck.'

'Luck! Everyone has a share of it. The trick is knowing what to do with it when you get it.'

'Nonsense. Not everyone has luck. It isn't lucky to be an army officer these days.'

'Ah, the purges again.'

'Purges, a euphemism. Massacres is a better word.'

They emerged from the green depths of the forest into bright light. Beyond the table-tennis players and the fretted-wood restaurant where you could buy beer, *kvas* and fizzy cherryade, pies and cold meats, the beach was packed with Muscovites unfolding in the sun. They shed their clothes, they shed the moods of winter. Flesh burned bright pink but no one seemed to care. Rounding a curve in the river came a white steamboat nosing aside the calm water.

The doubts that had reached Viktor in the forest dissolved. Ordinary people wouldn't have been able to enjoy themselves like this before 1917. Possessively, Viktor, lover and philosopher, took Anna's arm.

'But do you?' She must have been talking while he savoured the fruits of socialism. Impatiently, she said: 'You haven't been listening, have you?'

'I don't want to hear anything more about purges.'

She pulled her arm away. 'Of course you don't. You don't want anything to interfere with your beautiful, cossetted life. Least of all truth.'

'I don't believe it is the truth.' Her attitude nettled him. 'Let's go and have a beer.'

They sat at a scrubbed wooden table and drank beer from fluted brown bottles. Around them families ate picnic lunches and guzzled; in one corner a plump mother was feeding a baby at the breast.

'I was asking,' she said, 'when you weren't listening, that is, whether you would like to see proof of what I've been saying.'

'If it will please you.'

'Please me!' She leaned fiercely across the table. 'It certainly won't please me. But it will give me a certain satisfaction to see that smug expression wiped off your face.'

'Not so long ago my eyes were always searching for the truth …'

'In everything except politics.'

'What you're alleging is more than political.'

'I can't understand how you're so blind. Everyone knows that Stalin is killing off all his enemies, real and imagined. They say the army is powerless now because he's murdered all the generals.'

Some of the men and women sharing the long table were looking curiously at them. 'Keep your voice down,' Viktor whispered, covering her hand with his to soften the words, knowing that any moment now she would accuse him of cowardice.

'I will for your sake,' which was the same thing. 'We don't want you thrown into Lubyanka, do we?'

A man with a walrus moustache who was peeling an orange pointed his knife at them and said: 'Cell 28. I spent three years there. Give my love to the rats.'

Viktor said: 'You see, everyone can hear you even when you lower your voice.' He felt faintly ashamed of his caution; but really there was no need to: if she had been speaking the truth then, yes, he would have sided with her.

19

'Am I to speak in whispers all my life?'

He thought: Yes, if I'm to share my life with you. But the possibility was becoming less attractive by the minute; he seemed to have expended a lot of ideals with his sexual passion.

The man with the walrus moustache bit into his orange and, with juice dribbling down his chin, sat listening. The woman in the corner transferred the baby to her other plump breast.

Viktor said: 'There are a lot of informers about. Even I admit that.'

'I suppose you think they're a necessary evil.'

He thought about it and said: 'Frankly, yes I do,' waiting for her voice to rise another octave.

Instead she spoke softly. 'I meant what I said, Viktor. I will show you the proof of what I say. Or rather I will arrange for you to see it.'

The man with the walrus moustache frowned and edged closer, evidently believing that he had qualified to take part in the conversation.

Viktor tilted the botttle, drained it and wiped the froth from his lips. 'Make the arrangements,' he said.

'What arrangements?' asked the man with the walrus moustache. He spat out an orange pip. 'I remember there was one rat who got quite tame. I called him Boris.'

'Let's get out of here,' she said.

Without speaking, they made their way along the dusty path beside the river. The bushes to their right were the changing quarters and from behind them came shrieks and giggles, the smack of a hand on bare flesh.

As they neared the bus terminal she said: 'You know Nikolai Vasilyev?'

'Your private tutor? I know of him. Isn't he supposed to be a great admirer of Trotsky?'

'He believes Stalin cheated him. He also believes that one day Stalin will murder him.'

'Another of your psychopaths by the sound of it.'

'He's a very fine man,' Anna said and from the tone of her voice Viktor guessed that he was, or had been, her lover.

'Does he teach you Trotsky's theories?'

'Sometimes when our sociology lesson is finished he talks about what he believes in. The dreams that peasants dreamed before Stalin made nightmares out of them.'

Exasperated, Viktor punched the palm of one hand with his fist and said: 'This proof. Tell me about it.'

'Nikolai's best friend is an army officer, a captain. The captain's father was a general.'

'Was?'

'He was executed by a firing squad along with thirty other officers. His crime – he questioned the disposition of Soviet troops on the eastern borders. He was proved right when the troops clashed with the Japanese at Manchukuo ten days ago. But the fact that he was right merely made his crime worse.'

'Perhaps he was executed for treason. Or treasonable talk,' Viktor said.

Anna ignored him. 'Nikolai knows where the executions take place. And he will know through his friend when the next one will be. For all I know they take place every day,' she added.

'In the imagination of Nikolai Vasilyev and his friend.'

'There's only one answer: you must see for yourself. If you have the stomach for it.'

Then he couldn't refuse.

*

In the red and white coach packed with Muscovites radiating heat from their sun-burn Viktor considered Anna's jibes about his privileged upbringing. In fact it had bothered him long before she had mentioned it.

He had been born in 1920 when the Red Army was still fighting its enemies in the civil war that followed the Revolution. There were many orphans in those days but not many who had the good fortune to be farmed out almost immediately to a respectable but childless young couple.

Viktor stood up to give his seat to a pregnant woman who had pushed her way through the strap-hanging passengers. The bus bounced as the hard tyres passed over pot-holes in the roads, but at least the crush of bodies stopped you from falling.

From what he had subsequently gathered the Golovins had become remarkably self-sufficient in the dangerous, disordered streets of Moscow. They had found a small house in a relatively tranquil suburb; his father had been given a job at the library where he helped Bolshevik authors re-write history; his mother had devoted herself to the upbringing of little Viktor.

In photographs he looked an uncommonly smug child,

21

scrubbed, combed, smiling complacently at the cameraman. It was a paradox that such self-assurance should have led to the self-doubts he was experiencing now.

It wasn't until he was sixteen that his father had told him that he was adopted. And it was only then that he began to question the uneventful security of his life.

To the inevitable question: 'Who were my parents?' his father, bearded and patient, replied, 'We don't know. There were thousands of children without parents in those days. You see it wasn't just the men who were killed in the Revolution and the fighting after it: women fought side by side with them.'

'But how did you find me?' Viktor asked.

'We didn't *find* you. You were allocated to us. We knew by this time that my wife, your mother ... foster mother? ... no, let's always call her your mother ... we knew that she couldn't have a child so we went to an orphanage. You had been taken there by an old woman who left without giving any details about your background. Perhaps she didn't know them; perhaps she was your *babushka*; we shall never know.' His father put his hand on Viktor's shoulder. 'But we do know that we were very lucky.' A pause. 'And I think you were very lucky too.'

But it wasn't the mystery of his birth that bothered Viktor because it was true, a baby could easily have lost its identity in those chaotic days when a new creed was being spawned. What bothered him was the cloistered life that he and his *parents* lived; questioned on this subject his father had no real answers.

'We're decent, upright citizens,' he said in his calm voice. 'Your mother keeps a good home.' Which was true; in her early forties when Viktor was sixteen, she was a fair-haired, handsome woman who cooked well and was obsessively house-proud. 'And I work hard,' which Viktor later discovered wasn't quite so true because his father had taken to nipping vodka behind the bookshelves in the library off Pushkin Square. 'So why shouldn't we have our security? We've earned it.'

When he was seventeen Viktor pointed out that the apartment on the Lenin Hills, to which they had just moved, *and* the dacha were hardly commensurate with a librarian's income. And it was then that he first heard about his father's biography of Tolstoy. 'I was given a considerable advance by my publishers,' he confided.

22

'Enough to support two homes?'

'They have high hopes of my project.'

Viktor's doubts were assuaged until he discovered that the great work consisted of an exercise book half filled with jumbled notes and a letter from the State-controlled publishers saying that they would consider the manuscript on its merits when it was delivered. Which, judging by the scope of Tolstoy's life and the paucity of his father's notes, wouldn't be this century.

The bus swung round a corner and the standing passengers swayed together, laughing, still drunk with the sun. Viktor loved them all; but he wasn't one of them – his parents had seen to that.

At school he had subtly been kept apart from other children. Even now at university where he was studying languages – English, German and Polish (he could have taken a couple more because foreign tongues gave up their secrets to him without a struggle) – his privileged circumstances created suspicion.

Through the grimy windows of the coach he could see blue and pink wooden cottages tucked away among birch and pines; then the first scattered outposts of Moscow, new apartment blocks climbing on the shoulders of old houses.

Pride expanded inside him. So much achieved during his lifetime! What scared him was the gathering threat to the achievement. War. Fermented in the east by Japan and in the west by Germany. Viktor, orphan of war, was a preacher of peace. Russia had most certainly had her fill of war, but would the belligerents of the world let her rest?

By the time he and Anna alighted from the bus and made their way towards her lodgings in the Arbat her mood had changed. She seemed to regret what she had proposed.

'Of course you don't have to go,' she said and, when he protested, she insisted: 'No, I mean it. You're entitled to your opinions. I was being possessive.'

'No, I must go,' confident that in any case there would be nothing to see.

It was early evening and heat trapped in the narrow streets of leaning houses engulfed them. In the distance they could hear the rumbling of a summer storm.

She slipped on the cobblestones and he held her and she leaned against him.

She said: 'There's no one in the house. Would you like to come in and I'll make some tea?' and he said he would, but he wasn't thinking about tea and his double standards surprised him; an hour ago they had been snapping at each other like wayward husband and nagging wife.

She slid the key into the door of the tenement owned by a baker and his wife. The stairs creaked beneath their feet, splintering the silence.

Her room was a revelation. He had expected garish touches, photographs of film stars, vivid posters from Georgia, beads and powder scattered on the dressing-table. But it was a shy, chaste place and he wondered if he had misjudged her. On the mantelpiece above the iron fireplace stood a photograph of her parents, and the only beads on the dressing table were those strung on a rosary ... So even she had to admit that you were still free in Russia to worship whatever god you chose.

She lit a gas-ring in the corner of the room, put a blackened kettle on it and sliced a lemon. 'What are we doing this evening?' she asked.

'Whatever you like.' He was fascinated by the change in her.

'You know something? You're the first man who's ever been up here.'

He believed her.

'I always kept it reserved for ... for someone special.'

'I'm honoured,' he said inadequately.

'How do you like your tea?'

'Hot and strong,' he told her.

'I wish I had a samovar. Perhaps one day. But I have a little caviar.'

She poured the tea in two porcelain cups and spread caviar on fingers of black bread.

As he sipped his tea, sharp with lemon, he said softly: 'You know you really should take care. Your talk, it's too bold. It will get you into trouble.'

'So, who would care?' She was estranged from her parents; he didn't know why.

'I would care.'

'But we must be free, Viktor.'

'Aren't we?'

She shook her head sadly. 'Let's not start that again.' She popped a finger of bread loaded with glistening black roe into her mouth.

24

'I'll tell you what I'll do. After I've been to this place that Professor Nikolai Vasilyev babbles about I'll prove to you that this is a free country.'

'You really believe it, don't you?'

'We'll each try to prove our points.'

'And yet by warning me to watch my tongue you disprove yours ... But enough of that. Here, have some more tea.' She poured a scalding stream into his cup. 'How about going to the Tchaikovsky?'

Her suggestion was hardly inventive: they went there most evenings since they had paired off together. It was a student café, strident with debate and none too clean; but the beer was cheap and the company stimulating.

'Why not?'

'Do you mind looking the other way while I change?'

He stared through the window thinking how strange it was that a girl who only that afternoon had lain half naked beneath him in the forest should suddenly be overcome by modesty.

Suddenly thunder cracked overhead. The first blobs of rain hit the window and slid down in rivulets. Behind him he heard the rustle of clothing.

Another crack of thunder and he turned and she was naked and he reached for her

*

The summons came ten days later.

His father took the call in the living room.

'It's that girl,' he said, exuding displeasure, and handed the receiver to Viktor.

'Do you still want to go through with it?' Anna asked.

'Of course. Where shall I meet you?' He wanted to stop her from committing any indiscretion on the phone. *But why should I worry?*

'Nikolai says—'

'Forget about Nikolai,' he broke in. 'Just tell me where to meet you.'

'At the Tchaikovsky in half an hour. But Viktor—'

'I'll be there.' He hung up.

He glanced at his watch. Six pm.

'That girl,' his father said, stroking his grey-streaked beard. 'Anna, isn't it?'

'How did you know her name?'

25

'I've heard you talk about her.'

Viktor who didn't remember ever discussing her said: 'Well, what about her?'

'I've heard,' his father said, 'that she's a bit of a firebrand.' His voice didn't carry authority; but it was a voice that wasn't used to being contradicted.

'Really? Who told you that?'

'We get a lot of people from the university in the library.'

'And they thought fit to discuss your son's friends with you? Your adopted son,' he added because he was angry.

'Just one of your friends. They seemed to think that she wasn't desirable company.'

'What were they implying? That she was a whore?'

'Viktor!' exclaimed his mother who had just entered the room, clean and bright from a good dusting that morning.

'I'm sorry, mama, I didn't know you were there.'

'What sort of excuse is that? I won't have that sort of language in my house.' With one finger she dabbed at a trace of pollen that had fallen from a vase of roses on the table.

Viktor turned to his father. 'Why did they think she was undesirable, whoever *they* are?'

'Apparently she has an *ungovernable* tongue.' He had a way of emphasising long words as though he had just invented them.

'She's got spirit if that's what you mean.'

'Misdirected by all accounts. I really think, Viktor, that you should give her up.'

'There must be some nice girls in your class,' his mother said.

What would they say, Viktor wondered, if they knew that he had celebrated his release from celibacy by making love to her twice in one day? Twice! He almost felt like telling them; but that wouldn't be fair; they had been good to him in their way.

His father said: 'Wasn't there some gossip about her and her private tutor?'

'Was there? I didn't know.'

'Your father's only telling you for your own good,' his mother said.

Viktor wondered if his father had been fortified by a few nips of vodka. 'And I'm grateful,' he said stiffly, 'but I'm nineteen years old and capable of making my own judgements.'

His father drummed his fingers on a bookcase crammed

with esoteric volumes discarded by the library. 'You're going to see her now?'

'You were listening to my conversation, you know perfectly well I am.' He consulted his watch again. 'And I'm late.'

His father's fingers returned to his beard but the combing movements were quicker. 'You realise you are displeasing your mother and me. Do you think we deserve that?'

Addressing his mother, Viktor said: 'Look, you've been wonderful to me. If it wasn't for you I might be living in a hovel, working on an assembly line; I might even be dead. I've never been disobedient before. But I'm a man now. And I have the right to choose my friends. After all, it is a free country. Isn't it?' turning to his father.

His father said: 'I've warned you.'

'And your warning has been considered and dismissed.' Viktor kissed his mother on the cheek. 'I'm sorry but there it is: your little boy has grown up. And now I must rush.'

He took a tramcar to the centre of the city. It was another fine day, cumulus cloud piled high on the horizon. Two more months and the jaws of winter would begin to close. But Viktor didn't mind the long bitter months. Perhaps his parents had been Siberians. That would account for his blue eyes.

He walked briskly through the Arbat, past sleeping dogs and a group of children wearing scarlet scarves and red stars on their shirts and old people in black becalmed in the past on the pavements.

She was waiting for him at a table by an open window. A breeze breathed through the window stirring her black hair. She wore a yellow dress with jade beads at her neck. She was smoking a cardboard-tipped cigarette with nervous little puffs.

'I'm sorry I'm late,' he said. 'Coffee?'

'We haven't time. Come, we can't talk here.' Outside she said: 'You have to promise me, Viktor, that whatever you see you won't tell a soul. You won't say where you've been and you won't say who with. Do you promise?'

'Of course, it was understood anyway. Where am I going anyway?'

She was silent for a moment. Then she said: 'To a place of execution.'

Apprehension was germinating inside him: she seemed so confident. 'How do we get there?' he asked. 'Wherever *there* is.'

She took his arm, propelling him along the pavements until they arrived at Theatre Square. There they caught a No 18 tram to the Kaluzhskaya Zastava and thence a No 7 to the Sparrow Hills.

'And now?' He looked at her questioningly, apprehensively. An old grey limousine answered his question. Anna pulled open the rear door and pushed him in. The car moved off, leaving her behind.

The driver had cropped brown hair and his accent was Ukrainian. 'I have one request,' he said, 'and it's up to you whether or not you obey it. But I'd be grateful if you didn't take too much notice of where we're going.'

'You seem to take it all rather lightly,' Viktor said, 'if we're going to see what Anna claims we're going to see.'

'Is there any other way? In any case Anna says, through Nikolai Vasilyev, that you don't believe there are any restrictions in the Soviet Union. If that is so why should I bother too much about what you see?'

'But you do bother ...'

The shoulders in front of him, clothed in blue serge despite the heat, shrugged. 'It's immaterial. If you go telling tales then we'll kill you.'

The driver handed Viktor a flask. 'A little firewater, perhaps, to prepare you for what lies ahead?'

Viktor took the flask. He had only drunk vodka once and had considered himself quite sober until he had walked into the fresh air, whereupon he had collapsed. He took a sip and handed the flask back to the crop-haired enigma in front of him.

The vodka felt like molten metal in his stomach.

From the crown of the Sparrow Hills, he could see the valley of the Moskva River, fields of vegetables, Tikhvinski Church, the Novo-Dyevitchi Convent and to the right, on the wooded slopes of the river, the Merchants' Poor House. It all looked very peaceful in the evening haze.

The Ukrainian took a rambling route as though trying to confuse anyone following. In the outlying suburbs where the Tartars had once lived men were coming home from work to wives and children standing at the doors of houses surrounded by wooden fences threaded with dog roses. The homecomings had an ordered rhythm to them that soothed Viktor's doubts. The proposition that he was being taken to a mass execution became ludicrous. And yet ... Why had Anna gone to such elaborate lengths? What possible motive could the Ukrainian have for taking him on this confusing journey? Perhaps some bizarre mime would be staged; perhaps they would claim they had missed the killing and show him some bloodstains. Well, they would have to do better than that.

'Another nip?' The Ukrainian handed back the flask, silver with a family crest engraved on it. Viktor took another sip; if the Ukrainian was trying to get him drunk he had another think coming. But the liquor did embolden him to ask: 'What sort of farce is this that we're acting?'

The Ukrainian laughed, massaging the bristles on his scalp. There were a couple of incipient creases on his neck; he wasn't so young. 'A tragedy,' he said, 'not a farce. Grand Guignol.'

'You don't seem to be taking it too tragically.'

'That way lies madness.'

'And how do you know about these ... alleged executions?'

'Because, my dear Viktor, I have become a desk-bound soldier, a military clerk, after being wounded in a skirmish with the Japanese. But a clerk with a difference. I was considered bright enough to be enrolled in military intelligence known to one and all as the GRU. Do you know how the GRU came into existence?'

'It seems irrelevant.'

'But then you wouldn't know, would you, because it was born of defeat and defeats don't have any place in our history books.' He swung the old car round a bend in a dirt road, sending up a cloud of dust. 'In 1920 the Poles invaded the Soviet Union and stormed through my country. The Ukraine, that is,' he explained. 'They were thrown out eventually; then Lenin made a mistake.' He turned his head and grinned. 'Heresy, Viktor Golovin? But a mistake it certainly was. His intelligence, the Cheka Registry Department, got it all wrong and told him the Poles were ripe for revolution. As ripe as green apples as it turned out. The Red Army attacked Poland and got torn to ribbons for their pains. As a result the GRU was formed and a certain Yan Karlovich Berzin was put in charge.'

Viktor said: 'What's all this got to do with executions?'

'The GRU is in charge of military purges, even though we're only a branch of the Secret Police, the NKVD. The NKVD itself didn't do too badly in the purging business under

29

a gentleman named Genrikh Grigorevich Yagoda. But apparently he didn't purge quite diligently enough and he was shot in Lubyanka Prison. Now they have a fellow named Nikolai Yezhov in charge. He's doing a good job – seeing off about thirty a day, they estimate – but it's only a question of time before they cart him off to Lubyanka.'

'I don't believe any of this,' Viktor said.

'Where have you been, comrade? In solitary confinement?'

'I've heard the rumours, of course.'

'You should listen to rumours. They're the alleyways in the maze surrounding the truth.'

'If what you say is true – and I don't for one second believe it is' – *Or did he?* – 'then why are you honouring me with a visit?'

'Because I'm in love with Anna Petrovna. So is my friend Nikolai Vasilyev. So, I believe, are you. Wouldn't you do anything she asked?'

Viktor thought about it, then said firmly: 'No.'

'Ah, but you are young. Perhaps you are the sort of young man she needs. Someone who will stand up to her.'

The Ukrainian's words surprised Viktor: he seemed to be the sort of man who would stand up to anyone.

The Ukrainian went on: 'But I assure you that what I'm doing is not entirely selfless. You see I think you'll be so horrified, so disgusted, that you'll do something rash – and leave Anna to me. And Nikolai Vasilyev —' He circumvented a cow that had wandered into the road. 'There is another reason,' he said abruptly, his tone flinty. 'You see I've heard all about you from Nikolai. You're something of a hothouse plant, aren't you? And in my book naïvety, feigned or otherwise, is as much to blame for tyranny as greed or corruption or any of the other usual culprits.'

Viktor shivered; but he knew he still had to attack. 'By your own admission you play your part in this blood-letting. Are you proud of that, comrade?'

'I have saved more than I have sentenced to death. It's all I can do.'

'So you select the victims?'

'I don't intend to be cross-examined.' His voice was suddenly weary.

'Not a very proud achievement, to condemn men to death and come to terms with yourself by saving a few souls.'

'Then you believe me?'

Too late, Viktor realised that he had been manoeuvred into accepting the Ukrainian's claims. 'And what if I tell the authorities that you took me to this place of execution?'

'Then you, too, would be executed. Comrade Stalin doesn't like to have people in the know around too long. Yan Berzin's days are numbered. So are my own. So, you see, I don't really care what you do or say.'

He pulled into a track leading to a farmyard and parked the car in a stable. 'And now, my patriotic young friend, we walk.'

The Ukrainian was shorter than Viktor had imagined him to be. He wore a brown tweed jacket and grey trousers and an open-neck grey shirt making Viktor self-conscious about the alpaca jacket that had looked so smart in the shop in the Alexander Arcade.

He also walked with an unnatural stiffness and when he saw Viktor staring at him he said: 'The bullet hit me in the spine. I wear a steel corset. Ridiculous, isn't it? But perhaps it will stop another bullet one day. Except that in Lubyanka they pump them into the back of your head.' They turned into the dirt road and headed east. 'You're not a very curious young man, are you? I suppose it's part of your upbringing. But you haven't even asked me my name. It's Gogol, like the author. Mikhail Gogol.'

Bats fluttered in the calm air, swallows skimmed the road ahead of them. In the fields peasants were scything lush green grass. A bearded *muzhik* wearing brown carpet slippers wandered past, eyes vacant.

'I'd better tell you where we're going and what we're going to do,' Mikhail Gogol told Viktor. 'We're on the outskirts of a village that was once called Tzaritzuino-Datchnoye. Does that mean anything to you?'

'Not a thing,' replied Viktor, with the terrible certainty growing upon him that it soon would.

'Well, the village was given by Peter the Great to Prince Kantemir of Moldavia. In 1774 Catherine the Second - Catherine the Great - bought it back for Russia. She started to build a huge dacha here but abandoned it. There's a theatre - also unfinished - next to it and there are lakes, lawns, gazebos ... but all overgrown. In fact the place is a jungle,' Gogol said.

'Why the history lesson?'

31

'You must know your background. One day, perhaps, you'll write about it.'

'I might,' Viktor said. 'But it will be fiction.'

'*Touché.*'

Gogol stopped for a moment, holding his back as though it pained him. He thumped the base of his spine with his fist. 'I can't walk very far these days. Would you believe that I was once an athlete? Hundred metres sprint champion at the military academy in Kiev?'

'Why are we going to a decayed dacha?' Viktor asked.

'To witness a massacre, of course. I forgot to tell you why Catherine abandoned the place. It was because it reminded her of a coffin.'

*

From behind his cover Viktor could just see the dacha over the top of the ivy-covered wall surrounding it. And it did resemble a coffin. A long, low building surmounted with spires that looked like funeral candles.

He was crouching behind a clump of dusty-leaved laurel bushes. Facing him, across a stony path, a massive wooden door, studded with iron spikes, opened into the wall; set into it was a smaller door; both were guarded by a grey-uniformed sentry who every ten minutes marched along the length of the wall, first to the right and then, re-passing the door, to the left. According to Gogol, who had brought Viktor through the under-growth to the rear entrance, the smaller door was unlocked and only needed a push to open it. Clearly the sentry, a shabby-looking fellow with pock-marked features, didn't expect intruders because he marched dispiritedly, staring at the ground; and no official visitors either because he had taken off his cap and was smoking a cigarette. Locals, said Gogol, had been warned not to come anywhere near the mansion and only a select few (GRU, for instance) knew that it was used for executions.

'Make your move when he's halfway to the right-hand extremity of the wall,' Gogol had instructed Viktor, before making his way to the front entrance of the mansion where, apparently, he was expected. 'Then make your way through the shrubbery to the theatre. At the back you'll find a potting shed, wait for me there. If you get caught then I've never heard of you. I admit,' he added, 'that I do still have some faint instincts for self-survival.'

The sentry took a deep drag on his yellow cigarette, pinched out the tip and slipped the remainder into the pocket of his jacket. Then, carrying his rifle as though it were a cannon, he started out to the right of the door.

Viktor tensed himself. Twigs cracked beneath his feet. Dust from the laurel leaves made him want to sneeze.

Halfway across the path he slipped, righted himself and made it to the door. The sentry, a hundred yards away, didn't look around. Viktor reached out one hand and pushed the smaller door. But it didn't move. Perhaps Gogol had locked it from inside. Perhaps he wants me dead with a bullet from the sentry's rifle in my back – or an NKVD bullet in the back of my head in Lubyanka.

The sentry was turning. Viktor pushed again. The door swung open with a creak. He was inside, closing the door, peering round, sprinting for a privet hedge enclosing a shrubbery. He crouched behind a rhododendron. In front of him a spider on a web suspended between dead blooms was devouring a fly; through the web he saw a man wearing a brown smock pushing a handcart. A gardener – reassuring; gardening and bloodshed were contradictions. Then it occurred to him that the garden was so overgrown that gardeners were superfluous; he thought of gardeners exterminating insects and wondered if this one had turned his hand to humans.

He was through the shrubbery and halfway across a stretch of knee-high grass strung with brambles when a shot rang out, freezing him. The explosion stayed with him for a moment like a splash of ink; then it was erased and he was away again.

Was that what he had been brought to hear? he wondered, kneeling behind a lichen-covered wall surrounding a stagnant pool. A single shot and then, perhaps, a glimpse of a body, or what looked like a body, being removed under a blanket? He almost smiled.

Through a crack in the wall he could see the pool; a stone cherub with a ruined face smiled crookedly at him; a fish with a white, diseased body surfaced briefly before returning to the moss-green depths with a flick of its tail. Viktor crawled to the end of the wall; keeping low, he ran to a thicket of holly bushes. Above him loomed the walls of the dacha, the coffin.

On one side lay the half-finished theatre where Catherine the Great had once planned to watch the cream of Russian thespians. It looked a dull place from the outside, dead-eyed and brooding, but then theatres often did. Beside it stood the potting shed, ferns growing from its windows.

Inside the shed Viktor waited. Outside, the shadows were lengthening. The swallows and bats had vanished but somewhere in the tangled undergrowth a bird sang.

Gogol said: 'Follow me,' his voice reaching Viktor through the ferns. Viktor joined him outside.

'Right,' Gogol whispered. 'Through that gap,' pointing at a gap in the wall of the theatre intended for a door. Gogol got there first; inside the doorway he paused, grinding his fist into the base of his spine. 'Now you've got to be careful,' he said. 'Just round the corner you'll see a passage, just like the corridors behind the auditorium at the Bolshoi. Take the first door on the right. You'll find yourself in a box. If you stand in the shadows at the back you can't be seen from below. But you'll have one of the best seats for the show.' He grinned fiercely. 'Wait there afterwards for me,' and was gone.

If there had once been a stage it was no longer there; nor were there any seats; just a rubble-strewn arena cleared at one end in front of a wall that would have been the back of the stage. Half a dozen civilians strolled restlessly about, smoking; leaning against another wall opposite Viktor's box stood a collection of old M 1891 rifles and two green boxes of ammunition.

So it was going to happen. His belly lurched and with it everything he believed in. No, it wasn't going to happen; this was bizarre play-acting, a charade. Why the ammunition, Viktor? And what are those stains, so black and regular on the floor?

He returned to his schoolroom where, as a treat, they had screened flickering newsreels of the Revolution. There was Lenin, fierce and yet avuncular, accepting the adulation of his triumphant rebels. He opened a history book and the first page was a red flag that reminded him of a field of poppies rippled by a breeze. There was the new order, there was justice.

The men below selected rifles. More civilians, all in shirtsleeves, entered the arena and picked up the rest of the guns. Crisply, they loaded them. Outside, he heard a vehicle, a lorry by the sound of it, draw up.

Viktor bit deep into the flesh inside his lower lip and tasted blood.

From behind the wall he heard shouts. Hands clenched,

body taut, he waited the entrance from the wings. Shouldn't there have been an orchestra? A conductor in white tie and tails?

In came the players. Middle-aged mostly. All men. All wearing military trousers, all in shirt-sleeves. They walked erect but there was a strange docility about them. They were obviously officers. Did those trained to command accept commands just as readily?

Desperately Viktor wanted to leave his vantage point. To return to the sanctuary of his adolescence, to the toy soldiers of his nursery.

The officers were blindfolded and lined up against the wall, hands behind their heads, elbows touching. Thirty of them, Stalin's daily ration. I don't believe it. His skull filled with ice, his legs bent and he had to steady himself with one hand against the wall of the box.

The firing squad lined up opposite the blindfolded men raised their rifles. Some of the condemned crossed themselves.

Now surely they would be granted their last wishes. That always happened. In books, in films ...

They slumped. Blood appeared at their breasts. And it seemed to Viktor that he heard the explosions from the rifles after the impact of the bullets.

The abruptness of the transition from life to death astonished him; he could barely comprehend it. A second volley of shots made the bodies jump as they slid to the ground.

Two of the executioners propped their rifles against the wall, drew pistols and walked along the line of bodies shooting out any vestiges of life.

Then the *gardener* made his entrance pushing his handcart. But Viktor, unconscious on the floor of the box, didn't see them load the bodies into it.

*

He waited the following evening at the Café Tchaikovsky for three hours. From seven in the evening, the hour at which they usually met, until ten.

But she didn't come and some inexplicable perversity – nothing had rational explanations any more – stopped him from calling at her lodgings. Perhaps the whole episode had been an act of cruelty on her part for which she had found some anarchic justification; perhaps, like Gogol, she had merely wanted to knock him off his smug perch. Perhaps even now she was naked in the arms of Nikolai Vasilyev. Or Gogol.

She hadn't attended her class that day but she had sent a note explaining that she had to visit a sick relative at Kuntsevo. Well, she had a grandmother in Kuntsevo (Stalin also had a house there), but that was only seven miles away so she could have been back by seven, eight at the latest, especially when she knew what he had been through.

Later, he decided that he had done so little about finding her because he was still in a state of shock. He believed nothing any more, least of all the earnest babble of the students in the Tchaikovsky.

When she didn't appear in class the following day he telephoned Nikolai Vasilyev and then, when he didn't get any reply, went round to Anna's lodgings in the lunchtime break. Her landlady, an old crone with features as sharp as a claw, told him that Anna had packed her belongings two nights before – the night of the massacre – paid a week's rent and disappeared.

Viktor didn't believe her. He threatened her, offered money, but fear and the bribe she had received (the new Viktor Golovin *knew* she had been bribed) had efficiently silenced her.

He called at Nikolai Vasilyev's house in the north of the city. But he, too, had disappeared; the woman who answered the door was in her thirties, blonde, pretty and distraught, possibly Vasilyev's mistress. She didn't know what had happened; he had been missing for two days. But she had an address for Gogol.

Gogol lived in an apartment near the Alexander Brest Railway Station. Viktor rang the bell but its chime had a lost quality to it. Neighbours told him that they had seen Gogol leave with four men in civilian clothes. Leave? Well, escorted would be a better description, said one old man. 'But don't say I said so,' he added, pocketing Viktor's rouble.

When Viktor continued to pursue his inquiries his father took him aside and said: 'Best leave it alone, Viktor. What's done is done. You can't bring them back …'

Them? Again Viktor wondered about his father's source of information.

But what astonished him most as, with suicidal intent, he asked his questions, was the lack of reprisals. What he was suggesting to those he cross-examined was tantamount to treason. And yet he remained untouched. Privileged.

When he had finally ascertained beyond all reasonable doubt that Anna, Vasilyev and Gogol had been *purged*, Viktor took the only step left to him.

He, too, disappeared.

Chapter Two

It is difficult enough to determine when a conspiracy is born. Is it at a moment of decision, of inspiration, or is it when two schemers meet on the same train of thought?

It is well-nigh impossible to decide when a conspiracy is *conceived*. A chance remark, an afterthought, a memory ... any such stimulus can do the trick without the potential conspirator realising what has happened.

So it would be foolhardy to suggest that, when he sat up in bed to eat his breakfast on September 28, 1938, the man in the crumpled blue pyjamas had conceived the plan that was to reach out for the soul of Viktor Golovin.

What was certain was that he was already contemplating an awesome concept. What was equally certain was that he was enjoying a hearty meal – partridge, bacon, hot-buttered toast and marmalade.

He ate rapidly but fastidiously – his hands were remarkably small for such a bulky body – and as he put away the food he read the newspapers, his features a mixture of petulance and pugnacity, unrelieved by the boyish smile that so often disarmed his critics.

The only item that gave him any pleasure was the news, prominently displayed, that the Royal Navy had been mobilised. He considered it to be a halting step in the right direction; unfortunately it was belied by most of the other items.

The previous evening the Prime Minister, Neville Chamberlain, had broadcast to the nation: 'How horrible, fantastic, incredible, it is that we should be digging trenches and trying on gas-masks here because of a quarrel in a far-away country' – bracketing Czechoslovakia with the Arctic! – 'between people of whom we know nothing ...'

Dear God, the glib insularity of the man!

'... I would not hesitate to pay even a third visit to Germany if I thought it would do any good ... I am a man of peace to the depths of my soul.'

After making the broadcast, Chamberlain had received a letter from Hitler and there was no doubt that it was an invitation to appeasement. Would they never learn, these men of lofty resolve, that idealism could only survive on strong shoulders?

With a sigh Winston Churchill pushed aside his tray, climbed out of bed, put on a dressing gown and sauntered on to the lawns of Chartwell, his country manor, near the village of Westerham in Kent, to which he had escaped from his flat at Morpeth Mansions in London for a brief respite from the crisis.

War clouds were gathering over London, Berlin, Paris and Prague; but they weren't in evidence in rural Kent. Bonfire smoke wreathed the seventy-nine acres of grounds; the trees were autumn red and gold; chrysanthemums still insisted it was summer despite the first frost on the grass.

He lit a cigar. The sole hint of war – and that only apparent to himself – was the foundations of the cottage he was building in which Clemmie and his four grown-up children could find tranquillity when it came.

As come it undoubtedly would. But not as most people seemed to think when the present negotiations over Czechoslovakia broke down. No, Chamberlain would return to Germany, a grovelling pact would be struck with Hitler, Mussolini and Daladier, and the Czechs would be sacrificed on the altar of compromise. It was ironic that those who had failed to heed his warnings about the Nazi threat now expected war immediately whereas he still gave twelve months or so.

But if Chamberlain does return with peace in his bag then watch out, Winston, because there'll be no place in Britain for a *warmonger*.

He made his way to the foundations of the cottage and with a mason's trowel scraped a few crusts of cement from the first row of bricks. Warmonger! His cross, unjustly borne, ever since ... He supposed it went back to those dashing days in

38

Cuba, India, the Sudan and South Africa when, as warrior or reporter, he had always breathed gunsmoke.

Then it hadn't mattered too much; in fact his escape from captivity during the Boer War had helped him to gain his first seat in the Commons. In 1900. In two months he would be sixty-four. But age didn't bother him because he didn't heed it.

Stretching for a crumb of dried cement just out of his reach, he felt a warning nudge of pain in the shoulder he had dislocated when embarking from a troopship in Bombay in those young, fire-eating days. He dropped the trowel, threw away six inches of cigar and started back towards the red-bricked old mansion that he had bought in 1922 when the roofs leaked and weeds had occupied the grounds.

Like one of those weeds the warmonger epithet had taken root during the Great War when, as First Lord of the Admiralty, he had extended hostilities to Turkey. But despite the catastrophic Gallipoli Campaign, he still believed that his instincts had been correct; the back-door assault on the enemy should have shortened the war by a couple of years. What he had lacked had been support and loyalty.

And what no one realised, then or now, was that he only revelled in battle, as indeed he did, when his sights were set on peace. Did a true warmonger lay bricks? Or paint landscapes? Or build his own swimming pool?

When the second world war finally broke out, when he was recalled to the helm as he had no doubt he would be, then he would pursue peace more vigorously than ever. But this time his quarry wouldn't be a butterfly that flitted capriciously between conflicts: it would be a lasting peace.

And to achieve that he would have to indulge in manoeuvres that would dwarf Gallipoli by comparison. He had no idea what those manoeuvres would entail – there had as yet been neither birth nor conception of any concrete plan. But he did know that if he divulged even a glimmering of his wondrous, horrendous vision then it would be stillborn. And he would be finished.

The public must never know.

At least not in his lifetime.

*

For several years Chartwell had been a Foreign Office in exile.

There, Churchill had conferred with his closest henchmen, Bob Boothby and two red-haired stalwarts, his son-in-law Duncan Sandys and Brendan Bracken.

There, energetically but impotently, he had drawn up the policies he would have pursued had Stanley Baldwin or his successor, Neville Chamberlain, given him office in the Government.

There, he had furiously denounced Hitler's occupation of the Rhineland, Austria and now the Sudetenland territory of Czechoslovakia.

There, he had sounded the trumpets for King Edward VIII when he was forced to abdicate the throne because he was determined to wed the American-born divorcée Mrs. Wallis Simpson. Not only was he a warmonger, he was a defender of lost causes.

And it was to Chartwell that he repaired with Bracken when the Munich crisis was over. Chamberlain, fresh from his betrayal of Czechoslovakia, had waved his meaningless agreement with Hitler at the crowds outside Downing Street and told them: 'I believe it is peace for our time.'

The First Lord of the Admiralty, Duff Cooper, had resigned in protest. Churchill had passionately mourned Munich in the Commons: 'All is over. Silent, mournful, abandoned, Czechoslovakia recedes into the darkness ... Do not suppose this is the end. This is only the beginning of the reckoning.'

As he had feared, his sentiments had been anathema in the euphoria that followed Chamberlain's homecoming.

'I wouldn't mind so much,' he told Bracken as he restlessly paced one of Chartwell's reception rooms, 'if Neville believed any of this eyewash himself. But he doesn't. Even when he was waving at the crowds on his way back from Heston he told Halifax, "All this will be over in three months." '

'He believed it once,' Bracken remarked. 'Even you must give Chamberlain credit for that.'

'This is the first time I have disputed his sincerity,' Churchill said. 'In the past I've always respected his idealism-
- however unwisely it was dispatched. He was the conscience of a nation still recovering from the haemorrhage of the war. Twenty years, that's all it's been, Brendan, twenty wasted years.'

Despite Churchill's sombre mood Bracken grinned, running his hand through his crinkly, ginger hair, because it was typical of his mentor that he couldn't resist salting a compliment. *Wasted* years. Perhaps so. But a little misplaced in the context.

Churchill poured himself a whisky and soda and continued to patrol the book-lined room littered with newspapers. 'And I've never doubted his strength. He's a tough old bird is Neville, and a wily one too, despite outward appearances.' Bracken grinned again. 'The toughness, stringiness if you like' – Churchill permitted himself a smile – 'is still there but the sincerity ... I'm afraid it's been dissipated, Brendan.'

'I assume he's only buying time.'

'Then why doesn't he come clean?'

'In public? Come now, Winston, that would be an abuse of honesty. If he admitted he had dallied with the Führer just to give Britain the chance to re-arm, Hitler would march into the rest of Czechoslovakia tomorrow. But he has expressed his doubts to his confidants; and I don't have to remind you, Winston, that you aren't one of them.'

Churchill grunted and lit a cigar from a fresh consignment from John Rushbrook in New York.

Bracken, Irish-born newspaper publisher and M.P., regarded Churchill fondly from the depths of a sighing leather armchair. He had known him for years, from the time Churchill had moved to the Admiralty after his tempestuous reign at the Home Office. Like Churchill, Bracken enjoyed talking and liked to educate people. His favourite topic was Churchill, youthful adoration was behind him, mature understanding in its place.

He understood the melanchola, veiled from the public, that frequently afflicted Churchill, a legacy handed down from the Dukes of Marlborough but tempered, thanked God, by his mother's American blood; he understood the flamboyance summoned to smother doubt, the bravado employed to mask fear. 'You can't be a hero without being a coward,' Churchill had once told him.

He believed he knew Churchill better than anyone except Clementine. Not that he wasn't bombastic, arrogant and impetuous; far from it; but what people didn't comprehend was his sensitivity – Churchill made damn sure of that.

But what you could never quite cope with was his unpredictability. It erupted now as Churchill, thumbs in the waistcoat of his crumpled grey pinstripe, stared at a portrait of his grandfather, the 7th Duke.

'What about Joe?' he said.

'Joe? Joe who?' Bracken asked, bewildered.

'Joe Stalin. I wonder how he views this grovelling policy of ours – if he's got time to think in between his purges.'

'I shouldn't think he's very pleased. He would like to see the capitalist powers fight each other to a standstill.'

Silence.

Somewhere a clock chimed. Bracken could hear the crackle of Churchill's cigar as he rolled it between his fingers.

The silence continued. Nervously, Bracken cleared his throat.

Finally Churchill said: 'That's a very interesting remark, Brendan.'

But hardly an original one, Bracken thought.

'Let's put it to one side for a moment,' Churchill said. 'But we may return to it,' as though they were in for a long session which, Bracken knew to his cost, could last until four am. 'Don't think for one second that Stalin, that wily old Georgian, is hoodwinked by Neville's scrap of paper. He knows that Corporal Hitler is going to wage war and he's got to decide whom to support. To put it more bluntly, who's going to win, Germany or us. Who do you think he'll put his money on, Brendan?'

Bracken thought about it. 'Well,' he said, giving his spectacles a polish, 'he's been chasing an anti-Hitler coalition for three years.'

'As indeed he might,' Churchill said, returning to his perusal of the 7th Duke. 'In 1936 Hitler was bellowing that the Ukraine and even Siberia should be part of the *lebensraum*, Germany's living space. But pray continue, Brendan.'

'But then again he thinks that we've deliberately allowed Germany to re-arm so that she can fight Russia. He must interpret Munich as an inducement to the Nazis to further that aim. On one side he's got the aggressor, on the other the betrayer. An unenviable choice, Winston.'

Churchill wheeled round, waving his cigar so vigorously that Bracken feared his suspect shoulder might pop out. 'I'll tell you what he'll do first: he'll sit on the barbed-wire fence and wait to see who looks like winning the war in Spain. It is, after all, a dress rehearsal for the next world war.'

'Suppose the Fascists win – and that seems likely. It would be very strange to see a Bolshevik going over to the other side.'

Churchill gave a fleeting smile which reassured Bracken who

had feared that he was on the brink of a deep depression. 'I did it once,' he said.

'But this is a bit different. Communists siding with Fascists. It's ridculous.'

'History is littered with strange bedfellows.'

'Not strange, grotesque. If Franco wins he'll be expected to throw in his lot with Hitler. You seem to be suggesting that Stalin of all people will join him. A preposterous notion, if you don't mind me saying so, Winston.'

'I don't mind in the slightest, my dear Brendan, because you are giving rein to assumption. I merely said that Stalin would observe which way the winds of war blow in Spain. If Franco wins – and I have little doubt that he will – then Hitler will be that much stronger. Another prospective Fascist ally instead of a Bolshevik foe in western Europe. Another Italy – although if you've got allies like Mussolini you don't need enemies.'

Bracken said: 'I've reined in my assumption and I still don't understand. You don't appear to have contradicted the proposition that Stalin would side with Hitler and Franco.'

'Ah, then you haven't reined hard enough. There will be no question of such an unholy triumvirate because Franco, another wily bird, won't actively side with Hitler; he'll sit on the barbed-wire fence, too. Do you know what I would do if I were Chamberlain?'

Bracken shook his head. It was, he decided, a gala night for unpredictability.

'I'd promise Franco that I'd give him Gibraltar if he stayed neutral. Who knows, maybe one day I'll be in a position to give that promise ... ' Churchill sat down opposite Bracken and took a swig of his whisky and soda. 'But I digress. What I'm saying is that Stalin will wait till the Fascists have thrashed the Reds in Spain, then he'll throw in his lot with Hitler. You see, Brendan, it's really the only option open to old Joe.' Stalin, Bracken reflected, was five years younger than Churchill. 'He knows that one day Hitler will turn on him and he's got to delay that inevitable moment until Mother Russia has girded her loins to meet such an attack.'

'And that will take a few years,' Bracken remarked. 'According to estimates here Stalin has purged upwards of 30,000 Red Army officers. Not only that but he's got rid of nearly all of the Supreme Military Council. Do you know the total estimate of Stalin's victims, killed or imprisoned?'

'No,' Churchill said irritably, 'but you will tell me.'

'Something like six million. And you know, of course, what he's reputed to have said when one of his sons tried unsuccessfully to shoot himself … ' Bracken was beginning to enjoy himself.

'An educated guess would be words to the effect that he couldn't shoot straight.'

'An inspired guess! And did you know—'

'For God's sake, Brendan,' Churchill said, 'let's get on with the business at hand.'

They were interrupted by Clementine who came into the room to bid them goodnight, somehow managing to be both dignified and homely in a pink robe. Sometimes she reminded Bracken of a Society hostess, sometimes of Gracie Fields. But contradictions had been thrust upon her by marriage: she should by now have withdrawn into gracious patronage and yet here she was by the side of a man who in his sixties was talking about leading his country in a second world war. Small wonder that there were occasionally wry edges to her smile.

'Goodnight, Brendan,' she said, 'please don't get up,' as Bracken sprang to his feet, and to her husband: 'It's nearly midnight dear, will you be much later?' The question, Bracken suspected, was purely academic.

'Not much longer,' Churchill said, kissing her lightly. 'You run along now.' And when she had gone: 'What a lucky devil I was, eh, Brendan? I was never much good at the niceties of courtship, you know, but Clemmie understood.'

As if she had any choice, Brendan thought.

Churchill regarded the smoking tip of his cigar. 'She's never liked these things, you know,' and ground out the long stub as a gesture of penitence. 'And now where were we?'

'Stalin. You prophesied he would go in with Hitler.'

'No doubt about it.' Churchill gave himself another whisky and siphoned soda water into it. 'Now let's get that phrase of yours back off the shelf.'

'What phrase was that?'

'*He,* Stalin that is, *would like to see the capitalist powers fight each other to a standstill.* It made my hair curl, Brendan, what little there is left of it. Of course you're absolutely right, that's just what old Joe would like to happen.'

Patiently, Bracken waited for enlightenment.

Holding his glass of whisky in one hand, pausing to tap some of the books in the cases with one small, plump finger as though they contained the answers to the questions that had defied the sages, Churchill began to pace the room again. There was his own novel, *Savrola,* written in his youth; there was *The Aftermath* in which he had poured out his post-war hatred of the Bolsheviks. 'It's strange,' he said, finger lingering on *The Aftermath,* but my fear – yes, fear, Brendan – of the Reds has always been greater than my fear of the Nazis. We shouldn't have squeezed the Nazis so hard, Brendan, we should have left them a little pith.'

Still Bracken waited.

'Supposing,' Churchill said, turning to study Bracken's reactions, 'supposing we reversed the process to which you have just referred. Supposing we took steps to make sure that Russia and Germany fought each other to a standstill?'

Tentatively, Bracken said: 'A formidable proposition, Winston,' aware that he was being used as a sounding board.

Churchill got up steam. 'I wonder if it could be done ... why not ... it has always been possible to manipulate great men ... just kick them in their Achilles heel – conceit ...'

'But what about this pact you're so sure they're going to sign?'

'It won't fool either of them. Hitler intends to march through the steppes, Stalin knows it. It's just a matter of buying time. Like Munich,' he added, scowling.

The distant clock chimed again. A single note. Half an hour had passed since Clementine had taken herself to bed. It was 12.30 a.m.

Like Munich ... That was the only truth, Bracken realised. He had been frog-marched into a debate about a war that hadn't been declared, a Soviet-German Alliance that didn't exist.

But Churchill had become an exultant prophet, his glass of whisky his crystal ball. 'What we must do,' he said, 'is make the sands of time run with great alacrity.'

'I'm afraid I don't understand, Winston, you're talking in riddles.'

Churchill's words lost their ring. 'No more you should, Brendan, no more you should. I'm not even sure that I do at this moment. But it will come, it will come.'

He sat down abruptly.

Then, voice sombre, he wound up the debate: 'But I tell you

this. Unless some stark and terrible measures are devised, this island of ours is doomed to be pillaged by the barbaric hordes of either the Nazis or the Bolsheviks.'

Watched by a stunned Bracken, he drained his crystal ball. 'We have but one hope of survival and that is to make sure that these two arch-enemies of freedom fight each other to the death.'

Without warning he strode to the door. Turning, he said: 'Come on, Brendan, there's a good chap, you're keeping me from my bed.'

Part Two

Chapter Three

By the second week of June 1940 much of Europe lay in ruins, the people dazed and beaten by Hitler's *Blitzkrieg*. Poland, Denmark, Norway, Holland and Belgium had fallen and France was poised to throw in the Tricolour.

But in Lisbon you could have been forgiven for forgetting that there was a war on at all.

The sun shone; the boulevard cafés in the cobbled squares and wide avenues were crowded with customers, British and German among them, the broad, flat waters of the Tagus estuary were scattered with ships of many nations; the little yellow tramcars butting along their shining rails and climbing the steep hills were stuffed with cheerful, sweating passengers.

In the grand arenas of the Baixa, business in the banks was brisk, hotels were full, shops were relatively well-stocked. In the precipitous maze of the Alfama, women garlanded their leaning cottages with laundry, dogs slept in the alleyways and the hot air was greased with the smell of grilling sardines.

It was only on closer inspection that you realised that the Portuguese capital had not entirely escaped the war. There was a restlessness abroad in those pavement cafés; conversations were muted, money changed hands surreptitiously. And in the grand hotels, the Avenida Palace and the Aviz, the atmosphere was majestically clandestine.

The perpetrators of this atmosphere were mostly refugees but quite a few were spies. The refugees had flocked to neutral Portugal from the countries over-run by the Nazis, following in the footsteps of the Jews who had fled from Germany itself. Together they formed a cosmopolitan society that shivered with intrigue and suspicion.

At first they all had but one aim – to get out of Europe through Lisbon, the gateway to freedom. The rich usually managed it, liberally tipping the custodians of the city's portals. Their poorer brethren, those more used to using the tradesmen's entrance, didn't escape so easily.

And it was they who were the most furtive. Selling jewellery, worthless bonds, secrets and their bodies if they were well nourished enough. Lying, cheating, cajoling, bribing. Anything to get a berth on a ship or, more ambitiously, on a New York-bound Clipper seaplane or an aircraft flying by night from Sintra airport. For preference a passage to the United States, traditional haven of desperate emigrants; second choices Britain, because, being at war, she was less hospitable to aliens, and South America, which was such a long way off and the sympathies of some of those far-off countries were suspect.

They wore incongruous clothes, these homeless fugitives. Long coats and cloaks, slouch-hats and absurd peaked caps, moth-eaten stoles and peasant blouses. Collectively they looked like extras from a dozen period movies. And the longer they stayed the more threadbare became their costumes, the more humble their homes.

The really tough persevered, in particular the Jews who were used to such privations. Others, dogged by ill-luck, double-crossed by swindlers, took to the hills or one of the shanty settlements on the outskirts of Lisbon where they could share their poverty without humiliation.

Their empty seats in the cafés were immediately filled, their rooms soon occupied by newcomers feverish with optimism. Some were luckier than others, in particular the British – many of them in transit, via Spain, from the South of France – who were accommodated outside the city. After all, Portugal was Britain's oldest ally even if she had to placate the Germans – you didn't upset Hitler, not if you were as small and un-prepared as Portugal, you didn't.

On June 13, the eve of the German occupation of Paris and a fine, dreamy day in Lisbon, the plight of the refugees seemed more stark than usual.

Or so it seemed to the tall young man in grey flannel trousers and white shirt striding loose-limbed along the Avenida da Liberdade, the Champs-Elysées of Lisbon, on his way to meet a girl in the Alfama.

It was *feira*, the Festival of St Anthony of Padua, Lisbon's own saint, and the groups of dark-clad aliens seemed so remote from it; particularly the children with their hollowed eyes, pale skin and sharp bones. They should have been part of it – the processions, the feasts, the fireworks – because *feira* is a time for children (and lovers and drunks); instead they sat quietly in their ghetto groups in their peaked caps and too-long shorts, having learned already that insignificance is survival.

But today Josef Hoffman was determined not to be affected by the refugees. He had earned a day off from their suffering.

He had been in Lisbon for a year now, working with the Red Cross. At first his work had been coldly selective, weeding out the frauds – German agents mostly – and the rich from the deserving. With his Czech passport and his way with languages – he was already fluent in Portuguese – he was a natural *agent provocateur*.

But he had soon sickened of this. He wanted no more contact with spies or men who would offer him 5,000 escudos to help them jump the queue in the American Export Line offices. He wanted to help the helpless, that was why he had joined the Red Cross.

And, although he was only twenty-two, he had grown old with them.

As he made his way across the Praça Rossio, the city's main square, he could hear firecrackers exploding like gunfire. He stopped and bought a red carnation, its stem wrapped in silver paper, from the flower-seller beside the fountains, to give to the girl whose name was Candida. She was slumbrous and warm-limbed and she would cut the stem off the carnation and wear the flower in her hair that shone blue-black in the sunlight. Hoffman wasn't in love with her which he thought was a pity.

He left the square and turned up the Rua da Madalena, intending to climb towards the ramparts of the Castelo de São Jorge, St George's Castle, which stands astride one of Lisbon's seven hills. Or was it eleven, or thirteen even? The travel guides begged to differ; Hoffman thought it was typically Portuguese, unaware, because he was young, that practically nothing is typical.

He was also unaware that he was being followed by a man carrying a gun, a Russian-made automatic pistol, in the pocket of his raincoat. The man had puffy features and a fleshy nose and he walked as though the pointed brown and white shoes he was wearing hurt his feet; in normal times the heavy gaberdine raincoat and wide-brimmed hat would, together with the shoes, have been conspicuous on a hot evening, but not these days when it was common enough to see a Bohemian or a Slovakian in outlandish clothes hurrying to some secret rendezvous.

Hoffman turned left and began to climb, the walls of the castle ahead of him. He was early for his appointment and intended to spend ten minutes or so wandering around the battlements of the castle with their sensational views of the city and the Tagus.

The man with the pointed shoes followed.

Absorbed with the thought of the pleasures to come that evening, Hoffman almost collided with a woman carrying a basket of fruit on her head; she cursed him but kept her balance with dignity. A procession of children in national dress scattered as a firecracker thrown by an urchin fell hissing in their midst; when it exploded everyone screamed delightedly.

The man in the pointed shoes felt the gun in his pocket, crooked his forefinger round the trigger. The gun felt hot and heavy, like himself. Why couldn't they have given him an older quarry instead of a mountain goat? Hoffman didn't have the build of a natural athlete, but he was slim and supple.

Hoffman strode along a short street lined with linden trees and entered the castle grounds. The castle was Phoenician and Moorish and Christian; apart from the walls there wasn't much of it left.

In a dusty clearing just past the gates teenage girls were performing an impromptu folkdance. They wore long skirts striped in green and gold and red, white blouses and green and red headscarves. A woman spectator bursting with knowledge told Hoffman that they were from the north, affronted that *feira* in Lisbon was such a discreet affair.

Not in the Alfama, he thought: nothing was ever discreet down there. He walked over to the stone parapet and gazed down at the labyrinth below, rooftops like a discarded pack of mildewed playing-cards. So closely were the hillside terraces packed, so sturdily were they planted, that they had resisted the earthquake which devastated the rest of Lisbon on All Saints' Day, 1755, and the tidal wave which had followed it. Down there every day was *feira*.

The man with the pointed shoes moved nearer, paused. He

52

hadn't expected Hoffman to come to this public place. Indecisively, he turned and looked at the dancers tripping about self-consciously in front of a statue. He put his free hand into the other pocket of his raincoat and fingered the purchase he had made that morning, a dozen firecrackers.

Hoffman gazed across the city and the Tagus, called the Straw Sea, because it was often gold at sunset. It was gold now. So broad was the estuary that visitors often thought that the open sea lay to the left of the city whereas, of course, the Atlantic lay to the right through a narrower channel.

Hoffman walked on towards the remains of the fortifications. Apart from the girls dancing it was aloof from the festival up here. You could feel space. A few Americans carrying cameras strolled the ramparts. Hoffman thought that there would be Americans at the Day of Judgement taking pictures.

He knew one of them, a rangy young man from the American Consulate, who did his best for the endless queue seeking visas to the United States. It was a hopeless task but at least he was polite and he treated all the old ladies as he would treat his mother.

He pointed at the ships becalmed in the golden waters and said: 'Kind of hard to believe that Europe's in flames, isn't it?'

Hoffman asked: 'Has Paris fallen?' The American, whose name was Kenyon, knew about such things.

'Not quite, but it's there for the taking. Tomorrow, I guess. Then France will quit. The only neutral countries in Europe will be Switzerland, Sweden, Spain, Turkey, Ireland and, of course, Portugal. And Britain will stand alone. But not for long unless some sort of miracle occurs.'

'Churchill talks in miracles,' Hoffman said. 'Dunkirk was a miracle.'

'A miracle? Perhaps. It was a retreat just the same, a defeat. That's the kind of miracle they can do without.'

'I suppose,' Hoffman said, choosing his words, 'the sort of miracle they need is American intervention.'

'Fat chance,' Kenyon said. 'Last year Roosevelt promised that there would be no "black-out of peace" in the States. If he does decide to stand for a third term he can hardly go back on his word.'

'But if and when he does become President again?'

53

Kenyon shrugged. 'Perhaps, who knows? But it may be too late. No, Churchill will have to pull that miracle first, and not just with words. If he doesn't, then one day the whole world will be full of refugees.'

A firework fizzed and exploded. A small boy watched artfully from behind a pillar. Behind him Hoffman caught sight of a man wearing a raincoat and a broad-brimmed hat. He had a lost air about him; a refugee probably. He turned to look at the decorative birds pecking the dust and Hoffman forgot all about him.

The birds were either black or white, the colours of Lisbon's mosaic pavements. There was even a white peacock.

Hoffman glanced at his watch. In five minutes' time he was due to meet Candida Pereira. He bade farewell to the American and retraced his footsteps. They would have some *bacalhau*, cod, served with baked potatoes, onions and olives and one of the honey-sweet desserts washed down with a bottle of vinho verde, and then ... well, they might dance in the streets, carouse ... and then ...

Hoffman walked quicker.

So did the man in the pointed shoes, wincing with each footstep. But at least they seemed to be heading for the teeming streets of the Alfama which was where he wanted Hoffman.

Hoffman plunged into the maze like a rugby player into a loose scrum. Above him the rooftops reached for each other; from the walls hung pots of pink and red geraniums and birdcages from which only the song of the captives escaped. From the dark mouths of bars came shouting and laughter and music, sometimes Tommy Dorsey or Bing Crosby on scratched phonograph records, sometimes the *fado*, the lament of Portugal.

He stopped at the foot of a flight of steps named Beco do Carneiro. Old hands still got lost in the Alfama. He turned and, over the heads of the crowds, noticed a broad-brimmed hat glide into a doorway. But it didn't really register; he was imagining the invitation in the slumbrous eyes of Candida Pereira and was by now alarmed that he might be late. However slumbrous their eyes, the Candida Pereiras of this world didn't wait around.

He hurried on, emerging eventually in the Largo de Santo Estevão. He had come a long way round but it wasn't far now.

Near the café where they had arranged to meet, the scene was particularly boisterous. A group of men who looked like American gangsters' barbers were singing lustily, children were wrestling and from the windows above women were shouting across the street.

The man in the pointed shoes took the firecrackers from his pocket. He gave three to children and told them to light them and throw them.

He moved up closer to Hoffman and, reluctantly, let go of the butt of the automatic. He lit three more firecrackers – Whizz Bangs they were called – and threw them just ahead of Hoffman. As they landed the children's firecrackers exploded, cracks as loud as pistol shots in the cramped space.

He returned his hand to his pistol pocket and through the gaberdine aimed the barrel at Hoffman's back. He waited for his own Whizz Bangs to detonate, finger caressing the trigger.

The three explosions were almost simultaneous. In fact everything happened at once. The shoulder charge that knocked Hoffman sprawling, the explosion behind him, the screaming.

When he got to his feet Hoffman was surprised to see the man he had noticed wearing the broad-brimmed hat in the grounds of the castle lying on his back, brown and white shoes pointing towards the sky.

*

'What I don't understand,' Hoffman said, 'is how you just happened to be there at the right time.'

The sun-tanned man in the navy-blue lightweight suit said: 'We didn't just happen to be there. We had been keeping tabs on the man who tried to shoot you.'

'Shoot me? Why should he want to shoot me? Why should anyone want to shoot me?'

The man who had told him his name was Cross – 'Double-cross', with the mechanical laugh of one who had made the joke many times before – said: 'We rather hoped *you* would be able to tell *us* that, Mr. Hoffman.'

Us? There was only Cross present; although in the Alfama earlier there had been two of them.

As he had picked himself up after the gunshot, one of the men – Cross, he thought – had thrust him through the throng and said: 'Let's get out of here before all hell breaks loose,' and Hoffman had thought: 'They must know about me.'

If not, he reasoned as they hustled him down steps and alleys to a waiting car, they wouldn't have been so sure that he would be willing to be bundled away from trouble.

Beside the car, a black Wolseley, he had made a token resistance: 'Before I get into that thing I want to know just who the hell you are.'

'We're from the British Embassy. We want to help you.'

And he had believed them. In the society in which he moved, British or American still had a reassuring ring to them.

'Is the man who tried to shoot me dead?'

'We think so.'

The car, with the second man, obviously junior to Cross, at the wheel, had taken them along the waterfront to an old, comfortable-looking block of flats in the Belém district, close to the Jeronimos Monastery.

The apartment itself, presumably Cross's, was splendid. The living room was spacious and filled with light; the curtains were gold brocade, the chairs and sofas Regency-striped. Through the windows, before Cross drew the curtains, Hoffman could see the first lights of evening pulled across the Tagus.

Cross, who had identified himself as a second secretary at the British Embassy, was interrogating him in the nicest possible way. He held up a cut-glass decanter and said 'Scotch?' as if there could be any other drink.

Hoffman shook his head; Cross made him feel immature, and yet Cross couldn't have been all that much older. Twenty-five perhaps, but contained and assured – some might have said condescending – in the way of some Englishmen; those, Hoffman divined, who were not quite of the noble birth to which they aspired, but formidable just the same. And well-heeled because few diplomatic services, least of all the British, would provide a twenty-five old employee with a flat as luxurious as this.

'Well, I'm going to have one. Are you sure you won't have a wee dram?'

'No, thank you,' sitting back to study Cross as he poured himself a drink.

Hoffman had met quite a few Englishmen since he came to Lisbon but somehow this one didn't quite fit. He was elegant enough, suit not too keenly pressed, striped tie deliberately askew; his manner was languid, his smooth hair was a warm shade of brown and his features were handsome in a military sort of way. Odd, then, that he wasn't in the Army. Hoffman could sense contradictions about him and they bothered him.

The sun-tan, for instance; diplomats were never bronzed. And his hands were too big, strangler's hands, making an absurdity of the white silk handkerchief tucked in the sleeve of his jacket. Hoffman couldn't imagine Cross playing the English game of cricket; blood sports would be more his line. His voice was modulated but controlled; when Cross appeared to be wasting words he was wasting them for a purpose. No, Hoffman thought, your appearance is camouflage; beneath those casual graces lurks a hunter.

Glass in hand, Cross walked to a coffee table standing in front of a coldly-empty marble fireplace and picked up a pistol. 'Taft, the man who drove us here, took it out of the pocket of your assassin's raincoat pocket. Would-be assassin,' he corrected himself. He held the automatic by the barrel. 'Crude but effective, as they say.' He pointed at the letters CCCP on the walnut barrel. 'No doubt where it came from.' He sat on the sofa opposite Hoffman, still holding the gun.

'Was he Russian?' Hoffman asked.

Cross laid the gun on the striped cushion beside him and drank some whisky. 'I think perhaps I should ask the questions,' he said. 'A rescuer's privilege.' He gave a cocktail party smile. 'How long have you been in Lisbon, Mr. Hoffman?'

'About a year.'

'Czech passport, I believe. And you work for the Red Cross.' Statements not questions.

Cross said: 'When did you leave Czechoslovakia, Mr. Hoffman?'

'In 1938, when the Germans marched into the Sudetenland.'

'You were from the Sudetenland?'

Hoffman shook his head. 'From Prague.'

'Weren't you a little premature in leaving?'

'On the contrary, that was the time to get out, before the whole of Czechoslovakia was occupied.'

'What language do you speak?'

'English,' Hoffman said.

57

Cross didn't smile. 'Your native language?'

'Both Czech and Slovak and a little Hungarian.'

'I wish I had your talent for languages,' Cross said. 'It's not our strong point – we think everyone should speak English.'

Is he dead?

We think so.

So casual. The reply had barely registered. A man who tried to shoot me is lying dead in a Lisbon street or in a morgue and here we are discussing languages.

'Did you leave anyone behind?'

'Sorry, I don't quite ... I will have that drink,' Hoffman said, 'if you don't mind.'

'Not at all,' in a tone that did mind just a little.

Cross poured him a whisky. 'Soda?'

'Please.'

He sipped his drink. 'Did I leave ... '

'When you left Czechoslovakia, did you leave any relatives behind?'

'Only my mother. My father died five years ago.'

'Wasn't that a little callous?'

'She had married again. To a man who had all the makings of being a good Nazi when the Germans finally took Prague.'

'And where did you go to?'

Hoffman, who felt that Cross knew the answer to this and most of the other questions, replied: 'To Switzerland.'

'How? Across Germany?'

'Austria.'

'Same thing by then.'

We think so. Hoffman took a gulp of whisky. 'It wasn't too difficult. I had forged papers and foreign languages didn't surprise people in that part of Europe in those days. The Balkan tongues had spilled over ... '

'Why the Red Cross?' Cross asked abruptly.

'Should I be ashamed of it?'

'It's a dedication not a job. You were very young to choose a dedication.'

'I knew what was happening in Europe. To the Jews in Germany. I knew what was coming. I wanted to help.'

'But not to fight?'

'Apparently you didn't wish to fight either, Mr. Cross.'

Cross didn't look as angry as he should have done. But the interrogation lapsed for a few moments. A ship's siren sounded

58

its melancholy note, bringing a touch of loneliness to the evening.

Cross poured himself another whisky. Then he said: 'For a pacifist that was a very belligerent remark, Mr. Hoffman.'

'Pacifist? I suppose I am. I happen to think I can do more good working for the Red Cross than becoming another freedom fighter.'

'An unusual appointment, isn't it? A Czech working for the Red Cross in Lisbon?'

'On the contrary. As you know, the city's full of refugees from central and eastern Europe. I can help them, we understand each other.'

'Quite a cushy number,' Cross remarked. Hoffman hadn't come across the word 'cushy' but guessed its implication and guessed that Cross was trying to needle him. 'Like mine,' Cross added. 'Did you go to Berne?'

'Geneva. I spent a year there. I learned English there. Second secretary of what, Mr. Cross?'

'Chancery,' Cross said without elaborating.

The phone rang.

Cross spoke into the receiver. 'Yes ... He is, is he? ... Yes, he's here ... No, we won't ... I won't forget... I'll ring you back.'

He replaced the receiver saying to Hoffman: 'Yes, he's dead all right.'

'Do you mind if I ask a few questions?'

'Fire away, but don't expect too many intelligent answers.'

'I presume you're with British Intelligence.'

'You may presume what you wish, Mr. Hoffman.'

'Who was he?'

'Your very-dead, would-be assassin? A man named Novikov.'

'Russian like his gun?'

'As far as we can gather. As you know Portugal doesn't recognise the Soviet Union. But quite a few Russians managed to infiltrate during the Spanish Civil War when they were backing the Communists. They settled here with false identities and kept their heads down.'

'And why were you following him?'

'He worked as an interpreter – like you he was quite a linguist – and did a lot of work for us. But, of course, he was a Soviet agent. Who isn't an agent of some sort or another in

59

Lisbon these days? He was also a hit man,' Cross said. A breeze breathed through the open window, ruffled the curtains and, with a tinkle, spent itself in the chandelier. 'But we had penetrated his set-up and we got word that today he had a contract. We didn't know who but it soon became obvious that it was you. Why, we didn't know, still don't,' raising an eyebrow at Hoffman. 'At one stage Taft and I thought he was going to clobber you in the castle grounds.'

'Then why didn't you try and stop him?'

'We wanted to know where you were leading him and then perhaps why he was after your blood.'

'Mistaken identity?'

Cross grimaced at such a preposterous suggestion. He picked up the automatic, pointed it at Hoffman and said: 'Don't worry, it's not loaded.'

'Never was?'

'Oh, it was loaded all right. Taft took the bullets out.' He aimed the gun at the window and pulled the trigger. Click. 'There,' he said.

Hoffman put down his glass; he wasn't used to hard liquor and the whisky had affected his reasoning. There was a catalogue of questions to ask but he had to search for them.

'Until today I was a stranger to you?'

'Not quite. We make a point of checking out Red Cross personnel. I admire your dedication, Mr Hoffman, but it's not unknown for a few devils to flit among the angels of mercy.'

'But I—'

'We just checked you out, that's all. Any more questions?'

'Why did you shoot him? It was you, wasn't it?'

'As a matter of fact it wasn't. Taft did the dirty work.'

'Did you have to kill him?'

'He was going to kill you. Don't let that dedication of yours blind you to reality.'

'And you think you'll get away with it?'

'I'm quite sure we will. There are a lot of unsolved murders in Lisbon these days as I'm sure you know. The PIDE can't follow up the death of every stateless mid-European. Perhaps he had stolen someone's family jewels, their papers, their seat on the Clipper ...' Cross spread wide his hands. 'My turn again?'

'What more questions can there be? I don't know why he tried to kill me, nor do you.'

Cross leaned forward, grey eyes looking intently at Hoffman. 'Novikov worked for the NKVD. Have you really no idea why the Russian secret police should be so anxious to remove you from the face of this earth?'

'No idea at all,' lied Viktor Golovin.

Chapter Four

'So,' Churchill said to the tweed-suited man sitting opposite him on the lawns of Chartwell, 'contact has been made in Lisbon?'

The man, who had fair hair needled with grey and a withdrawn expression that looked as though it had been recently but permanently acquired, nodded. 'Some weeks ago.'

'You didn't inform me,' Churchill said reprovingly.

'With respect, Prime Minister,' said Colonel Robert Sinclair, head of the Secret Intelligence Service, 'you told me not to worry you with details. Only the grand stratagem.'

'You're right, of course.' Churchill smiled at him brilliantly through the smoke from his cigar and the spymaster's pipe. 'I've had a few things on my mind recently ...'

In the distance they heard the wail of air-raid sirens; then the alarm at Westerham groaned into life.

A few things on my mind, Churchill thought, and all of them disasters.

Since his becoming First Lord of the Admiralty on the declaration of war and then Prime Minister on May 10, 1940, after Chamberlain's policies had finally collapsed, the Nazi jackboot had crushed most of Western Europe; now its toe was aimed across the English Channel at Britain.

Well, he had told the Commons three days after becoming Premier that he had 'nothing to offer but blood, toil, tears and sweat'. But even he hadn't anticipated the scale of the catastrophes that lay ahead in the next three months.

Now Britain stood alone. Hitler had, on July 16, issued a directive for an invasion. And, judging by the armadas of

Messerschmitts, Dorniers, Heinkels and Junkers swarming across the skies, had every intention of carrying it out.

But had he? Wasn't it more likely that the attacks were aimed at softening up Britain to induce her to make the sort of deal with Germany that Hitler had always dreamed about?

Indeed only three days after issuing the directive Hitler had told the Reichstag: 'In this hour, I feel it to be my duty before my own conscience to appeal once more to reason and common sense in Great Britain as much as elsewhere ...'

The Führer was dumbfounded by the stubbornness of the British people. Hurt, even, that they didn't appreciate his benevolent schemes that would leave the British Empire, or most of it, unscathed.

No, Hitler's heart wasn't truly in the occupation of Britain: his ambition lay elsewhere – to the east.

And it was this belief that formed the cornerstone of the first phase of Churchill's Grand Stratagem that had been gestating ever since he had first suggested to Brendan Bracken, two years earlier, that Germany and Russia should be manoeuvred into fighting each other to a standstill.

From the south there came the drone of approaching aircraft.

Clementine called from the house: 'You'd better come in, Winston.'

Churchill who was wearing a painter's smock and grey trousers pretended not to hear and shaded his eyes to look at the enemy squadrons. They were flying high in the summer sky in parade-ground order.

Churchill said: 'I wish I had my field-glasses but if I go in to get them Clemmie will collar me.'

'So she should,' Sinclair told him. 'We can't afford to have our Prime Minister strafed by a Messerschmitt.'

His tone was almost flippant and it surprised Churchill. Sinclair, who looked like a Scottish laird, was canny but dour. In the past he had shown animation solely when talking about his only son Robin; Robin had died on the beaches of Dunkirk.

Perhaps imminent danger brought out the flippancy in him; it was a drug that affected men in many different ways. It made some grovel, it made some exultant, some foolhardy. For me it does all those things, he thought, but the public must only see the bravado.

Suddenly from the direction of the afternoon sun Spitfires attacked. Machine-guns chattered; the neatly-arranged squadrons of German aircraft broke up and Churchill was on his feet shouting: 'Bravo!'

Clementine came running out and handed them both steel helmets. 'If you won't take shelter,' she said, 'you'd better wear it.'

The sky above the serene countryside was now daubed with skeins and whorls of white smoke; from the midst of the high-battling planes one fell spinning towards the ground, trailing black smoke.

'One of theirs or one of ours?' Sinclair asked.

'God knows, poor devil.' Churchill sat down again on the garden seat beside Sinclair. 'But I do know this, we can't afford to lose many more. Max Beaverbrook is doing a superb job but even he can't replace the aircraft at the rate we're losing them. You see people only count the planes we lose in battle: they forget the ones destroyed on the ground when the Huns bomb our airfields.'

'At least we know where they're going to hit,' Sinclair said, flippancy discarded.

'Ah, Ultra, my most secret source. But we'll have to do better than that. If they continue to hit the airfields then we're done for. I wonder,' said Churchill thoughtfully, 'if a bombing raid on Berlin would taunt Hitler and Göring into bombing our cities instead of our defences ...'

Two aircraft detached themselves from the battle. A Dornier chased by a Spitfire. They roared so low over Chartwell that Churchill and Sinclair could see the pilots. The Spitfire's guns were blazing, shell cases clattering on the roof and terrace.

Black smoke burst from the Dornier. It turned over slowly with funereal majesty and disappeared as the Spitfire climbed exultantly and returned to the battle.

But the battle was almost over. The battered armada was returning home, discharging its bombs on to the countryside as it went. The trails of white smoke spread, entwined, drifted ...

'Floral tributes,' Churchill remarked.

But Sinclair was looking towards the pall of black smoke where the Dornier had crashed and Churchill knew what he was thinking.

Churchill guided him back to Lisbon. 'This contact, this

63

man Hoffman, or Golovin as he used to be called, is he sympathetic?'

'He's being cultivated,' Sinclair said.

'In what way? It's a warm day, you can divest yourself of your cloak of secrecy.'

'As you know, he works for the Red Cross and he's a pacifist.'

'So was Chamberlain,' Churchill remarked enigmatically. 'But he was strong.'

'I think Hoffman – we both know that his real name is neither Hoffman or Golovin – is strong. But at the moment he doesn't realise that he's being manipulated, so he's co-operating.'

'In what way is he being manipulated?' Churchill asked impatiently.

'Moulded would perhaps be a better word. As you well know, there have been a lot of peacemakers in evidence in recent years, and some of them are still swanning around Lisbon. Hoffman has been put in touch with them. Persuaded that he might be able to contribute something towards ending hostilities.'

Churchill said drily: 'He might be able to do just that.'

An all-clear sounded in the distance, others joined in, an eerie but welcome orchestra on a tranquil afternoon.

'I believe they've been dubbed Wailing Winnies,' Churchill said. 'Anything personal, do you think?' He took off his tin hat and threw it on the grass. 'I wonder how many more there'll be today.'

'I hear', Sinclair said, 'that they intend to put up something like 1,800.'

'And I wonder how many will get back.'

'More than we tell the public,' Sinclair said.

'You really are a pessimist, aren't you. What about some champagne?' He waved towards the house but Clementine was already on her way with a tray, a bottle of Möet Chandon and two glasses. 'What a woman!' Churchill exclaimed.

Clementine put the tray on the wooden table in front of them. 'I'm going back for a cup of tea,' she said. 'But I thought you'd like a victory celebration.'

'As if I needed an excuse,' Churchill said, easing the cork out of the bottle.

When Clementine had gone, Sinclair said: 'I think I'm realistic, not pessimistic. You forget I've been in Intelligence for a long time.'

'Then you must realise that it's necessary to broadcast encouraging statistics. God knows, the British people have little enough to be optimistic about. There's not so much difference between the statistics we put out and my speeches.'

'Your speeches are magnificent. A rallying call. The greatest weapon we have. Bar none,' he added, so that Churchill wondered if he was casting doubts on the Grand Stratagem in which, Lisbon apart, he was the only other conspirator. How old was Sinclair? Fifty-five, something like that. When war was declared Churchill had wondered if Sinclair wasn't too decent for his job; he had, after all, been employed by a Government that deified naïvety. But if there had been too much chivalry in his character it had been sent packing by bereavement and he now wore it as a disguise.

Sipping his champagne, Churchill stared at the white trails that had merged into a single cloud in the sky and thought: 'I enjoyed that battle, no doubt about it; but I'm not a warmonger ... ' But the introspective arguments were all too familiar. 'I am a man for the times,' he reassured himself. 'And they will discard me once again when it's all over ...'

Despite the warmth, the champagne, the presence of Sinclair, he felt suddenly alone. A man for the times ... a figure beckoned into an arena by circumstance.

'And the final circumstance,' he said, 'will be victory. And to win that victory,' he said to Sinclair who was looking at him curiously, 'we have to return to the plan, the reason for your visit.'

Sinclair relaxed saying: 'Of which Lisbon is the last instalment.'

'But the most important. Without it the first phase will be for nothing. Now let's run through Phase One again,' by which he meant he would run through it.

*

The comprehensive idea, Churchill said, was to match Germany and Russia against each other in a prolonged engagement in which they would bleed each other dry. In that way the world would be rid of two tyrannies of which, by their magnitude, the Bolsheviks were the more dangerous.

On August 23, 1939, Stalin and Hitler had signed a non-aggression pact with Poland as the shared spoils. Both dictators were merely buying time because there had never been any secret about the Führer's ultimate designs on the Soviet Union. It was, in fact, a classic pact of shared deceit. (Earlier that year Stalin might just as adroitly have signed a pact with Britain and France had they shown any inclination to throw in their lot with the Bolsheviks.)

But if Britain was to be saved – and she was militarily in no position to save herself – then she could not sit back and wait for one or other of the two despots to break their infamous alliance. While she waited she could succumb to invasion or slow death through isolation.

The first step then of Phase One was to blast the Luftwaffe out of the skies and sink as much as possible of the invasion fleet that Hitler would undoubtedly assemble across the Channel. By doing that Britain would convince Hitler that the invasion of Britain – Operation Sea Lion – was a mistake.

'His heart isn't in it anyway,' Churchill said, lighting a fresh cigar and pouring them both more champagne. 'So now we reach the crux of Phase One. Having been persuaded that his instincts are right – that it would be a mistake to invade Britain – he must then be convinced that the time is ripe to break his pact with Stalin and attack Russia. Prematurely!' Churchill stood up and took a turn round the garden seat. 'I'll tell you something,' he said, stopping in front of Sinclair. 'Two questions will always torment historians chronicling the Second World War – until, one day, the truth comes out as it always does ...'

Sinclair tilted his head politely. 'And they are?'

'One, why Hitler exposed himself on two fronts by invading Russia too soon.' He stared into the bubbles rising in his glass of champagne.

'And two?'

'Why Stalin ignored all the warnings that Hitler intended to attack when he did.'

'Warnings from whom?' asked Sinclair, trying to cope with an invisible invasion force that had been assembled across the

Channel, dispersed and converted into an army poised to attack the Russians.

'Myself among others,' said Churchill enigmatically.

Then he sat down again and continued to expound on Phase One.

If Hitler was to be persuaded to invade the Soviet Union prematurely then he must be convinced that his tactics against Britain had been successful. In other words that Britain had been forced to the edge of the negotiating table. If he believed that then the nightmare of war on two fronts would recede.

But the Führer was a wary negotiator – 'the only mortal he wholly trusts is Adolf Hitler' – and any suggestion that Britain was ready to come to terms would have to come from the top. From Churchill!

It would be the duty therefore of British Intelligence to get word to Hitler that Churchill was willing to discuss an armistice *after* he had turned against Russia. After, that was, he had proved his determination to eliminate the Bolshevik menace – an aim which Churchill shared.

At the same time he would have to be persuaded that the Red Army wasn't prepared for such an attack. This was easy enough because Stalin himself had torn the heart out of it.

Churchill slumped back in the seat. 'Well, what do you think?'

Sinclair said: 'You want me to work out details of how your alleged intentions should reach Hitler?'

'Without committing anything to paper,' Churchill said. 'Of course we can't make any move through normal diplomatic channels: I'd get thrown out of the Commons if word got out that I was contemplating a deal with Adolf. Hitler will understand that.'

'It shouldn't be too difficult,' Sinclair said. 'All we need is an intelligence source that Hitler trusts – as much as he trusts anyone.'

Churchill nodded, yawned. He needed a snooze; that was the way to defeat fatigue; naps enabled you to work a long day – and night. He was grateful to Jacky Fisher for teaching him to work at night: the eccentric old First Sea Lord in the last war had started work at two a.m. and finished at two p.m.

But Churchill couldn't snooze just yet: he had to convey the most important part of the conspiracy to Sinclair. He straightened up and said: 'But all this will be for nought if Stalin realises that the Nazis are poised to stab him in the back.'

'So we have to persuade him otherwise?'

'Exactly, and that is Phase Two, the eye of the whole conspiracy. If Stalin believes that Hitler is reneging on his agreement so soon then he will mass his troops, purged or otherwise, on the borders and there will be two possible outcomes.'

Churchill paused as he caught sight of Clementine at one of the windows of the house. She was pointing at her wristwatch. The message was clear: time for your nap. He waved at her.

Sinclair filled in the first possible outcome. 'There would be one hell of a battle.'

Churchill nodded. 'But not the sort we want. It would be another Waterloo with one or the other side emerging victorious. We would still have an enemy and an implacable one at that.'

'And the other outcome?'

'They'd patch it up. Slap each other on the back and blather about military manoeuvres. Withdraw their hordes and prolong their alliance. The first outcome,' Churchill said sombrely, 'would be unfortunate, the second would be a disaster – we could well have two implacable *and* united enemies.'

Churchill projected his imagination to what he hoped would happen. He saw blood on snow. He blinked – and saw a sparrow taking a dust-bath in a bed of roses.

He stretched, massaged his aching shoulder. He sipped what was left of the champagne in his glass but it was flat.

If they have accused me in the past of being a warmonger what would they say if they knew what I was contemplating now? They must never know in my lifetime, he decided. Perhaps one day when the war was distant history. When what I hope to achieve can be assessed against the sacrifices involved.

He sighed and said to Sinclair: 'What we have to achieve is a long, drawn-out war and that can only happen if Stalin is caught unawares. If Hitler is fooled by that lack of preparation and lured across the border to come face to face with the Russian winter. The Bolshevik hordes will retreat, regroup, re-arm; the Nazis will be extended until they're ready to snap. Then, God willing, they'll fight each other to a standstill. Or, at the very least, be so palsied that it will be at least a decade before either of them can muster the strength to turn on us once again. By which time we and the rest of the world should, in any case, be prepared.'

Sinclair said levelly: 'What you are suggesting, Prime Minister, could involve the deaths of millions.'

Churchill said quietly: 'Millions of deaths? You are probably right. But what you have to remember is the alternative. And that, quite simply, is the end of civilisation as we know it. The extermination of democracy. The death of liberty. The end,' pointing at the green tranquillity in front of them, 'of all this.'

The sparrow finished its dust-bath and flew away.

'Winston.' Clementine's voice reached him from the back door but Churchill ignored it: his deafness, not as bad as some people believed, was sometimes a great asset.

After a while Sinclair said: 'Odd to think that the key to the whole thing is a young man named Hoffman who hasn't the slightest inkling of what's afoot.' He knocked out his pipe on the heel of one of his brogues.

'The key to Phase Two certainly,' Churchill replied. 'But first of all we have to convince Corporal Hitler of our good intentions if he does attack Russia. Do you have any ideas?'

'Some,' Sinclair replied.

'Please be a little more explicit, colonel, we are on the same side you know.'

Sinclair scraped the charred bowl of his pipe with the blade of a silver penknife. Where would either of us be without our dummies? Churchill pondered as ash fell from his cigar.

'I believe in keeping an operation like this as tightly parcelled as possible,' Sinclair said at last.

'Lisbon?'

'It's the obvious centre. Much better than Switzerland, always has been. You can get in and out of the place because it's not landlocked. By sea and air,' he added.

Churchill said: 'I do know where Lisbon is.'

'But, of course, we wouldn't use Hoffman in this phase. He isn't ready for it.'

'Of course not. That goes without saying, surely.' Churchill suspected that Sinclair was wasting time, hoping that Clemmie reached them before he had to elaborate. 'Who then?'

'Another agent,' Sinclair told him.

Clementine was walking across the lawn towards them, determination in her stride.

'Who, man, who?'

'With respect, sir, you did say you weren't interested in the details.'

'I am now.'

Clementine was a hundred yards away, rounding a bed of red, white and blue petunias.

'Well, the man I have in mind won't be an innocent abroad like Hoffman.'

Churchill stood up and prodded his now-cold cigar at his spymaster. 'For the last time, Sinclair, who is this man?' He wasn't all that interested but he didn't like to be defied.

'Admiral Wilhelm Canaris, head of German military intelligence,' Sinclair said. His usually enigmatic features added: *Satisfied?*

'Thank you, colonel,' and to Clementine who was now standing beside them, empty basket and scissors for cutting flowers in her hand: 'There you are, my dear.'

'Here I am,' she said, 'and there you are, which is not where you're supposed to be at all. It's long past time for your nap.' Her tone implied that this was a far more serious matter than staying out of doors during an air-raid.

Churchill gave her a peck on the cheek and Sinclair a wink. 'Very well, my dear, just off.'

'And so am I,' said Sinclair, bowing to Clementine.

As Churchill walked thoughtfully across the lawns the siren at Westerham began to moan another warning. Churchill turned and looked inquiringly at his wife but she shook her head firmly and he continued on his way to the house.

Chapter Five

The softest touch for a creator of disinformation is a subject who wants to believe the creator's lies.

So I am lucky in that respect, Sinclair thought as he walked his red setter in the woods near his Berkshire home: Hitler wants to believe my lies – that Britain is at last ready to acknowledge his genius and do a deal.

And I'm also lucky that, for the time being, Hitler still trusts the purveyor of the lies, Admiral Canaris, head of the *Abwehr*, the intelligence section of the German High Command.

But I am unlucky in my own state of mind. The head of an intelligence agency should be impersonal, clinical in his judgement. But that is no longer true of me, not since the death of Robin. Now I am fuelled by hatred and that distorts judgement.

He picked up a stick and threw it for the dog, who disappeared among the rotting silver birch trees; a gun emplacement had blocked the natural drainage and the trees were dying like over-watered house plants. But it was a quiet place, becalmed among green fields, especially on evenings such as this with shafts of fading sunlight reaching its bed of moss. A place to contemplate. A place to plan. A place to hate.

The dog came bounding back and placed the stick at his feet and he threw it again, thinking: 'Admiral Canaris and I have a lot in common. We are both confused by hatred. I loved my son and so now I hate Germany: he loves Germany but hates Hitler. But you've got to stop this,' he admonished himself. 'Start to plan!'

Once more he threw the stick. How to entice Canaris to Lisbon? That shouldn't be too difficult; he was already involved with Franco in neighbouring Spain, and Lisbon was the European capital of espionage, which was Canaris's profession.

To anticipate the reactions of Canaris he would have to study him more deeply. As he walked down the flinty lane towards his home in Finchampstead he poked a particularly bright flint with his walking stick and found that it was a jagged sliver of shrapnel.

When he reached the big rambling house he called to the setter: 'Robin, come here.' But the dog's name was Rufus.

*

In his study he consulted the file on Canaris.

He lit his pipe and, as the day died outside and his wife cooked an austerity meal in the kitchen, the admiral emerged from the dossier and took a bow.

71

He was fifty-three years old but looked older. His silken hair was prematurely grey and he was known as Old Whitehead.

He had served in the Navy in the last war with distinction. On one occasion his cruiser had been scuttled off the South American coast before the superior guns of a British warship; he had been interned on an island close to Chile but had escaped to the mainland in a rowing boat disguised as a Chilean. He had crossed the Andes on horseback ... taken a train to Argentina ... sailed to Amsterdam on a forged passport, calling at the *British* port of Falmouth!

A man to be reckoned with.

His escapades had continued in spectacular fashion and his star had been in the ascendant until he had fallen foul of Admiral Erich Raeder who had blocked his promotion in the conventional Navy, thereby setting him on course for espionage.

Ironic, mused Sinclair, that Raeder had advocated defeating Britain before attacking the Soviet Union.

On January 1, 1935, on his forty-eight birthday, Canaris had become head of the *Abwehr*.

He was 5 feet 3 inches tall. He had pale blue eyes. His manner was mild. He had difficulty in sleeping. He was a hypochondriac although his only known complaint was bad circulation which accounted for the coldness of which he continually complained.

He was a pessimist. He detested Hitler because of his persecution of the Jews and he feared for his country because he believed its leader was a madman.

He was subject to fits of melancholia.

In Lisbon the approach would have to be circumspect. Canaris was co-operating with British Intelligence but he certainly would not co-operate to the extent of bringing about Germany's downfall.

So he would have to be persuaded that Churchill genuinely wanted to settle for peace; that, with the spectre of war on two fronts removed, Hitler would be able to concentrate on crushing Russia.

But Canaris was a sly old fox. What if he still had lingering doubts about *perfide Albion?* Well, there was one way in which the admiral could be *persuaded* that it was in everyone's interests to tell Hitler about Britain's change in policy. Blackmail.

From the kitchen came his wife's voice. 'Dinner's ready, dear. Spam fritters and scrambled eggs – dried eggs, I'm afraid.'

*

Old Whitehead winced at the first scream.

He abhorred cruelty. But then he reminded himself that the man being beaten up in the adjoining room was a draft-dodger and felt a little better because he also abhorred that particular brand of cowardice.

But who are you to moralise? Admiral Canaris asked himself, sitting in an easy chair and picking up a copy of *Signal*, the Services' propaganda magazine. You with your double standards.

His hands trembled as he turned the pages of the magazine. What a mess he had become since the death and glory days when he had been a U-boat commander and then captain of the cruiser *Schlesien*; since he had been diverted into espionage.

But perhaps that is your true vocation, intrigue, because you even intrigue with yourself. Deceive yourself, manipulate your conscience, trade secrets with the enemy, assuring yourself that it is for the good of the country you love ...

Furthermore you are a pessimist, Canaris. Your punishment? The admiral turned a page of the magazine and stared at a photograph of a sailor with his arm round the waist of a girl with her hair in braids; the sailor's face was bold; like mine once was in those far off days of youth and optimism.

He turned another page and Adolf Hitler stared at him.

From the room next door another scream and a voice shouting in English: 'I don't know! I ... tell you ... I ... don't ... know.'

A thud, followed by the sound of a body falling.

Canaris glanced at his wristwatch. Another couple of minutes and he would call it off because in all probablity the Englishman was telling the truth.

He was one of the many informants who during the past couple of weeks in Portugal, Switzerland, Sweden and, indeed, in London itself, had reported a dramatic change in Britain's policy.

According to the reports Churchill, despite his swashbuckling oratory, wanted to do a deal with Hitler because he realised that the position of his bombarded and besieged islands was hopeless.

In his offices in Tirpitzufer in Berlin Canaris had studied the reports with scepticism. There were too many of them all at once.

Then two highly plausible sources had come up with the same information in Lisbon and he had flown to the Portuguese capital.

But before confronting them he had decided to put a lesser informant to the test. A dispensable informant such as the draft-dodging Englishman – of whom there were quite a few in Lisbon – who was at this moment having his teeth knocked down his throat in the basement of the German Minister's residence.

Canaris shivered despite the heavy leather overcoat he wore. He felt cold. But then he always felt cold. From a silver pillbox he took a white tablet to aid his circulation.

He opened the door to the adjoining room and told the two shirt-sleeved inquisitors to put down their rubber hoses.

The Englishman who had been propped against a wall of the bare room slid to the floor. Just as they did in the movies, Canaris thought. Although unlike movie interrogators the two sweating Gestapo bully-boys did not appear to have been enjoying themselves. Presumably they preferred more refined and less exhausting methods of extracting information which he didn't permit – that was the domain of Reinhard 'Hangman' Heydrich, Himmler's deputy and head of all SS security, which included the Gestapo.

Perhaps one day men such as this will interrogate me, Canaris thought, and felt even colder.

He said to the Englishman: 'Get up.'

The body on the floor moved. The bloodied head turned. Eyes slitted between swollen flesh regarded Canaris. With hatred or gratitude? With a face in that condition you couldn't tell.

To one of the interrogators Canaris said: 'Bring him a chair.' When the Englishman was sitting on the kitchen chair beneath a naked electric light bulb Canaris gave him a cigarette and lit it for him.

The Englishman, whose name was Spearman, inhaled and coughed and inhaled again as if the smoke was a medicament. He was young, about twenty-three, with fair wavy hair and a face that, before the beating, had been half-saint and half-

74

delinquent. According to *Abwehr* records in Lisbon he was a homosexual.

To one of the interrogators, Canaris said: 'What was it he didn't know? What was the question?'

'He didn't know whether it was true or not.'

'Whether what was true?'

'The information he brought, whatever that was,' the man said sullenly.

So the Gestapo, who unfortunately handled all interrogations in Lisbon, were learning at last: don't tell your inquisitors too much, thereby keeping risks to a minimum.

To the Englishman he said: 'Why aren't you fighting for your country?'

Spearman spat out blood. 'This is a neutral country and I shall report you to the authorities.'

'Really? What authorities, I wonder? The Portuguese? We Germans really are calling the tune here, you know, and their police won't risk upsetting us. The British? I don't think so, do you? They would lock you up or, worse, make you fight. But you didn't answer my question. Why aren't you helping to defend your country? You see I am a patriot and the reasoning of a traitor interests me.'

'I'm not a traitor.' The voice was slurred.

'What are you then?'

'A pacifist.'

'Then you should have registered as a conscientious objector in England.'

'I prefer the sunshine,' Spearman said.

'Where did you get this information?'

'At the Casino at Estoril, where else?'

'A hundred and one places,' Canaris said. 'The Aviz or the Avenida Palace, in Lisbon, the Palácio or the Hotel do Parque in Estoril ... '

'I like to gamble.'

'Who gave you the information?'

'I gleaned it.'

He spoke beautiful English. Perhaps he had been to Cambridge where the Russians were so assiduously recruiting agents.

'Who from?'

Spearman put two fingers inside his mouth. They came out

75

holding a tooth. Then the spirit seemed to go out of Spearman, so often the case when a homosexual realises his looks have been damaged.

Sensing that the moment had come to change the approach, Canaris dismissed the two Gestapo thugs. They hesitated, unsure of Canaris's authority.

Without raising his voice, Canaris said: 'Get out.'

They went.

Canaris sat down opposite Spearman, gave him another cigarette and said in a friendly, almost paternal, tone: 'Come now, stop being so obstinate. An admirable quality, I agree, and very British, but entirely misplaced at the moment.'

Tears gathered in Spearman's eyes. 'I just don't understand,' he said. 'I pass on information, that's all. I don't pretend it's true, I never have. And what happens ...?' His voice trembled and he brushed at his eyes with blood-stained fingers; Canaris felt almost, but not quite, sorry for him. 'This is what happens ... It isn't fair.'

'If you co-operate it won't happen again. Believe me, I don't want to see you hurt.' True enough. 'And if you do help us we might even increase your reward.'

Spearman stared at Canaris beseechingly. 'But I have co-operated; I don't understand ...'

'Your informant, who was he?' Canaris hardened his tone a little.

'I told you it was only hearsay.'

'A homosexual?'

'Does that make it more suspect?' a little spirit returning to him.

Canaris shook his head. 'It makes no difference. Gossip is gossip. It's up to us to process it.' He handed Spearman a handkerchief. 'Who was he?'

Spearman pressed the white silk handkerchief to his eyes. 'Yes, he's queer all right.'

'Your ... *friend?*'

Spearman nodded.

'British?'

'Swiss.'

'You move in exalted circles, Mr. Spearman,' because there was no such mortal as a poor Swiss here, or anywhere else for that matter.

'I move in influential circles.'

76

'You mean, I think, that for reasons we won't pursue you are briefly admitted to the fringe of such circles. Among the fugitive kings of Europe *reigning* in Estoril.'

'And bankers and businessmen and diplomats and spies, of course. There are more spies in Estoril than whores in Piccadilly.'

'And your *friend* ... what is his profession?'

'Does it matter?'

'Oh yes,' Canaris said, 'it matters very much.'

'Very well then, he's a businessman.'

'You're not giving very much away, Mr. Spearman. I understood you were going to co-operate.'

'I thought it was an unwritten law,' Spearman said, puffing away at his cigarettes, 'that informants weren't obliged to give away their source of information.'

'I just re-wrote that law.'

'Very well, his business is cork.'

'Along with every other businessman in Lisbon. But hardly a profitable enterprise for a Swiss. After all, they don't produce that much wine, and none of that particularly memorable. Are you sure it's cork, Mr Spearman?'

'I understand he's a middleman.'

'Ah, but he wouldn't be anything else, would he?' Canaris touched his grey eyebrows, a habit of his; his wife had clipped them for him at their home on Lake Ammersee in Bavaria just before he left for Portugal; he wished profoundly that he was back there now. He unbuttoned his overcoat, leaned forward and snapped: 'His name please.'

'I can't give it to you. You'll have him beaten just as you've beaten me.'

'A Swiss businessman? I doubt that, I doubt that very much,' Canaris said. 'British draft-dodgers, yes, we beat the hell out of them. But not Swiss businessmen. In any case we might need his cork, if cork it is, for some of our Rhine wines. He is German Swiss?'

'No, French ... Shit!' Spearman stamped on his cigarette butt. 'That was bloody clever.'

'At least it narrows the field. You might as well tell me his name, I'll find out soon enough. If you die during further interrogation,' his voice still pleasant, man-to-man, 'then it will merely be a process of elimination.'

Spearman began to shiver. 'If I do, you won't —'

'Reveal the source of *my* information? Certainly not. I am an officer and a gentleman, although that may have escaped you.'

Spearman gave him a name. Cottier. Canaris stood up and began to pace the floor. Cottier? It meant nothing to him.

'... in any case,' Spearman was saying, 'he only heard it indirectly at a party. You know those Estoril parties ...'

'No, I don't,' said Canaris, thinking of France, Belgium, Holland bleeding from the wounds of war. 'And who was *his* informant, for God's sake?'

The transfer of responsibility seemed to cheer Spearman up a little. He uttered a name which stopped Canaris in his tracks because it was the name of one of the two sources that had brought him to Lisbon.

*

Half an hour later Canaris lunched with Fritz von Claus, head of the *Abwehr* operation in Portugal, in his small terrace house overlooking the flea market.

He usually enjoyed himself there. It was so cramped, so full of books, so bachelor, and the schnapps was so smoky on the tongue that it reminded him of his youth when, on leave from naval college, he had planned – not conspired – breathtaking visions for the Fatherland.

To Canaris, von Claus always seemed like a professor, although he was the younger of the two (the deformity on his back, not quite a hunch, had added years to his fragile frame) and, of course, junior in rank.

By the time they were halfway through a bottle of schnapps washed down with pale beer imported from Munich the present was an unwelcome stranger to their conversation. But an intrusive one.

'So, what do you think?' Canaris asked.

'About the rumours? As you say, they're a little too thick on the ground. I wouldn't have suggested you came to Lisbon if they hadn't been backed up by two of our prime contacts.'

'I'm glad you did,' Canaris said. 'I like it in your home. It's a forgotten outpost of the Germany we once knew. Before—'

'Careful,' von Claus whispered.

'Hey, what's this? Spy warning spy about eavesdroppers? Are the British so alert?' But his voice was hushed.

'The Gestapo are, you must know that.'

His words sobered them both. Von Claus switched on the radio.

Finally Canaris said softly: 'But they answer only to Himmler and Heydrich. I answer to Hitler. For the time being,' he said sombrely. 'What has it come to, Fritz, fearing your own countrymen more than the enemy?' He tossed back a measure of schnapps. 'But back to the business of the moment – then we can luxuriate about the past over lunch. What's for lunch, Fritz?'

'Frankfurters,' said von Claus. 'Frankfurters that spit their juice at you when you sink your teeth into them. Sauerkraut and potato salad.'

Canaris licked his lips. 'If you eat like that every day why don't you put on any weight?'

'I wish I did, I have a lot of trouble getting suits to fit me,' said von Claus who was as dapper as he was deformed. 'But tell me, Wilhelm, if this is an elaborate disinformation operation how could it possibly benefit the British?' He turned up the volume of the radio.

Canaris shrugged. 'God knows. But I wouldn't put anything past Churchill. On the face of it his strategy is logical enough: persuade us to smash Russia so that Britain and Germany can co-exist without the Bolshevik menace. I'd like to think it's as simple as that ...'

'Except that in our world things never are? Have another drink, Wilhelm. Blast the suspicions out of that old grey head of yours.'

'Not so old,' Canaris said. 'You see, what Churchill is saying to Hitler is this: "We will cause no trouble in the west, leaving you free to pursue your dream of expansion in the east." Or more concisely: "We, the British, will allow you to go to war on only one front." '

'So?'

'You don't fool me, professor. You just want me to express your own doubts.'

'And they are?' smiling his pinched smile.

'Timing, my dear Fritz, timing. Just supposing Hitler was delayed? Drawn into the Russian winter. And then just supposing Churchill didn't keep his side of the bargain. Just supposing he attacked. *Voilà*. A war on two fronts.'

'Britain isn't strong enough to attack,' von Claus objected.

'She would be if the United States had by then entered the war. Timing, you see. She would be with Canada, Australia, New Zealand, South Africa, India and all the rest of her Empire beside her.'

Von Claus stood up and said loudly: 'Come on, let's eat and soak up some of that liquid cordite.' As Canaris stood up he again lowered his voice to a whisper: 'You know what I think, Wilhelm? I think it might be a good idea if Stalin was warned that the Führer intended to attack. That way there would probably be no war at all and thousands, possibly millions, of German lives would be saved.'

'That possibility,' said Canaris equally softly, 'had not escaped me.' He put his finger to his lips in a gesture that was only slightly theatrical.

*

The first of the two sources on which Canaris had decided to gauge the strength of the reports about Churchill's new policy was a sleek, well-fed cat.

His hair, grey at the temples, was sleek; his physique, aided by Savile Row suits, was sleek; when paid compliments he purred.

He was one of the *Abwehr's* most trusted agents in Lisbon and unique because he never asked for money; certainly, being a banker, he had more than enough but it was the sad experience of the accountants in Tirpitzufer that the richer the agent the more he charged. Apparently all that the banker required was recognition when Germany won the war.

Canaris met him by appointment at a ball given by a Brazilian coffee millionaire in one of the red-roofed mansions lying behind the Casino at the coastal resort of Estoril, fifteen miles from Lisbon. The occasion struck Canaris as a bewildering anachronism. While most of Europe was blacked out the mansion glittered. The guests, who had arrived in splendid limousines, danced beneath chandeliers jewelled with light; the champagne frothed brilliantly; the gardens, designed for assignations, were strung with coloured lights.

And in view of international tensions, the guests themselves were an astonishing mêlée. Especially on the dance floor. There, in white ties and tails, in gowns from Paris, London and New York, the partnering confounded politics. Americans, Spaniards, Portuguese, Germans, French, South Americans,

80

Japanese ... only the British seemed to have given it a miss because they shunned the Germans whenever possible.

There was King Carol of Rumania; Camille Chautemps, one-time Premier of France; the elegant Duke of Alba, former Spanish Ambassador to Britain; Joseph Bech, the Grand Old Man of Luxembourg.

There was Otto Bauer, head of the Gestapo in Lisbon.

Ignoring him, Canaris, immaculate but uncomfortable in his evening clothes, skirted the dancers spinning to a Viennese waltz, took a glass of champagne from a red-jacketed waiter and made his way on to the terrace.

The banker, looking sleeker than ever, smiled at him and together they strolled through the scented gardens until they were outside the glow of the fairy lights. Beyond, they could see the moonlit waters of the Atlantic where they lapped the small Tamariz beach.

'A beautiful night,' the banker purred.

'But a little cold.'

'Cold? But, my dear admiral, the air is like mulled wine.'

'I would be cold in hell,' Canaris told him. 'What do you have for me?'

'An intriguing morsel.' The banker's German was almost perfect. 'No, more than a morsel, an entrée which I'm sure you and the Führer will devour hungrily.'

Canaris sipped his champagne; in the darkness it seemed to lose its taste. 'Well, out with it, man,' he thought and said: 'How very intriguing,' wishing that just sometimes spies could be more straightforward, and reflecting how different this exchange was from the interrogation of Spearman.

The banker chuckled richly. 'It's more than intriguing, admiral, it's downright sensational.'

'Am I right in assuming that it has something to do with British policy towards Germany?' hoping that von Claus had got it right; at the same time hoping he would deflate the banker into speeding up his revelations.

'Quite correct,' undeflated. 'I told von Claus roughly what it was all about. But I didn't tell him my source; that's what's so sensational.'

Another source. Canaris stifled a sigh. 'You mean your information is second-hand?'

'Of course, isn't all information second-hand unless the informant is the originator of his intelligence?'

81

'I suppose you're right.' Perhaps I should have brought a length of rubber hose, Canaris thought.

'But my information is documented. And what a document!'

The banker moved closer to Canaris, his cologne overpowering the perfumes of the garden.

Canaris backed away.

The banker said: 'I think you will agree, when you have read it, that my place in the post-war financial world should be assured.'

'You have this document with you?'

'Of course. A letter. With a fascinating signature.'

When the banker didn't immediately produce it Canaris wondered if he was going to disappoint Tirpitzufer accounts department and ask for money.

'Whose signature?' he asked. 'Winston Churchill's?'

'Not quite. I'm afraid he doesn't bank with me. A pity because I hear he is very interested in money.'

Canaris's patience was fast running out. 'Then if you would be so good ...'

The banker said: 'Here you are, admiral. Read it when you get back into the light. You will not be disappointed.'

He handed Canaris an envelope, gave a little bow and disappeared, purring, in the direction of the mansion.

Canaris moved swiftly into the light and, after glancing around, ripped open the envelope.

The letter consisted of only two paragraphs. They confirmed what he had expected from the banker. But he had to admit that the signature was a knock-out.

Windsor.

As he picked his way through the gardens he assessed the credibility of the letter. A hand-writing expert would soon be able to confirm whether the signature was that of the Duke of Windsor, formerly Edward VIII, who on December 10, 1936, had abdicated because the British wouldn't allow him to wed the twice-married American, Wallis Warfield Simpson.

But why should he write to a Lisbon banker?

Why not?

He had recently been staying in Estoril at the home of another banker, Ricardo Espirito Santo e Silva, known to the British as the Holy Ghost, while his war-time future was debated in Whitehall.

His pro-Nazi sympathies were famous, or infamous according to your view, a viewpoint that in no way detracted from his patriotism: it was merely that the Duke thought that Britain and Germany should never have gone to war.

So impressed had Hitler been by the Duke's philosophy that he had ordered his Foreign Minister, the empty-headed Joachim von Ribbentrop, to try and persuade the Duke to stay in a European country within the sphere of German influence, the idea being that one day he could return to the throne - along with his Nazi sympathies.

Of course von Ribbentrop, the one-time champagne sales-man, had botched what had been a hare-brained scheme in the first place. He had offered to put 50 million Swiss francs into a deposit account for the Duke; then asserted that, if all else failed, *coercion* could be used.

In other words: kidnap him.

And to compound the idiocy he had put Walter Schellenberg in charge of things. Schellenberg, one of Heydrich's lieutenants in the Reich Security Administration, the RSHA, which incorporated nearly every police department in Germany--with the exception of the *Abwehr*, that was - was able enough, a charmer even. But he, too, thought von Ribbentrop was an ass and his plot fatuous.

He had never really tried to implement it beyond getting word to the restless Duke that British agents were gunning for him, and, in the event, the Duke had sailed from Lisbon on August 2 on his way to the Bahamas to become Governor, which was just about the most ineffectual job the British could find for their ex-king. But, of course, the British never forgave.

But at least the circumstances for contact between the banker and the Duke were established. And following the approaches from Schellenberg's henchmen the Duke would have known that the banker was his best clandestine short-cut to Berlin.

Canaris reached the terrace framed with bougainvillea and jasmine, slipped the envelope into the inside pocket of his jacket and weaved his way through the guests.

Bauer, heavily built with cropped hair, intercepted him. 'Do you always collect your post in the garden?' He tapped the lapel of Canaris's jacket.

'Sometimes I read it in the garden,' Canaris replied. 'Especially when it's confidential. Especially when it comes from Berlin.'

He watched Bauer field that one. Hitler, Himmler, Heydrich? All the H's. The Bauers of the various SS security departments were always unsure how to treat Canaris; they sensed that Heydrich was poised to unseat him and gobble up the *Abwehr* and yet Canaris seemed to ride all such rumours with magnificent disdain; what's more, he was a confidant of Hitler who used him as an emissary as well as a spymaster.

If they knew the truth, Canaris thought, smiling at Bauer, they'd put me in front of a firing squad.

'Was the letter from your wife, admiral?'

'No,' Canaris said, still smiling, 'not my wife.'

'You were lucky to get an invitation to the ball at such short notice.'

'My dear Bauer,' Canaris said, discarding his smile, 'I was dining with our host when you were attending your first interrogation,' and was pleased when the Brazilian millionaire clapped him on the shoulder and said: 'Ah, Admiral Canaris, how are you these days?' studiously ignoring Bauer.

Together they strolled away, leaving Bauer staring after them. 'A thug, I'm afraid,' the Brazilian said, 'but I have to think of the future and I want to export my coffee to both the Germans and the Portuguese.'

In the Embassy car taking him back to Lisbon Canaris reconsidered the letter.

If you thought about it, what better go-between for Churchill and Hitler? The Duke had been friendly with both; in fact Churchill had backed him before the abdication. Churchill and Hitler in agreement! The mind boggled.

Personally Canaris thought the dethronement of the lovesick king had been the best thing that had happened to Britain for years: he was a playboy, his brother, George, was a king.

Canaris glanced out of the window of the Mercedes-Benz 170. Lights everywhere. Coming to Portugal was like walking out of a dark cave.

He touched the clipped tufts of his eyebrows. According to *Abwehr* intelligence in Lisbon the Duke had recently been in touch with Churchill who, although he was conducting a war, had found time to reply. So the rapport was still there.

Canaris was inclined at this early stage in his deliberations to believe that the letter was genuine.

But would the suggestion it contained work? There was no reason, Canaris decided, spreading a travelling rug across his knees, why it shouldn't. Hitler had never wanted to go to war with Britain and, judging by his half-hearted invasion preparations, had no real wish to occupy it.

If he was given an alternative then he would grab it. And that's what Churchill, via the Duke, was offering him. With a proviso. Russia.

Canaris switched on a reading light above his head and took the envelope from his pocket again. It bore no postmark and must have been handed to the banker by one of the Duke's friends when the Duke was well away from the complications it would cause. That, too, was in character.

He re-read the brief typewritten text several times.

It has come to my knowledge through impeccable sources – Churchill, of course – *that my country is willing to consider any course of action that will bring an end to the suffering that is, as I write, being endured by millions of innocent people, a tragedy that could in my opinion have been averted in 1939 by the use of the pen instead of the sword.* But not in Churchill's opinion!

It is common knowledge that the Führer is anxious to reach a peaceful settlement with Great Britain …

Referring, Canaris assumed, to Hitler's speech to the Reichstag on July 19. Churchill had ignored his appeal and Hitler had been grieved and enraged.

… and that feeling is now shared in the very highest echelons of Westminster where it is believed that Great Britain could honourably cease hostilities with Germany if she abandoned her plans to invade our islands and turned her attentions immediately to the menace which both countries have long considered to be the ultimate foe.

In other words, leave us alone, attack Russia as soon as possible and we'll do a deal.

Hitler, Canaris thought, would probably consider such a proposition favourably. He had always sworn to crush Bolshevism. If the Duke was to be believed the British were proposing that he attack sooner than he had anticipated with the element of surprise on his side.

In his room in the German Minister's Residence on the Rua do Pau da Bandeira, linked to the Legation by a secret underground tunnel, Canaris took off his evening clothes with relief, washed and brushed his teeth and slipped between cool sheets. Hands behind his head, he lay in the moonlight and waited for suspicions to present themselves, as they always did when he wanted to sleep.

Surely the whole set-up was too facile. Could it be that the Duke was playing a card in a masterly game of deception? That he was contributing far more to the British cause than he could have done in any other capacity? If so, history would gravely misjudge his post-abdication record. He would be dismissed as dilettante instead of saviour.

Wearily, Canaris climbed from the bed and went to the bathroom where he took a dose of Phanodorm. He should have taken it half an hour earlier but even now when he was old enough to know better he still hoped for the miracle – a night of natural sleep.

Soon the drug began to dispel the suspicions. But on the borders of sleep he glimpsed a terrifying vision: a mass grave filled with grey-haired corpses with clipped eyebrows.

When he finally slept he dreamed that he was King of England.

*

Canaris met the second source the following morning at a rendezvous as macabre as the mansion at Estoril had been sumptuous.

Why couldn't spies be content with the mundane? he wondered, sitting in the back of the Mercedes-Benz taking him to the Church of St Vincent Beyond the Wall outside Lisbon.

According to Baron Oswald Hoyningen-Hüne, German Minister in Lisbon, the old church was decorative enough from the outside, the walls of its cloisters covered with glazed tiles depicting the Fables of La Fontaine; it was inside that the atmosphere became sinister because the crypt housed the mummified corpses of a dynasty of Portuguese kings, the House of Bragança.

The black limousine was appropriate for the occasion, Canaris thought: it looked like a hearse.

As it glided to a halt outside the church Canaris glanced at his watch. It was 11.55 am; at least the informant had picked a civilised time, midday. The driver opened the door and Canaris stepped out, still wearing his leather overcoat despite the gathering heat; his bodyguard, a young man with a slight limp who had been wounded in Norway, stood at a respectful distance.

Overhead a hawk floated on the hot air before swooping on its prey. Yellow butterflies flitted among blazes of poppies and air droned with insect noise.

Canaris hoped that the informant, as valuable in his way as the banker, would pull up outside; then he would suggest a stroll in the great outdoors out of earshot of the driver and the bodyguard because almost anything was preferable to conversing in the company of corpses, however venerable they were.

Again he consulted his watch. One minute to go. He sighed. The informant was inside already. He turned on his heel and, followed by his bodyguard, headed for the cadavers.

The crypt, lit by flickering candles, smelled of burning tallow, embalming fluid, spices and prolonged death. The kings gazed at Canaris from black, glass-topped caskets scattered across the floor in historical disarray. A dynasty of Braganças contemptuously reshuffled by a new Republic.

Beyond the flame of a thick white candle Canaris detected a movement. His hand reached for the automatic he carried in the pocket of his coat as a back-up to the bodyguard.

A moth brushed against his face; he shivered but not this time with the cold. He thought he could hear breathing. As he stepped over a king staring benignly through the centuries, a man's voice said: 'Perhaps you would be good enough to tell your Man Friday to go away; there's enough death here already.' He stepped out of the shadows. 'I haven't got a gun.'

Canaris told the bodyguard who was hovering at the door to wait outside.

He let go of the gun in his pocket and said: 'Was this set-up really necessary?'

'It's one of the few places where we won't be seen. A superstitious lot, the Portuguese.'

'Why,' Canaris said, speaking in English, 'do spies always have to be so melodramatic?'

'Because our profession is supposed to be melodramatic. When we discover it isn't we have to create our own melodrama. I'm sorry I couldn't lay on a ball in Estoril for you. Do you have the money?' he asked abruptly.

'If you have the information.'

'Nothing in writing. Just what I've been told.'

'I seem to have heard that before,' Canaris said. 'May I suggest that you come a little closer. I don't like addressing you across half a dozen corpses, even though they're a bit past eavesdropping.'

Canaris had only met Cross once before but again he was struck by the man's blend of sophistication and brutality. He wore a double-breasted grey suit and his tan was a shock in this funereal place.

Canaris said: 'Well?'

Cross told Canaris what he had implied to von Claus – that in the British Embassy in the Rua S. Domingos a Lapa he had heard reports that Churchill was ready to do a deal with Germany.

'Provided we divert our attentions away from the English Channel to the Soviet Union?'

'Yes,' Cross said, in a tone of surprise, 'how did you know?'

'You aren't the only agent with his ear to the ground in Lisbon.'

'The banker?'

It was Canaris's turn to be surprised. 'Just other sources,' he said. 'Let's stick to the rules, Mr. Cross.'

Double cross?

Cross brushed the dust from the glass on one of the caskets. Dom Carlos, one of the more recent Braganças, medals still pinned to his faded uniform, stared inquiringly at him.

'Rules? The Braganças stuck to the rules and look where it got them.'

'Nearly three hundred glorious years,' Canaris said. 'After Duke John of Bragança threw the Spanish out.'

'Look where the rules got Carlos the First. Assassinated. In 1908, I think.'

Canaris said: 'I'm honoured that I have been selected to convey this information to the Führer.'

'I wonder,' Cross said, 'how *he* will shed his mortal coil. Let's see if we can find Carlos.' He moved from one casket to another, brushing the years from the glass lids. 'Why do you think you've been honoured, admiral?'

'Because someone is aware that the Führer will listen to me.'

'And will he?' inspecting a noble face that had been partly eaten away by rats. Canaris smelled putrefaction. 'No, that's not him,' Cross said, moving on.

'Of course.'

'But you don't believe what you've heard?'

'I don't believe, I don't disbelieve. Do you believe what you've heard in this instance, Mr Cross?'

'He looks as if he died from undernourishment,' Cross said, pointing at an emaciated monarch. 'Yes, I do. The source was informed ... that's what sources are, aren't they?'

Canaris looked longingly at the daylight at the top of the steps. Cross had in the past proved just as reliable as the banker; but if you were going to deceive you made sure the purveyor of the deceit was trusted.

Canaris said: 'Do you regard yourself as a traitor, Mr. Cross?'

'On the contrary, a patriot. It's merely that I don't believe we should be at war with Germany. The real enemy is Russia.'

'And you feel that we should put them to the sword? Do Churchill's dirty work for him?'

'It's more complex than that,' Cross said, straightening up from a casket. 'In the first place Britain isn't in a fit state to fight anyone. In the second Hitler has always sworn that he would see off the Bolsheviks. But what's more important is that Churchill could not be seen to be co-operating with the Germans, so there is really no way Britain could fight on their side. No, it has to be done this way because it's the only way.'

Canaris began to move towards the shaft of daylight; the smell of the place was beginning to make him feel sick.

Cross said: 'I got the impression that speed was of the essence. The quicker Hitler attacked Russia the better for everyone. According to my *informed sources*. That makes sense, doesn't it? Break the pact with Stalin without prior warning and before he's reorganised the Red Army.'

'Perhaps. Hitler hadn't intended to attack quite so precipitately.'

'That was because after his speech to the Reichstag he had finally given up hope that Britain would seek peace. Now Churchill's resurrecting that hope. Historians will always wonder why Hitler abandoned his plans to invade Britain. Our naval and air superiority – that's what they'll plump for. But we'll know better, won't we, admiral?'

Could you be infected by the breath of coffins? Canaris took a small, anti-catarrhal inhalant from his pocket, breathed some vapour into his lungs and said; 'I haven't decided what I'm going to tell the Führer.'

Cross peered into a casket. Shaking his head, he said: 'One more to go.' He reminded Canaris of a sleek young officer taking a roll-call of the dead on a battlefield. How did he acquire such a tan?

Cross said: 'Tell him what *you* believe.'

'It would be better if I had some documented proof of Churchill's intentions,' looking keenly at Cross to see if he reacted, if he knew about the Duke of Windsor's letter, but Cross merely replied: 'The point is that Hitler will believe you.'

No, the point, my friend, Canaris thought, is: Do I want to tell him? Theoretically, he supposed, the answer was a resounding Yes: a swift and comprehensive victory over Russia would leave the Third Reich triumphantly astride Europe and the western reaches of the Soviet Union. But do I want Hitler to lead us to that sort of victory? Do I want to be instrumental in giving him a free hand to extend the genocide of the Jews with his executioner, Himmler, the mad chicken farmer, at his side?

Again the solution that he and Fritz von Claus – encouraged by schnapps – had touched upon – presented itself: Advise Hitler to attack and at the same time warn Stalin. No war, no more German casualties, no more genocide.

'Of course there are other considerations,' Cross was saying and his words were so pertinent that for one alarming moment Canaris wondered if he had been voicing his thoughts.

'Such as?'

Cross, stooped over a king, glanced up at Canaris. 'I am in British Intelligence – as well as yours,' smiling, 'and it is not unknown that you don't always see eye to eye with Hitler.'

'Really? I'm afraid that observation doesn't say much for British Intelligence.'

Cross stood up, shaking his head. 'No Carlos, I'm afraid. A pity. I like to have everything neatly tied up, you know, a beginning and an end. What about the bomb in the Bürgerbräukeller in Munich on November 8 last year?'

Startled, Canaris said: 'What about it?' He replaced the inhaler in his pocket and brought out his silver pill-box; he swallowed a mauve tablet, a tranquilliser.

Cross said: 'Intriguing, wasn't it?'

'Not particularly. A botched assassination attempt by British Intelligence agents and a German carpenter. Or if you prefer the other version: a touch of uncharacteristic brilliance by the Gestapo to make the German people believe Hitler is immortal. As you know the Führer cut short his speech and left by train for Berlin. Shortly after he left the bomb went off.'

'There are those in MI6,' Cross said, walking towards the stairs, 'who believe both versions are bullshit. That the assassination attempt was genuine enough. That it was carried out with the connivance of German Intelligence – not any of the SS groups' – Cross raised an eyebrow at Canaris – 'and when it failed strenuous efforts were made by *someone* to confuse the whole issue. German carpenters, the Gestapo ... a double dose of eyewash in other words.'

'So?'

'We were discussing your allegiances. Führer or country. That sort of thing. I merely wondered if you had any theories about the assassination attempt.'

'I've just told you what I know.'

'Mmmmm. Did the Führer have any theories?'

'He was ecstatic, of course. Divine intervention, that sort of stuff,' unable to restrain a faint note of contempt in his voice.

'Perhaps he would like to hear our theories ...'

And now I'm being blackmailed. The crypt became Canaris's own grave. 'He's not interested in theories ...'

'More than theories, really. As you say, British Intelligence was involved. Two of our men were arrested, in fact.'

Canaris shrugged. 'You want me to convey some information about involvement to the Führer?'

'Come off it, Herr Admiral,' Cross said. 'You know perfectly well what I'm talking about. It's not the sort of information you'd want to pass on, is it?'

Hardly; you don't sign your own death warrant. He had often wondered if the British would ever try to use their knowledge of *Abwehr* complicity in the bomb plot as a lever; he had hoped they wouldn't because they knew there would be other plots ... They really were quite desperate to convince Hitler that they were prepared to do a deal ...

Thankfully, Canaris reached the foot of the steps.

Choosing his words with extreme care, Canaris said: 'Of course if we brought the Soviet Union to its knees with one pre-emptive strike Hitler's position would be unassailable.'

'But you would applaud that, wouldn't you, Admiral?' sardonically.

I'd like to spit in his grave, Canaris thought and said: 'Of course,' just in case they didn't know about his personal involvement in the bomb plot.

'However it wouldn't necessarily follow that his position would be unassailable ...'

Now what the hell did he mean by that? Another bomb plot? Like everyone in this profession Cross spoke in code.

'Wouldn't it?' Although he spoke non-committally, Canaris managed the slightest suggestion of hope.

'Let us say we plan for every eventuality. But we're peering too far into the future, aren't we? All that need concern you at the moment is that you can bring greater glory to the Fatherland. And no one has ever doubted your patriotism, Herr Admiral. No one.'

A tiny glow of pride lit Canaris's soul.

Cross said: 'Well I must be on my way. I'll go first, if you don't mind.'

'If you wish.'

'So could you please tell Man Friday to get away from the top of the steps.'

Canaris called out and they heard the shuffle of feet.

Cross stretched out his hand and momentarily Canaris thought: 'My God, we're going to shake hands, how very British,' before realising that Cross wanted his money. That, too, was very British.

Pocketing the escudo notes, Cross grinned, saying: 'More grist for the casino,' and ran up the steps two at a time.

Canaris gave him a couple of minutes. Then he heard a motorcycle start up; it must have been hidden. Riding a motorcycle in a suit? Ah well, Cross wasn't a conventional man.

Canaris walked up the steps into the sunlight and breathed the fresh air as though it were life-giving oxygen.

Chapter Six

September 18, 1941. On board Churchill's special train.

'So it worked.'

Churchill, dressed in a bright blue, zip-up siren suit and black-and-gold Moroccan slippers, read the document Sinclair had brought him with satisfaction.

It was from General Hastings Ismay, Chief of Staff to Churchill in his capacity as Minister of Defence.

ACCORDING TO INFORMATION RECEIVED HERE TODAY HITLER YESTERDAY GAVE ORDERS FOR THE INVASION FLEET FACING THE BRITISH ISLES TO BE DISPERSED. RECONNAISSANCE AIRCRAFT REPORTED TODAY THAT THIS PROCESS HAS ALREADY BEGUN.

The source of the first item of information, Churchill assumed, was Ultra at Bletchley Park. It was Ultra which had decoded Hitler's Directive No 16 signed on July 16, 1940, announcing his invasion plans.

Churchill glanced at Sinclair. 'My most secret source?'

Sinclair, wearing tweeds and brogues – did he ever wear anything else? – nodded. 'But some of the ships are being left so that a force can be re-assembled at short notice.'

'Of course – if we renege on our promise. But one hopes it will be too late by then.' Churchill poured them both a whisky and soda and sat back in his seat; he liked trains, their clacking rhythms, their foraging, serpentine progress. He particularly enjoyed this train equipped as it was with an office, bed, telephone and, on his insistence, bath. 'Corporal Hitler has to keep his fingers on the screws to keep us in line. So don't expect any let-up in that cacophony,' pointing with his cigar through the blacked-out windows and cocking an ear to the bark of the anti-aircraft guns. 'He dare not give us breathing space. And of course to an extent I'm responsible for it.' He fell silent as melancholy touched his euphoria.

Sinclair said: 'If you hadn't ordered the bombing of Berlin then the Luftwaffe's attacks wouldn't have been switched from the airfields to our cities.'

'And we would have lost the Battle of Britain,' Churchill said. 'And then we would have had to extend genuine peace feelers.'

Churchill stood up suddenly, switched off the lights in the combined office and living quarters and pulled back a corner of the black-out. Through the anti-blast adhesive they could see vicious flashes of light.

'But at what a cost,' Churchill murmured. 'At what appalling cost.'

'That's something you'll have to live with, Winston.' Since they had become partners in deception, associates in schemes of awesome potential, they had become more familiar. 'There's worse ahead, far worse.'

'What would the people say if they knew?' Churchill asked seeking no answers. And to Sinclair: 'You really are the archetypal Job's Comforter.'

'You ask what the people would say. Perhaps one day, when they are ready for it, they will say you saved the free world.'

Churchill let the black-out fall back and switched on the light again. He brightened, latent energy returned. He stood in front of Sinclair, pulling the zip of his one-piece suit up and down. 'Did you know I designed these myself? One of the best things I ever did. I call them my rompers.'

Sinclair said: 'If you hadn't been a politician you could have been a designer, or a painter —'

'Or a bricklayer,' Churchill said sitting down. 'Did you know that I was once a member of the Amalgamated Union of Building Trade Workers? They tried to chuck me out but I wouldn't go.'

He sat down. 'So we've pulled our first trick; the grand illusion awaits us. The stage: Lisbon. Are you quite sure about the identity of this man Hoffman?'

'Quite,' Sinclair said.

'And Cross, what do you think of him?'

'He's a great admirer of yours.'

'Hardly a commendation for reliability. You spies are worse than we politicians when it comes to answering a straight question.'

'Well,' Sinclair said carefully, 'by definition an agent, especially a double-agent, must have certain flaws in his character.'

94

'I suppose so. I knew him once, you know,' Churchill said enigmatically.

'I didn't know you'd even heard of him until recently.'

'When he was a boy.' Churchill didn't elaborate. 'So it's all down to Cross and Hoffman?'

'And the girl.'

'Yes,' Churchill agreed, 'and the girl.'

The train pulled into a station. Churchill went to the door. Sergeant Thompson, Churchill's former bodyguard recalled from his grocer's shop in Norwood, was already standing on the platform.

Churchill and Sinclair joined him. 'Where are we?' Sinclair asked.

'Somewhere in England,' Churchill told him. 'To be more precise, somewhere in Kent.'

'Why are we stopping?'

Thompson answered the question. 'Mr Churchill wants to make a telephone connection to Chartwell, sir.'

'To tell Clemmie I'll be home for dinner in half an hour,' Churchill said.

Chapter Seven

The girl to whom Churchill and Sinclair had referred arrived over the strip of water on the Tagus reserved for flying boats six days later.

Her name was Rachel Keyser, she was twenty-three, British and Jewish and aggressively proud of both, of medium height with shingled hair so dark that it shone blue-black in the sunlight and an extravagant figure contained in a square-shouldered, narrow-waisted, lime-green costume.

As she peered down at the molten waters of the estuary straggled with shipping she was frightened and angry with herself for not being able to subdue her fear.

It was 11.25 a.m. Fifteen minutes earlier the captain of the

Pan American Airways Clipper in which she had crossed the Atlantic had announced minor technical trouble.

The passengers had been aware of the trouble for the past five minutes. All they disputed was the *minor:* one of the four propellers above them had feathered.

Suddenly the beautiful body of the Clipper had felt heavy. Like a pregnant woman fearing a miscarriage, Rachel thought.

Perhaps the mid-Atlantic take-off from Horta in the Azores had caused the trouble. Despite the weather forecast at Bermuda the sea at Horta had been rough. Clipper pilots were not supposed to take off if waves were more than thirty inches high; the waves at Horta might have been twenty-nine or thirty-one inches; whatever their height they hadn't deterred the captain and the big shining sea-bird had taken off at 100 mph, slapping aside the waves and skimming past the face of a cliff.

At least, thought Rachel trying to divert her fear, the prospect of a crash-landing had brought a small side-benefit: it had dampened the ardour of the Venezuelan diplomat who had been trying to proposition her throughout the twenty-two hour trip from the States.

Not that he wasn't reasonably attractive – or had been until he had suddenly subsided, white-faced and trembling, after the captain's announcement – but who wanted such attention when you were flying to meet your first love, or lover rather?

The affair had been a revelation. She had met David Cross when they were both in Berlin. He had been a young diplomat at the British Embassy, she the daughter of a first secretary there, engaged outside office hours in smuggling Jews out of Germany.

Cross had seduced her with ease and she had found to her surprise that she responded pleasurably to aspects of his character that she had never encountered in anyone else, least of all in diplomatic circles. He was calculating, inventive and a little cruel. She wasn't proud of her response to such qualities, but then again she wasn't ashamed.

During her stay in Germany she had, through her father, witnessed terrible things happen to the Jews. She had seen them humiliated, degraded, abused; she had seen families led away to God knows where; she had seen the bruised trust on the faces of children as, helplessly, they followed their parents;

she had seen windows smashed, faces smashed, shops looted, books burned.

She had seen the tormentors laugh.

She had sworn vengeance. Which was why, after she had qualified in Britain as a cryptanalyst, the Foreign Office had sent her to Washington. Away from trouble.

Why then had they suddenly changed their minds and transferred her to Lisbon where every day she would rub shoulders with Germans? And why the rush?

According to messages from Whitehall she was needed to supplement the cipher department in Lisbon, which had become the European cross-roads of coded communications.

But surely there were other more talented operators not so savagely anti-Nazi and therefore not so much of a liability? Apparently not: according to Whitehall she was the best.

One other aspect of her new posting bothered Rachel. She was delighted that she was going to be reunited with Cross, but it did seem rather a coincidence. As though she were being used.

The Clipper lurched to one side. The diplomat closed his eyes; his hands were pressed together, lips moving, and Rachel realised that he was praying.

She remembered reading about the Samoan Clipper that in 1938 had developed an oil leak over the Pacific; all that had been found of it was burned-out wreckage.

Rachel joined the diplomat in unspoken prayer.

Below them were the relatively narrow reaches of the Tagus which linked the Atlantic with the broader expanse of the estuary. To the left the faded red roofs, spires and domes of Lisbon tumbling down the hills to the waterside.

The Clipper righted itself, then dipped suddenly. The passengers in the spacious cabin sighed collectively. A woman fainted, a child began to cry.

The water was only a few hundred feet below them now. Rachel saw docks, plodding orange-coloured ferries, fishing boats with Phoenician rig ... the crying of the child reminded her of the Jewish children in Germany.

Another lurch. She noticed oil leaking from the engine cowling above her.

This surely wasn't how it ended. Not at my age.

She wished she had been kinder to her parents.

Masts of ships flashed past the window.

A noise like a tattoo on a tin drum.

The Clipper lifted, bounced, then touched the surface again, settled and imperiously thrust aside the waters of the Tagus.

After the Clipper had been moored at Porto Ruivo, Rachel walked swiftly up the wooden gangplank to wait for her luggage. The diplomat made no attempt to follow her.

With her diplomatic passport she went straight through immigration, porter in tow. Cross was waiting for her beside a green MG sports car. He kissed her and said: 'Welcome home.'

*

'How brown you are.'

She stroked his chest and belly.

'Estoril. In my business you have to go there. And I go on the beach.'

My business? Well, now that she was a cryptanalyst she knew what that business was – she had always vaguely realised that he wasn't a conventional diplomat.

She kissed him and wished that he wasn't so controlled. He was obviously aroused – her hand crept towards his hip where the paler flesh began – and yet he didn't give. That was part of the cruelty, to try and bring her to such a pitch that she fell on him.

Well, it wasn't going to work, not this time.

He kissed her breasts, taking one generous brown nipple in his mouth, and opened her thighs with his hand. And, of course, she was wet.

His fingers began their measured persuasion.

But she didn't moan. She touched his glossy brown hair; it felt warm as though the sun had been on it.

Gently, she took his penis in one hand and began to stroke it, up and down, as he had taught her long ago in an apartment with a view of the Tiergarten in Berlin.

Since then there had been three lovers. None of them had been as satisfactory as Cross and two of them had been shocked at her practised ways.

My trouble, she thought, trying to remain detached, was that my first lover was an expert. That should never have been: the first experience should have been an explosion of young passion, clumsy, premature and wonderful.

Now I have expertise instead of spontaneity and there will never be any substitute until I find a man I truly love and, thank God, I don't love this man who is doing these wonderful things to me – control yourself, you slut – even though I come alive with him.

He glanced up from her breasts, hair falling across his eyes, and smiled and she thought: You bastard, as he lowered his head once more, hair brushing her belly, as he moved his face, his lips, his tongue to where she wanted them to be.

No!

What, she wondered absurdly, would her parents, now back in London, think? Would they be disgusted or would they understand the passions they had passed on to her? Understand, perhaps, but not condone. Nor would they be condoned in many other Jewish quarters. Hypocrites! Soon, with the war, all that would change; morals were early casualties. 'Let's make love, I might be killed tomorrow ...'

She felt the warmth of his tongue. The rationalising which had been her defence was dispersing. She was losing. Excitement and warmth spread through her. Such expertise. She found that she was moving her body rhythmically. This wasn't what ... the damned moralists ... taught you ... to expect. You waited till marriage, then on the marital bed you gave yourself as a sort of reward to the panting male for doing the right thing by you. Coupling, copulation, intercourse ... but this was ... this ...

She used her mouth on him.

And he gave. She could feel it.

Did it have to be like this, victory or defeat?

'Oh God!'

But it was his voice.

And he was inside her and there was neither victor nor loser and it was ...

'Beautiful,' she told him later as they lay beneath a sheet on the bed in his apartment.

'We didn't waste any time,' he said, lighting a cigarette.

She looked at her wristwatch on the bedside table. She had been in Lisbon for one hour.

*

That evening she explored Lisbon on foot. It fascinated her. It was a pre-war shop window with glimpses of austerity between the showcases. She saw restaurants packed with diners gobbling down seafood: she saw refugees sharing a loaf of bread. She saw elegant women buying perfume from Paris: she saw women in black with autumn-leaf faces queueing to buy rationed sugar.

The city seemed to be built on two main levels so she took the street elevator built by Alexandre Eiffel 'of Eiffel Tower fame' according to her printed guide – you could see his handiwork in the battleship-grey metal tower – to the upper level, the *bairro alto*.

There were only three other passengers in the wood-panelled cabin that smelled of disinfectant. A burly middle-aged man with cropped, greying hair who was smoking a black cigar and a young woman with a hospital-pale face holding the hand of a small boy wearing a peaked cap too big for him and knee-length trousers.

The man, who had bloodshot eyes and incongruously small ears pressed close to his scalp, drew deeply on the cigar and blew out a cloud of smoke. Deliberately, it seemed to Rachel, in the direction of the woman.

The woman began to cough, rasping coughs from deep in her chest. The boy moved closer to her and touched her dress with his hand.

As the elevator began to rise the man exhaled another cloud of smoke in the direction of the woman. She put her hand to her breast as if in pain.

Rachel said with studied politeness: 'I think your cigar is upsetting this lady; I wonder if you could put it out.'

The man smiled at her and said in German-accented English: 'Upsetting the Jewess and her brat? I'm doing Lisbon a service.'

She couldn't believe it. Surely he could see that she, too, was Jewish. Although some German men tended to forget their anti-Semitism if you had the good fortune to be a young and reasonably attractive woman.

She said: 'I'll ask you once again —'

'Please don't trouble yourself,' the woman said in Yiddish and began to cough again. The boy peered at the man from under his peaked cap.

Another jet of smoke.

After that it seemed to Rachel that she moved in slow motion. Still she couldn't believe what was happening as she snatched the half-smoked cigar from the man's lips, heard him yelp with pain, saw the blood on his lower lip, tossed the cigar on the floor of the elevator, crushed it with the heel of one of her shoes, ground the mess into shreds with the sole, stepped back, breast heaving.

The woman shrank into the corner of the elevator. The man touched his lips then raised his hand as though to strike Rachel. It was then that the boy stepped in between them and then that Rachel found to her further astonishment that she had a long nail-file in her hand and was ready to use it as a knife.

The man reached for the boy and Rachel heard herself say: 'Don't'. The man hesitated. The elevator stopped with a jerk. He dropped his hand to his side. 'Jewish bitch,' he snarled at her.

The door opened. The woman, still coughing, grabbed the boy's hand and pulled him outside.

The man said to Rachel: 'Your name please, Jew.'

'We're not in Germany now.'

She smiled at him, actually smiled.

He grabbed at her handbag but she dodged and strode out of the cabin.

He shouted after her: 'Don't worry, Jew, I shall find out who you are.'

Ahead of her, halfway across an iron bridge, she saw the woman pulling the boy along. Suddenly he broke free, turned round and grinned and she called out to him, 'Thank you for helping me,' and with one finger he tapped the side of his nose and she loved him. Still grinning, he rejoined his mother.

'Good to see such spirit,' she said as the German strode past her.

On the bridge high above the Chiado, Lisbon's select shopping district, the elation left her. She paused and gazed down at the pigmy figures and felt dizzy.

On her very first day in Portugal she had allowed her hatred of the Nazis to erupt. How could she continue to live a normal life in a city teeming with Germans – and Jewish refugees? A few more incidents like the encounter in the elevator and she would be requested to leave, *persona non grata*.

She could only hope to co-exist if she believed that she was in some way contributing to the ultimate downfall of the Nazis. Then and only then would she be able to suffer their presence, content with her secret purpose.

She turned and continued walking across the bridge to the

Largo do Carmo where she found a taxi and told the driver to take her to a restaurant in the Alfama.

There, one hour later, the purpose she sought was given to her.

*

'But why is this man Hoffman so special?'

Cross poured red Dão wine into their glasses. 'I can't tell you, not yet.'

'You want me to sleep with a man but you can't tell me why?'

'That's about the size of it,' Cross said.

'You think I'm a whore?'

'I think you'll do anything for your people.'

She was silent while the waiter served *lagosta à moda de Peniche*, layers of baked lobster cooked with onions, herbs and spices soaked in port, according to Cross who was selective about food even when he was about to ask his mistress to seduce another man.

He tasted the food. 'Mmmmm. It's good.' He sipped some wine. 'Anyway I always thought *sleep with* was a misnomer. Surely people mean the opposite?'

'You,' she said, 'have got to be the most insensitive man in the world.'

He had put the proposition to her almost as soon as they were seated in the restaurant, a neat, clean little place with whitewashed walls and green tablecloths that had once been a furniture factory.

And she had arrived in a yellow summer dress with amber beads at her neck believing that, after all, she might be a little in love with Cross! He had destroyed any such possibility with a few incisive sentences, making only a token concession to chivalry.

'You must be wondering why you've suddenly been brought back to Europe,' he had said.

He seemed to have forgotten that, when she had asked him why in his apartment, he had told her the reason was her prowess with ciphers. She got the impression that since then he had taken advice from London. He held her hand; at least he did that!

She waited tensely.

'I remember you telling me,' he said, 'how you wanted to

102

pay back the Germans for what they were doing to the Jews. Well, now you have your chance.'

'What do I have to do?'

'Ultimately a lot. At the moment ...' With a shrug he abandoned the pretence of caring and told her that all she had to do was seduce a man named Hoffman.

She bit into some lobster. He was right, it was good. She was surprised that she wasn't more angry. Of course she hadn't been the slightest bit in love with Cross; that had been a fleeting illusion – Lisbon and lovemaking. But she was intrigued, excited even. Rachel Keyser, perhaps you *are* a whore.

She sipped some wine – that was good, too – and said:'Let's start again. Who is this Hoffman?'

'He works for the Red Cross.'

'Nationality?'

'He pretends to be Czech. In fact he's Russian; but don't let on you know. Perhaps I shouldn't have told you.'

Oh yes you should, she thought, appraising him impersonally. Sleekly handsome features, grey eyes ... Did the pigment of an eye really indicate character? If so I, with my brown eyes, should be as soft as a meringue, born for motherhood and unquestioning devotion. What a hope! She took in the white shirt, striped tie and brass-buttoned blazer; all very British and decent – and toally misleading. *You intended to tell me, to feed me a few morsels of intrigue to jolly me along.* How well he knows me, she thought.

'What does he do in the Red Cross?'

'Helps the refugees.'

'Age?'

'A little younger than you.'

'Why did he leave Russia?'

'The same reason as any refugee. To escape oppression.'

'Oppression should be fought.'

He grinned at her. 'Not everyone is as belligerent as you.'

'Is he a pacifist?

'You make it sound like a crime.'

'Acquiescence didn't do the Jews much good in Germany.'

'He believes he's doing more good here than he could taking on the Red Army. In point of fact he's going to do much more good; more than he could ever dream of.'

Another morsel.

'Do you know what this is all about?' she asked.

'I don't know the whole picture. But I do know more than you.'

'You will have to tell me why this man of peace is so important.'

'Blessed are the peacemakers,' Cross said, pouring more wine for both of them.

'Answer the question, David.'

Four men came in and sat at a table on the opposite side of the restaurant under some chairs hanging from the ceiling, relics of the factory days. They were young and blond. 'Germans', Cross told her.

'I hope one of the chairs falls on them,' she said.

'And they,' Cross said, pointing at a young man and a pretty girl who had just entered the restaurant, 'are French.'

'It's grotesque,' she said. 'Victors and vanquished sitting down to eat in the same restaurant.'

'They're doing it in France.'

'But not like this. Not as if they're all tourists who have bypassed the war.'

'And he,' said Cross, nodding towards a tall man who looked like a cowboy wearing a suit for the first time, 'is an American. A Texan named Kenyon.' He waved. 'They're all fighting in their own way,' he added.

'Spies?'

'They're like company directors in Mayfair, they're everywhere.'

'You?'

'What about a sweet,' he said. 'My mother always insisted that it should be called pudding.' He consulted the menu. 'The *sonhos* are very good. *Sonhos* meaning dreams. In fact they're fritters dished up with syrup.'

'Fritters,' she said, 'and coffee and why is this Hoffman so important?'

'You'll just have to accept that he is.'

'Is that all I have to do, sleep ... get him into bed?'

'For the moment, yes.'

'I'm going to find it difficult making love to a pacifist,' she said.

'Why should you? Opposite poles are supposed to attract.'

'Repel in my case.' She waited while Cross ordered the sweet and coffee. Then: 'Why me?'

'You speak a little Russian, don't you?'

She nodded.

'Well, that's one reason.'

'And because your employers, whoever they are, decided that you would be able to persuade me?'

'That as well. Persuade you, that is, to make a vital contribution to defeating the Nazis.'

The waiter brought the dreams, the fritters. On the other side of the restaurant the Germans were speaking to each other in low voices. The Frenchman was kissing the pretty girl's hand. The American was drinking a Martini cocktail and reading the *New York Times*.

'So,' Rachel said biting into a dream, 'I can assemble some of the evidence. A woman is needed to seduce a Russian. Qualifications? Obviously she must be reasonably desirable. She must be violently opposed to the Third Reich. She mustn't be inhibited by morals ...'

Cross said nothing.

'... but it seems to me that there is a missing factor. One you've omitted to mention. Codes come into this, don't they, David? A Nazi-hating, code-breaking slut is what your people are after, isn't that it?'

Cross said: 'Here comes the coffee. All the way from Brazil.'

'Why codes, David?'

'I told you, I haven't got the whole picture yet.'

'Messages to and from the Soviet Union?' She spooned brown sugar into the coffee. 'It has to be. Through this man Hoffman.'

Cross said: 'You're making sense.'

'What's his name?'

'Hoffman's? Josef.'

'His real name.'

'I'm afraid I can't tell you that.'

'And I know why. Because you think that, in certain circumstances, I might use it. Don't worry, David, I won't be that abandoned, not with the sort of man Hoffman seems to be.'

'I'm delighted to hear it,' Cross said. 'Brandy? The Portuguese brew's not bad. And don't get it wrong, the man's not a coward. Stretcher-bearers don't get VC's but they deserve them – they don't even carry guns. And for that matter what about young men swanning round Lisbon in the diplomatic service when they should be in the Army?'

Rachel said: 'No, I won't have a brandy and yes, but you are in the Army. A secret army.'

'Let's not be melodramatic,' Cross said. He ordered a brandy for himself. 'Can I take it you're willing to ... co-operate?'

'On condition that you tell me what the hell this is all about when I get Hoffman into bed.'

'If I know ...'

'You know,' she said.

'I have conditions too,' he said.

'I don't think you're in a position —'

'—You've got to stop your private war.'

She looked at him questioningly.

'Stop molesting Germans in elevators. Snatching cigars from their mouths. And no,' holding up one hand, 'it doesn't matter how I heard. You'll find out soon enough that the tom-toms beat all the time in Lisbon.'

'He was a pig,' she said.

'No one is going to deny that.'

'You know him?'

'Of course I know him,' Cross said. 'He's the head of the Gestapo in Lisbon.'

Chapter Eight

Cross drove Hoffman to the Casino at Estoril in his open MG.

A visit to some of the fleshpots, he had told Hoffman, was essential when you were helping refugees. Top of the agenda was the Casino, second the nearby Palácio Hotel. In both you could meet the wealthy fugitives of war – and shame a few of them into digging their hands into their pockets on behalf of their less fortunate countrymen.

Hoffman had accepted Cross's invitation because, since Cross had saved his life, he took most of his advice. This was Cross's world, not his, and he was grateful for a courier. He was also grateful to Cross for putting him in touch with some of the peacemakers in Lisbon who were still trying to persuade the Germans and British to lay down their arms; he thought their cause was forlorn but anything was worth trying.

My world, Hoffman thought, as the evening air streamed past him, no longer exists. That world, or the world of Viktor Golovin, was a stuffy librarian's home and a university and a girl and a future. But it had all dissolved in a volley of gunfire in an abandoned theatre.

And all that was left was escape. From tyranny, from mass murder. But to where? Every night he had dreamed about the bodies jerking in their death throes; then in the middle of one such nightmare the bodies had stopped jerking and he had opened his eyes and it had been morning and the answers were laid in front of him like breakfast on a tray.

Escape, yes, escapism, no. He had been handed a cause: to help the victims of tyranny. And what better place at which to offer his services than the Red Cross in Switzerland.

With his savings he had bought counterfeit documents from a forger who, thanks to Stalin, was doing brisk business in a cellar in the Arbat. He had crossed the Ukraine on a students' excursion, slipped through the border into Czechoslovakia – and found himself surrounded by the henchmen of another tyrant, Hitler's SS.

He had reached Geneva without too much trouble – the Nazis bid to re-design Europe made a fugitive's lot that much easier – and after training had been posted to Lisbon.

At first – after, that was, he had stopped acting as an *agent provocateur* – he had thought himself fulfilled in his work. Until a spectre that haunts all émigré Soviet citizens presented itself.

Mother Russia.

No matter how feverishly he worked the spectre kept reappearing. The scourge of all Russians since their history began: their love of country which makes them endure any despot, whatever his trappings.

It was this love, much deeper than any conventional patriotism, that accounted for all their attitudes. Their masochism. Their belligerence. Their over-reaction to criticism.

When a foreigner asked Russians how they could condone a régime even harsher than Tsarism they replied: 'Because we are Bolsheviks,' but what they meant was: 'Because we are Russians.'

As he fed and housed and dispatched the bewildered refugees, Josef Hoffman remembered that he was Viktor Golovin and grieved for his people.

And a question repeated itself in his mind: humanity or country?

Cross's voice reached him. Hair flapping across his forehead, he was pointing along the coast.

'I can't hear you.'

'The Jaws of Hell,' Cross shouted. 'Good name, isn't it? There's an abyss there. The sea comes under a rock and booms like thunder during a storm. And here are the jaws of heaven,' he said as they swung into Estoril.

Cross stopped the car beside the little railway station separating the beach from the road and the gardens. Cross pointed out the landmarks. The miniature castle on the promenade – 'Pretty but phoney' – the ornate gardens leading up to the Casino, the Palácio Hotel … 'Which is where we'll go first,' he said, gunning the MG into a tyre-screeching U-turn.

In the crowded bar Cross ordered two whiskies. It was a decorous place furnished in autumnal colours with a floor made of black and white marble squares and a black marble bar.

Cross nodded at the barman juggling with the bottles and glasses with great dexterity. 'Joaquim Jerónimo, the most knowledgeable man on the Lisbon coast. He's heard more secrets than you've had hot dinners.'

'You would know, I suppose,' Hoffman said. He accepted that Cross was in Intelligence – most foreigners were involved somehow or other – and the only question was how deeply? Hoffman suspected that Cross's involvement was very deep.

A man and an elegantly-gowned woman vacated their bar stools and Cross appropriated them. He said: 'You've been looking a bit broody lately, Josef, anything the matter?'

'Wouldn't you look broody if an assassin tried to kill you and you knew someone else might try and finish off the job?'

A pianist began to play gentle ripples of music. Then he sang quietly: 'Who's taking you home tonight …' No one paid any attention but he didn't seem to mind.

Hoffman still hadn't rationalised the attempt on his life. How could the NKVD have discovered that he was in Lisbon? And in any case was he that important that he merited a bullet in the back and the possibility of a scandal?

'I think,' Cross said, finishing his whisky and ordering another from the energetic Joaquim Jerónimo, 'that you're missing some of the more basic pleasures of life.'

Hoffman swallowed the rest of his whisky; the liquor assuaged some worries, aroused others. He supposed Cross was right, he needed relaxation (Candida Pereira hadn't taken kindly to being abandoned on the night of the shooting), but how could you visit the fleshpots of Lisbon while so much of Europe was in torment?

He closed his eyes and heard again the volley of shots in the half-finished theatre. He opened them again but his hand shook as he reached for his second Scotch.

'I don't need more basic pleasures,' he told Cross. 'But that's something you wouldn't understand. It's a question of priorities.'

'And what's that supposed to mean?' Suddenly there were flints in Cross's voice.

'Patriotism doesn't seem to be top of your priorities.'

The flints sharpened, 'I wouldn't talk about things you don't understand if I were you, Josef.'

'Your country's beleaguered and you're having a hell of a time in Lisbon,' the whisky talking.

'It so happens that I love my country more than you could ever understand. But I have a job – ' Hoffman got the impression that Cross had been on the brink of an indiscretion. 'But don't ever say anything like that again,' fingers of one hand painfully tight on Hoffman's arm, 'or else ... Another drink?'

'No more,' he said but Cross had ordered.

'So,' Cross said, 'how do you think the unholy alliance is holding up?'

'Which one? There are so many these days.' A trick to make him partially admit his nationality by presuming Cross meant the Soviet-German Treaty of Friendship?

'Russia and Germany, a bizarre partnership. Both biding their time, wouldn't you say?' and to the woman who was standing behind them, looking around uncertainly: 'Unaccompanied?'

'I've been stood up,' the woman said.

'By a man with a white stick,' Cross said. 'Let me get you a drink. And let me introduce Josef Hoffman. Josef, Rachel Keyser.'

Hoffman looked into eyes so brown that they were almost

black. At raven hair full of light. At olive skin and parted lips. At compassion and strength and vitality and perception.

And the night seemed to chime.

*

Hoffman was suddenly conscious of the shabbiness of his grey, off-the-peg suit beside Cross's navy-blue, tailored lightweight; of the unruliness of his fair hair beside Cross's barbered locks. At least he had the edge on height, but, standing on the terrace overlooking the moonlit lawns, he felt clumsy.

'So, Mr Hoffman, what brings you to Lisbon?'

He told her. It sounded pretty dull.

Cross said: 'Josef is a Czech and a man of peace,' and Hoffman wished he hadn't because he contrived to make a weakness out of what should be a strength.

Rachel Keyser sipped her sherry and said: 'The trouble in this world is that the men with the guns take advantage of the men with the flags.'

He decided she was about twenty-four. Certainly older than him. Jewish ... British. What was she doing here? He asked her. She told him she worked at the British Embassy in the communications department. How long had she been here? Two days, she told him, and he frowned because he had sensed a familiarity with Cross that was more than two days old. Early days, too, to be arriving unaccompanied at the Palácio. And who but a madman would stand up a girl like Rachel Keyser?

Cross said: 'Look here, if you really have been abandoned why don't you join us at the Casino? If you've got any money to lose, that is.'

She shivered as a breeze crept in from the ocean and hugged her stole to her shoulders; the breeze pressed her green gown against her body. 'Yes,' she said, 'I think I'd like that. Are you a gambling man, Mr Hoffman?'

Better to be honest. 'I haven't the slightest idea, Miss Keyser, I've never had any money to gamble with.'

'In that case you aren't or you would have lost the clothes you stand up in by now.'

No great loss, he thought, and said: 'And you?' and when she said: 'I like the occasional flutter,' he thought: 'She's acting,' wondering at his own perception.

Inside the Casino, Cross slipped Hoffman 2,000 escudos. 'Just to start you off,' he said. 'Pay me back when you've won.'

Hoffman tried to give him back the money but Cross pushed his hand away.

The main hall of the casino had a sunken floor, show-cases in which stuffed birds nested, divans and walls covered with beaten silver and gold. Most of the patrons wore evening dress, the men's shirt-fronts gleaming in the light of the chandeliers, diamond necklaces and tiaras glittering. Hoffman felt shabbier by the moment. Perhaps the security guards would mistake him for a pickpocket and throw him out.

Rachel Keyser gave Cross some money and he brought some chips for her. She sat down at one of the eight tables and began to play roulette. Cross and Hoffman stood behind her.

Hoffman became aware that she was employing some sort of system. 'A martingale,' Cross whispered. 'A short cut to the debtors' prison.'

But she was winning, playing only the even chances and doubling up when she lost.

Cross said: 'If she gets a losing streak and finds herself having to double up on the twelfth throw she's bust because that would take her above the house limit.'

A uniformed attendant came past bearing a small blackboard bearing the name CROSS.

'Excuse me,' Cross said.

She continued to win; not a lot, but more money than Hoffman had possessed since he came to Lisbon.

The bored croupier droned his instructions in French and Portuguese. *'Rien ne va plus ... Nada mais.'*

Rachel Keyser turned and smiled at Hoffman. 'Why don't you have a bet?'

'Later perhaps.' How could he explain to her how incongruous he felt, how he detested the players who could throw away a peasant's earnings for a year ... ten years ... on the turn of the wheel and barely notice the loss. Was she rich, this devastating Jewish girl? The stole, and the green silk gown ... and yet she wore them with care as though they were special. Like I wear my suit because it's the only one I've got. And you don't get rich working in an embassy, but perhaps she had private means. He looked at her hands; well cared-for but not pampered.

A German sat next to her. Did she flinch or was it his imagination? *Miss Keyser, I want to know a lot more about you.*

'I'm sorry,' Cross said, 'I've got to leave. Urgent business. The Ambassador ...' As Rachel stood up he placed one hand on her bare shoulder. 'No, you stay here, we can't sabotage a winning streak. Josef will see you home.' He pressed a wad of notes into Hoffman's hand. 'Won't you?'

Hoffman hesitated; there was nothing he would like better. 'Of course,' he said, 'but ...'

But Cross was gone.

And then Rachel Keyser began to lose.

Her chips dwindled; those of the German sitting beside her mounted.

Rachel's shoulders slumped.

She turned round. Hoffman got a fleeting impression that losing such a quantity of money meant quite a lot to her, scared her. 'What shall I do?' she asked.

'I don't understand roulette.'

'I've doubled up eight times. I stand to lose a packet. By my standards that is.'

'I told you I wasn't a gambler.'

'Once more?'

'If you wish.' After all it wasn't his money; but he hoped she would win.

She lost.

She turned round again.

He shook his head.

'Thank God for that,' she said, leaving the table.

'How much did you lose?'

'A few thousand escudos. I'm not sure how much that is.'

'In British money?' Hoffman had learned many currencies from the refugees. 'One escudo is about a penny.' He fingered the money in his pocket. Why was Cross being so considerate?

She said: 'I think I'd like to go home.'

'Good. This isn't my sort of place. Cross thought it would do me good to see some of the millionaires I can touch for the benefit of the refugees. Would you like dinner first?' holding tight to Cross's money. A band was playing, couples were dancing.

She shook her head. 'I want an early night.'

112

Because of the petrol shortage, the black Citroën taxi summoned by the doorman was fuelled on wood gas, and towed a stove on a small black trailer. Its progress was slow; Hoffman was glad. In the glow of the dashboard he noticed a small, paper Union Jack. 'If we'd been Germans he'd have stuck a Swastika there,' Hoffman told her.

'How long have you been here, Josef?'

'Several months. It's a beautiful city.'

'But isn't it a bit of a backwater?'

'If you've got nothing worthwhile to do.'

'And you have, of course,' she said quickly.

'It's very satisfying work.'

'A curious way to put it. You aren't seeking self-satisfaction surely?'

Rocks ahead, he thought. 'I'm happy to be helping people in need of help. And by God they need it.'

'I see,' she said, and he felt somehow that she didn't.

'You've seen the refugees?'

'Only sitting around the cafés.' She made it sound like an indictment.

'Look,' he said, 'these people aren't criminals on the run. They had to get out of their countries. If they hadn't they would have been rounded up, sent to camps, massacred ... They're women and children and old people —'

'Not all of them,' she interrupted.

He no longer cared about impressing her. 'You're beginning to sound like a Nazi.'

The cab driver glanced over his shoulder and forced the taxi to go another mile an hour faster.

'It's just that I don't believe in weakness. Kid gloves never won any ideals, Mr. Hoffman.' *Josef* discarded. 'I don't mean you have to brandish the mailed fist. What I do mean is that peace can only be achieved through strength. If Britain had been strong she wouldn't be at war now.'

'These refugees are children of a war they never sought, don't even understand.'

Unaccountably she softened. 'I'm sorry, Josef.' Josef again. Rachel Keyser was a very unpredictable lady. She told him about Berlin. 'I always thought that if the rest of Europe had been strong, if the Jews themselves had been strong, the persecution would never have happened.'

113

'And now you believe in vengeance?'

'Don't you, Josef? After all, the Nazis invaded your country,' almost catching him off-guard.

'I don't know what I believe in,' he said.

She let that one ride.

The taxi pulled up outside the Avenida Palace next to the railway station, between the Rossio, the main square, and the Praça dos Restauradores. Hoffman had been there a couple of times; it was old and elegant, hung with chandeliers and floored with marble, and reminded him of Vienna which he had passed through on his way to Geneva. Miss Keyser must receive a good allowance: the Avenida cost 200 escudos a day - although he had put refugees in the salon for nothing.

'Only till they find me an apartment,' she said, reading his thoughts. She handed him half the fare but he told her to keep it; let Cross pay. The hotel doorman hovered outside. Rachel Keyser stepped out. 'Well, Josef, it's been —'

'Stimulating.' Should he offer to buy her a coffee in the hotel? See her to her room? Into it … Fat chance, you gauche peasant. 'Goodnight,' he said, waving as the taxi took him away.

*

The drivers of two cars, one a Volkswagen 60, the other a Chevrolet Standard, watched the parting of Rachel Keyser and Josef Hoffman with indecision. Should they follow Hoffman or wait and see if the girl re-emerged? Both made different decisions. The Volkswagen followed Hoffman to his lodgings; the Chevrolet stayed outside the hotel. Both drivers had been aware of each other since they had followed the taxi from the Casino; both wished they could co-operate and ease the strain of surveillance; both accepted that there was no chance of this happening because one worked for the NKVD and the other for the Gestapo. In the event both stayed at their posts for two hours before deciding that, disappointingly, both quarries had retired to their respective beds alone.

*

The knock on Rachel's door came fifteen minutes after she had left Hoffman and she knew it was Cross.

'So, what happened?' he asked, closing the door behind him.

'You can see what happened. Nothing.'

'You can't have tried very hard.'

114

He sat down on a frail chair. The whole room had an air of genteel fragility about it – dressing-table with match-stick legs, thin gilded mirrors, antique bed. From a picture frame on the wall the Portuguese leader, Antonio Salazar, gazed down with aesthetic approval.

She sat on the edge of the bed and said: 'What did you expect? He's a gentleman, something you wouldn't understand.'

'I wasn't aware that you appreciated gentlemen.' Cross lit a cigarette. 'When are you meeting him again?'

'He didn't make a date.'

Cross said angrily: 'Christ Almighty! You're brought halfway round the world to make one simple conquest and what do you do? Act like some Victorian maiden flirting with the vicar's son. Did you flutter your eyelids behind your fan?'

'Sometimes,' Rachel said, 'I think you're a complete fool. Well, I can tell you this – he isn't. If I'd made a pass on the first night he would have smelled a rat.'

'What a romantic phrase. Jesus wept! Some seductress! Didn't it occur to you that you were supposed to manipulate the situation so that *he* made the pass? Believed that he was an irresistible, mid-European lover?'

'As a matter of fact,' Rachel said, returning Antonio Salazar's steady gaze, 'we had a row.'

'Great. On her first date Mata Hari has a quarrel. Wonderful.'

'An interesting row. The reverse of the norm. You know, over-masculine male showing coy female what a wow of a he-man he is.'

'You mean he's a pansy?'

'I mean he's the pacifist and I'm the belligerent. Different.'

'You seem remarkably casual about it all. You're supposed to be taking part in an operation that will change the course of the war.' Another morsel, she thought. 'And you behave as if you've just returned from a church fête.'

'It's going to be an interesting relationship,' Rachel said, kicking off her shoes and lying on the bed.

'You said he didn't make another date.'

'But we'll be seeing each other again; I knew that when I first set eyes on him.'

Cross stared at her speculatively. 'Really? I didn't know I was quite such a matchmaker.' He stood up, crossed the room and kissed her, loosening his tie at the same time. 'But until your next meeting with him ...'

'In Washington,' she said, 'I learned a lot of new phrases.' She smiled up at him. 'Go screw yourself, David Cross.'

As the door closed behind him she thought: 'Not bad for a demure Victorian maiden.'

Chapter Nine

Hoffman telephoned her two days later.

With studied nonchalance he asked her if she would like to take a trip up the Tagus to a small town where on Sunday, the first Sunday in October, they would be running the bulls. 'You'll see a bit more of the country,' he said with a diffidence that was almost patronising. 'You know, Lisbon isn't Portugal,' in the way that inhabitants of capital cities always isolate themselves from the rest of a country.

She said she would love it.

Hoffman hung up, with a surge of pleasure, in the musty bar opposite his lodgings near the Largo do Carmo. Then he went into the small square and sat on a worn marble bench opposite the headquarters of the Guarda Nacional Republicana to consider his good fortune.

Pigeons pecked at his feet; a guard in a green and white sentry box, wearing shiny black boots and a peaked green cap, scowled at him because no one had a right to look so happy.

It was quite extraordinary, Hoffman thought. Normally he would never have been in a position to approach such a woman. He didn't visit five-star hotels and she certainly didn't frequent bars where you spat your olive stones on the floor and drank wine for an escudo a glass. And even if such an unlikely meeting had taken place he would never have taken her back to her hotel.

Extraordinary ... it was then that the doubts returned and the guard relented because the smile faded from the face of the tall, fair-haired young man sitting opposite him.

It was more than extraordinary; it was miraculous and

Hoffman didn't believe in miracles. Had Cross arranged the whole thing? But why? Hoffman frowned; a vestige of a smile crossed the guard's granite features.

The doubts took a different direction. How could he entertain such a woman on the money he earned with the Red Cross? And what an escort he would be with his dreadful clothes, as shabby as a penniless refugee's!

And if all that wasn't enough he was younger than her. It wasn't the years that mattered – two or three of them at the most – it was the experience: Rachel Keyser, he sensed, was a very experienced lady.

In many ways, he thought, he was older. He had witnessed death and betrayal and he had become a fugitive. But as far as women were concerned he was a novice. Don't exaggerate, Viktor Golovin. What about Anna Petrovna and the plump little waitress in Geneva and Candida Pereira ... No, it was only when he thought about Rachel Keyser that he felt gauche.

He looked so miserable that the guard almost forgot to salute an officer leaving the building in a black staff car and only just made it with a flourish of his sword.

The movement jerked Hoffman out of his melancholy. It was no good brooding. He made his way through the pigeons, past a newspaper kiosk where a German was remonstrating with the owner for displaying too many British newspapers, and up the hill to his lodgings.

He had one room with use of a bathroom along the corridor. The room was clean and whitewashed with a view of assorted rooftops; it contained a bed, a wardrobe, a tin chest covered with old hotel labels and a wickerwork rocking chair.

His landlady was a tiny, toothless old woman permanently in mourning for one of her legion of relatives. In addition to paying her rent Hoffman brought her chocolate bars from the Red Cross which she munched with gums as hard as bone. For the rent he also got breakfast – coffee from Brazil and bread hot from the bakery, buttered on Saturdays and Sundays.

Hoffman shut the door behind him, unlocked the tin chest and surveyed his possessions. A Bible that he had bought in Prague to cleanse himself of Bolshevism but never opened, a Leica camera with a broken lens, a fountain pen, some letters from the waitress in Geneva, a hunting knife, two fancy Swiss shirts two sizes too small for him, a blank photograph album ... nothing Russian in case the room was searched by the

117

PIDE, the Portuguese secret police, who were very thorough, having been trained, so it was said, by the Gestapo.

The most he could expect from that lot at the flea market in the Campo de Santa Clara in the Alfama was a couple of hundred escudos.

Despondently he picked up the Bible. It was locked with a chain and a tiny padlock and key. He turned the key and the vellum pages opened at the Book of Jeremiah and two American 100 dollar bills fell out.

Hoffman felt them, rubbed them together, held them up to the light. Who, he wondered, was his benefactor (he had bought the Bible in a street market)? A missionary from the New World who had decided to reward a convert? He's converted me, Hoffman thought, locking his conscience in the tin chest, stuffing the two bills in his trouser pocket and heading for a money-changer on the Rossio.

When he emerged, pocket bulging with escudos, he discovered that a conscience cannot be contained by a lock and key. Surely God wouldn't want it all back; God was beneficent not grasping. But perhaps a little rent for his House. Hoffman made his way to the Cathedral and placed the equivalent of 50 dollars in the offertory box; then another 50 because if he couldn't make a girl happy on 100 dollars he might as well give up trying.

*

They took a boat from the Terreiro do Paço. Fragile sunshine lit the broad square and King José I on his bronze horse and the crowded waters of the Tagus. The air was chilled, a few white clouds sailing in from the Atlantic, but by lunchtime it would be warm enough.

The boat probably wasn't what Rachel had expected: more rust-bucket than yacht. It had one cramped cabin, patched green tarpaulin over the deck and a suspicious amount of water in the stern. It was skippered by a fisherman named Carlos who was doing Hoffman a favour because he had translated some documents for him, British share certificates which Hoffman presumed were stolen.

Surveying the decrepit craft moving sluggishly at the foot of the slipway, glancing at Rachel, dazzling in white, Hoffman decided that this was his most idiotic venture yet.

This opinion was confirmed as the vessel, the Santa Clara,

weaved its way erratically through the big ships moored in the river. The cabin was too dirty for Rachel's pristine dress so they sat under the tarpaulin roof: it was more than chill in mid-river: it was biting cold. From time to time spray spattered them.

'We can go back if you like,' he said, as a wave hit the bows, splashing water on to his new flannel trousers and brown herringbone jacket.

'I wouldn't dream of it. But what an idiot I was to wear a dress like this.'

What would Cross do in a situation like this? Answer: Cross would never have got himself into a situation like this. But if he had ... Hoffman took off his jacket and draped it round her shoulders.

'Thank you,' she said, 'but you needn't —'

'I insist,' he said.

Carlos, middle-aged, unshaven and morose, steered the Santa Clara past a Panamanian cargo ship. Ahead lay clear water. The sun came out from behind a cloud. Things began to look up.

They reached the town at one p.m. It was an uninspiring place on the Ribatejo plain; but during *feiras* it was injected with vitality; the bulls ran, boats sailed on the Tagus like petals of blossom; sardines were gorged in great quantities.

They went to an open-air restaurant and sat beneath a fig tree that was losing its leaves and drank white port.

Skinny cats patrolled the dust at their feet in the hope of sardines; dead fig leaves rustled in the breeze; half-naked children stared at them. Through the branches of the fig tree they could see green meadows where black fighting bulls were bred, and ricefields.

'I'm glad I came,' she said, filling Hoffman with great joy. She raised her glass. '*Nasdarovya.*' And again he was almost caught if, that was, she was trying to catch him.

'Why Russian?'

'Toasts should always be in Russian. They have fire. We should now hurl our glasses against the wall.'

'You speak several languages?'

'English – badly,' laughing. 'Russian, German, Hebrew and Yiddish. You?'

Carefully, he said: 'Slav, as you know. Czech but not so well. Portuguese, Polish, German, English and Russian.'

119

'How did you come to learn Russian?'

Why so curious? A set-up? Stop it. 'I studied languages in Prague. Anyone who has a way with languages should learn Russian. It's one of the languages of the future.'

'Not German?'

'They're not going to win the war,' Hoffman said.

'They're having a good crack at it.'

'You forget the Americans,' Hoffman said. 'And the Russians.'

'But they're not in the war.'

'They will be, it's inevitable.'

'You're very … assertive for a pacifist,' she said, sipping her port and holding the glass up to the sunlight.

'There's no reason why pacifists shouldn't be strong. That's a misconception. Cross has put me in touch with a lot of people seeking peace. They're not weak, tough as old boots some of them.'

'But it's a contradiction in terms, surely?'

No,' he said, happy to see the waiter approaching with their meal, 'no contradiction. You have to be strong to be peaceful. Anyone can fight; it's not that difficult.'

'A bellicose pacifist,' she said, 'that's different,' and: 'What's this?' as the waiter wearing a grease-spattered black jacket and a floppy bow tie laid a plate in front of them.

'*Dobrada,*' he told her, grateful for the interruption.

'What's that?'

'Tripe,' he told her. 'Cooked with beans.'

'Ugh.'

'Try it."

She did and for five minutes they stopped arguing.

Afterwards figs and goat's cheese and coffee and *medronho*, brandy made from arbutus.

She looked as at home here, he thought, among the dust and the cats and the grubby children as she would in the best restaurant in Lisbon.

Reading his thoughts she said: 'I don't really like casinos.'

'Not when you're losing?'

'Or at any other time. Shall we stop talking about pacifism and war?'

He liked that, too – she was the one who had raised the subjects each time.

'Let's go and see the bulls running. Do you like bull-fighting?'

'I'm sure you think I do. In fact I've never been to a bull fight.'

'They're different here,' he told her as he paid the bill which was practically nothing. 'They don't kill the bulls for one thing – not till next day, that is. The bull's horns are covered with leather and the eight bullfighters have to master the bull. One of them tries to seize the bull by the horns.'

'Shouldn't we all?' she asked.

*

While they were eating, Carlos the boatman was telephoning Lisbon. Two calls, two payments; the trip would more than pay for itself.

First he telephoned the German Embassy on the Rua do Pau da Bandeira and asked to be put through to a man named von Claus who worked in Chancellery.

The conversation was brief. He told von Claus that Hoffman and the Jewish woman were spending their day as planned.

'Will you bring them back?'

'*Sim*'

'Call me when they get back.'

'*Sim.*'

The second call was to a Russian named Zlobin who, like most Russians in Lisbon, posed as a Balkan refugee, a wealthy one staying at the Aviz Hotel.

The conversation was almost identical.

Both calls were monitored by Britain's MI6 and relayed to Cross.

Sitting at a desk staring over the garden at the rear of the British Embassy, Cross thought: 'You'd better hook him bloody quick, Rachel my girl, or it will be too late.'

*

The streets were barricaded with ranch-like wooden fences with escape exits and although the bulls were past their prime someone invariably got hurt.

Hoffman and Rachel took up a position on the safe side of the fence near an exit. Crowds packed around them, swaggered in the street and leaned from balconies dripping with geraniums. The air smelled of wine and dust; all the girls looked beautiful.

Beside them stood a thin man in a white shirt and black

121

trousers, his fat wife who was smiling from beneath a shawl and their son who was about six years old with short black hair as bright as needles and a smile given to him by his mother.

The man handed Hoffman a bottle. 'Drink,' he said, 'it will give you courage to face the bulls.'

Hoffman tasted the liquor, raw brandy. He tilted the bottle and felt it burn his throat and drop into his stomach like molten lead. 'Thanks,' he said in Portuguese, 'but I'm not going out there. Are you?'

'In the past I have always gone. But this year now. I promise my wife.' His wife went on smiling. 'Instead I get drunk,' tilting the bottle.

Hoffman turned to Rachel: 'Do you think I should go?'

'Of course not. You can't call the Red Cross if you get hurt: you are the Red Cross.'

'Your skin is very fair, *senhor*,' the man said. 'And your hair. You're not from Portugal?'

'From mid-Europe.'

'And the *senhora?* I think she must be Portuguese, she is so beautiful.'

Rachel smiled graciously at him. 'I'm afraid not. I come from Palestine.'

'Why did you say that?' Hoffman asked in English.

'I don't know: it just came out.'

It was as the bulls came down the street, goaded from behind with sticks, that the little boy broke free from his mother.

The smile vanished. 'Alfredo,' she shouted to her husband. 'Do something ...'

But her husband didn't seem to understand what had happened; he stood transfixed, bottle to his lips, remembering the good years when he had run before the horns.

In front of the bulls came the heroes, youths and young men and older men, fired by liquor. They challenged the bulls, they fell before them, they darted into the escape hatches, they vaulted the fences.

It was Hoffman who saw the boy first. He had wandered through the exit and was standing gazing at the bulls bearing down on him. Then he shouted for his mother and began to run towards her but on the other side of the fence.

His father dropped his bottle, tried to climb the fence but fell back, shaking his head as though it were too heavy to carry.

The boy fell directly in front of them. The bulls were twenty yards away; but their tormentors, occupied with their own courage, didn't see the boy.

Hoffman pushed back against the crowd to give himself room. The boy's mother was screaming. He cleared the fence with one leap, then fell.

He scrambled to his feet. Lunging at the boy was an old black bull, eyes angry, horns dipped for the kill.

Hoffman picked up the boy and, as the other bulls stampeded past, threw him over the fence. He was vaguely aware of hands clutching for the boy's body but the bull, deprived of its prey, had rounded on him.

An aged bull perhaps but a powerful old warrior. And a furious one.

Hoffman dodged the horns once and tried to run for the fence but the bull cut him off. He saw a blur of faces, Rachel's among them, and he thought: 'What the hell is a man of peace doing fighting a bull?' and he grabbed at the scything horns and held on, tossing from side to side, while others caught the bull's tail and pulled and others shoved at its heaving flanks.

Then he began to twist the horns to topple the old bull on its side and as he twisted and the others pushed it began to lean to one side. Hoffman's arms ached and the skin had been rubbed from the palms of his hands but he was winning.

But did he want to win? Why humiliate the old bull who had been thrust into the streets to chase the crowds and had done what was expected of him?

He let go.

The bull paused, righted itself. He and Hoffman gazed at each other. The bull wrenched himself free from the others and was gone.

The spectators began to applaud.

Hoffman dodged through the exit and pushed his way towards Rachel. She was holding the boy's hand while his mother wept and the father stared at the shards of broken bottle glass at his feet.

Hoffman touched the boy's head. 'You'll be a bullfighter yet,' he said and was sure it was the wrong thing to say. To Rachel he said: 'Come on, let's get out of here.'

She took his arm and said: 'Not bad for a man who hates violence.'

'I had to take the bull by the horns,' he said.

*

With bulls and crowds behind them, they walked through the centre of the town with its pillory where miscreants had once been suspended in a cage, past a terrace of blue and white cottages, across scrubland where lean cats and scruffy chickens lived in peace, to a green and silver glade among the olive trees.

As they walked she told him about herself and she wasn't a bit as he had imagined her. She had the spirit and mentality of a girl from a ghetto: she had been born and brought up in the wealthy pastures of Hampstead but her heart had been in the East End on the other side of London. Her mother had owned a gown shop in Oxford Street, her father had worked at the Foreign Office. Before she was into her teens she had become aware of anti-Semitism. Or had she sought it out? he wondered. But it wasn't until her father was sent to the British Embassy in Berlin – 'One of the few Jews in the Diplomatic Service' – as an adviser on the Jewish situation in Germany and she witnessed the persecution of her people that she found an outlet for her aggressive instincts.

She had connived, lobbied, physically fought the Nazi tormentors embarrassing her father and many of the Embassy staff who couldn't manage to convey the gravity of the situation to Whitehall. Nor, for that matter, could the envoys of other European countries get the message to their capital cities. 'No one really wanted to know,' Rachel said.

And then, after training in communications, she had been sent to Washington. 'As far away from trouble as possible.'

Hoffman was puzzled. 'And you were content? It's hard to believe that someone as red-blooded as you could sit there while Europe went up in flames. The Jews with it.'

'I was biding my time.'

'For what?'

'For anything that came along.'

Hoffman sensed that she was hedging. 'Such as?'

'I'm a Zionist, too. I thought I'd go to Palestine one day and help them win their independence.'

One day. There was something wrong there; the urgency that was part of her was missing.

124

'I was young,' she said a little too hastily. 'I had to gain experience.'

'And now?'

'Still learning.'

'But why Lisbon?'

'Apparently I'm quite good at my job.'

He didn't bother to point out that she could hardly be learner and virtuoso; he was pleased that as a liar she was an amateur. He thought Cross would be mad as hell at her performance and that pleased him too. But why was she lying? Just because her work was secret?

He asked her: 'You work with Cross?'

'He's a specialist.'

'Spy?'

'Isn't everyone in Lisbon?'

'Not everyone. I'm not.'

'Every diplomat then.'

'You?'

'We're told to keep our eyes and ears open.'

'Are you doing so now?'

'This is developing into an interrogation,' she said.

A flock of sheep wandered past, nudging one another along, shepherd and dog behind them. When they had gone it was very quiet and they lay down beside each other under the silvery leaves and then, because it had been that sort of day, he leaned over and kissed her.

There had never been a kiss like it. It was in the mind, it was in the body and it was on the threshold of emotions for which there were no names, only understanding.

*

Carlos the boatman interrupted the kiss.

He said from the edge of the glade: 'We have to go, Senhor Hoffman, the tides ...'

She looked up at Hoffman and her eyes were lazy and sharing, flecked with gold, and she smiled at him. There will be other times, the smile said.

Hoffman stood up. 'How did you find us?'

'It's a small town, *senhor*. You were watched, the foreigner with the balls, who fought the bulls.'

'What did he say?' Rachel asked, but Hoffman didn't translate. Nor did he believe the boatman's explanation: he had

125

followed them. Ever since leaving Russsia he had possessed this new awareness. 'We have to go,' he told Rachel.

And they sailed back on the *Santa Clara* which was no longer a rust-bucket. On the golden waters of the Sea of Straw.

*

Two days later Cross sent a message by King's Messenger to the head of Special Intelligence in London, Robert Sinclair.

Decoded, it read:

OPERATION REDCROSS PROCEEDING AS WELL AS CAN BE EXPECTED.

Like a hospital bulletin, Sinclair reflected.

SUBJECT DRAWN CLOSER INTO NET BUT WITH MINOR COMPLICATIONS, SOME ALREADY ANTICIPATED. BOTH SUBJECT AND CONTACT ARE UNDER SURVEILLANCE BY AGENTS OF *ABWEHR* AND NKVD.

Contact was a bloody pedestrian word for a girl apparently as ravishing as Rachel Keyser.

ABWEHR SURVEILLANCE PROBABLY ROUTINE INITIALLY TO CHECK OUT NEW RECRUIT TO EMBASSY BUT INTEREST MAINTAINED BY CONTACT'S ASSOCIATION WITH SUBJECT IN RED CROSS. WE HAVE SURVEILLANCE IN HAND BUT SUGGEST TIME APPROACHING TO MAKE REVELATION BEFORE OTHER PARTIES INTERFERE.

A nice euphemism for kidnap or kill.

RECOMMEND MAKE NECESSARY DOCUMENTS AVAILABLE SOONEST SO THAT WE CAN INSTIGATE NEXT VITAL PHASE.

COMPLICATION NOT ANTICIPATED IS GROWING AFFECTION BETWEEN SUBJECT AND CONTACT. THIS UNEXPECTED DEVELOPMENT COULD HAVE UNPREDICTABLE RESULTS.

Was it his imagination, Sinclair wondered, or did he detect a sour note in that last paragraph?

Thoughtfully, he raked the glowing coals from the fire in his office to preserve them for tomorrow and, as the sirens wailed their warnings in the distance, left his office to walk to No.10 Downing Street, to report the latest developments to Winston Churchill.

Chapter Ten

Before applying his mind to the conquest of Russia, Adolf Hitler decided to inspect his bird boxes.

He left the chief of the Luftwaffe, Hermann Goering, and the head of military intelligence, Wilhelm Canaris, in the house. He took with him Eva Braun and his Alsatian dog Blondi.

It was a crisp October day, leaves of the deciduous trees turning red and gold, conifers thrusting dark-green spears among them. In the distance stood the crumpled white peaks of the Untersberg Mountains.

This was the part of Germany that Hitler loved best. Obersalzberg in the Bavarian Alps, above the village of Berchtesgaden, close to the Austrian border.

It was here that he had sought refuge when he was released from prison after attempting to seize power in November 1923. It was here that he had finished writing *Mein Kampf,* My Struggle, his credo, which he had begun in gaol.

It was here that he had bought a modest house and converted it into his luxurious alpine retreat, the Berghof; and it was here that he had at last found direction to become saviour of the Fatherland.

When he was exhausted from one of his crusades it was to Obersalzberg that he retired to regroup his thoughts. To breathe the clean mountain air, to talk to the visitors who filed past the Berghof which had become a shrine, to walk through the wooded slopes where he had built feeding centres for birds and game. (Hunting was forbidden and one of these days he would have to do something about Goering who liked to shoot anything that moved near his own lodge above the Berghof.)

As Blondi gambolled through the autumn-pale grass Hitler gazed across the valley with deep satisfaction. It was a microcosm of the Aryan dream. He saw it peopled with fair-haired, blue-eyed youths and girls; he saw the roads leading to cities where great minds owned by blond intellectuals thrived.

It was a pity that he was so modestly proportioned and had

127

errant dark hair – leadership stamped by his small but agressive moustache – but his mind was Aryan.

And it was this purity of spirit, he believed, that enabled him to rise above the tribulations that beset any leader: treachery, stupidity and obstinacy (as displayed until recently by the British).

As for the bloodshed that had accompanied his crusades, well that was a necessary evil. It had been shed copiously but then his endeavours had been on a grand scale. It had been obvious to him from the start when, as an unsuccessful architect/artist and twice-wounded corporal in the last war, he had been *chosen* to establish a Third Reich, that the whole concept was heroic.

Hitler, dressed in a grey jacket and black trousers, followed Blondi into a wood. Pine needles crunched softly beneath his feet; the dog's barks lost themselves in the trees.

Eva, wearing Bavarian costume, took his arm – held on to it – and said: 'These are the moments I like best. You and I, together, alone,' and he thought: 'She almost said: "Husband and wife".'

He glanced fondly at her pretty, homely face. She had been born for flirtation, sex, marriage to a good burgormaster, three children and many good works in her small town. He had given her none of these; she had aimed too high.

As far as he was concerned there had only been one woman, Geli Raubal, daughter of his widowed half-sister. They had been together for six years until one terrible day in September 1931 she had shot herself because he was too possessive, because he wouldn't even let her go to Vienna for singing lessons.

'You're thinking about her,' Eva accused.

He patted her hand. 'That was a long time ago. Don't let it bother you. It doesn't bother me,' he lied.

Eva, too, had introduced the spectre of suicide into his life, less than a year after Geli's death; but the attempt on her life had been more of a forceful entry into his than a serious attempt to kill herself. Not that he minded: he needed a woman's company between crusades.

She clung to his arm. 'Are you sure?'

'Of course,' reflecting that such conversations, puerile though they were, constituted an escape.

They walked deeper into the wood until they came to a

128

couple of bird boxes. They seemed to be in good condition and popular enough because all the food had been taken. Hitler replenished each with bread, shelled nuts and seed.

It was Eva who saw the movement in the grass. She ran over and picked up a bird. Cupped in her hand, fluttering weakly, it looked like a robin; but the red on its breast was blood and it was a sparrow.

Hitler took the bird from her and gently felt its fragile body with the tips of his fingers. From one wing he took a pellet of shot, then another. 'Why shoot little birds?' he said. 'I can't understand it.'

'But it can't have been shot here,' she said. 'They wouldn't dare,' pointing towards the boundaries of the inner circle of the retreat which was guarded by SS sentries.

'It must have flown here after being shot somewhere else,' Hitler said. By Goering, he thought.

'Can we save it?'

'I doubt it,' Hitler said. 'They don't have much resistance. This was a tough little devil. Usually they die of shock.'

As he spoke the sparrow in his hand died. He placed it in the branches of a tree out of Blondi's reach, shook his head sadly, glanced at his wristwatch and turned back towards the Berghof to discuss a campaign in which innumerable men, women and children would die.

*

Hitler talked first to Canaris because it did Goering good to be kept waiting.

Canaris, wearing a thick blue suit and looking as wary as ever, was standing beside a log fire lit specially for him – the man was always cold – in the main reception room with its sunken floor and marble stairs designed by Hitler.

A manservant poured coffee and left them. Hitler gestured to Canaris to sit down and said: 'I summoned you to hear the latest on Churchill's intentions.'

Hitler had first announced his decision to invade Russia on July 29, just over two months ago. The announcement had been made to his personal Chief of Staff, General Alfred Jodl and, two days later, to Goering and Admiral Eric Raeder, Commander-in-Chief of the Navy. The proposed date for the attack: May 1941.

All three had taken the notice of intent seriously but not the date. It was impossible – and even Hitler admitted this to himself – to predict any date until Britain had been brought to heel. If that hadn't been accomplished by the end of the year then no move against the Soviet Union could be accurately forecast.

Then Canaris had come up with the intelligence that Churchill was willing to seek peace if Hitler removed the Bolshevik menace. Hitler was jubilant. He believed Canaris partly, he acknowledged, because he wanted to believe him. But that was only his instinct asserting itself, and his instinct hadn't let him down since the outbreak of war. He had always believed that Britain should, in her own interests, co-operate with Germany; and at last Churchill had produced the sort of formula that he would have produced had he been the leader of a beleaguered island. And, of course, he hadn't made the approach through normal diplomatic channels: the outcry over such devious double-dealing would have broken every window in Whitehall.

So Hitler had withdrawn his Sea Lion invasion fleet, sorely battered in any case by the RAF – officially he had only postponed it till April 1941, but that was to deceive the Russians – and revised his strategy.

Now the plan was to appease Russia by, among other things, offering her a vast area from the Caspian Sea to Singapore when the Old World was finally carved up between Germany, Italy, Japan and the Soviet Union – and at the same time secretly assemble an invasion army.

Canaris said: 'There isn't a great deal more, *mein Führer.*' He picked up a black briefcase and took out two sheets of teletype. 'But this is further confirmation.' As if it was needed, his weary voice seemed to say.

Hitler scanned the contents. The introductory sheet was headed *Former Naval Person to President Roosevelt.* The message referred to a request for 250,000 rifles from the United States. The second sheet concluded with the words: AS YOU KNOW THE GERMAN INVASION FLEET HAS NOW DISPERSED AND I THINK YOU CAN NOW CONFIDENTLY LOOK FORWARD TO THE ANNIHILATION OF THE MUTUAL ENEMY – the Russians of course – WITH A NEGOTIATED SETTLEMENT BETWEEN THE OTHER TWO FACTIONS FOLLOWING CLOSE BEHIND.

Frowning, Hitler handed the two sheets of paper back to Canaris. 'Former Naval person? Churchill?'

Canaris said: 'When Churchill was at the Admiralty at the beginning of the war he always signed himself *Naval Person* when communicating with Roosevelt. Now, of course, it's *former* ... It might have something to do with the fact that they both held naval appointments during the last war ...'

'It sounds extremely childish,' Hitler said.

Canaris shrugged.

'Where did you get this from?'

'Lisbon.' *Where else?* 'From an *Abwehr* agent established in the communications department of the British Embassy.'

Hitler began to pace up and down the room, hands behind his back. 'Cross? I remember him from our last conversation. How did he get access to a cable sent by Churchill from London?'

'He's just returned from London. As a double agent – I think I told you that last time – he has access to many secrets in London.'

'Double agents must be the most devious members of the human species. Are you sure we can trust him?'

And can I trust you? Hitler wondered. According to Himmler, the resolve of the *Abwehr* chief was 'wavering'. The euphemism of the Reichsführer of the SS for disloyalty? More likely, Hitler suspected, the Reichsführer's opening shots in a campaign to discredit the *Abwehr* and absorb it in his own secret services. Canaris had always been a great patriot, his information had always been good. *And everything he tells me now corresponds with my own instincts.*

'Cross is one of the best we've got,' Canaris said, taking a white tablet from his pillbox and swallowing it with the remains of his now-cold coffee. 'And we mustn't forget the Duke of Windsor ...'

'Dear David,' Hitler said ruminatively. 'That was what the Duchess, Mrs Simpson, called him,' he explained to Canaris. He opened a drawer in a chest beside the sunken floor and took out a photograph album. 'There's dear David and his wife walking down the steps of the Berghof. We might have made him king again if he hadn't bolted to take up some comic opera post in the Bahamas. Perhaps we still will ...' handing the album to Canaris. The photograph was dated October 23,

1937. 'Turn over the page,' Hitler said, 'and you'll see Chamberlain on the same step.'

'To my mind the letter from the Duke clinched it,' Canaris said.

'I quite agree.' Hitler walked over to the window and stared at the mountains. Above the Berghof, approached by tunnel and an elevator 124 metres high, was the Kehlsteinhaus, the Eagle's Nest, the odd building perched on the spur of the Kehlstein Mountain and built at extravagant cost by Martin Bormann. Hitler didn't much care for it; Bormann's folly, he thought. What interested him more was the Untersberg mountain where Emperor Frederick I was said to be buried, biding his time to be re-incarnated and save Germany. He had been a crusader, too – in the Holy Land – and had been known as Barbarossa, Red Beard.

Hitler turned from the window and said to Canaris: 'I'm going to call it Barbarossa,' and when Canaris looked puzzled added: 'The conquest of Russia.' Briskly, he said: 'Keep me informed of any developments.'

'Of course, *mein Führer*.'

'Particularly in Lisbon which seems to me the melting pot of Europe.'

'And the world,' Canaris said. He hesitated and Hitler said: 'Is there something you wish to tell me, admiral?'

'Not really.' Canaris fingered his clipped grey eyebrows. 'The mention of Lisbon reminded me of a few details; I have them here in my briefcase.' He picked it up and thumbed through the papers inside. 'There's a Jewish girl there working for British Intelligence. She has formed a liaison with a man we suspect to be a Russian ... but they're only details ...' He looked questioningly at Hitler.

Hitler struck the coffee table with his fist. 'Admiral, you know perfectly well that I'm not interested in details. Details are for subordinates. Particularly,' he said harshly, 'when they concern Jews. Whatever she's up to I doubt whether she'll have the intelligence to complete it. Surely she doesn't bother you? Or do you perhaps have some sympathy for the sub-humans?'

'None at all, *mein Führer*.'

'Very well, but no details please.' Hitler returned to the window. 'That will be all, admiral. Please send the *Reichsmarschall* in to me.'

*

While he waited Hitler patrolled the big room letting the spurt of anger spend itself.

Here he was, aged fifty-one, in the prime of his life, poised for the final battle, now that his troops had moved into Roumania with its great reserves of oil, and he had allowed the mention of a Jewess to upset him. When he was finally accepted as Saviour of the Fatherland he wouldn't let such minor irritations provoke him. But then, of course, there wouldn't be any Jews anyway.

With a click of his heels and a brisk Nazi salute, *Reichsmarschall* Hermann Goering presented himself, wearing a ridiculous pale blue uniform tailored to conceal his growing paunch.

The *Reichsmarschall*'s self-indulgences were becoming an increasing embarrassment. They could, Hitler supposed, have been condoned if he had fulfilled his promise to shoot the RAF out of the skies; but he had failed miserably.

However Goering, though dissipated, was still canny and useful; he was also loyal and had been in the crusade from the beginning with the scar from the wound received in the attempted putsch in 1923 to prove it. But he was a problem.

Tersely, Hitler told Goering to keep up the *Luftwaffe's* night attacks on British cities. Churchill had to be constantly reminded about Germany's ability to crush his country – but Hitler didn't confide his motives to Goering; only Canaris knew about Churchill's peace moves.

Just as tersely, Hitler dismissed Goering. But as he marched – it would soon be a waddle – to the door Hitler called out after him: 'Just one more thing, Hermann.'

Goering stopped.

'Stop shooting sparrows,' Hitler said.

*

Goering carried out Hitler's orders zealously, continuing the bombardment of Britain's cities and adding a new dimension – fire. On October 15, in addition to 390 tons of explosive, his planes dropped 70,000 incendiary bombs on London.

But instead of causing moral collapse the Blitz had the opposite effect. In London, and later in most of Britain's major cities, the people were more united than ever before. 'We can take it,' they said, and did so every terrible night.

Whenever Churchill was assailed by doubts about the fate he had decreed for Russia and Germany he did two things: he studied the anti-British propaganda pouring out from the Kremlin and the treachery of Communist agents trying to undermine Britain's war effort, then he visited one of the battlefields of Britain.

One day the battlefield was Peckham. A landmine had fallen, devastating acres of terraces of little houses that in South London shoulder each other towards the Thames.

On his way by car with the Chancellor of the Exchequer, Kingsley Wood, he peered out of the limousine at what London was taking. At the spaces in the terraces – like gaps left by cleanly pulled teeth; at the boarded windows and holed roofs and tiny, debris-spattered gardens complete with stirrup pumps for extinguishing flames.

The car skirted a crater in the road; it had been roped off and tin-hatted air-raid wardens were chasing gaping children who ran away, gas-mask cases swinging from their shoulders, to re-group.

At a street-corner tobacconists' shop, its bomb-blasted windows shored up with cardboard, people were queueing for cigarettes as they queued for almost everything else – their four ounces of butter, their twelve ounces of sugar, their scrap of meat. Guiltily, Churchill regarded the glowing tip of his cigar; he was about to squash it in the ashtray when he thought: 'No it's a symbol. And so am I and that is the main thing I have to offer these people.'

A young woman in trousers and jersey recognised him and pointed. Smiling, he raised two fingers in his V for Victory sign and she returned the salute.

The car stopped on the edge of the devastation. The crater in the centre of the smoking rubble that had been thirty or so homes was fifty yards wide. On the stump of a wall a poster fluttered: DIG FOR VICTORY. Above floated a silver barrage balloon.

Rescue workers were digging for the dead and the injured. On swaying walls hung staircases and patchworks of homely wallpaper. The air smelled of bonfires and whitewash.

From the rubble Union Jacks were already sprouting.

Within minutes of his arrival crowds gathered around him. They cheered him and touched him and it was when he thought: 'It's as though I have brought them great riches,' that he had to dab the tears from his eyes with a handkerchief.

A fire officer told him: 'Jerry must be pretty proud of these mines. They float down on parachutes and so the blast does maximum damage.'

'And kills more innocents than a conventional bomb. How satisfying that must be for Corporal Hitler and his fat friend.'

A group of children began to sing:

Just whistle while you work
Mussolini is a twerp,
Hitler's barmy,
So's his army
Rub 'em in the dirt.

As he was driven away a stout woman shouted: 'Let the Jerries have it back, eh, Winnie?'

Oh yes, he thought, I'll let them have it back all right. And the Russians who have thought fit to make a pact with such inhuman aggressors. The people of Peckham had to be saved from both tyrannies. For ever.

*

Churchill set aside an hour to discuss the latest developments in Lisbon with Sinclair.

There was no Cabinet meeting that evening. At nine p.m. he was dining with the Secretary of State for War, Anthony Eden, who had shared his anti-appeasement views in the late thirties – but he hadn't told Eden about Lisbon. Between 7 and 7.45 he had an audience with the King, who had lately taken to practising at a shooting range in the grounds of Buckingham Palace in case he had to go down fighting. So he received Sinclair at eight. It was a cold, clear October night and the sky was swept by the beams of searchlights which seemed to polish the cold stars. The air-raid warnings sounded just as Sinclair arrived.

Sinclair, who looked more like a dour Scottish laird every time he saw him, hesitated in the hall. 'Aren't we going to the Annexe?' – the Government block at Storey's Gate, overlooking St James's Park, where an underground, bomb-proof War Room had been built.

Churchill shook his head. 'I can't stand the place. In any case the apartments there aren't finished yet and life here's much more exciting.'

A few nights earlier Churchill had rescued his kitchen staff from probable death. Bombs had been falling around No. 10

135

when, over dinner, he had suddenly remembered the huge plate-glass window in the kitchen. He told the butler to put the meal on a hot-plate and dispatched the staff to the shelter. A few minutes later the kitchen was wrecked by a bomb, the window blown into lethal shards of glass. Mrs. Landemare, the cook, had expressed annoyance at the mess.

Churchill took Sinclair by the arm. 'I'm surprised the whole place didn't come down. It's 250 years old and was thrown up by a jerry builder named Downing. Jerry finishing off Jerry's work, eh?' He laughed. 'Come on, my dear chap, and have a grog before we get down to work.'

Churchill took Sinclair to his study. The mahogany furniture was covered with white dust shaken from the ceiling by a bomb; the curtains were drawn across black-out frames and steel shutters. The anti-aircraft guns were barking outside; from time to time the building trembled as a bomb erupted nearby.

'We've actually got some of the rooms shored up with wooden props,' Churchill said, pouring them both whisky. 'That's how safe it is!'

'I think you should take more care of yourself, Prime Minister,' Sinclair said, sipping his whisky. 'You owe it to the people.'

'So everyone keeps telling me. But that's not the Churchill the people want. If I die they want me out there brandishing my brolly at the bombers not skulking in some rat-infested dungeon.' He leaned back in his red upholstered chair. 'Now tell me the state of the parties in Lisbon.'

*

Hoffman stroked the full, lovely contours of her body, and everywhere, it seemed, there was an answer to his touch. A movement, a pulse, a stirring. And when she touched him he felt his body respond with an intensity he hadn't believed possible.

Not that there was anything hurried about their caresses. On the contrary, they were tentative, exploratory, the approaches to pre-ordained fulfilment.

Nor was there any attempt by either of them to dominate. He had feared that, in love-making, Rachel's character would demand assertion; had feared that out of perversity he would

136

try to take control. Instead they reached for each other and looked into each other's eyes.

There was no shame, no expertise, just awareness. The natural culmination of a kiss two weeks earlier beneath an olive tree.

When they were both ready she lay back and he thrust into her, lowering himself at the same time to kiss her; then he raised himself again, until she sighed and, suddenly, called his name. Then he was beneath her, and she was moving and this time it was he who called her name ...

'I love you,' he said, as he became aware of rain tapping on the window of her room in the Avenida Palace, of the chiming of a clock nearby, of the shivering lights in the chandelier above them.

'And I love you,' she said.

But there was sadness in her voice and it scared him.

*

Sinclair said that, yes, he was ready to make the next move; the documents and tape were ready – he patted his black briefcase – and would be put into tomorrow's diplomatic bag to be flown to Lisbon. They would be given to Cross; then Rachel Keyser would show them to Josef Hoffman.

A bomb fell close by. No. 10 shook and a piece of plaster fell on the carpet between Churchill and Sinclair.

'There is one complication,' Churchill said, touching the piece of plaster with the toe of his shoe. He was wearing a light grey pin-stripe and a blue, polka-dot bow tie.

Sinclair who thought there were more than one looked at him inquiringly.

'Timing,' Churchill said. 'You've accomplished Phase One in masterly fashion. Hitler will now attack Russia as soon as he can. But, and it's a big but, we don't want him to do it too soon. Next June would be ideal; May could be disastrous because it would give him time to reach Moscow before the Russian winter sets in. If Moscow fell then, who knows, the Russians might even admit defeat; at the very least there would be a lull in the fighting which is exactly what we don't want.'

'According to our intelligence. Not Ultra,' Sinclair said and paused because Churchill was notoriously sceptical about other clandestine sources of information and had devised his own method of sifting reports. But Churchill didn't interrupt and he continued: 'According to these sources we may have an unexpected ally.'

'Mussolini?' once again surprising Sinclair with his grasp of every aspect of the war.

'Exactly. Our sources in Rome report that the Duce is as angry as hell about Hitler's occupation of Roumania and wants to put on a show of his own.'

'A Grecian adventure?' Churchill nodded thoughtfully. An anti-aircraft gun opened up in St James's Park and they heard shrapnel falling on the roof. 'See if you can't make your fellows encourage him to take on the Greeks. He'll make such a botch-up of it that Hitler will have to come to his aid. That should delay his invasion of Russia a few weeks; just about the right period of time to ensure that the *Wehrmacht* founders in the ice and snow.'

'We're already pursuing that line of persuasion,' Sinclair said and thought he sounded rather prim. 'Through Switzerland; and Lisbon, of course.' He had been poised to make the point Churchill had just made.

'The Battle of the Conjurors,' Churchill murmured.

'Sir?'

'An apt phrase to describe espionage. But that's the battle that's going to win the war. Where would we be today without my most secret source? We'd be under the Nazi jackboot, that's where. If we hadn't known in advance where the Fat Man's planes were going to strike they would have overwhelmed us.' He cocked an ear as the gun in the park barked again and glass tinkled outside. 'When we've won this particular round of the Battle of the Conjurors then we must wait for America to enter the fray. After Roosevelt's re-elected, that is.'

'*If* he's re-elected, surely, Prime Minister.' Sinclair dearly wished that he could exercise the same degree of familiarity that other men of the moment had achieved with Churchill. Bracken, for instance, and Beaverbrook and his own namesake, Archibald Sinclair, Secretary of State for Air, who had been dining at No.10 the night Churchill saved Mrs Landemare and her staff. But since he had lost Robin he found it increasingly difficult to be sociable; all his energies were concentrated in his work – to avenge Robin and all the other fine young men who had died.

'He'll be re-elected all right. Willkie's been calling him a warmonger. You wait till FDR fires a few salvoes – at him. He's already arming us: one day he'll fight with us. The Japanese will see to that,' Churchill said.

'The Battle of the Conjurors.' Sinclair repeated the phrase and asked: 'When you come to write the history of this war, will you write about this particular battle?'

Churchill answered briskly. 'Out of the question. In fact I shall have to float over the dark, deep depths with some aplomb. Disguise them, even. The people must believe that it was sheer guts that won the day. As indeed it will be – with guidance from those dark, deep depths.' He shook his head decisively. 'No, my account of the war would be far too premature to reveal the conjurors' sleight of hand. One day it will all come out: it always does. First Ultra and then, later, what you and I have concocted. By then it will be seen in its right perspective: people will understand that we pitted two tyrants against each other to preserve liberty.'

'But at what cost? Millions of lives?'

'*Their* lives,' Churchill snapped. 'Would you prefer that it was British lives?' and then, remembering about Robin, 'I'm sorry, I forgot ...' Outside, the gunfire was receding. Churchill said: 'We'll have the all-clear any minute now. But they'll come again tonight – according to my most secret source. I really am most terribly sorry ...'.

It was the only time Sinclair could remember seeing Churchill flustered. To help him he said: 'As you know, we've taken several measures to strengthen the whole disinformation operation. Hoffman is the spearhead but we don't want to rely completely on one man. Who knows, perhaps he won't co-operate ...'

Churchill said with uncharacteristic humility: 'Tell me about them, Sinclair, tell me about them.'

Sinclair lit his pipe. The whole object of the next phase of the exercise, he reminded Churchill, was to convince Stalin that Hitler was not preparing to invade Russia.

To help achieve this, British Intelligence had been feeding trusted Soviet agents with false information to damage their credibility. In particular Richard Sorge, the Kremlin's master spy in Tokyo. 'He's been fed so many incorrect facts that if and when he warns the Kremlin about Germany's intentions Stalin won't believe a word he says,' Sinclair said.

139

'We're also using a young man named Philby,' Sinclair went on. 'But in a different way. He works for British Intelligence but he's been turned by the Russians. A double-agent in other words.'

'And you intend to make him a triple one?'

'Precisely.' Sinclair wished that Churchill would stop jumping the gun. 'Apparently he's very well thought of in Moscow so we're giving him access to all sorts of classified material in Lisbon. He's our Iberian specialist,' Sinclair explained. 'Or thinks he is.'

'What sort of information?' Before Sinclair could reply Churchill answered himself. 'Information, I presume, allegedly culled from the Germans in Portugal that Hitler has absolutely no intention of attacking Russia in the near future.'

Sinclair sighed. 'That's about it. Who knows, we might even give Philby real promotion one of these days; when he would become the perfect vehicle for misleading the Russians – after the war.'

'Except that he'll be discredited over this business.'

Sinclair shook his head. 'We'll make sure he finally gets the right intelligence. But too late. Much too late.' Sinclair managed a smile.

Churchill said: 'And when he's finally discredited, when he makes a bolt for it, everyone will say how simple-minded your people were in allowing him to operate undetected ...'

'Public opinion should be the last consideration of an Intelligence chief.' Sinclair returned to the matter in hand. 'Other double agents, those loyal to Britain, have also been busy reassuring the Russians about Hitler's reluctance to invade. And, of course, we're being helped by *Abwehr* agents who are just as keen to conceal the German military build-up in the east.'

Sinclair made a last attempt to surprise Churchill. 'But we will warn Stalin that Hitler *does* intend to attack.' The attempt failed.

Churchill grinned at him and said: 'One of our best ploys. I will personally warn the Russian bear; he will immediately conclude the opposite. I'll advise Cripps to do the same in Moscow. And FDR. The Bear – he's too wily for his own good – will think we're trying to create dissension between Hitler and himself.'

The all-clear sounded outside.

Churchill stood up and said: 'Now let's see those documents of yours.' He poured more whisky for both of them. 'There is absolutely no doubt, is there?'

Sinclair took a sheaf of papers and a taperecorder spool from his briefcase. 'That Josef Hoffman is Stalin's son? Absolutely none.'

Part Three

Chapter Eleven

Hoffman perused the documents, watched anxiously by Rachel Keyser.

CERTIFIED COPY OF BIRTH OF INFANT. (Fee one rouble.) DATE OF BIRTH 1919.

No month, Hoffman thought. Some document!

PLACE: PETROGRAD. SEX: BOY. NAME OF FATHER: JOSEPH VISSARIONOVICH DJUGASHVILI.

At least whoever had forged this ludicrous document had gone to the trouble to get Stalin's real name right. (Student rebels at Moscow University never failed to recall that Stalin, born in Gori in Georgia, was the son of a drunken cobbler named Djugashvili.)

But why Petrograd? Hoffman cast his mind back to history lessons. In the Civil War that followed the Revolution, Stalin had been sent to Petrograd, once St Petersburg, now Leningrad, to save the former capital from the White Russians.

OCCUPATION OF FATHER: COMMISSAR OF NATIONALITIES.

They'd got that right, too; they'd obviously gone to considerable trouble. But why?

Hoffman glanced at Rachel. They were sitting in the bedroom of a palace at Sintra, fifteen miles from Lisbon, where staff from the British Embassy were allowed to spend weekends. 'Why?' he asked her.

'Finish reading them,' she said and there was the same sad expression on her face that had scared him before.

MOTHER'S NAME: NADIA LATYNINA.

Who the hell was she supposed to be?

OCCUPATION OF MOTHER: STUDENT.

But it was around 1919 that Stalin had married his second wife, Nadezhda Sergeyevna Alliluyeva, the vivacious revolutionary who, according to gossip, had been driven to suicide thirteen years later by Stalin's boorish behaviour to her and the discovery of his despotic rule. So the British were alleging that he was the bastard son of Stalin, born about the same time that Stalin had married her. He had certainly got around! How ludicrous it all was.

There had, of course, been rumours about Stalin's affairs. In particular with Rosa Kaganovitch, a doctor and sister of a leading Bolshevik. But Nadia Latynina? Never heard of her. And there had bever been any rumours about illegitimate children.

The only children Stalin had sired were Jacob (Yasha) by his first wife, Ekaterina Svanidze – she had died in 1907 – and Vasily and one daughter, Svetlana, born in 1925, on whom Stalin doted.

By all accounts Jacob was a neurotic who had once tried to commit suicide and was now a bureaucrat and a Red Army Reservist. Vassily, a boozer and a rebel, was now a pilot in the Red Air Force; Svetlana was an attractive, red-haired student.

All three of them would have been astonished to learn that they had a brother born out of wedlock!

The forgery written in faded ink the colour of dried blood was pathetic.

Hoffman picked up the next document.

It was another birth certificate recording his birth. FATHER: LIBRARIAN. Etcetera.

They were certainly thorough.

'There's a lot more yet,' Rachel said. She picked up a *queijada*, the sweet cheese pastries made in Sintra, but replaced it without tasting it. She lit a cigarette; Hoffman hadn't seen her smoking before.

The third document was a letter written in 1919 by Joseph Stalin and addressed to Feliks Edmundovich Dzerzhinsky who in 1917 had been appointed head of the Cheka, the Bolsheviks' first secret police force.

Stalin had signed himself Commissar of Nationalities and the letter was an appeal couched in relatively humble terms, because even though you were one of Lenin's lieutenants, you didn't antagonise a secret police chief, certainly not one as cold-bloodedly ruthless as Dzerzhinsky.

Stop it! You're speculating as if you're believing.

The letter implored Dzerzhinsky to use all his powers to obtain and destroy all documents *relating to the birth we discussed.* As they had also agreed it was *in the interests of Boshevism to do so.*

The letter concluded with a request to Dzerzhinsky to destroy the letter. Stalin (or the perpetrator of the forgery) should have known better: a secret police chief destroys nothing.

Next, another faded letter from Stalin, this time addressed to Nicolai Semonovich Golovin, Hoffman's father. *My heartfelt thanks for your action in this matter. May I assure you that I shall follow the boy's progress with the deepest possible interest.*

This was followed by a note apparently written recently and signed by someone named Sinclair.

It said: *It would appear that Cheka agents called on Golovin and confiscated any subsequent correspondence from Stalin. The following transcripts of telephone conversations were probably recorded by elementary wire-taps instigated by successors to the Cheka embodied in the NKVD. (Dzerzhinsky, incidentally, survived as director until he died in 1926.)*

The alleged transcripts were typed, badly, on sheets of yellowing paper headed simply CASE 1385. The conversations, dated in the '20s and early '30s all had a similar theme.

Hoffman applied himself to one dated October 21, 1930, when Stalin was firmly in power after Lenin's death in 1924 and his bitter rival, Leon Trotsky, had been exiled.

Stalin: How is the boy?

Golovin: He's fine. He had a wonderful time on the Black Sea. We are very grateful to you —

Stalin: And how does he like his new school?

Golovin: Early days yet but I'm sure he will settle down. Like his father he adapts well and is capable of great concentration.

Grovel, Hoffman thought.

Then he remembered: 'But I did go to the Black Sea in 1930. To Tuapse.' He recalled sunlight on green water and an argument with his father about an ice-cream. 'And I did go to a new school that autumn – State School 42 in Moscow.' He remembered the fears on the first day there; an unsmiling teacher who wore *pince-nez*; a bully with a birth-mark on his cheek.

Stalin: You must make sure that he works at home, too.

Golovin: Of course, Comrade —

147

Stalin: You must also make sure that his political education is not neglected. Politics are everything.

Golovin: We are already attending to that.

With scant success, Hoffman thought.

Stalin: I will be in touch again in one month.

Golovin: Very well ...

Stalin: Look after him well, Comrade Golovin. He means a lot to me.

Then June 1936.

Stalin: I understand that he is assured of a place at Moscow University.

Golovin: That is correct. He has done very well.

Stalin: But not as well as I had hoped in the political field.

Golovin: He is a very sensitive boy ...

Stalin: And isn't that compatible with political aptitude?

Golovin: I didn't mean that exactly.

Stalin: Never mind, there is still time.

And how they had tried, Hoffman remembered, in that first year at university! But politics to him were like meat to a vegetarian.

Stalin (after a pause): He is looking very well. A little pale perhaps ...

How could Stalin have known? But, of course, those frequent walks in the Kremlin from Red Square past the Cadet Institute Pavilion, past a gloomy, two-storey house ... Stalin's home. Had Stalin been watching him? Loving him?

Stop it!

Golovin: He has very fair colouring.

Stalin: So did his mother ... Are the funds sufficient, Comrade Golovin?

Golovin: Quite adequate.

Stalin: Very well, guard him well, I will be in touch.

There were several more similar transcripts; Hoffman didn't bother to read them. He leafed through the rest of the documents. The message was clear; there was little point in reading many more forgeries. He picked out two at random. One purported to be a memorandum from Stalin to Lavrenti Pavlovich Beria, the sinister head of the NKVD, whose two successors had been executed in Lubyanka. It was dated just before Hoffman had fled from the Soviet Union.

For reasons which need not concern you I want full surveillance mounted on a student at Moscow University named Josef

Hoffman. Whatever movements he chooses must be completely unrestricted. This order must be carried out without question and with maximum application wherever the subject chooses to go.

The evidence was becoming increasingly implausible. The NKVD had tried to kill him in Lisbon!

Hoffman scanned the second document. Again from Stalin to Beria.

An attempt was made to liquidate Josef Hoffman in Lisbon two weeks ago. According to foreign intelligence sources this was a NKVD operation. Those responsible must be dealt with summarily in the normal manner.

Shot.

'I don't understand,' he said aloud.

She crossed the room and touched his cheek with her hand but he brushed it aside.

He picked up another paper. It was a denial by Beria that anyone in the NKVD had been involved in the assassination attempt. Nevertheless three officers had been dealt with 'in the normal manner'.

In a white-tiled cell in Lubyanka.

'But they did try to kill me,' he said. 'Why?'

'There is a lot to explain,' she said. 'I don't understand a lot of it. But I didn't understand any of it when I first met you. Only that you were Russian, not Czech ... Please believe me.'

She stood in front of him, pleading.

He leaned forward, picked up a *queijada* and bit into it; he wasn't aware of any taste. Through the window of the pink-and-gold room he could see lawns and a garden laid out with box hedges and, beyond the palace grounds, farmland stretching away to the sea. It had been raining and in the gardens a bird was singing, its notes like the last drops of rain.

'But it was arranged, wasn't it? You and me?'

She looked away from him saying, 'Later, we'll talk about it later,' as though she were talking to a child and, walking across the deep pink carpet: 'First listen to this. Let's get it over with. Then we can talk.' She made some adjustments to a wire-recorder. 'I don't really know how to work this thing' then she pressed a button – she seemed to be able to work it well enough.

It was his father's voice right enough; pedantic and pompous, but bereft of its didactic quality. 'I don't know where he is. He came back one day from a journey into the country and he was, well different; as though he had seen a vision.'

Guns firing, bodies falling in slow motion.

Another voice. (Stalin's? It certainly had a thick Georgian accent.) 'Had he been with the girl?'

'Anna Petrovna? I don't know. I warned him about her ...'

'Nikolai Vasilyev?'

'Perhaps. I warned him about all such dangerous influences.' A stammer of apprehension in that sonorous voice. 'Then he just disappeared.'

'Don't worry, Comrade Golovin, we know where he is.'

'Will he ... will he be coming back?'

'Perhaps. But not to you, Comrade Golovin. You have played your part. But your days as foster father are over.'

Was that a woman sobbing in the background? His mother?

Stalin, if it were he, said: 'I am very grateful to you and I have arranged for a suitable reward to be paid to you.' And, unbelievably – if it were he – there was a catch in his voice.

'Thank you ...'

'Yes, thank you ...' a woman's voice. His mother's. No doubt about it.

Click.

The voices had been severed as though the throats of their owners had been cut.

Suddenly Hoffman thought: 'They weren't such bad parents, really.' He supposed that, ever since Stalin had first contacted Dzerzhinsky, State security had kept up surveillance; not even dictators were immune from the attentions of their own protectors.

Rachel switched the OFF button and looked at him. 'Do you believe it now?'

'That was my father's voice, yes.'

'And everything you've just read?'

Believe that his true father was a tyrant and a mass-murderer?

'No, I do not believe it,' he shouted.

But he did.

*

Sintra isn't like any other part of Portugal. It is dark green and verdant, a little decayed, a little decadent. It is built on high ground, nesting amid soft hills, and contains a clutch of

150

palaces including the former summer residence of the Portuguese kings, an odd building with two conical chimneys like oast houses.

Lord Byron had much admired Sintra. It reminded Hoffman of a small town in the foothills of the Swiss Alps which had borrowed a little from Ruritania. It was a classic setting for intrigue which, Hoffman assumed, was the reason he had been brought here for The Revelation.

Although it had stopped raining the foliage was still dripping as he and Rachel, both wearing raincoats, walked down a narrow road lined with mossy walls.

Hoffman's brain ached with questions, but every time he tried to put one into words it slipped away. They passed a waterfall, green and white and cold, and he thought again: 'I am the son of one of the most evil men in history,' and then the first question came quite easily: 'Who was my mother? Who was this girl Nadia Latynina?'

The stranger walking beside him said: 'I wish we knew.' *We!* 'The birth certificate said she was a student, that's all that's known. By us anyway.' *Us!* 'But,' glancing at Hoffman, 'she was obviously very fair, slim, tall. Sensitive,' Rachel said softly.

He ignored the last part of it. 'Weren't there any other records? You seem to have been very thorough with records.'

'They couldn't find any.' *They* now. 'She seems to have vanished.'

'So all I have left is a Georgian gangster. If he destroyed her – and, make no mistake, that's what he did – you would have thought he would have destroyed all the evidence.'

'He probably tried, but in those early days he must have under-estimated the secret police. They made copies. And even later it can't have occurred to him that he was under observation. Or perhaps it did occur but he had to risk everything to keep in touch with Nikolai Golovin. You see,' she said, 'it seems that he is very proud of you. He had antagonised his other two sons, Jacob and Vassily, he loved his daughter Svetlana, still does, but, well, she's a girl ... You were the only son he hadn't polluted and he wanted to keep it that way; to keep you isolated in a showcase where he could watch over you.'

'And he didn't want any scandal,' Hoffman said.

'That as well,' she said.

They turned up a lane past a crouching, red-roofed house.

151

The blue sky was hung with watery clouds, and the woods on either side of them smelled of dead summer. To one side, on a crag, they could just see the Moorish Castle.

'Tell me one thing; how the hell did you get all this information?' he asked.

'British Intelligence have a double-agent in the NKVD. It wasn't too difficult for him to copy the duplicated documents. They've known about you for a long time, Josef ...'

'Kept me on ice?'

'I suppose so. I don't know very much about it, not that side of it.' *What side then?* 'I suppose there was no way they could use their knowledge while you were still in Russia.'

'They didn't exactly jump on me when I escaped.'

'I suppose,' she said carefully, 'that they wanted you to establish yourself.'

'Before introducing the *femme fatale*. Yes, I can see that. Get the stupid bastard waving his Red Cross flag in Geneva or Stockholm or Lisbon, somewhere useful, before making their play ... But why?' he asked her.

'First,' she said, 'let's get everything else cleared up.'

'Just like that? Like clearing out an In tray?' And abruptly: 'Why were you posted to Lisbon?'

'The In tray,' she said, 'we'll clear that out first.' Her tone was surer now, resigned.

She had told him the truth, she insisted. As far as she had known then, she had been sent to Portugal because of her expertise in communications. Cryptanalysis, if you preferred it. Almost immediately Cross had recruited her into Intelligence with the specific task of cultivating him; and, yes, she and Cross had been lovers but they weren't any more and he could believe or disbelieve that, it was up to him.

Why should he believe anything she said, he asked, and she said she couldn't think of any reason.

But she hadn't been told why she had to cultivate him. 'Cultivate, some euphemism.' Only that the two of them were to play some vital part in the final victory over oppression. It wasn't difficult to persuade her, she admitted: Cross and his superiors were well aware of her hatred of the Nazis; but there had been a question mark over him, still was.

'So you knew from that first meeting in the Casino that I was Russian. That must have been quite a joke. Did you have a good laugh about it after you and Cross —'

'Please.' She stretched out a hand but he evaded it.

A biplane took off from Sintra airport and climbed unsteadily into the sky. A few drops of rain fell from a dark cloud hovering over them.

He said: 'All we ever talked was lies.'

'No, not always. Not —'

'Always,' he said firmly. 'I'm surprised you didn't invite me up to your room that first night. Oh no, of course not, how stupid of me, Cross was there, wasn't he?'

'He came there. Nothing happened. It doesn't matter, does it, not if you don't believe me.'

'He must be quite a lover. Aggressive, sadistic even. Your type. It must have been hell having to bed down with a pacifist.'

The slap was hard and unexpected and it made him stumble. And it was then that Hoffman utterly surprised himself: he slapped her back, hard; then held her wrists as she came at him.

When he let go she said: 'Let's get back, there's going to be a storm.'

He thought how incongruous her words were. But she was right about the storm; the dark cloud had swollen and fat raindrops were spattering on the cobbled surface of the lane. The pilot of the biplane thought better of it and turned back towards the airstrip.

He said: 'And you still don't know what it's all about?'

'I know more than I did.'

'But you're not telling?' And then he remembered the question he had asked before. 'Why did the NKVD try and kill me? Surely Beria must have primed them to leave me alone.'

'They didn't try to kill you,' she said, hurrying through the rain that had begun to fall heavily.

He stopped, 'But they did,' he called after her. He ran a few strides to catch up with her. 'They did.'

Her black hair was pasted closed to her scalp by the water, her lipstick was smeared, there was a red mark on her cheek where he had hit her and there was hopelessness in her eyes. She looked beautiful, he thought.

'The NKVD had nothing to do with it,' she said.

'What the hell are you talking about?'

They reached the bottom of the road and turned towards the palace.

'No one was going to shoot you.'

'But the man with the gun —'

153

'He wasn't Russian,' she said.

'Wasn't Russian. What was he then, for God's sake?'

The rain had soaked through his clothes to his skin and he was swimming in lies.

She stopped and turned, hands on her hips, rainwater streaming down her face.

'He was British,' she said.

*

Lying in a hot bath in the palace, a glass of whisky beside him, Hoffman considered her explanation. He was a little drunk and her reasons had become blurred, as though the steam from the bath had got at them.

Apparently it had all been a set-up to establish a relationship between Cross and himself, to make him grateful to the British for saving his life; a stepping stone to Rachel.

The *assassin* had been armed with a gun and the whole build-up had been elaborate, even down to firecrackers in his pocket, because Cross was a perfectionist in such matters. But Hoffman had never been in much danger: the gun had been loaded with blanks.

A hefty tackle. *Assassin* sprawling. Whisked away in a car to Cross's flat. Man-to-man rapport established. Russian peasant only too happy to accept guidance from sophisticated saviour.

You stupid prick, Hoffman thought. He drank some whisky. And how could he have ever believed that a woman like Rachel Keyser would fall in love with him?

You deserved all you got and more, he decided climbing out of the bath. He stood in front of the mirror, swaying slightly.

He peered into it.

Joseph Stalin peered back.

*

It wasn't until next morning that anything made any real sense. He awoke at 7.30 a.m. with a sense of sleepy serenity; then he felt the first stab of pain in his skull and it awakened the previous day's revelations. At first they were like an old black-and-white movie, erratic and silent; then gradually they gained colour and sound and continuity.

He turned his aching head to one side and saw Rachel lying beside him. She had pushed the blankets down to her waist and he could see that she was wearing a filmy black nightdress.

154

They had come to Sintra as lovers. But she must surely have realised that what she was going to tell him would put an end to all that. Or was the arrogance of such women so indestructible that they believed their sexuality could overcome any obstacles?

Another pulse of pain in his skull. He hadn't drunk all that much whisky, but he wasn't accustomed to spirits in any quantity.

Hands behind his head, he stared out of the window at the grey sky, drained of rain, and let the movie run free. It was all about the privileges he had enjoyed as a teenager, about his parents' cosseted life.

How complacent they had been. With good reason!

He swung himself out of the bed, put on his dressing gown and stood at the window. The fields below the hills were covered in mist; the sun was rising amid pink petals of cloud; a donkey was delivering olive oil to the palace kitchens.

'We've got a lot to talk about,' she said. She was sitting up in bed, blanket clutched to her breasts.

'Have we?'

'But not here,' her voice businesslike. 'The reason we came to Sintra was to avoid surveillance.' She had driven the black Austin loaned to them by the British Embassy very quickly, he remembered. 'But they may have picked us up by now.'

'They?'

'Germans, Russians. Apparently the Germans are curious about us. As for the Russians – Cross thinks they've stepped up surveillance because of the German interest. A vicious circle ...'

A knock at the door. A maid in a black and white uniform brought in a tray. Orange juice, coffee, hot rolls. They ate in silence.

He spoke to her while she was splashing in the bathroom; it was easier that way. 'I want to get back to Lisbon,' he said. 'As soon as possible.'

'I'll drive you,' she called out. 'But we'll stop on the way. I have to explain. There was no point last night. Too much whisky.'

She sounded, he thought, like a super-efficient secretary who has just slept with the boss.

She drove the little, stiff-backed car at a brisk pace. The town hadn't yet awoken and stray dogs stared at them, affronted by the noise.

The grey Citroën van picked them up on the outskirts of the town.

'They took their time but they made it in the end,' she said.

'Russians?'

'Germans. They like using Citorën vans.'

'You seem to know a lot about it,' Hoffman said as the Austin accelerated round a bend in the road.

He glanced behind. The van was still with them.

'He has a problem,' she said. 'He's supposed to be inconspicuous. But what can he do when we're rattling along at ...' glancing at the speedometer '... sixty-five miles an hour. Either he shows his hand or he loses us.'

'You sound,' Hoffman said, 'as though you've been doing this sort of thing all your life.'

'Or perhaps I've just found a purpose.'

She swung the wheel and the Austin swerved round a donkey laden with cannisters of kerosene. A peasant shouted after them, jumping back as the Citroën van swept past him.

The still-wet road descended the hills in bends past gardens of spent flowers. Part of the mist had been smoke from the fields below and they could smell it inside the car. She had pushed the accelerator flat on to the floor so that there was no speed left in the engine. The Citroën disappeared and reappeared in the mist and smoke.

She took a turn beside a field of gnarled vines too fast, braked and went into a long skid. But she fought it; the Austin righted itself and accelerated down a straight stretch of road.

'Let's hope he's not so lucky,' she said.

But he was.

There were patches of clear visibility now, the fields on either side golden. They raced past a plantation of cork trees, through a hamlet with chickens pecking at the sides of the road.

Ahead lay a hollow filled with mist. They dipped sharply into it and it was like driving through grey wool.

Tyres screeching, they took a sharp corner, splashing through a stream that had overflowed in the storm. To the right a cart laden with slabs of marble and pulled by two horses was just emerging from a yard. The Austin swerved round it and plunged out of the mist.

Two hundred yards down the road Rachel pulled into a lane and waited.

The sound of the Citroën's engine reached them from the hollow.

'Now,' she said.

The noise of the impact was savage. They heard metal ripping, glass smashing, thuds as what they supposed were the slabs of marble hit the road.

They climbed out of the Austin and walked back. The Citroën was lying on its side, oil and water streaming from its engine; marble littered the road; the horses still in their shafts were pawing the ground; the man in charge was shouting and trying to calm them. The driver of the Citroën sat on the roadside, hands covering his face, blood oozing from between his fingers.

Rachel Keyser and Hoffman went back to the Austin.

At the next village Rachel telephoned the police and told them about the accident.

Ten minutes later she turned suddenly into a dusty track. She stopped the Austin beneath the sails of a windmill. 'Now listen to what I've got to say,' she said.

*

As she began talking he became aware of a whistling that he couldn't place.

Then he forgot it as her words struck home.

She wanted him to return to Russia.

He couldn't believe it!

'Why for God's sake?'

'For Russia's sake.'

She explained. British Intelligence believed that the Germans were secretly preparing to attack Russia. But Stalin, isolated from reality in the Kremlin, sinking deeper into his persecution complex, trusting no one's judgement but his own, would never believe the British warnings. He had struck his pact with Hitler; and although he knew that one day it would be broken he didn't think that time was imminent. Any word to the contrary – from the British of all people – would be interpreted as mischief-making.

Stalin was well aware that most clandestine information, and disinformation, filtered through Lisbon. Hard-put to distinguish one from the other, he would rely more and more on his own egocentric judgement. Unless he found a source he could trust.

157

'Me?'

She nodded.

'You're crazy.'

'Think about it,' she said. 'Stalin believes he is surrounded by betrayal. With the exception of Svetlana, even his own children have let him down. But throughout all this period of treachery, imagined or otherwise, he has isolated and protected one person. You. Kept away from you so that he doesn't antagonise you as he did the other two boys.'

Hoffman stepped out of the car and sat on a hummock of yellowing grass beneath the sails of the windmill. The whistling seemed louder. He glanced up and noticed clay jugs attached to the ropes of the sails; as they turned they whistled.

He said: 'You don't understand why I left Russia.' He told her about the massacre he had witnessed. 'Now you can see why I can never return.'

She was quiet for a moment. Then: 'On the contrary. It makes me realise how much you care for your people. For Russia.'

That was true, always had been.

She said: 'You can help save them from a holocaust.'

'They have one already.'

'Nothing compared with what the Nazis would inflict on them. The Jews to start with ...'

'Are the Jews all you care about?'

'No,' she said, 'humanity.'

She plucked a blade of grass and began to chew it. A breeze teased her hair. He could smell the smoke from the fields and dry earth after rain. He wondered how much of what she was telling him was the truth. They said power corrupted; so did intrigue.

The way she had deceived him had honed new instincts in him. He said: 'You don't seem to include Germans in humanity.'

'I know,' she said. 'That's something I have to work on. But if you were a Jew and you had seen what I have seen ...'

'I saw worse,' he said softly. 'Much worse.'

An aircraft took off from Sintra. A German JU-52 with crosses on its fuselage. Rachel stared at it speculatively, one hand shading her eyes.

She said: 'Odd, isn't it, how differently we reacted to what we saw. I wanted revenge, you wanted escape.'

158

Anger flared inside him but he controlled it because, with his newly-aroused instincts, he knew that was what she sought.

'I wanted escape,' he said, 'so that I could work for peace. Were there so many opportunities for revenge in Washington?'

She reacted angrily and he thought: 'At last I've won a round.'

'I went there to be trained and you damn well know it.' she said.

'And there you would have stayed if it hadn't been for me.'

'Don't worry, I would have got out all right despite you.' She was silent, breathing quickly, trying to control herself. 'The point,' she said slowly and quietly, 'is that we can both do something for humanity. We've been thrown together, we're collaborators – if, that is, you agree to help ...'

He lay back and stared into the blue sky. The windmill's sails continued to whistle as she talked.

'... I know that you're a pacifist. I can understand that.' Forcing herself, he thought. 'But what I'm asking you to do doesn't undermine any of your ... principles. The reverse in fact. You will be giving your country an opportunity to defend itself —'

'What I don't understand,' he interrupted, 'is Britain's sudden concern for Russia.'

'I'm not going to insult your intelligence,' she replied. 'Britain is concerned about Britain. If Germany wins a runaway victory against the Soviet Union then she will turn on the British. But that needn't concern you. What must concern you is that you can help to save your country. Surely that would be the greatest act of pacifism ever conceived.'

She was leaning over him, brown eyes staring into his; but as she moved closer, lips parted, he turned his head away. You have betrayed me once, he thought, you could do it again.

*

She didn't drive straight back to Lisbon. Instead she drove through the little town of Mafra which Hoffman knew because he had put refugees in the monastery there. It was a solid-looking place built by King João V. According to legend the King had vowed he would build a monastery if God granted him a child and God obliged with a daughter.

'An impressive building,' Rachel said, to break their long silence.

'It was designed by a German,' Hoffman said. 'Where the hell are we going?'

'To a mansion.'

'I want to get to the centre of Lisbon.'

'First the mansion.'

'Do you mind telling me why?'

'Because,' she said.

'I could jump out of the car.'

'You could,' she agreed, pushing her foot down on the accelerator.

'Was this planned too?'

'Not by me,' she said, and he thought: 'What sort of an answer is that?'

He estimated that they were five miles outside Lisbon when she swung the Austin off the road onto a long, winding drive burrowing through thick undergrowth.

When he saw the mansion – grey and massive with colonnaded wings – he said: 'How did the owner get this pile? – cork or port? Or wolfram perhaps?' because fortunes were being made selling it to the British and Germans for alloying steel.

'Olive oil,' she said.

She pulled up outside portals surmounted by baroque angels. They were welcomed by an elderly, fragile-looking man wearing a blue blazer with a pink and grey silk scarf at his neck. Behind him stood Cross looking more sleekly healthy than ever beside the old man.

'Good morning, Mr. Hoffman,' the old man said in almost perfect English. No one introduced him.

Hoffman nodded, ignoring Cross. They walked into a cool marble hall; it reminded Hoffman of the foyer of a museum.

'You were very punctual,' the old man said.

'Was I? I didn't know.' Hoffman looked at Rachel.

The old man led them up a broad, curving staircase. At the top was a long landing guarded by suits of armour. Sunlight coloured by a stained-glass window quivered on the parquet flooring.

They went into a library, its walls lined with books that had an unread look about them. Windows with small leaded panes looked across lawns as smooth as moss and a dark, deep-looking lake.

A log fire was burning in a grate. In front of it a chair; beyond the chair a pair of slippered feet.

160

The old man approached the chair; Cross and Rachel Keyser stood behind Hoffman.

The old man cleared his throat and when the occupant of the chair stood up Hoffman knew that he would be travelling to Moscow, because who could resist the oratory of Winston Churchill?

Chapter Twelve

The following day Hoffman made contact with German Intelligence.

A necessary precaution, Cross said, if Stalin was to be persuaded that he had access to Nazi secrets. But at the same time the Germans would have to be convinced that Hoffman was worth recruiting.

'Oh, what a tangled web we weave,' Cross said, handing him an envelope. 'That's Churchill's itinerary for Lisbon. He's gone now but it shows how valuable you could be to the *Abwehr*. Supposing they had known beforehand ... God forbid!'

Hoffman looked at him in surprise. Vehemence wasn't Cross's style.

Cross caught the look and said: 'Probably the greatest man the world has ever known,' and Hoffman who didn't believe that Churchill was greater than Leonardo da Vinci or Christopher Columbus was even more surprised.

They were walking along the waterfront at Belém near Cross's apartment. It was a grey day, gulls calling about loneliness.

Cross seemed to think that an explanation about his views on Churchill was required. 'We won the last war,' he said. 'Just. Then the yellow streak in politics – Baldwin, Chamberlain, all that lot – dissipated the victory. But Churchill will save us again.'

Hoffman thought Cross talked about Churchill the way some Germans talked about Hitler; he wondered why.

'My father was in the Navy,' Cross said abruptly. 'He knew Winston quite well. Did you know that when Churchill returned to the Admiralty last year a signal was sent to all Naval ships: "Winston's back"?'

Hoffman said he didn't.

'Anyway Churchill came to our house one day in the late twenties. I had always assumed I would follow in my father's footsteps and I would have done if I hadn't gone down with tuberculosis. My father didn't take kindly to illness; he seemed to think it was my fault. A disgrace to the family, all that. But Churchill was quite different. He took me to a top Naval specialist and I was finally cured. But not even Churchill could get me into the Navy with a history of tuberculosis. Instead he got me this job; he made sure I could play my part.'

It was then that Hoffman realised just how dangerous Cross was. A frustrated blood-and-guts serviceman diverted to espionage; a paranoiac; not so very different from a Gestapo officer worshipping Hitler.

Half an hour later Hoffman walked down the steep, narrow Rua Joaquim Casimiro, named after a nineteenth-century composer and organist. The paint on the walls of the tall terrace houses was flaking; the balconies looked as though they had been stuck there with glue. Halfway down he came across two Judas trees, shiny round leaves just falling. Around Easter the branches, still bare of foliage, would be covered with mauve-pink blossom, blushing with shame, according to legend, because Judas, the apostle who betrayed Christ, had hanged himself on such a tree.

At the bottom of the street which formed a T-junction with a busy road he entered a small café-bar. It was just below the surface of the road and the rattle of trams was part of the acoustics, like the squawking of a parrot in the corner.

It was midday. A few men in blue working overalls sat at the long bar drinking beer or coffee and brandy. Hoffman ordered a Bagaceira, firewater distilled from the residue of grapes in a cask that has contained whisky, and sat, as instructed, beside a mirror bearing the words VINHOS DE PORTO. As arranged, he carried with him a copy of yesterday's *Diario de Lisboa* opened at the sports page and was smoking a Portuguese Suave cigarette.

Earlier that morning he had telephoned the German Legation and, on Cross's instructions, asked to speak to Fritz von

162

Claus. 'If I made the call he'd smell a rat,' Cross had said, from which Hoffman had inferred that Cross acted in a dual capacity. An indiscretion? Hoffman, with his new awareness, didn't think so; Cross merely wanted to emphasise how frank he was being. Hoffman had told von Claus that he had valuable contacts with the British Embassy and the Red Cross.

Cross had said that there would be no difficulty in recognising von Claus: he was short and dark with a deformed back that was almost a hunch. He was also one of the *Abwehr's* aces, devoted to Canaris; but, like the admiral, his loyalties to the Third Reich had been sorely strained by the activities, condoned by Hitler, of Himmler and Heydrich and their henchmen.

Hoffman waited. Cross had predicted that von Claus would be late. 'He'll give you the once-over first. A cautious man, Fritz.'

He sipped his drink and coughed and thought about Churchill. He had been softer and pinker than he had expected, but there was no denying his persuasive powers. His words didn't fade: they stayed with you like hammer blows on a golden gong.

'For the sake of Mankind, Mr. Hoffman, I beg you to help us to help the one parent you should never deny.' A pause. 'Mother Russia, Mr. Hoffman. To accomplish this you must make contact with your other parent ... Comrade Stalin. But he is so much part of Russian history that he has adopted its motivations of which persecution is the vanguard.' How many times had this been rehearsed? Hoffman had wondered. 'He trusts no one – except, we believe, you, Mr. Hoffman. If you establish yourself in Lisbon as his link with reality you will be able to apprise him of Hitler's true intentions. Who knows, the Führer may abandon the whole shooting match; on the other hand he may mount another *Blitzkreig*; whatever he does you will be able to warn Comrade Stalin and you will be believed.'

For a moment it occurred to Hoffman that what would suit Churchill best would be the destruction of the German Army and the Red Army by a debilitating war deep inside the Soviet Union. But no, that was ridiculous. If it were so why would Churchill go to so much trouble to ensure that Stalin was prepared for an attack?

'You are fond of sport?'

Hoffman glanced up. The man standing beside the table was on the short side and his back was deformed.

'As a spectator,' as arranged.

'Do you mind if I join you?' Von Claus spoke in clipped English.

Hoffman gestured to the empty seat opposite him. 'A drink?'

Von Claus pointed at Hoffman's glass. 'Anything but that; it makes Schnapps seem like mother's milk. A brandy, I think.' He sat down.

While ordering the drink at the long bar Hoffman glanced at the little man sitting at the table. His thin black hair looked as though it had been painted on his scalp; his face bore the erosions of suffering; he was as dapper as a fraudulent nobleman.

When he placed the brandy on the table von Claus said: '*Danke schön*,' and the parrot swore in Portuguese.

'A good cover, that bird,' von Claus said, touching the brandy with his lips. 'You can blame any indiscretion on him. Do you have any indiscretions to commit, Herr Hoffman?'

'I thought I should join what seems to be a growing profession in Lisbon.'

'Espionage? Yes, it's very popular. But as in everything else you only succeed if you have anything worth selling. Do you have anything worth selling?'

'I have access to information.'

'Ah, access,' as though he had heard that one many times before. 'Proof is also a good saleable commodity.'

Hoffman took the envelope from his pocket. 'Here's the proof. I obtained it since speaking to you this morning. Where's the payment?'

'You're hardly in a position to bargain.'

'For dynamite? I think I am. How about ten thousand escudos?'

'You seem very sure of yourself.'

'But at this moment you are not. For all you know this could be details of a new U-boat deterrent.'

'And is it?'

'No.' Listening to himself, Hoffman was amazed; it was like listening to a stranger.

Von Claus said: 'Five thousand and hand over that envelope, please. You can't expect any more. Only buyers at de Beers buy unseen.' He handed over his copy of *Diario*. 'You will find

164

the money in an envelope inside. It's what I had intended to give you.'

Hoffman shrugged: if nothing else it was the easiest 5,000 he had ever earned. A few days ago he would have spent it on Rachel Keyser; now he would spend it on Josef Hoffman.

Von Claus took the typewritten memorandum from the envelope Hoffman handed him. Hoffman watched him closely. The hollow features had obviously been trained not to show emotion but this time the training failed; the skin on his domed forehead moved, his thin lips compressed.

Von Claus took a decent mouthful of his brandy this time and licked his lips. Finally he said: 'Am I expected to believe this?'

'Easy enough to check out,' Hoffman said.

'Now that it's over – if it ever took place? Yes, I suppose it is. But tell me, Herr Hoffman, why do you imagine I would be interested in out-of-date information?'

'One, because you were. I could see it in your eyes. It was a shock to you. You *should* have known about it. Think of the opportunities, if you had been prepared for a visit by Winston Churchill. Kidnap, assassination – the possibilities are limitless. Two, because it proves that I do have access to top secret information. And three, it's quite possible that Churchill will return to Lisbon.' He was proud of that one; it was his own brainchild.

'And I thought—' Von Claus produced a small gold box from his waistcoat pocket and took a pinch of snuff.

I know what you thought. You thought you had all such eventualities covered – by Cross.

Von Claus returned the snuff-box to his pocket. 'If you can obtain such good information why didn't you tell me about Churchill before?'

'Because I didn't know before. But if I had I wouldn't have parted with it for 5,000 escudos. One hundred thousand perhaps ...'

'May I ask who your informant at the Embassy is?'

'I may be a novice at the game but I do know that's an improper question.'

'Improper?' Von Claus smiled thinly. 'That's the first time I've heard that word used in connection with espionage. However, I take your point.'

According to Cross, von Claus would assume that the

contact was Rachel Keyser. According to Cross the NKVD would be observing his meeting with von Claus. A tangled web ...

'Firstly,' von Claus said, 'I shall check this information,' tapping the memorandum with one frail finger. 'If it turns out to be true then you can take it that we shall accept your services. In future when you make contact use the name Best. All subsequent meetings will be here unless you hear to the contrary. If I can't make it a man named Schneider will meet you. He's easy to recognise, he's got a stupid duelling scar across one cheek.'

'Payment?'

'According to value.'

'Then,' Hoffman said, 'you or Schneider had better bring more than 5,000 escudos with you next time.'

'I should certainly like to know if Churchill intends to return to Lisbon,' von Claus said. 'But in advance next time ...'

With an abrupt movement he finished his brandy; he stood up slowly and painfully. 'I sincerely hope we meet again, Mr. Best.'

As he walked out of the café the parrot squawked a Portuguese obscenity which made the workmen at the bar smile.

*

The German Legation on the Rua do Pau da Bandeira was a pink palace. A cobbled drive led up to its doorway; immediately inside was a big echoing hallway; to the right of this a glittering ballroom, which had been likened to the inside of a cube of sugar, where Baron Hoyningen-Hüne, the aged and cultured German Minister, threw lavish balls attended by diplomatic representatives of most countries in Lisbon except the British.

In the garden at the rear stood a rubber tree said to have been planted by Vasco da Gama; underneath the building was a secret passage leading to the Minister's residence close by.

A ball was in progress while Otto Bauer, the Lisbon head of the Gestapo, studied a report on von Claus's latest foray for the *Abwehr*. Himmler's instructions had been blessedly simple: 'Accumulate as much evidence as possible to discredit Canaris's organisation in the eyes of the Führer.'

From the ballroom below came the strains of 'The Blue

'Danube'. Bauer didn't dance; he wasn't built for it and, in any case, he preferred distractions of a more intimate nature. In the Chiado he had chanced upon a doorway whore who, for a price, submitted to all sorts of indignities. But he did like Viennese music and, lips pursed, he whistled along with the waltz as he read the agent's report stolen from *Abwehr* files and copied before being returned.

So von Claus had gone once again to the café at the bottom of the Rua Joaquim Casimiro. Why didn't the man vary his movements? That was the trouble with the old aristocrats, they were too rigid in their outlook. They even confined their instruments of interrogation to rubber truncheons whereas the Gestapo ... Bauer, who had once been complimented by Himmler on his ingenuity in this field, took the spittle-soaked butt of his black cigar from his lips and crushed it in the ashtray on his desk.

'Wine, Women and Song' reached him from the ballroom; he began to whistle again, then stopped, his attention riveted by a sentence in the report. *In the café subject spent 23 minutes in the company of Josef Hoffman, a Czech Red Cross employee, who, you will recall, has also been under* Abwehr *surveillance.*

Of course he recalled it. He had learned about it from other documents stolen from *Abwehr* files. He had considered mounting his own surveillance operation. But what was the point when the *Abwehr* were doing all the donkey work and he could read their reports?

His deputy had been surprised by the intensity of his interest in the case; after all it was only routine. But his deputy hadn't been humiliated by a Jewish bitch in a Lisbon elevator. A Jewish bitch who was currently being screwed by this Hoffman.

Now von Claus had entered the picture.

Bauer leaned his bulky body back in his swivel chair and pulled at the lobe of one of his small ears, all his predatory instincts aroused.

Von Claus paying money to a Czech – the agent had seen the usual newspaper change hands – who was consorting with a Jewess. Take it a step further and von Claus was accepting the word of the Jewess because she was obviously Hoffman's source of information.

Himmler would like that. Bauer lit another black cigar and inhaled with satisfaction.

But how much better if he could prove that von Claus was

being taken for a ride by Fraülein Keyser. It wouldn't be too difficult to portray such naîvety as treachery. Who knows, perhaps it was treachery – like Canaris, von Claus wasn't renowned for his pro-Nazi sympathies. Nor for that matter was the Minister in Lisbon which was why Bauer had to maintain a façade of protocol; although in the end fear of the Gestapo usually prevailed.

Bauer regarded the glowing tip of his cigar. Now that von Claus is personally involved, he thought, I shall have to act. No more of this second-hand surveillance via *Abwehr* files.

Find out what the hell Hoffman is up to. And perhaps *persuade* the Keyser bitch to come clean. The prospect of such persuasion caused Bauer to become physically aroused.

Downstairs, old Vienna had been abandoned. The orchestra was playing a modern quickstep.

*

At seven a.m. the following morning a man named Muller began to keep watch on the terrace house where Josef Hoffman lived.

He was a thin, wiry man, prematurely grey, in his late thirties. He was fit except for a persistent cough caused by excessive smoking; without the cough he would have been a top-class burglar instead of a mere housebreaker employed by the Gestapo to carry out robberies where little risk was involved.

He was insignificant enough as it was but he went to great pains to make himself even less noticeable. This morning he wore grubby overalls and spectacles, fitted with plain glass, and strolled up and down the street as though looking for an address – he had learned long ago that the observer who remains stationary, as they do in the movies, is the most likely to attract attention.

As he paused outside a shop-window filled with cheap jewellery he remembered the green years in Hamburg when he had aspired to becoming Germany's most renowned cat burglar. What had gone wrong? He coughed: that was what had gone wrong.

The Gestapo had approached him while he was serving his third jail sentence. Cigarettes had been rationed in the prison and he scarcely coughed at all when the two agents had visited him in his cell; if he had they would probably have found someone else. As it was they didn't give him much choice: steal for Himmler or spend the rest of your life in jail, enforcing the threat with a list of burglaries, supplied by the Kripo, which he had carried out. They had then sent him to Lisbon where there was great scope for his talents.

He moved down the street. It was a brisk, sunny morning and the air smelled of coffee and freshly-baked bread. He lit a cigarette, flipping the match into the gutter. In the Largo do Carmo the owner of the newspaper kiosk was hanging out his wares, *Berliner Morgenpost* to the fore, no doubt, with a good supply of British newspapers bringing up the rear.

Two expensively-suited Germans strode past. Wolfram buyers probably. They looked as though they owned the place; perhaps one day they would.

The door of No. 18 where Hoffman lived opened. Hoffman emerged, scarcely paying any attention to the golden day. When he reached the square a small Fiat that had been parked down the street took off after him; Muller had been told to expect this; then a Renault took off behind the Fiat; he hadn't been told to expect that; still it was none of his business; thieving was his business.

He glanced at his watch. 7.45. Hoffman's landlady went to the market every weekday at 8.30. He relaxed and lit his third cigarette of the morning. Luckily for him she left the house at 8.15.

He gave her three minutes, time enough for her to discover that she had left her shopping list behind. Then he walked briskly to the rear of the terrace which he had cased at dawn. The back door was hidden from the rest of the terrace by a high wall; he walked down a short path and tried the door; it was locked, naturally, but the lock was a rudimentary affair. He selected a key from the bunch in the pocket of his overalls and slipped it into the key-hole. He turned the key gently but firmly and the door opened.

The kitchen was the woman. Scrupulously clean, old and smelling of garlic. The whitewashed hall was cold and dark; like the Spaniards the Portuguese hid from the sun. The stairs creaked as he climbed them; they always did. There were three doors on the landing. One was closed; that would be the landlady's – women always closed their bedroom doors. He peered into the room next to it. It was piled high with suitcases, books and papers. The woman's life was in there.

169

Coughing, he turned and entered Josef Hoffman's room.

*

Hoffman, on his way to the Avenida Palace to learn about codes – from Rachel Keyser of all people – had begun to walk down the steep hill leading from the Largo do Carmo when he realised that he had left his recently-earned 5,000 escudos in his room. In the Bible.

He hesitated. He was late already. So what? Codes could wait, so could she. A woman passed him wearing a familiar perfume. Rachel's perfume. He saw her lying naked on the bed; a knife turned inside him.

He turned and began to retrace his footsteps towards his lodgings.

*

The trouble was that Muller wasn't *exactly* sure what he was looking for. 'Evidence,' Bauer had said. But not evidence of what. 'Forged documents,' he had elaborated. 'Ciphers, anything suggesting foreign connections, anything that would incriminate a man – and you would know about that, Muller. Anything Jewish,' Bauer had added, pulling at his ear.

Muller went straight to the tin chest under Hoffman's bed. It was locked. A good omen. It took him thirty seconds to pick the lock. The contents smelled musty, not a good sign unless you were looking for a family heirloom. Still, there were plenty of those around in Lisbon these days, the refugees' passports to escape. Perhaps Hoffman had brought some diamonds from Prague. Muller brightened: he had been given permission to steal anything within reason to make his thefts seem like run-of-the-mill burglaries.

But first *evidence*.

With meticulous care he began to examine Hoffman's life, his soul.

The documents were at the bottom of the chest in a blue cardboard folder. Most of them were in a foreign language, Czech or Slovak, he presumed. There, too, were his Red Cross papers, passport, and a photograph of a beautiful girl, Jewish by the look of her. Muller laid all these things on the bed and, with a miniature Leica, photographed them.

170

The last paper contained hand-written notes which appeared to refer to some sort of journey. Surely if they were incriminating Hoffman would have destroyed them. But with amateurs you never knew. Frowning, Muller photographed them.

*

Hoffman slid his key into the lock in the front door. The door opened with a faint sigh. He closed it behind him and walked across the hallway towards the staircase.

Foot on the first step, he stopped. Someone had coughed. Was it out in the street? He froze. Another cough. From upstairs, no doubt about it.

Surely no one would bother to rob his landlady. Or him for that matter. Unless the Germans or the Russians had decided to extend surveillance to intrusion.

Stealthily, he climbed the staircase, pausing as a step halfway up creaked. Another cough. From my room!

He took the last stairs in two strides.

The grey-haired man in overalls was just closing the lid of the tin chest. Even by opening it he had desecrated it.

The man looked startled but not scared. His eyes took in Hoffman, but remained focussed on the open door behind him.

'No,' Hoffman said. He kicked the door shut. 'Who are you? What do you want?'

'Nothing here,' the man said calmly in bad English. 'You haven't got anything. It was the cough, I suppose?'

Hoffman walked towards him, fists clenched. They were separated by the bed. 'I don't have much but it's mine. What have you stolen?'

'Not a thing. Search me if you like,' one hand instinctively searching for his cigarettes.

'I'm not that stupid.'

'Have you got a match?'

'I'm not that stupid either.' Hoffman edged round the bed. 'Why have you got a camera?'

'If you really want to know,' the man said, 'it's to cripple cunts like you with,' as he swung the small camera on its strap at Hoffman's head.

The camera hit Hoffman just below the eye. Hoffman heard metal hit bone. Pain leaped through his head. The eye closed at once.

171

But he was on the intruder. They fought quietly and intensely. Hoffman was younger, stronger, but his opponent was a street fighter, lithe, deceptively strong and dirty. Hoffman hit him on the side of the jaw with his fist and the man fell against a wall mirror, splintering it. When he got up he was holding a shard of glass like a dagger in his gloved hand. Hoffman backed away. The intruder waved the glass knife at him. 'Get out of the way, prick ...' Hoffman backed further away, behind the bed; then, swiftly, he bent and tipped the bed towards the man. The dagger fell to the floor, breaking into a hundred smaller daggers. The man was breathing hard; youth over age, Hoffman thought. 'The camera,' Hoffman said, 'give me the camera.' 'Come and get it,' the man said. With one foot he pushed the bed towards Hoffman. Hoffman rounded the bed, closed. 'It's almost over,' he thought – as the man leaped through the open window.

Hoffman rushed forward. He expected to see the man spreadeagled on the pavement. All he saw through his one good eye was a woman lying on the cobbles, water spilling from the cask she had been carrying and, already halfway towards the Largo do Carmo, the fleeing figure of the intruder.

*

Bauer gazed thoughtfully at the photographs of Hoffman's documents. In particular at the handwritten notes. A few place names together with times.

So Hoffman was going places. But where? The trouble with the notes was that they were written in different languages. Portuguese, English, and Czech or Slovak. Madrid, Geneva ... it looked like Red Cross business. Disappointing. He frowned at the last place name; it was almost illegible.

He picked up a phone and summoned one of the translators on the Legation's 800-strong staff.

The translator looked at the word. '*Moskva*,' he said crisply. And when Bauer looked puzzled: 'Moscow.'

'Is it written in Czech or Slovak?'

'It's written in Russian,' the translator said.

*

Cross reacted vigorously to the news that Hoffman had been burgled. 'We'll have to move even quicker than we thought,' he said, standing at the window of his living room. 'If the

Germans know you're going to Russia they'll want to know why. And they won't be choosy how they find out.'

'But I'm working for the *Abwehr*.'

'But not for the Gestapo,' Cross said briskly. He sat down in the chair where he had sat the first night Hoffman had met him and opened his briefcase. 'Here are some more documents for you. They should get you to Moscow, after all you do work for the International Red Cross.'

'When am I going?' Hoffman asked.

'Tonight,' Cross said.

*

In his office on Prinz Albrechtstrasse in Berlin, Heinrich Himmler, head of the Waffen SS and all Nazi security organisations except the *Abwehr*, considered Bauer's cabled report.

He had issued orders that anything that could be construed as *Abwehr* disloyalty to the Führer should be referred immediately to him. Bauer's decoded cable, sent from Lisbon the previous night, had been on his desk at 8.30 that morning.

A Slav coupling with a Jewess; that was disgusting enough. What sort of child would two such sub-humans produce? pondered the Reichsführer who was small and unprepossessing and wore steel-rimmed spectacles to correct his shortsightedness.

Disgusting, yes, but there were times when he had to control his loathing of such vermin in the interests of logical calculation. Such a time was now.

Bauer's report was only a strand in the evidence Himmler was accumulating against Canaris and his *Abwehr*, the so-called intelligence service of the generals, many of whom were disloyal to the Führer. But slowly and with infinite patience he was weaving a web with each strand.

So what do we have here?

A Czech working for the Red Cross in contact with a Jewess employed at the British Embassy in Lisbon. A Czech who then offered his services to the *Abwehr*. So, indirectly, the *Abwehr* were using a Jewess. What more could you expect from a hunchback like von Claus?

But what was far more interesting was the journey on which Hoffman was embarking immediately after making contact with von Claus. Moscow. Why would a Czech Red Cross worker in touch with both British and German intelligence suddenly decide to travel to Russia? Not on Red Cross business, according to Bauer who had checked.

Why?

Himmler took off his spectacles, rubbed the bridge of his nose where the frame had left a red mark and stared myopically at an oil painting of Hitler hanging on the wall.

It was almost as if this Hoffman had made his play with the *Abwehr* to prove something. To prove that he had access to German secrets. To prove it to the Russians ...

Himmler snapped his fingers.

Supposing Hoffman *did* have such access. Supposing von Claus was a traitor. Supposing he had told Hoffman about the Führer's plans to invade the Soviet Union.

Himmler replaced his spectacles, picked up a telephone and told the operator to put him through to Communications. The cable he dictated to be encoded and sent to Bauer top priority, top secret, was brief: STOP HOFFMAN AND INTERROGATE.

*

What would I do, Bauer deliberated, if I were organising Hoffman's journey to Moscow?

Firstly, knowing that the notes for the trip had been copied, I would change the times. In particular the departure flight. I would dispatch him sooner, Bauer thought. Much sooner. In fact I would put him on an aircraft tonight.

Bauer consulted a timetable. There was a Tráñco Aéro Español flight to Madrid at 2135 hours.

That's the flight I'd put him on, Bauer decided.

He picked up the telephone and told his deputy to change the mode of surveillance on Hoffman. The battered old Mercedes-Benz with the souped-up engine instead of the small Fiat because by now Hoffman had probably identified his shadow.

If Hoffman didn't try to catch the flight at 2135 hours no harm was done. If he did then they would take him on the stretch of road bordered by thick woods five miles from Sintra airport.

*

'Why you?'

Hoffman stared in astonishment at Rachel Keyser sitting at the wheel of a grey Morris 8.

'Only Cross and I are involved. He seemed to think I was the better driver.'

Hoffman glanced up and down the darkened street outside his lodgings. There was no sign of the black Citroën, a taxi was parked down the street and beyond it a battered Mercedes-Benz.

Hoffman threw his bag into the back seat of the Morris and climbed in beside Rachel.

She drove out of the maze of small streets and accelerated up the broad, well-lit reaches of the Avenida da Liberdade.

She said: 'We'll have to work on the codes when you get back.'

'Very business-like,' he said.

'One other thing. You'll have to produce a convincing story when Stalin asks you how you found out you were his son. And why you suddenly decided to return.'

'I've thought about it,' Hoffman told her as the Morris rounded the Parque Eduardo VII. 'It isn't difficult. I'll tell him I always suspected he was my father. That I overheard a conversation between my parents and that seemed to tie up with the privileges we enjoyed … But I was too scared to do anything about it. After all, if Stalin didn't want it out in the open who was I to interfere?'

'But what will you say clinched it?' Rachel asked.

'Nothing clinched it. When I reach the Kremlin I still won't be sure …'

'Then why will you say you've returned? And, come to that, why did you leave in the first place?'

'That's the easiest part,' Hoffman said, 'if you understand the Soviet mentality. I left because I was disgusted by the atrocities being committed. I returned because I heard rumours that the Germans were planning to invade. Country over conscience, very Russian. And I felt I had to warn him whether he was my father or not.'

Rachel swung the wheel; the Morris passed the flaring oil lamps of a shanty settlement and bored into the darkness of the countryside. In the driving mirror she saw the flash of headlights behind her; she drove faster.

'We had something more elaborate cooked up for you,' she said.

'Leave it to me,' Hoffman said brusquely. 'I know what I'm doing. After all, he is my father.'

'You think I don't understand how you feel, don't you?'

Hoffman didn't reply. Their whole relationship had been a lie from the start; he wondered if it still was. He wanted to reach out and touch her, to feel her warmth. But to hell with it. Not now or ever. Even a peasant – the grandson of a Georgian cobbler! – had his pride.

The headlights swooped past. Tail-lights glowed for a moment or so before disappearing round a bend in the road.

The night was starless, the forest on either side of the road part of the night.

The light flashing in the middle of the road came as a shock.

Rachel braked sharply; the Morris stopped to one side of the road within a few feet of the light.

Rachel wound down the window and said to the man holding the flashlight: 'What's wrong?' and when she saw the pistol tried to drive away but by that time he had yanked the driving keys out of the ignition. 'Get out,' he said in German-accented English, levelling the gun at her head. And to Hoffman: 'You too, but don't try anything otherwise she gets it.' He switched off the headlights.

Rachel climbed out of the car.

'Hands behind your head. That's right. Be good and you won't get hurt. And you,' waving the pistol at Hoffman. 'And forget any two-against-one stuff because there are two guns trained on you over there.' In the darkness Hoffman could just see the outline of the battered Mercedes-Benz.

The flashlight, he decided, was his target. One kick and they'd all be in darkness. The old Hoffman would have reasoned: 'But Rachel might get hurt.' The new one thought: 'Rachel might get hurt but that's a risk I've got to take.'

He took one step towards the man holding the light.

The man said: 'Now both of you get in the back of the Mercedes.'

Hoffman was about to kick when the first shot rang out. He thought for a split second that he *had* kicked because the flashlight exploded in the man's hand. Then there was only darkness.

'Get down,' he shouted to Rachel.

They waited for another shot. Nothing.

176

The Germans were shouting at each other.

A body hit Hoffman, hands searching for his throat, Hoffman brought up his knee sharply. Felt it sink into the man's crotch. The man screamed out in agony.

Hoffman kneed him again. The man vomited.

In the Mercedes another light flared, weaker than the flashlight but dangerous enough. Its beam sliced through the darkness and found Rachel's face. Hoffman flung himself between the ray of light and Rachel.

Another shot.

The light disappeared as though it had been switched off and the bullet ricocheted off the bodywork.

Hoffman rolled towards the grass verge taking Rachel with him.

'What's going —' she began. But another shot cut her short; the bullet hit one of the Mercedes' rear wheels; the tyre sighed and the silhouette of the car sank to one side.

Hoffman thought: 'It must be the *Abwehr* - or the NKVD perhaps.' He whispered: 'Let's get into the forest.'

But suddenly they were illuminated as though by a spotlight. Hoffman, Rachel and the three Germans. For a moment they were frozen like insects under a stone suddenly exposed to daylight.

Hoffman looked behind him: someone had switched on the Morris's headlights.

Crouching, he ran for the trees - as the gun fired again.

The man who had attacked Hoffman reared up and fell back, blood pumping from his chest, bright red in the glare of the headlights.

Another shot hit one of the occupants of the Mercedes; the door swung open and he fell on to the ground.

But the third occupant had got behind the car and was firing back. His first bullet doused one of the Morris's headlamps.

They heard running footsteps. A shuffling behind the Mercedes. Another shot. The sound of blows. A snap as though a bone had broken. A final scream.

'Come on,' Cross said, breathing heavily, 'get in the MG, we haven't much time.'

*

Ahead they could see the lights of the airport.

177

The night rushed at Hoffman and Rachel squeezed into the passenger seat of the MG beside Cross. Cross had to shout to make himself heard.

'Bauer's smart. I knew he'd try and stop you leaving; I also thought he would guess you'd make a dash for it tonight. So I followed you.'

'What about the bodies?' Rachel pointed behind her.

'Armed robbery ... the Germans won't make a fuss. Three armed Gestapo thugs in nice neutral Portugal? It's the last sort of publicity they want. As for the Morris – it hit the Mercedes and you, Rachel, hitched a lift to the airport.'

Rachel was conscious of Hoffman's body pressed against her. She remembered how he had flung himself between her and the beam of the torch. She wanted to kiss him fiercely.

The MG slowed down and Cross said: 'Here we are, the runway to freedom. Don't ask questions, just follow me.'

The small departure and arrival lounge bore the legends Aero Portuguese, Tráñco Aéro Español, Deutsche Lufthansa, British Airways and Ala Littoria. Outside in the floodlights they could see a German three-engined Junkers 52 and a British de Haviland Flamingo standing beside it.

Refugees swarming around them bargaining, cajoling, threatening for seats on the British Airways aircraft and planes from any other friendly countries that might have landed. The British, Germans and Italians flew mostly by night to avoid confrontations in the air; they all wanted to use Lisbon and none of them wanted to spoil the unwritten agreement that they didn't molest one another.

Cross said to Hoffman: 'Get out your Red Cross papers.'

'The Red Cross don't even know I'm leaving,' Hoffman said.

'They do – Bauer told them. But that doesn't matter. Just show your papers.'

A plump refugee with two diamond rings on his fingers saw the papers and thrust a wad of escudos at Hoffman. Hoffman pushed him aside.

Cross with his diplomatic passport led the way through emigration; Rachel followed with hers; Hoffman brought up the rear with his Czech passport and documents from Geneva.

'This way,' Cross said pushing through the throng of passengers waiting in a bare-walled room on the other side of the desks. Outside, a group of passengers was striding across the tarmac towards a Berlin-bound Junkers.

Cross led Rachel and Hoffman to a door at the side of the room; he took a key from his pocket and opened it. 'The Gestapo will presume you're on the Tráñco Aéro Español flight,' he said, handing the key and a wad of escudo bills to an airport policeman on the other side of the door. 'Let's surprise the bastards.'

From behind the squat airport buildings they heard shouting and the squeal of tyres. 'Cops,' Cross said. 'Looking for armed gangsters. We'd better get the hell out of here.'

He began to run towards a DC-3 standing in the penumbra of the floodlights. It bore the colours of a Portuguese charter company. As they approached one engine fired, then the other. The slipstream hit them, pressing their clothes against their bodies.

'It's all fixed with control,' Cross shouted. 'There shouldn't be any hitch: I paid them enough. And we'll be okay with our diplomatic passports.'

At the foot of the boarding steps Hoffman hesitated.

Rachel stared at him. A wave, a smile, a hint of understanding ... Anything, please.

Cross said: 'For Christ's sake move, here come the police.'

Hoffman turned and ran up the stairs.

The door closed behind him, Cross pulled the steps away and almost immediately the DC-3 began to taxi forward.

Rachel thought she saw his face at one of the windows but she couldn't be sure.

The aircraft reached the end of the runway, accelerated and climbed into the night.

Rachel waved. 'Good luck,' she called out.

Cross looked at her quizzically. 'You make it sound as if you're both aiming for the same goal,' he said. 'You haven't forgotten that we're betraying him, have you? That when he's finally poised to warn Stalin that Hitler's going to attack we're going to make damn sure the opposite message is sent in his name?'

'No,' she said through her tears, 'I hadn't forgotten.'

Part Four

Chapter Thirteen

In the dining room of his dingy home in the Kremlin Joseph Stalin watched, absorbed, while a man named Zalutsky tasted his food and wine.

One of these days, Stalin thought, the plump, blotchy-faced Ukrainian would fall down dead on the floor. An appropriate fate for a suspected Trotskyist who was only alive today because the idea of forcing a traitor to intercept poison was appealing.

What thoughts went through his mind now as with trembling hand he raised a glass of red Georgian wine to his lips? His mentor, Trotsky, was dead, but perhaps some other traitor had doctored the food.

Stalin watched the glass all the way to Zalutsky's mouth. A sip, no more. Did he intend to keep it in his mouth and, with his back turned, spit it back into the glass? 'Drain it,' Stalin commanded.

While Zalutsky finished off the wine and turned his attention to the roast suckling pig, Stalin began to doodle on a coarse-grained sheet of notepaper. He drew a sharp-fanged wolf; the animal joined a pack of wolves he had already consigned to the notepaper.

If Zalutsky did one day fall to the floor clawing at his throat who would he hold responsible? Regrettably there were many contenders for the role and, as before, he would have to liquidate them all because it was the only way to stamp out intrigue.

Ever since he could remember he had been surrounded by treachery. Father beating son unmercifully – and those beatings by his father, a drunken Georgian shoemaker in Gori, had been unmerciful – that was surely a form of treachery.

The pencil broke on the fangs of another wolf and he said to Zalutsky: 'Try a little more of that pig." In a perverse way it would give him some sort of grim satisfaction if the Ukrainian did collapse.

And at the seminary in Tiflis where, thanks to the selflessness of his mother, after his father's death, he had studied to be a priest, he had been betrayed by the monks and expelled for failing to attend examinations. By which they meant preaching revolution instead, which in those days was as much Georgian patriotism as Marxism. More treachery.

He had been nineteen then – sixty-one now – and throughout his subsequent career the daggers had been raised behind his back. By Tsarist *agents provocateurs* in prison camps, by Mensheviks in the Revolution, by White Russian agents in the Civil War, by Trotsky and other careerists after Lenin's death in 1924. But inexorably he had blunted the knives of all the conspirators.

'The revolution is incapable either of regretting or burying its dead' – Joseph Stalin, 1917. And just as true today.

'Now the potatoes,' he said to Zalutsky, darkening the wolf's face with the broken lead of the pencil.

Who had he trusted during his life? The heads didn't take long to count. His mother who had wanted him to be a village priest – but had been proud of him when he became what he was; his first wife, Ekaterina, he supposed, who had died in 1907; certainly not his second wife, Nadezhda, the dark-eyed quicksilver revolutionary who had turned on him before her death in 1932; a handful of stalwarts such as Molotov ...

As for his legitimate children – Jacob was an introverted wash-out and Vassily, although a pilot, was a drunken braggart. Svetlana, his red-haired, teenage daughter, was his darling, but she was a girl, which left ...

Viktor. Only that morning he had received news about the son of the girl he had loved more than twenty years ago. (She hadn't betrayed him: she had died in childbirth.)

He went to the window and stared at the Kremlin. Despite its bloody history, from primitive fort to palace to shrine of Communism, it was a glorious place. Particularly on such a day as this with its gold cupolas riding high in the bright sky, the first snow of the winter scattered on its lawns.

But in a way its glories made him uneasy. They weren't intended for a cobbler's son, nor for a Bolshevik, which was why he had kept his home as unprepossessing as possible.

He thought Viktor would have liked such a home. And the view of the Kremlin's baubles, of course.

He remembered the vow he had made the boy's mother.

He turned round. Zalutsky had poured him a glass of wine. He picked it up and threw the contents in the Ukrainian's face. 'Now get out,' he shouted.

Perhaps Zalutsky was poisoning the food after he had tasted it. Stalin swept the food off the table. Perhaps after all Zalutsky would have to be executed.

*

That vow.

Who would have believed that he, who, of necessity, used promises and pacts as utensils, would have honoured it?

Restlessly Stalin, small of stature, with yellowish eyes and pock-marked skin (he had contracted smallpox when he was seven), bushy moustache giving him a deceptively benign appearance, strode up and down his study.

But honour it he had.

'Don't let him be tainted,' she had said. 'Keep him apart from it all. Do you promise, Joseph?'

'I promise,' he had replied and she had smiled and died, nineteen years of age, in a bed in Leningrad.

Not that his motives for keeping his word had been purely selfless. He wanted one son who would grow up straight and tall, unable to betray him. One boy whom he could trust from afar.

Even when Viktor had fled to Switzerland and then to Portugal he hadn't been too alarmed. Like his mother, whom he resembled in so many ways, he was headstrong. At University he must have been exposed to subversive elements. He had wanted to get away and make up his own mind about values.

One day he would return.

Stalin picked up the message delivered by hand from the NKVD headquarters where Laventi Beria ruled.

Madrid. What was Viktor doing in the Spanish capital? Was it possible that he was coming home? Or just making a routine Red Cross trip to Geneva.

To calm himself, Stalin stuffed a pipe with his favourite tobacco from Jusuri, and lit it. Trailing a cloud of blue smoke, he sat at his desk in the book-lined room. On the desk were photographs of Svetlana and his own mother, Keke, the only woman he had ever revered apart from Viktor's mother.

Then he turned his attention to another promise, one of the more common variety, one that neither signatory had the slightest intention of keeping.

The problem was: Just when did Hitler intend to break the Treaty of Friendship signed in September last year?

Not for a long time, in Stalin's opinion. Hitler was quite mad but not mad enough to expose his armies on two fronts, not mad enough to repeat Napoleon's mistake.

To assess the intentions of the world's leaders, Stalin invariably applied his own standards. For instance he understood perfectly well why Britain and France had allowed Germany, a beaten force in 1918, to re-arm: they wanted the armaments to be turned against the Soviet Union.

Which was why he was sceptical about warnings that Germany was considering attacking the Soviet Union. The warnings all came from interested parties – in particular Britain through their new ambassador in Moscow, Sir Stafford Cripps – who wanted to turn him against Hitler, to make them go to war.

Well, Winston Churchill wouldn't succeed with that ploy: his cunning was altogether too obvious.

And yet Hitler had menacingly moved his troops into Roumania and Finland, thereby breaking promises ...

And Richard Sorge, Russia's spymaster in Tokyo, had warned that Hitler was planning an invasion ...

But lately Sorge's information had been suspect.

If only, Stalin brooded, he could find one source of information in which he believed.

*

Churchill said: 'According to Cripps, Uncle Joe has bought it. So far, that is.'

'Bought it?' Sinclair, pouring drinks in the drawing room of his house in Berkshire, looked at Churchill questioningly.

'He doesn't believe any of our warnings because he thinks we're merely trying to embroil him in a war with Hitler. Which, of course, we are – but not in the way he thinks. We don't want any brief border battle: we want the Nazis storming into a country unbelieving and unprepared. We want them attacking that much too late so that they are swallowed up in the vastness of the Russian steppe: we want the jaws of the Red Army dislocated in the process.'

Churchill took the whisky and soda from Sinclair and swallowed half of it. 'What's happening with Hoffman?' he asked.

'He's on his way,' Sinclair said.

Chapter Fourteen

With Red Cross credentials it was relatively easy to travel across Europe.

From Madrid Hoffman took an Ala Littoria flight to Rome that refuelled in Sardinia. From Rome he flew north-east to Vienna; from there a train through Czechoslovakia into Poland. The plan was to disembark in the German-occupied sector near Warsaw and cross the River Bug into the Russian-occupied sector where, equipped with forged documents identifying him as an NKVD officer, he would have no difficulty in reaching Moscow.

Hoffman would probably have reached his destination with ease if a diligent Gestapo officer, acting on instructions from Berlin, had not spotted Hoffman changing trains on the Czech-Polish border.

The train was halted in a suburb of Warsaw which was still lying in ruins after the German *blitzkreig* the previous year. The passengers in Hoffman's compartment – a teenage German soldier, an old woman in black carrying a stinking cheese, a pretty girl in her twenties who had been crying a lot recently, and a sweating, middle-aged man – glanced nervously at each other.

The sliding doors were pulled open. In the corridor stood two men in civilian clothes; one looked plump and jolly, the other, wearing a black leather coat, had dissipated features and pouched eyes.

The man in the leather coat went directly to Hoffman. 'Your papers, please,' he said in German.

'I represent the International Red Cross—'

'Papers,' holding out his hand.

Hoffman unzipped his canvas bag. His Red Cross documents and passport lay on the top of his clothes and toilet bag; forged Russian papers were sewn into the lining of his overcoat. 'Hardly subtle,' Cross had said, 'but where else?'

The man in the leather coat scanned them with minimal interest, thrust them into his coat pocket and said: 'You will come with us.'

'But—'

The man leaned forward and grasped Hoffman's arm. 'Come.'

The other passengers looked away. Hoffman sensed their relief that it was him not them; he couldn't blame them.

Shrugging, he picked up his bag and followed the two men along the corridor and on to the platform of a small, bombed-out railway station. 'I want to know who you are and what authority you have to detain me,' Hoffman said, as the train moved away.

The second man laughed hugely. 'Authority? God in heaven, Kurt, they'll be asking to see our birth certificates next.' It was then, to his surprise, that Hoffman realised that the plump, jolly man, not the archetypal Gestapo sadist, was in charge; he looked more like a dairy farmer than a secret policeman, Hoffman thought. 'Now come along with us, there's a good chap, and stop asking questions, because that's our job,' the jolly man said.

A grey Packard stood incongruously outside what was left of the station. It looked like a gangsters' car. 'It belonged to a Jewish businessman,' the jolly man explained. 'My name, by the way, is Lieber and this is Adler and that's really all you need to know about us.' He smiled conspiratorially.

Adler got behind the wheel; Lieber sat beside Hoffman in the back. Adler drove away from Warsaw into the countryside which was powdered with snow; Hoffman considered trying to escape but it was hopeless – he would be gunned down as he fell on to the road; he would just have to bluff it out or escape later.

They took him to a village hall. The village itself seemed deserted except for a couple of dogs and an old man in a black cloth cap standing beside a burned-out cottage.

The hall smelled of antiseptic and, faintly, excreta. There was a platform at one end facing rows of wooden chairs;

posters depicting German soldiers being welcomed by grateful Poles hung from the walls. Grateful for what? Hoffman wondered.

Two trestle tables flanked by electrical units of some kind stood between the platform and the chairs. Leather thongs hung from the tables and there were stains on the floor that might have been blood.

Lieber led the way backstage; in the wings stood a few rudimentary stage props. What looked as if it might have been a Canadian Mountie's uniform lay in a dusty heap, above it a cardboard cut-out of a snow-capped mountain.

'*Rose Marie*, if I'm not mistaken,' Lieber remarked. ' "Dead or alive, then we're out to get you dead or alive", or something like that.' He began to hum softly to himself. He pulled a rope and the moth-eaten red curtains closed, isolating them from the rest of the hall. 'That's better,' he said. 'Now we can get down to business. What are you doing in Poland, Herr Hoffman?'

'I'm on Red Cross business as you'll shortly find out.'

'Not according to the Red Cross,' Lieber said pleasantly. 'Try again. We called Geneva. They called Portugal. You should have been at work in Lisbon today, Herr Hoffman.'

From the other side of the curtain Hoffman heard the tramping of feet, a rubbery sound as though the people entering the hall were bare-footed.

He said: 'It was a secret mission. Negotiating the transfer of Poles caught in the Russian sector.'

'It's a funny thing,' Lieber said pleasantly, 'but in the propaganda films made by Germany's enemies the senior Gestapo officer is always depicted ordering his subordinate to soften up a prisoner. Not here,' hitting Hoffman on the side of the face with the back of his hand so that he fell against the cardboard mountain. 'Not by any manner of means,' kicking Hoffman just below the ribs, making him retch. 'Not that Adler wouldn't like to flex his muscles, of course, and so he will, shortly, if you don't co-operate. Adler is much more refined than me; a specialist, you might say. What are you doing in Poland, Herr Hoffman?'

'I told you. Check it with Geneva again.'

'What made you join the Red Cross, Hoffman?'

'To help Mankind.'

'It's you that needs help now. Are you a pacifist?'

Hoffman stood up. 'When I meet people like you, yes.'

189

'Heroics,' Lieber said, 'bring out the worst in Adler.' He chuckled and consulted a notebook. 'Five days ago you met an *Abwehr* agent named von Claus in Lisbon and gave him certain information.'

From the other side of the curtain Hoffman heard a volley of commands. 'What's happening out there?' he asked.

'You later made contact with the British agent Rachel Keyser whom you already knew.'

More commands in Polish.

'Then your room was burgled.'

The sound of leather hitting flesh.

'Almost immediately you were driven to Sintra airport.'

The blows stopped. They were followed by screams, two sets of them.

Hoffman moved towards the curtains but Adler kicked his feet from under him. Adler lit a cigarette.

Hoffman said: 'The Red Cross will hear about this.'

'On the way to the airport three of my colleagues were shot. Murdered,' he added.

More screams.

'You were in a great big hurry to leave Portugal, were you not, Herr Hoffman?'

Silence. Adler peeped through the curtains like an actor checking the mood of an audience.

'You took off on a chartered DC-3 instead of the scheduled flight mentioned in your notes. In fact your whole itinerary was changed ...'

The screams began again.

Hoffman, still on the floor, tensed himself to leap at Lieber but Lieber said: 'I wouldn't if I were you – Adler's got a gun pointed at the back of your head.'

Hoffman turned: he had.

'And Poland wasn't your final destination, was it, Herr Hoffman?'

The screams stopped again; the silence that ensued was more chilling because it was a dead silence.

'You were going to Russia. Where are your Russian documents?'

'I haven't got any Russian documents.'

'The documents authorising you to negotiate the return of Poles to the German sector then.'

'There aren't any. Geneva cabled the Russians in their sector.'

Lieber said: 'Search him, Adler. Linings first.'

Adler found the NKVD papers within a minute.

Lieber was enormously amused. 'Secret policeman meets secret policeman, eh? Now surely, Herr Hoffman, the game is up, as they say. Why were you going to the Soviet Union?'

'You'll have to ask the *Abwehr*,' Hoffman said.

Lieber said: 'I'm asking you.' He pulled the rope and the curtains parted a little. 'Odd, isn't it, standing on the stage and watching the show in the stalls.'

At the far end of the hall a group of naked men were being held at gunpoint by two SS Rottenführers armed with machine pistols.

Two other prisoners were strapped, naked, on the trestle tables. Beside each stood a man in plain clothes holding twin, rubber-handled electrodes. The men looked questioningly at Lieber who nodded.

The electrodes were placed on the prisoners' genitals.

'A bit like electrocardiograms, aren't they,' Lieber remarked.

The operator nearest the platform flicked a switch. The naked body on the table bucked against the leather straps. His scream filled the hall.

Lieber nodded to the second operator. This time the prisoner bucked so violently that a strap broke and his back arched unnaturally. The operator cut the current and examined the broken strap with astonishment.

'Like you, they refused to answer questions,' Lieber said. 'But as you saw, those operators are amateurs. Unlike Adler here. He likes a good work-out before resorting to electric shocks. Why were you going to Russia, Herr Hoffman?'

'I told you.'

Lieber said: 'One last show before Adler gets to work. Come backstage again, Herr Hoffman.' Adler prodded the pistol into Hoffman's back.

Lieber pointed through a window. 'They refused to answer questions too but as we didn't think they knew anything important we didn't bother with refinements.'

Hoffman saw a dozen men lined up against a brick wall. They had their hands behind their heads. The German firing squad stood twenty feet in front of them.

Hoffman watched from the box in the ruined theatre – *And now surely they would be granted their last wishes. That always happened. In the books, in the films …*

He heard the shots outside the village hall. His skull filled with ice. He closed his eyes. Blood-red shadows swam before him. He heard Lieber shouting, the jolliness quite gone from his voice. 'What's happening ...'

He opened his eyes. The scene through the window sharpened into focus and there were the bodies, lying on the ground, but they were the bodies of the firing squad. And all was confusion. Shots, shouts, running figures ...

The ice in Hoffman's skull melted. Adler was staring through the window. Hoffman chopped at his forearm with his fist; the pistol clattered on to the floorboards. He snatched it up as Lieber went for his own gun. Hoffman shot him in the chest and thought: 'I didn't even warn him,' and turned the gun on Adler.

'Turn round,' he snapped. As Adler turned he hit him on the side of the head with the butt of the pistol. He heard bone crack. Adler slumped to the floor beside Leiber.

A wild exhilaration upon him, Hoffman ran to the curtains. Peering through an opening, he saw the two guards, SS emblems on their steel helmets, waving their machine pistols at the group of naked men. The guards looked confused, dangerous.

One of the prisoners on the tables was turning his head from side to side. The one who had broken the strap was lying still.

From the group came a shout in Polish: 'They've come to free us. Let's get these bastards.'

In slow motion Hoffman saw the guards tense themselves to shoot; saw the knuckles on their hands gleam white.

He took the sentry to the right first, resting Adler's pistol on his right forearm. Despite the wildness inside him he was quite methodical. He lined up the sights on the guard's cheek and squeezed the trigger.

No neat hole. The guard's face seemed to fall apart.

The second guard spun round firing at the curtain, filling the hall with noise. The bullets cut a line of holes above Hoffman's head as he hurled himself to one side, falling beside the Mountie's red uniform.

The bullets took out a spotlight and shattered the window above the bodies of Adler and Lieber.

The shooting stopped suddenly. The noise that followed was sickening. Hoffman peered through the curtains. The second guard had been overcome while he was shooting at the stage.

He was lying on the floor and the naked men were kicking him to death.

Hoffman jumped down off the stage and released the prisoner on the first table. The man nodded and began to weep. The prisoner on the second table was dead.

Hoffman ran to the end of the hall. Most of the guard's clothes had been ripped off and naked feet were thudding into face, belly, crotch; but his eyes between slits in swollen flesh were still alive.

'Stop it!' Hoffman shouted. 'Don't be like them.'

One of the avengers looked up. 'Was it you who shot the other bastard?'

Hoffman looked down at the gun in his hand. He nodded.

'Nice shooting. I don't know who the hell you are but why don't you come and help finish this shit off? But not with that,' pointing at the pistol. 'Shooting's too good for shits like this.'

'You mustn't—'

The door burst open and half a dozen men brandishing hand-guns burst in. They wore winter clothes and boots; they were unshaven and their faces, although polished by the cold, had a starved look about them.

One of them fired a bullet through the roof. 'Get your clothes,' he shouted to the naked men. 'We haven't got much time – German reinforcements are on their way. Get dressed and follow us. And who might you be?' he asked Hoffman as the Poles left the guard's twitching body.

Hoffman told him he was from the Red Cross.

'With a gun?'

'He saved us,' said a man with a beard, emerging from an ante-room carrying a bundle of clothes.

While the naked men dressed, the Pole who had fired the shot through the roof went to the door and peered up and down the street. He was powerfully built and completely bald; Hoffman gathered that his name was Kepa.

Hoffman joined him and said: 'What happens now?'

Kepa lit a cigarette. 'What always happens. We split and go underground. We don't win any wars but we kill Germans and that makes everything worthwhile. But you wouldn't understand that, Mr. Red Cross.'

Hoffman told him his name. 'I just killed two men,' he said.

'Only two? You don't graduate here until you've killed twenty – provided they're Germans.'

'Can I come with you?'

'You're Czech, aren't you?'

Hoffman nodded.

'They didn't even make a fight of it. A Czech Red Cross worker. What a find! What are you doing in my country, bringing much-needed supplies to the Krauts?'

Hoffman said angrily: 'You forget what happened here. I killed two men, don't you understand? Two Germans. I've never killed before ...'

'All right,' Kepa said, 'you're a temporary paid-up member. Stay with me and leave your ideals behind, we can do without them.'

The blue had gone from the sky and it was beginning to snow. With a roar a Stuka dived out of grey cloud and swooped across the silent village.

The suvivors were dressed now. Hoffman collected his bag and his forged documents lying on the floor beside the body of Lieber; Adler was sitting up, hand to his shattered cheek, but his eyes did not focus on Hoffman. Kepa would have killed him. But I am not Kepa.

The partisans began to move away, fanning out, keeping close to the cottages. The clock on the church had stopped at 2.50.

'That's when the Krauts came,' Kepa said. 'That's when they killed my wife and little boy.'

They had reached the end of the main street when the machine-gun opened up.

The burst was long and effective. Behind Hoffman and Kepa partisans and survivors from the hall leaped and fell as the bullets cut through them.

Hoffman and Kepa took cover behind the wall of a kitchen yard. A black cat, back arched, spat at them; behind them the curtains of the kitchen moved as though someone was peering through them.

The shooting stopped, then started up again, bullets hammering against the wall.

Kepa, massaging his shining scalp, said: 'There's only one way – get behind them. Have you ever used a grenade, Mr. Red Cross?'

'I'd never used a gun before.'

'But you used it well. Survival is a great leveller. Would you have guessed that I was a schoolmaster?' He handed Hoffman a grenade; Hoffman felt its cubed surface. 'It's an old one,' Kepa said. 'A British Mills bomb, part of the Polish Army's defences! It might explode and it might not. We've only got two and I've got the other. We'll take them from different sides.'

Kepa showed him how to take the pin out of the grenade. 'Count to three and throw it, like this,' making a lobbing movement from behind his back. 'Make it four if you feel like it but not less than two; that way they throw them back at you. If they turn the gun on you prepare to meet your maker - if he wants to see you any more - because that's an MG 42 they've got over there and it can fire anything up to 1,200 rounds a minute.'

As he spoke the gun opened up again. A window in the cottage behind them shattered. Close by a man screamed. The cat sat down and watched them warily.

Snow was falling faster. 'Our cover,' Kepa said. 'You go that way,' pointing to an orchard of bare-branched fruit trees ahead. 'I'll go this way,' ducking round the end of the wall.

The firing stopped again. Through a gap in the stone wall Hoffman saw Kepa make a crouching run across the street. He heard shouts in German. The gun coughed into life; plumes of dust followed Kepa as he leaped over a leaning wooden fence and disappeared.

The gunner stopped firing and Hoffman took off into the orchard, dodging between the squat trees, veiled by the falling snow, holding the grenade tightly in one hand, hoping that Kepa would reach the machine-gun position first.

From the village he heard sporadic shooting as the partisans fired small arms at the machine-gunners. Pea-shooters, Hoffman thought, against an instrument of mass execution.

He stopped at the end of the orchard and peered through the snow towards the village. The street on the other side of the wall had become a rutted track, frozen and grey, climbing towards a small hill. At the point where it linked up with the cobbled road through the village Hoffman could just make out the machine-gun. It was manned by three soldiers wearing camouflaged battle-dress and steel helmets. The gunner was lying down, peering through the sights; one of the other soldiers was looking through a pair of field-glasses; the third was opening an ammunition box.

Hoffman had run farther than he thought, the wall round the

orchard hiding him from the gunners. Now he had to retrace his footsteps, creep up behind the wall and ... Where are you, Kepa, where are you?

Crouching, he reached the wall but it was in a bad state of repair with ragged gaps every ten feet or so. He moved slowly, carefully, still hoping that Kepa would get there first; Josef Golovin, peacemaker, with a lethal egg in his hand that could blow three men into small pieces. But wasn't that self-deception, taking your time so that another man could kill them? Wasn't it better to kill these three men quickly before they murdered more partisans cowering in the main street? But perhaps the three German soldiers had lived in a village such as this, perhaps they had letters from their parents, their lovers, in their pockets ...

A breeze sprang up and blew the falling snow into his face. He wiped it from his eyes and tripped over a flint that had fallen from the old wall. As he fell the grenade slipped from his grasp and dropped through a gap in the wall on to the track.

He heard one of the soldiers call out. He waited for the sound of running feet. For a shot. Nothing. He raised his head. The grenade was lying in the middle of the lane beside a packet of frozen mud.

Where are you, Kepa?

Hoffman crawled through the gap in the wall. The soldiers were quite near now. And they were shooting again so perhaps they wouldn't notice him retrieving the grenade. He picked it up and crawled back behind the wall.

But one of the soldiers had noticed something. Through another gap Hoffman saw them looking in his direction. The shooting stopped. One of them was pointing.

He saw Kepa about fifty yards on the other side of the machine-gun. He was kneeling behind a stone well. If I can see him so can the soldiers, Hoffman thought, as the gunner shouted and swung the barrel of the gun round.

Hoffman saw Kepa take the pin from the grenade and hold it behind him, heard his voice when they had been together. 'Make it four if you feel like it but not less than two ...'

The gun fired, belt of cartridges rising from the ammunition box like a rearing snake, as Kepa threw the grenade; but a bullet must have hit him at the last moment because the grenade fell half way between him and the soldiers.

Kepa fell to one side; the gunners pressed themselves to the ground.

The snow-muffled silence thickened.

Cautiously, the soldiers raised their heads. 'It might explode and it might not,' he had said. It hadn't. What about mine? Hoffman wondered as the soldiers began to laugh.

Kepa was lying on the ground beside the well.

Leisurely the gunner took aim. Hoffman drew the pin from his grenade, realising that the distance was a little too far, although at university he had thrown the discus reasonably well, his only sporting achievement, and stretched his arm behind him and counted, 'One, two, three and, yes, four,' and threw the grenade and watched it fly high into the falling snow and disappear from view and waited. And waited.

The explosion was sharper than he had imagined it would be. Debris rained around him. Stones, parts of the gun and parts of the soldiers. What was left of their bodies lay in heaps.

The explosion spent itself.

Hoffman walked slowly towards the devastation.

I did it, he thought. I did it. There was revulsion now but there hadn't been as he threw the grenade. Not at all. Only the same wildness that he had experienced as he shot Lieber, clubbed Adler. Survival, that was it. But was that all it was? He picked up a steel helmet with a jagged hole in it; around the hole were fragments of bone and hair. Survival, yes, but it was accompanied by celebration, so who am I to judge others? Perhaps that was how it had been with the Germans; it had all begun with survival, then the celebration had taken over.

'Well done, Mr. Red Cross.'

Kepa was limping across the grass towards him. 'I played dead; I hoped one of them would come to investigate, then I would have got him,' waving a pistol. 'But they didn't play it that way – they were going to fill my body full of bullets before they came to take a look. Thorough, the Germans. But not as thorough as you, my pacifist friend,' as he stared at the remains of men and metal. 'You saved my life. It seems to be a habit of yours, saving lives.'

Hoffman didn't reply. He was staring at a blood-stained letter lying beside the twisted barrel of the machine-gun. He didn't pick it up; mother, lover, it was all the same.

Are you badly hurt?' he asked Kepa.

'A flesh wound in the thigh.' He bent down. 'But let's get rid of this just in case.' He picked up the grenade he had thrown and hurled it away.

It exploded in mid-air.

*

They sat in a coal cellar in a house fifteen miles from the village.

'At least the Poles will always have coal,' Kepa said.

He sat with his back to the wall, his wounded leg sticking out in front of him like a spare part. They had been driven to the house in a farm truck, covered with sugar beet, their escape made easier by the falling snow, as the Germans began to raze the village. The women of the house whose husband had been killed by the Nazis had bathed and dressed Kepa's wound.

'What about the others?' Hoffman asked.

'They each knew where to go. A lot of them were already dead.'

'Is it really worth it, this resistance? You lose so many men. Now the Germans are punishing the innocent.'

'We were all innocent,' Kepa said, feeling his wound through the bandage. 'We were all punished. All we have left is honour. We have to show the Krauts that we still have balls. Do you know that I saw horsemen in the Pomorze Army charge Guderian's tanks and send them scuttling? Not for long, mind, but they fought, those cavalrymen, and we have to make sure that they didn't fight for nothing.'

The woman came into the cellar and put a bowl of stew on the charcoal fire she had lit. 'No smoke,' she had explained when Hoffman pointed at the gleaming piles of coal.

The smell of the stew reached them immediately. Hoffman realised that he was famished.

'Potato skins,' she said. 'Very good for you. And beet and carrots and a little meat, only don't ask where it came from.'

She was dressed in black, passive-faced and huge-breasted, with a red scarf tied round her hair. Her face was touched with coal dust, Kepa and Hoffman were covered with it.

Kepa licked his lips and said to Hoffman: 'What you have to realise is that we are used to all this. It's our heritage. We never fight: we fight back. In the eighteenth century we lost the whole country to Russia, Austria and Prussia. Then Napoleon set up the Duchy of Warsaw. Then the Russians came again after Napoleon's defeat. The Kingdom of Poland, they called it. But by the end of the last war we were back in the reckoning again with our own country. Until last year. Now here we are again, fighting back.'

Hoffman held out an earthenware bowl into which the woman ladled stew; it was thin but it tasted good and strong.

'Pepper vodka,' she explained, watching Kepa wolf down his. She looked at him fondly but there was nothing maternal about the look and Hoffman wondered if once, long ago there had been something between them and that, although they had both been decently married, there was still a little of it left.

'But what about women and children?' Hoffman persisted. 'They'll be hurt because of what happened today. Perhaps taken away, perhaps lose their husband, fathers ... Is it worth it?'

'If you could ask them,' Kepa said, sipping noisily from a spoon, 'they would tell you yes. As they've told people like you throughout the history of Poland.'

Hoffman dropped it; but he wasn't convinced that Kepa was right. History, Kepa's subject by the sound of it, rang with the clarion calls of heroes who had led to their deaths people who wanted nothing to do with glory. It was the historians who had helped to make pacifism a crime.

And who are you, Viktor Golovin, to talk about pacifism? You who rejoiced in the killings.

Kepa said: 'Why don't you ask her what she thinks?' pointing at the woman.

'I only know,' she said, 'that war changes everyone.'

'It unlocks feelings,' Kepa said. 'You forget I was a schoolmaster. I suppose I taught history for so long that when the time came I knew what to do.'

'There was never any question about you,' the woman said, 'when the time came.'

'Nor you,' Kepa said, and again Hoffman sensed the feeling between them.

'But—' Hoffman began but he was interrupted by a banging on a door upstairs. The woman moved quickly for her size. She poured water on the charcoal and covered the bowl of stew and the plates with sacking. 'Cover yourselves with coal,' she said.

She climbed a ladder and disappeared through a trapdoor, kicking the ladder away from beneath her.

But they didn't cover themselves with coal. Kepa said the Germans would search the house first. 'If they come down here ...' He picked up a pistol lying beside him.

They listened to the tramp of feet.

'One man,' Kepa said.

'Will he know about the cellar?'

Kepa shrugged. 'Everyone in Poland keeps coal, but perhaps he doesn't know that.'

A door opened, slammed. They heard a motor-cycle being kick-started. It roared into life. The noise retreated. The women opened the trapdoor and Hoffman replaced the ladder.

'Well?' Kepa looked at her suspiciously as she handed them back their bowls of stew. 'Why did he go so easily?'

'He said he was coming back.'

'To search again?'

'That wasn't the reason he gave.'

'You?'

She nodded, staring challengingly at him.

'You would ... collaborate?'

'What do you think? You know – knew – me well enough.'

'I wouldn't believe it. Nor would Jan.'

Her husband? Hoffman was astonished that anyone would want to have sex with this plain, heavy-breasted peasant. And then he realised that, because he was young, he had never accepted that middle-aged couples made love.

She said: 'Why wouldn't you believe it? Because I am still in mourning more than a year after my husband died? Because I am no longer attractive?'

'Because you are Polish,' Kepa said.

'But not a martyr like you.' She sat in front of him, hands clasped round her knees. 'You just want to fight, to expose yourself to danger, until you join Marja and Fryderyk.'

Kepa bowed his head. 'They shot my wife and son in the garden,' he said to Hoffman. 'In the garden, just like that. Fryderyk had run out to see what was happening ... Marja ran after him ... a machine-gun opened up ... I saw them fall ... '

And the woman was beside him, stroking his face, and for a moment Hoffman was forgotten. 'I know, I know. But you scare me, you want to die and I don't want you to. I loved Jan. You know that. And he was a good husband and I was a good wife to him. Your wife and Fryderyk, they were precious to you. But they are gone and we are still here whether we like it or not ...'

Kepa raised his head and Hoffman saw that there were tears in his eyes.

The woman touched his eyes with her fingers. 'Do you really think that I would sleep with that pig?' From the folds of her black dress she produced a knife sharpened to a vicious point. 'If he touches me …' She stabbed upwards with the knife. 'But I kept him away from the cellar, didn't I?'

'You did well, Halina,' he said. It was the first time Hoffman had heard her name. 'Very well.' He held her hand.

They became aware again of Hoffman.

'So,' Kepa said, 'what is to become of you, Mr. Red Cross?'

'I want to cross the demarcation line,' Hoffman said.

'Why, for God's sake?'

'I can't tell you.'

'Then you can't expect much help, can you?'

'I saved those men from being killed, from being tortured. I think you owe me a little.' And saved your life, he thought.

'Is it for the good of Poland that you want to cross?'

'I shall be helping to defeat the Germans. Is that good enough for you?'

Kepa considered this. 'And defeating the Russians?' He looked shrewdly at Hoffman.

Shaken, Hoffman asked what he meant.

'They are worse than the Germans. As you'll see if you manage to cross over. There are many Poles who consider themselves lucky to be this side of the line.'

'Worse?' Hoffman's head ached. 'How can anything be worse than what I've seen today?'

'At least the Germans ask questions first. The Russians don't bother with such niceties.'

'I don't believe it.'

'Why should you disbelive it, Mr. Red Cross? Do you have some affinity with the Soviets?'

The woman said suddenly: 'Where do you come from in Czechoslovakia?'

'Bratislava,' Hoffman said promptly. *Russians worse than Germans?*

'The city?'

'Outside the city.'

'I know the area well,' she said. 'Where?'

'A village called Cicov.'

'That's a fair way from Bratislava.'

201

'On the Danube,' he said.

'I know, I've been there.'

'And the geese still walk on the pavements,' he said, managing a smile and hoping that the guidebook had been accurate.

It seemed to satisfy her. 'Does it hurt very much?' she said to Kepa. Blood was seeping from beneath the bandage.

'It will be all right,' and to Hoffman: 'So you don't believe it? I can tell you this, the Poles on the other side of the Bug have a greater need for your Red Cross than we do. You say you will be helping to defeat the Germans? Nothing wrong with that. I can think of only one better outcome of this war – the defeat of the Germans *and* the Russians.'

Hoffman said: 'You've been listening to German propaganda.'

Kepa spat into the coal. 'I listen to no one but my conscience.' He paused. 'But why should the Germans spread anti-Soviet propaganda? They have a pact, don't they? They're friends, allies, brothers-in-arms.'

But of course, he didn't mean it. 'You know as well as I do,' Hoffman said, 'that Fascists and Bolsheviks can never share a cause. It's an arrangement, that's all. A convenience for both sides. Hitler probably hates the Russians more than the English.'

'He never hated the English,' Kepa the historian said. 'But we're getting away from the point. You don't believe what I tell you about the Russians? Then you must go and see for yourself. At least I will have made a convert.'

When the woman began to protest, Kepa said: 'You should have seen what he did today.'

But they were Germans, Hoffman thought. The enemy. What if they had been Russians?

'I can get you to the river,' Kepa told him. 'and I know people on this side of the river who will help you. You have papers?'

Hoffman said he had.

'The Krauts didn't seem to think much of your papers. But the Russians will, eh?'

'It's a chance I have to take,' Hoffman said, evading the question. 'How do I get to the river?'

'By night,' Kepa said and told him how it could be done.

*

The German staff car was hidden beneath a pile of rusting vehicles in a scrapyard.

As dusk fell the day after the battle in the village, Hoffman went there with two other partisans; together they manhandled the car away from the wrecks.

The moon was shining and Hoffman could see that she was beautiful. A Maybach tourer with a long, low-slung bonnet and a leather hood. Through the windscreen was a hole surrounded by radials of splintered glass.

'A wonderful shot,' one of the partisans remarked. 'Right between the eyes.' From the boot he took a grey-green uniform. 'The driver's,' he said. 'He was a general's chauffeur but he hadn't got the general with him, more's the pity.' Appraising Hoffman, he said: 'It should fit you. And we've cleaned the blood off.'

Pulling on the jacket, Hoffman thought: 'You're a Russian posing as a Czech posing as a German who will shortly be posing as a NKVD officer. Not bad.'

'Yes,' the partisan said, 'it fits, well almost.' Like a tailor trying to disguise bad cutting, he gave the jacket a tug. Then he handed Hoffman some papers. 'Your name is Otto Stieff and you're a private soldier in the *Wehrmacht*. Read these papers and memorise as much of them as you can. Head east and you can't go wrong. Good luck,' and he was gone.

Hoffman read the papers in the moonlight, then switched on the engine. It throbbed powerfully. What the partisans didn't know was that driving was the least of his accomplishments: students didn't drive the few cars there were in Moscow and in Lisbon there had never been any reason to practise.

He found reverse and backed the car erratically out of the yard. Then he headed east towards the River Bug, the demarcation line between German and Soviet Poland, a hundred miles away. And it wasn't until he had reached Siedlce, half-way there, that he was stopped.

The road block was primitive but effective: a lorry parked sideways across the road and three sentries guarding the space to its right. According to Kepa, the number-plate of the Maybach had been changed, but if the Germans had a description of the stolen car he was finished; if Otto Stieff's name had been circulated as missing then he was finished twice over.

The officer in charge of the road block approached the car

deferentially but his attitude changed when he realised there was no one important in the back.

He flashed a torch in Hoffman's face. 'Papers.' He was a middle-aged second lieutenant with petulant features; a road-block, Hoffman decided, was the highest command he would ever have.

He scanned the papers, then said: 'Get out and let's have a look at you.'

Hoffman climbed out of the car. 'So your name's Stieff. Where are you from, Stieff?'

'Dresden,' Hoffman said.

'I have a rank.'

'Dresden, lieutenant.'

'What are you doing driving through the night by yourself, Stieff?'

'Going to pick up the general, *lieutenant*.'

Hoffman couldn't help the sarcastic emphasis. Stupid.

'So you're only accustomed to showing respect to generals?'

'No, lieutenant.' Controlled this time.

'That's a strange accent you have,' the officer said. 'I haven't heard anything like it before.'

Hoffman who had imagined his accent was pure Berlin said: 'My mother was Polish, lieutenant. I was brought up on the Polish border – the old Polish border, that is.'

'And you drive a general?' The officer seemed amazed that a mongrel should be permitted to drive a high-ranking German officer.

'My accent doesn't affect my driving, lieutenant.' Stupid again. What had come over him?

The officer turned to a corporal standing beside him. 'Search the car.'

Hoffman said: 'I don't think the general would like that, sir.' His papers were under the rubber lining in the boot; he felt his heart thudding.

'I'm quite sure he would endorse any security measures we thought fit to take.'

Hoffman sighed. 'With respect, lieutenant, you don't know the general.' If they found the papers he might just be able to shoot all three of them with the pistol concealed inside his jacket. 'I have to pick him up in—' he glanced at his wrist-watch – 'in one hour exactly. In two and a half hours he has to be back in Warsaw. It's a very tight schedule, lieutenant.'

'This will only take ten minutes or so,' the lieutenant said.

Hoffman shrugged. 'Very well, lieutenant. I'll tell General Wolff to explain to Heydrich that you thought the search was necessary.'

The officer's head jerked up. 'Who?'

Hoffman said: 'I understand that Reichsführer Himmler has dispatched Heydrich to Warsaw to meet General Wolff.'

The officer thrust the papers at Hoffman. 'Get on your way, man, and don't forget to show respect to officers.'

Hoffman stepped back and gave the Nazi salute. 'Heil Hitler.' He climbed into the Maybach and drove away. God help the next driver stopped at the block, he thought.

He drove along the pot-holed road into a belt of forest. He was about forty miles from the river. Ahead lay God knows what. He thought instead about what he had left behind. Kepa and the woman in the cellar. Reunited by bereavement. How could you reconcile that with conventional morals? He hoped they found some sort of happiness in their cellar. Before the inevitable.

Twenty minutes later he saw a gleam of silver in the distance. The River Bug. On this bank Germans keeping watch for unauthorised departures, on the other bank Russians watching for unauthorised arrivals. He drove faster and still just as badly.

*

Hunched in the old grey coat he had worn during the Civil War, Stalin read and re-read the report from the NKVD headquarters in Dzerzhinsky Square.

Hope, then despair, then ungoverned anger, overcame him.

They had checked out Viktor from Lisbon, lost him briefly, picked him up in Madrid. From Madrid he had flown to Rome, then on to Vienna.

It was when he read that Viktor had boarded a train travelling east that Stalin had truly begun to believe that his son was coming home.

When he had got that far in the report he pulled the coat closer to him and murmured: 'Keep him apart from it all ...' the words that Viktor's mother had used all those years ago.

He read on.

The NKVD had lost him on the outskirts of Warsaw. 'German officers believed to be Gestapo took him away in a car. Regrettably we were unable to follow.'

Regrettably! Crass, cowardly, treacherous bastards. He would have them recalled to Moscow and beaten to death in Lubyanka.

He poured himself a glass of vodka. He tossed the spirit down his throat and smashed the glass against the wall.

He picked up the telephone and told the Kremlin operator to get Beria. He told Beria to bring back his surveillance operatives from German-occupied Poland. He told him that he would personally supervise their executions.

He drank more vodka straight from the bottle. Then he beat his knuckles on the top of his desk until blood flowed.

Chapter Fifteen

Bauer picked up Rachel Keyser outside the Avenida Palace.

It was seven p.m., an hour of expectancy in Lisbon. The cafés were awakening, crowds hurrying along the black and white pavements, trysts being kept or broken.

Rachel approached the hotel from the Praça dos Restauradores. Opposite the obelisk commemorating the end of Spanish rule in 1640 she bought an evening newspaper. The headline read HITLER MEETS FRANCO. The story speculated on whether the Spanish leader, consolidating his position after his victory in the civil war, would do a deal with the Führer and let German troops attack Gibraltar from Spain.

Another story on the same page expressed the views of Portugal's dictator. According to the article, Salazar was confident that Spain, like Portugal, would continue to observe strict neutrality.

A gentle reminder to Franco, Rachel thought, that in this war it was better to sit on the fence until a decisive battle was fought. The article, she realised, also reaffirmed the Portuguese fear that, if the Germans entered Spain, they could take Portugal as easily as they had taken Poland.

Poland. Where was Josef now? Cross was confident that he would reach Moscow without a hitch. He was Red Cross all the way to the demarcation line – not even the Germans liked to upset them – and he was Red Cross even when he passed into Soviet-held territory. Once there his position was even stronger: he was Red Cross *and* NKVD.

Bauer said: 'I wonder if you could spare a moment, Fraülein Keyser.'

He was smoking one of his black cigars; he smelled of cologne and his cropped grey hair glistened; he looked like a man who had wallowed too long in a very hot bath.

Rachel said: 'Go to hell,' and tried to walk past him, but he gripped her arm and said: 'We have made contact with Josef Hoffman.'

She stopped, knowing that she was displaying fear; but she tried to disguise it just the same. 'Who?'

'You know who.' He led her into the hotel bar, a subdued place with walls fashioned from different coloured marbles, the haunt of journalists, minor diplomats and professional eavesdroppers.

Bauer led her unprotesting to a table and ordered a beer and a schnapps for himself and a glass of white wine for her. She waited for him to elaborate but he kept her waiting and she knew he was enjoying himself.

He took off his black topcoat and undid the jacket of his grey, double-breasted suit, displaying his big, drum belly beneath a striped shirt. While the waiter poured the schnapps he licked his lips; he drank it in a gulp and told the waiter to pour another. Then he drank some beer, licking the froth from his upper lip with the tip of his tongue.

At last he spoke. 'A very enterprising young man, Josef Hoffman. Or should I say he has enterprising masters?'

'Where is he?' Rachel asked, abandoning pretence.

'Somewhere in Europe. That's how war stories are datelined, aren't they?' He drank some more beer. 'Do you mind me speaking in German?'

'Why should I?' What did he mean, *made contact?*

'Ah, of course not, you spent a long time in Berlin, didn't you. An enjoyable period of your life, Fraülein Keyser?'

'An interesting time,' she said, hating him.

'But, of course, you must have had reservations about our handling of the Jewish problem.'

'Your problem,' she said.

'Last time we met,' he said, 'I got the distinct impression

that you felt very strongly about Jews. Being one yourself, that is. And I seem to remember that you didn't much like my cigars either.' He lit another one and blew smoke across the table.

She wanted to scream at him: 'For God's sake what's happened to Josef?' But instead she said: 'You haven't brought me here to discuss the Nazis' anti-Semitic policies.'

'True, true. I'll come to the point, Fraülein. Josef Hoffman is currently in the custody of the Gestapo. As you will appreciate he can come to very great harm. But you can save him.'

Despair lurched inside her. 'I don't believe you.'

Bauer took two sheets of paper from the inside pocket of his jacket. One was a cable. 'In code so it goes without saying that I can't show it to you.' The other was the decoded message. He handed it to her.

JOSEF HOFFMAN DESCRIBING HIMSELF AS RED CROSS COURIER TAKEN FROM TRAIN AT 1238 HOURS WARSAW TIME (the decoded cable bore yesterday's date) AND DETAINED FOR INTERROGATION.

Interrogation. She knew what that meant and she thought: 'I have done this to him,' but all she said was: 'That's against international law.'

Bauer examined the wet tip of his cigar. 'In my opinion the Red Cross are as useless as the League of Nations was. However I agree that if he had been pursuing genuine Red Cross business we would not have detained him. As it happens he wasn't. Neither Lisbon nor Geneva has any record of his mission; in fact they are both rather disturbed by his departure. I don't think,' Bauer said, leaning across the table, 'that your friends at the British Embassy are quite as clever as they think they are. They made the mistake of underestimating German Intelligence.' *Me*, he implied. His voice took on a grating quality. 'They thought it was sufficient to murder three Germans and to change Hoffman's timetable and he would reach Moscow just like that.' Bauer's bloodshot eyes stared at her intently. 'Why Moscow, Fraülein Keyser?'

'All right,' she said, sipping her wine, 'I do know Hoffman. In fact I am very fond of him—'

Bauer interrupted impatiently: 'We know perfectly well that you've been sleeping with him.'

'—but Moscow? I haven't the faintest idea what you're talking about.'

Bauer said: 'On the contrary, you drove him to the airport. Who killed my men, Fraülein Keyser?'

'I read that they were ambushed and robbed.'

'Was it Cross? I believe he works for … certain sections of German Intelligence,' but his expression said he wasn't sure.

'*If* he works for German Intelligence he would hardly kill three of your men, would he?'

Bauer let that one go. He ordered more beer and schnapps from the waiter. Pulling at the lobe of one ear, he said: 'You understand the implications of interrogation by the Gestapo?'

She closed her eyes for a moment.

'I sent a cable to Warsaw instructing our agents there to postpone interrogation until I conducted certain consultations in Lisbon. There is, in fact, only one consultation and this is it.'

The waiter gave him another beer and refilled his schnapps glass. 'That one's on the house, Herr Bauer,' he said.

'At least he knows who's going to win the war,' Bauer remarked.

Despite everything, Rachel managed a small lie. 'He doesn't charge the English for any drinks,' she said.

Bauer ignored it. 'First they will soften him up a little,' he said. 'You know, the rubber hose treatment. Then if he doesn't talk—'

'Everyone knows about your methods.' If he didn't stop she would pick up his glass of beer, smash it on the table and grind the jagged glass in his face. But then Hoffman would surely die.

'—they will use more refined methods. We have an expert there, a man named Adler. He's in a class all on his own.'

'You disgust me.'

'Fingernails first. One by one with a pair of pliers. There's something about the wrench of a nail from a finger that makes people talk.'

Please God, don't let it be so.

'Then electric shocks if he's really stubborn.'

What have I done to you?

'On the genitals. You would know all about those, Fraülein.'

'I'm going,' she said. 'I don't have to listen to filth from a fat pig like you.'

'You don't want to save him?'

She took a gulp of wine.

'Adler's very good with the electrical side of things. He knows just how much current to give without killing the subject. It's said to be the worst pain known to man.'

When I met you, Josef, you dreamed of peace and I derided your dreams.

'If you co-operate,' Bauer said, 'then you can save him all that pain.'

'But I can't help you,' hearing him scream.

'Why was he going to Moscow?'

'I understood he was going to Geneva ...'

'The fingernails one by one ...'

'... on Red Cross business ...'

'... until the tips of his fingers are pulp ...'

'... and then coming back to Lisbon ...'

'... electrodes on the testicles ... '

'... said nothing about Russia ...'

'... the body arches ... the backbone has been known to break in the hands of amateurs ...'

'... doesn't confide in me ...'

'... but Adler is no amateur ...'

'I don't know anything!'

Bauer said softly: 'What a pity. Then Hoffman will die. Very slowly.'

Her mind in panic, she thought: 'There must be another way. Think, think. What can I tell him? How can I prevent the pain? Quickly, lies, think of something convincing, you stupid bitch.'

'He wasn't going to Moscow,' she said.

'Really?' Bauer regarded her cynically, the look of a man who has heard many lies squeezed out by intolerable pressures. 'Where was he going? The Moon?'

'He was leaving the train at Warsaw.'

'Going on vacation?'

'On *Abwehr* business,' she said, and this time he reacted; a slight refocussing of his eyes, a suggestion of compression about his lips, but reaction just the same.

'How do you know about such things?' Then answered himself: 'Of course, Cross. What sort of *Abwehr* business?'

Encouraged by his reaction, she said earnestly: 'I honestly don't know. I just heard that it was some sort of mission for the

210

Abwehr.' And innocently: 'But surely you must know if he's acting on behalf of German Intelligence.'

Bauer said: 'Can you find out?'

'If,' she said trying to control her eagerness, 'you guarantee that no harm will come to Hoffman.'

'I can guarantee that he won't be interrogated for a while. But please don't tell Cross that I asked you to find out.'

For the first time since they sat down Bauer seemed to have lost direction. *Abwehr* business. The two words had kindled interest that appeared to be stronger than national considerations.

By instinct she had bought Hoffman respite. For how long?

Bauer said: 'The elevator where we first met. I'll meet you at the top, on the bridge, at eight tomorrow evening. Please be there – with full details of this *Abwehr* business.'

He paid the bill and left.

*

Bauer learned two hours later that Hoffman had escaped from the Gestapo. Not only had he escaped, apparently, but he had killed one of his captors, maimed Adler, the specialist, for life, and, so it was believed, helped Polish partisans to destroy a machine-gun post.

Bauer stormed out of the Legation and drove to the house of the compliant young prostitute who for an outrageous price catered for his sexual requirements.

At first she protested at his arrival at her home near the Botanical Gardens, pointing out that she had perfectly good business premises in the Chiado. But when he threw an extra handful of escudo bills on the table she forgot her objections.

Wearing high-heeled shoes, black stockings and garter belt she bent over a pile of cushions at one end of her bed and, with one eye on the heap of bills, heroically endured the humiliations he performed with his coarse, probing fingers.

Then, stripped naked, he began to whip her. He was aware that the lash was made from special lightweight rubber to minimise the pain but she squirmed and whimpered most convincingly.

So Hoffman had shot Lieber at point-blank range. The rubber made a satisfying thwack across her tender buttocks.

And had fractured Adler's cheek-bone causing irreparable

brain damage. Two lashes. Pale pink weals were beginning to show.

'That's enough,' she cried, but he tossed a couple more bills on the table and thought of the machine-gunners' dismembered bodies. He grunted as he brought the lash down as hard as he could.

On *Abwehr* business! This time her cry of pain seemed genuine.

And the fucking bastard had escaped. The lash sang through the air; any moment now the final frenzy would be on him; but he had learned his lesson with a girl in Hamburg whom he had nearly killed and, just in time, he thwarted himself in that respect by entering her brutally from behind.

And it wasn't until he was on his way home that it occurred to him that there was no reason why Rachel Keyser should know that Hoffman had escaped. Really, these sessions with the young whore were most salutary.

*

'*Abwehr* business? Very ingenious.' Cross and Rachel sat beside each other in a pew at the rear of St. Rock Church where they had arranged to meet in an emergency. 'Now we'll have to think of something to substantiate your ingenuity.'

A priest walked down the aisle. Rachel stared at the paintings on the wooden ceiling depicting the Apocalypse.

'We could cause a lot of heart-searching in the Kraut secret services,' Cross said. 'But whatever we do it will only be temporary as far as Hoffman is concerned.' He knelt, cupping his hands in front of him, as the priest, smiling gently, walked past. 'Because despite what Bauer promised you,' he explained, 'they'll still interrogate him and only by a miracle could he come up with the same explanation as ours. Although if we're to produce a miracle this is the place to do it,' nodding towards the altar.

Kneeling beside him, she thought: 'So I've failed.'

'But, as you say, you may have bought him time. They may wait to see what you come up with and then try it out on him. *Abwehr* business …'

But she was no longer listening; she was praying in this Christian place of worship for Hoffman's life; praying to the Deity who surely listened whether you were in church, mosque or synagogue.

'... if we could persuade Bauer,' he was saying into his cupped hands, 'that Hoffman' – his name brought her back from prayer – 'had gone to Warsaw at the instigation of the *Abwehr* to report on the atrocities there ... After all, he does work for the Red Cross. Perhaps if we could convince him,' Cross said, conspirator's imagination taking hold, 'that von Claus had provided Hoffman with details of the places to investigate. Mass graves and suchlike. We know that Canaris abhors Himmler's treatment of the Jews ... As for Moscow – well, that would be a good escape route for a Red Cross official who wanted to avoid contact with the Gestapo.'

'But it won't save Josef, will it?'

'As I said, it might buy him time. Time to escape. Time to be rescued by partisans. Who knows ...' Cross glanced at her curiously. 'Tell me something: if telling Bauer the truth meant saving Hoffman but losing the war what would you do?'

She didn't reply but she knew what she would do and the knowledge terrified her.

She closed her eyes and began to pray again.

*

As instructed, Hoffman left the Maybach in a barn at the end of a lane ten miles from the river and began to walk across the fields, searching in the moonlight for the landmarks Kepa had mentioned.

It was 1.30 a.m. The scattering of snow had thawed and the ground underfoot was muddy. A few minutes later he was knee-deep in marshes. Kepa hadn't said anything about marshes. A duck took off with a flapping run and flew low overhead, squawking. Somewhere there should be a ruined farmhouse; he stopped and stared around but all he could see was water and dark tufts of marsh grass.

Kepa wouldn't have sent him across a bog. Unless Kepa didn't want him to reach the Russians. The other enemy! Hoffman took a step forward but there was only water beneath his foot.

He stepped back – and fell back into more water. Clumsily, he waded to a hillock of muddy grass. He had left the jacket of the uniform in the car and he began to shiver.

He retreated again, reaching firmer ground. An aircraft droned overhead; a small animal broke from some reeds to his left, rushed into the marshes and swam away, making an arrow on the moonlit water.

He gestured hopelessly at the starlit sky and changed direction. A couple of minutes later he found the farmhouse; it was more of a ruin than Kepa had led him to expect, almost swallowed up by the bog. But Hoffman was more pleased to see it than any friendly tavern on a hostile night.

A path just riding above the water led to the east. Hoffman stepped on to it aware that he presented a perfect target, clear-cut and slow-moving. As he walked a stiff breeze flattened his wet shirt against his chest; he couldn't stop shivering.

But it was another hour before the shot came and by that time he had reached firmer ground. He threw himself into a ditch and waited, pistol in hand. At first there was nothing except the hooting of an owl; then, faintly, he heard footsteps and muted voices. He gripped the pistol tightly.

It was when the voices were almost upon him that he realised they were speaking Polish not German. 'Where did she go?'

She?

'I don't know. Perhaps you missed her.'

'If we stay here much longer the Germans won't miss us.'

A cloud passed over the moon. A thin beam of torchlight came from the direction of the voices. It ran along the ditch, stopping at Hoffman. He levelled his pistol and said: 'I've got you covered, put out the light.'

The light snapped out and one of the voices said: 'Now who the hell might you be?'

'Not a duck for sure,' said another voice.

And a third from behind him: 'Now you'd better drop that gun because *I* have got *you* covered.'

*

In a cottage on the edge of the blacked-out village the three duck-shooters regarded Hoffman curiously. They had examined the papers which he had taped to his chest in a waterproof pouch and read the letter from Kepa.

One of them said: 'Does Kepa still wear his hair long like Jesus Christ?' and Hoffman, who was cold and exhausted and weary of being tested, snapped: 'He's as bald as a coot and you know it.'

214

A gaunt young woman entered the room, stuffed with cheap furniture, walls covered with rose-patterned wallpaper, and said: 'Well, where's breakfast?'

A man named Emil, unshaven and with an aggressive tilt to his face, said: 'We didn't get a duck, we got this instead.'

He explained to Hoffman that they had to hunt by night; by day they would be the quarry. And they could only risk one, or at the most two, shots before the German patrols came to investigate.

'We can't eat him,' the woman said; but there was no humour in her voice; Hoffman got the impression that she had laughed a lot once, before the Germans had stamped on happiness.

The man named Emil said: 'He does look a bit tough.' One of the men sniggered but when the woman looked at him he pretended he was clearing his throat.

'So what's our baby going to live on?' the woman asked Emil.

Emil pointed at her breasts. 'Milk.'

'To get milk you have to feed me.' Her hands strayed to her breasts. 'There's nothing there any more.'

Hoffman felt hostility gathering around him. One more shot and they might have had food.

Emil fingered the black stubble on his chin. 'You were lucky,' he said after a while. 'This is the house Kepa meant you to come to.'

The woman said: 'He's not staying here.'

Emil said: 'You keep out of it.'

'It's my house as well as yours.'

They stared at each other with something approaching hatred. Hoffman looked away; on a crowded shelf on the wall stood a photograph of Emil and his wife on their wedding day; they looked posed and awkward and proud of each other. *I only know that war changes everyone.*

She pointed at Hoffman's trousers. 'German,' she said; but he had explained that to the men and they explained it to her. She didn't look convinced.

Suddenly she was gone, door slamming behind her, making a china ballerina on the shelf dance.

Emil took off his padded, hunter's jacket. 'Put this on, you'll freeze to death.'

Outside, perhaps, but not in this room which, with the

215

red-hot stove in one corner, was like an ornate furnace. So they meant him to go.

Somewhere in the house the baby began to cry. Above the wail Hoffman heard crisp footsteps on the street outside.

'A German patrol,' one of the men said.

They waited. The footsteps got nearer.

A door banged in the house, quieting the baby for a moment. Floorboards creaked.

The footsteps were directly outside.

The sound of a bolt being drawn.

Emil flung open the door of the living room and grabbed his wife as she turned the key in the lock of the street door.

He flung her on to the floor and she stayed there, at the foot of the stairs, whimpering.

The footsteps seemed to hesitate. Then continued, faded, died.

The woman looked up at her husband and said: 'They would have given us food if we had turned him in.'

'Bitch,' her husband said.

'No,' Hoffman said, 'she isn't.'

The baby began to cry again.

Emil said: 'Come, you have to go now,' and in the bare kitchen said: 'The baby is sick.' He opened the back door.

Clouds had covered the moon and stars. There were three hours till dawn.

'The rowing boat's over there,' Emil said pointing into the darkness, 'just as Kepa said it would be. It's about half a mile away. You'll have to pull strongly because the currents are strong. They say it's worse on the other side. Can anything be worse, I ask you?' He handed Hoffman back his pistol. 'I don't know why you want to get there but Kepa says you're okay.' Anything Kepa said was obviously okay.

It took Hoffman half an hour to reach the river; again he had to pick his way through marshes. He found the boat hidden in some rushes; the rushes whispered to him in the darkness.

The water was as black as the night. There were no lights on the opposite bank. Rivers such as this were supposed to have been Poland's defences against invasion. To the north lay Brest-Litovsk where in the last war the Russians had made their peace with Germany.

Dipping the oars gently into the water, Hoffman began to row for the far bank. He was between two juggernauts.

216

Between two tyrannies? He shook his head as he rowed. Between two tyrants, perhaps, but the Russian people weren't like the Germans: their failing was their national persecution complex. Which was why they had allowed Stalin to carry out his purges.

And if Stalin's megalomania is so obsessive that he believes no one, not even those who seek to warn him about Germany's hostile intentions, then I must tell him. For the sake of my people, he thought, as the beam of a searchlight hit the rowing boat, blinding him.

*

The chain-smoking, plain-clothes NKVD officer sitting at the table in the dug-out on the eastern bank of the Bug said: 'You contradict yourself.'

Fatigue overwhelmed Hoffman; his bones ached, his head was heavy, lolling. 'Contradict?'

'You say you are a NKVD officer. Then you must know that no NKVD officer would be taken in by this shit.' The officer, black-haired and squat, threw the forged documents at Hoffman. 'That's the contradiction.'

'Check me out,' Hoffman said. His voice seemed to belong to someone else. 'Check me out and you'll be in the shit, my friend, up to here,' lifting one heavy hand to his chin.

The officer lit another yellow, cardboard-tipped cigarette and, staring at Hoffman, said: 'You're too young for your rank.' But his tone wasn't as confident as his words; that was the snag in being trained in suspicion – you suspected your own reasoning.

'Check,' Hoffman said. Sleep was a warm fog and its tendrils were reaching for him.

A field telephone rang beside the officer. He took a deep breath of cigarette smoke and picked up the receiver.

The effect of the voice on the other end of the line was electrifying. The officer stubbed out his cigarette and looked as though he might leap to attention and salute.

Hoffman watched in amazement.

When the officer replaced the receiver he was trembling.

He said shakily: 'I must apologise, comrade ... you are to have an escort ... to Moscow,' he said in wonderment.

217

Chapter Sixteen

Eight p.m.

Bauer was waiting on the caged-in platform at the top of Eiffel's grey elevator tower when she arrived.

He was staring down through the wire mesh at the rooftops of the elegant shops in the Chiado; behind him in the darkness she could see the lights of ships on the Tagus.

A wooden barrier had been placed across the platform; beyond it the cage was being repaired and a gap yawned into space.

One push, she thought, and his heavy body would crash through the planks of the barricade. She imagined him leaning into space with one hand; heard his scream, saw his body turning slowly as it plummeted towards the rooftops.

'Don't worry, Fraülein,' he said as she joined him, 'I'm far too heavy for you to push. Too many cream cakes,' he added. 'Too many schnapps. But it's a beautiful night, isn't it? Cold – but then a man of my size doesn't take too kindly to the heat.'

She stood beside him and stared at the lights of the cars and trams – shining beads pulled slowly along on strands of gossamer. A breeze coming in from the river made her shiver and she pulled her Persian lamb coat more tightly round her.

'Well, Fraülein Keyser,' he said, 'and what have you to report?'

'What about Hoffman?'

'He is alive and well,' Bauer told her.

She tried to believe him and found a little comfort. 'Where is he?'

'He is detained in a village twenty miles outside Warsaw. Now,' his voice more businesslike, 'what about your side of the bargain? What about this *Abwehr* business?'

She told him what Cross had told her to say. That von Claus had provided Hoffman with details of Nazi atrocities in Warsaw; that Hoffman had gone there to expose them. 'A personal crusade rather than a Red Cross mission,' she added.

'You wouldn't be trying to set one German intelligence organisation against another would you, Fraulein?'

218

'I'm trying to save Hoffman,' she said.

'And failing miserably,' he said in a matter-of-fact tone. 'Since you mentioned the *Abwehr* I've checked every move they've made in the past month. They enrolled Hoffman, true. Since then there hasn't been any contact.'

'If the *Abwehr* suspect you have access to their files they wouldn't record it,' she said; but her words were flat, hopeless. The Gestapo still held Josef; they would check her story with him and it was too much to hope that he would chance on the same explanation.

She tried a last ploy. 'There is something else.'

'Really?' He turned to face her; she could smell his cologne.

'Bring Hoffman back to Lisbon and I'll tell you.'

'Why should I do that? If you want to save him you'll tell me anyway. What is this morsel?'

'No morsel, Herr Bauer. It is something beyond your comprehension. If you were responsible for relaying it to Berlin you would join Himmler, Goering, Goebbels beside Hitler.'

She saw the greedy interest in his face; he pulled at one small ear; she saw cunning join the greed.

'If you brought Hoffman here,' she said desperately, 'we could do a deal. His life for the greatest secret of this war. You would know how to arrange such an exchange so that there were no tricks ...'

The elevator stopped beside them. The doors opened; a handful of passengers walked across the bridge spanning the Chiado to the Largo do Carmo.

When they had gone Bauer said: 'I have another suggestion to make. As we hold Hoffman it makes far more sense. You tell me what this secret is and I will authorise Hoffman's release. Refuse to tell me and I will authorise a slow and lingering death for him.'

She would have to tell him; she couldn't let them do those terrible things to Josef.

'Come on, Fraülein. Otherwise I shall assume you are bluffing. What is this priceless piece of information that will place me on the rostrum with the leaders of the Third Reich?'

Of course she would have to tell him. You didn't consign a man to the sort of suffering contrived by the Gestapo for *any* cause. Not even victory over the Nazis ... From the streets of Berlin the bewildered faces of the children stared at her.

219

'Tell me now or Hoffman dies.'

The children had gone to God knows where but Josef was still alive. I have betrayed him once, she thought, and it must never happen again. I have no right.

'Tell me.'

She knew she had to tell him.

She spat in his face and walked briskly across the bridge.

*

On the bed in the Avenida Palace where they had made love she stared at the colours of the spectrum shivering in the chandelier and thought: 'At least he will never know that I sent him to his death.'

If he did would he understand?

Would I understand in his position? Of course, but it was so easy to make such affirmations when you were free from pain, from ... terrible ... terrible ... pain.

Were they torturing him now? He who had wanted none of this. He who had been seduced into a war of which he had wanted no part. By me.

And when I could have saved him all I did was spit.

The bedside phone rang.

It was Cross. Using the chess terminology they had agreed upon, he said: 'The pawn is passed.'

Hoffman in Russia? Cross had got the terminology wrong.

Cross's voice came to her from a long way off. 'Can you hear me ... hear me?' Words echoing. 'Passed ... do you understand?'

Passed the border, of course she understood, as a great joy suffused her, as the colours in the chandelier merged into blood red, as the telephone receiver swung from the bedside table.

When she regained consciousness she thought: 'I will have to tell him,' wondering if any man would ever understand that a woman who professed to love him could have knowingly dispatched him to one of the most terrible deaths ever devised by Man.

*

Hoffman sat in the back seat of a black Volga staff car beside a young Red Army lieutenant.

The lieutenant obviously had no idea why Hoffman was getting such preferential treatment; nor for that matter did

220

Hoffman. He could only assume that British Intelligence had done such a good job paving his way that NKVD headquarters in Poland had been warned to expect a second Ivan the Terrible.

The car was heading towards Pruzhany; beyond lay the northern reaches of the Pripet Marshes.

Hoffman, dressed in a coarse grey suit and black sweater provided by the NKVD, tried to make conversation.

'Have you been in Poland long?'

The lieutenant, who possessed fierce Slav features and cropped hair as thick as fur, examined the shiny peak of his cap as though looking for the answer: you didn't reply to questions from the secret police without weighing them up. Finally he said: 'From the beginning.'

'I sometimes wonder if it was necessary for us to occupy so much of Poland.'

The lieutenant stared at the Red Star gleaming above the peak of the cap. By now he was probably convinced that Hoffman was an *agent provocateur*, that an informer under his command had denounced him for making treasonable remarks.

'It was necessary,' he said. And after a pause: 'We had to create a buffer zone to keep the Germans away from our border.'

The car was approaching a village of wooden houses surrounded by silver birch trees. A group of peasants standing at the side of the muddy road, carrying scythes and shovels, stared at them sullenly.

'I thought,' the lieutenant said carefully, 'that you might like to stop here for coffee.'

Hoffman looked at his wristwatch. It was 11.30 am. 'All right,' he said. Never before had he commanded such respect.

The driver pulled up in the village square. At one end stood a platoon of Soviet troops wearing forage caps, tightly-belted tunics and mud-spattered jackboots. A pump stood in the centre of the square, behind it an ornate wooden church. Soldiers apart, the square was deserted, but here and there a curtain fluttered and a gate moved and Hoffman decided that the inhabitants had fled at the sound of the car. The atmosphere reminded him of the village near Warsaw.

The lieutenant led him into a hut that served as an inn. It contained a wooden bar and a handful of tables and chairs and smelled of sour liquor. A middle-aged man with shiny cheeks

221

that looked as though they had been shaved unnecessarily stood behind the bar, a pot of coffee steaming in front of him.

The lieutenant conferred with the barman. Hoffman, sitting at a table, watched and listened for any attempt at conciliation by the lieutenant; he was disappointed; his voice, curt and contemptuous, might have been a German's. He saw the lieutenant's head tilt and guessed that he had gulped a quick vodka to make him more at ease with the mysterious civilian he was escorting.

The lieutenant brought Hoffman a mug of coffee. He returned to the bar. His head tilted again. When he joined Hoffman he was more relaxed.

They sipped their coffee, appraising each other through the steam. 'We have a long journey ahead of us,' the lieutenant said at last. 'Seven hundred miles as the crow flies, longer by road.' He lit a cigarette. 'At any rate we shall be out of this stinking country soon enough.'

'Are the Poles so bad?'

'Bastards,' the lieutenant replied. 'Lazy, shifty, treacherous. They booby-trapped a patrol car in the next village this morning. Three Soviet soldiers were killed.'

'And Poles?'

'Ten for every one Russian. We shot thirty of them and made them dig their grave first,' said the lieutenant as casually as though he were describing some new roadworks.

Hoffman put down his mug on the table. The bleakness in his soul must have shown because the lieutenant said: 'Something a little stronger, comrade?'

Hoffman nodded. When the lieutenant placed the carafe on the table he poured the first shot straight down his throat; he took the second more slowly, feeling it burn his tongue. 'Surely,' he said, 'all Poles can't be bastards. They produced Chopin, Conrad, Paderewski, Madame Curie ...'

Wariness descended on the lieutenant again but this time it was complicated by alcohol. Hoffman thought that he was about twenty years old; his stomach hadn't yet acquired an anti-vodka lining.

'After all,' Hoffman went on, 'it must be hard to have your country occupied by two foreign armies.'

The lieutenant stared at him suspiciously. 'The Jews are the worst,' he said.

Rachel Keyser appeared before him. Standing on the tarmac

at Sintra as he took his seat in the DC-3. Without realising it, he stretched his hand across the table.

The lieutenant frowned. 'Are you all right, comrade?'

'Yes,' Hoffman said, 'I'm all right.' If he hadn't met her he wouldn't be here; if only she had been honest with him from the beginning. But how could she have been honest when it had been a set-up? 'Why are they the worst?' he asked the lieutenant.

'Aren't they always?'

'You mean they fight back?'

The lieutenant shrugged. Perhaps this man he was guarding *was* a Jew. 'By lunchtime,' he said, 'we shall be back in the Soviet Union. A little more firewater?' He poured them both vodka. '*Nasdarovya.*' Together they tossed back the liquid explosive.

*

With the telephone receiver held to one ear, Stalin pored over a map of Eastern Europe.

'So where is he now?' he said into the receiver.

'Close to the border,' said the voice of Lavrenti Beria, head of the NKVD.

When his son had escaped from the Soviet Union, Stalin had confided in Beria, the sadistic fellow-Georgian; but he had discovered that Beria already knew about Viktor Golovin.

It hadn't really surprised Stalin. Years ago he had personally destroyed all the relevant documents but of course photographic copies had been made. He had also taken the precaution of liquidating anyone with any possible access to the deception. But in Moscow's vicious political climate you couldn't completely suppress such knowledge; it lingered in secret hiding places, in film negatives, in scheming minds.

There was only one way to control such knowledge and that was through fear. Beria, formerly chief of the secret police in Georgia, was the man to look after that. The trouble then was that Beria had to be controlled. But my record of disposing of NKVD chiefs would take care of that, Stalin thought, running a finger down the border between Poland and Russia.

'How long will it take him to reach Moscow?'

'Two days,' Beria said.

Stalin was overcome with joy; he had never experienced emotion quite like it before; his son was coming home; a son

223

who had turned out to be an idealist but could not, apparently, resist the call of Mother Russia. 'Keep him apart from it all,' the boy's mother had said. But now that he had reached such enlightened maturity the truth could surely be revealed.

Stalin smiled and said into the telephone: 'You've done well, Lavrenti.'

Which he had. There had been that terrible period when NKVD operatives in Warsaw had reported that Viktor had been taken prisoner by the Gestapo. But he had escaped. My son, Stalin thought proudly. And all observation posts on the Russian side of the demarcation line in Poland, in particular the River Bug, had been re-alerted to watch for a man answering his description. He had apparently assumed the identity of an NKVD officer which had made it easier for Beria to lay on transport to Moscow.

'Thank you,' Beria said.

'And what about your men in Warsaw who allowed the Gestapo to take him?'

'Liquidated,' Beria said.

'And the officer who began to interrogate him in the observation post on the Bug?'

'Liquidated,' Beria said.

'And the escorting officer?'

'He will be dealt with in the same way,' Beria said.

'Good,' Stalin said, 'we can't be too careful.' He pulled at his thick moustache. 'You wouldn't lie to me about any of this, would you, Lavrenti?'

'I would swear to everything I've told you on my mother's grave.'

'Good,' said Stalin beaming. 'Because if you're lying you'd better start thinking about your own grave.'

*

The driver came into the café and peered around.

'All we need in the Red Army,' the lieutenant said, 'is short-sighted drivers. Over here,' he shouted, 'put your spectacles on, man.'

The driver stood in front of the table; he looked curiously vulnerable without his glasses. 'Trouble, lieutenant,' he said.

'What's happened? Have they punctured your tyres while you weren't looking?'

'Sugar in the petrol tank I think.'

224

'You mean you left the car unattended?'

The driver stepped back as though expecting a blow. 'I had to relieve myself.'

'You'll be relieved all right,' the lieutenant said, standing up. 'We'd better see what's to be done. You'll be all right here?' looking at Hoffman.

'I don't have much choice, do I?'

'Sugar?' said the lieutenant striding towards the door. 'I doubt it; they wouldn't waste it. Shit more like,' he said, disappearing with the driver.

A couple of minutes later Hoffman went up to the bar. The barman stared at him phlegmatically; he was middle-aged with larded hair and a bad skin; he was placidly suspicious and answered questions with questions.

Hoffman said: 'How about some more coffee to drown the vodka?'

'How about some more coffee?' The man shrugged. 'If you wish.'

Hoffman leaned on the bar and sipped the coffee. 'You live here?'

'Live here?' The barman considered this trick question. Finally he said: 'Not so far away.'

'Will you have a drink?'

He shook his head.

'I have great sympathy for the Polish people,' Hoffman said; he didn't expect any reaction – in the barman's eyes he was NKVD – and was astonished at the vehemence he suddenly unleashed.

'The Polish people?' The barman leaned on the bar. 'Always we hear about the Polish people. I am a Ukrainian.' He prodded his chest with his thumb. 'I said I come from around here but I come from farther south, from the western Ukraine. That is what Russia has taken, that and Western Belorussia to the north. I can't speak for the people of Belorussia but I can tell you that the Western Ukraine is not Poland, nor is it Russia. It is what it says it is. For the next thousand years we may be occupied – by Poles, by Germans, by Russians – but they will never break us.'

He stood back defiantly, waiting for the handcuffs.

Amazed, Hoffman searched for words. Sadly, he knew the barman's optimism was unrealistic. As far as the world was concerned Germany and Russia had split Poland into two and

225

no one had any time for such niceties as Western Ukraine and Belorussia. And as far as the Kremlin was concerned the niceties were now part of the Soviet Union.

He said: 'Are they trying to break you now?'

'You know they are. If you want full employment, comrade, join one of your firing squads. But let me say goodbye to my family before you take me off.'

'That won't be necessary,' Hoffman said softly.

When the lieutenant returned to report that the car had been fixed Hoffman said to him: 'We've been having quite a chat, the barman and me.'

The lieutenant said without interest: 'Really? What about?'

'The Russians,' Hoffman told him, looking at the barman. 'He thinks we're wonderful people.'

*

By the same time the following day they were close to Smolensk, 250 miles west of Moscow.

The sun was shining thinly and the lieutenant who, like most winter-conscious Russians, was always anxious to savour the dregs of summer, suggested that they eat out in the open. They bought bread and cheese and beer and stopped in a wood.

With a bottle of beer in his hand, Hoffman sauntered through the woods. Summer hung in delicate tatters around him; last leaves clung to the branches of the trees, wasted brambles tugged at his ankles, a squirrel made a looping run for its winter home.

Twigs cracked behind him. He looked round: the lieutenant was following. 'We'd better make a move,' said the lieutenant, who didn't look as though he wanted to move at all.

'Another ten minutes,' Hoffman said.

They walked on together until they reached a belt of pine trees.

The noise filtered through to Hoffman gradually. At first he couldn't place it. Then it came to him: shovels on earth and stone …

He quickened his pace. On the edge of a clearing a sentry appeared, rifle pointing at them. The lieutenant spoke to him; the sentry lowered his rifle, impressed: not many men who came this way had escorts to Moscow.

The lieutenant said to the sentry: 'What's going on anyway?'

The sentry answered him but Hoffman didn't catch his words. He walked into the clearing. And stopped, stunned.

226

In front of him teams of workmen were shovelling soil into a deep depression that had been recently excavated. Piled high in the crater in parade-ground order were thousands of corpses.

Quite calmly, Hoffman thought: 'This isn't happening.'

The bodies were clothed in the uniforms of Polish army officers. Each had been shot in the back of the neck. So regimented were they that, at a word of command, Hoffman expected them to leap to attention.

He noticed that some of the Red Army guards were grinning and pointing at the uniformed corpses.

Hoffman turned to the lieutenant and, still calm, said: 'What's going on here?'

'Just what it looks like,' the lieutenant said. 'There are more than 4,000 of them. Apparently they refused to accept the authority of the Red Army.' He shrugged. 'Who wants 4,000 rebel officers behind your back?'

'You mean they're all dead?'

The lieutenant looked at him curiously. 'They're only Poles,' he said, 'and a lot of them are Jews at that.'

Turning, Hoffman ran blindly through the woods towards the car.

He didn't speak until they were on the outskirts of Moscow. Then all he said was: 'What was the name of that place?'

The lieutenant told him it was called Katyn.

Chapter Seventeen

There is a short period of autumn in Moscow that is not a good time for neurotics.

Cold freezes the city at night, snow falls; in the morning, sunshine brings a thaw and the melted frost and snow condense into fog; sometimes this lingers all day, sometimes it is washed away by rain; at dusk the cycle begins again. This continues until one raw morning when there is no thaw, when the air crisps your nostrils, and you know that winter has finally arrived with its white baggage for a six-month stay.

During this transient time neuroses, fed by the indecision of the weather, sprout in sickly growth. The morning sunshine brings hope, the afternoon mists depression, the night despair.

Standing at the window of his study, watching clouds droop and settle over the towers and domes of the Kremlin, Stalin felt the morning's optimism seep away. Where was Viktor? The staff car had deposited him on the western outskirts of the city, then he had disappeared. He hadn't visited the Golovins, he hadn't called at any of his old haunts; he hadn't been near the Kremlin ...

The fog thickened and assumed monstrous shapes that dissolved when you stared at them. Pain throbbed in his left hand, the legacy of an ulcer, itself the manifestation of blood-poisoning that had nearly killed him during his under-nourished childhood. At least, he thought, he had something in common with Churchill, a suspect arm.

Puffing at his pipe, he paced up and down. He stopped in front of his desk and stared at three framed pictures – Keke his mother, Svetlana and Lenin engrossed in a copy of *Pravda*. But they would never be joined on his desk by Viktor: seeing a new picture there, his enemies would sense scandal and pick up its trail.

Also on the desk were some disturbing documents, reports from various sources that Hitler was contemplating an invasion of the Soviet Union.

Seeking distraction, Stalin scanned the documents. Two of them were from Soviet agents who had recently been discredited by transmitting information which had been proved to be false; others emanated from British sources who patently wanted to cause a rift between Germany and Russia. One report differed from the others: it was from an up-and-coming young British agent whose activities had been brought to his attention by Beria; his name was Philby, he had good contacts in Lisbon, capital of espionage, and he was quite positive that Hitler had no intention of attacking 'in the forseeable future'.

Stalin was under no illusions about Hitler's strategy. One day he intended to invade, but not until he had brought the whole of Europe outside the Soviet Union to heel, in particular Britain which he was currently demolishing with bombs. What Stalin planned to do was wait until Germany was fully extended, and perhaps a little bruised, and then launch his own attack; already he had established his launching pads by taking a slice of Poland, part of Finland and the Baltic States. Stalin envisaged hurling the Red Army against the *Wehrmacht* some time in 1942 – when it had been completely refurbished.

Within two or three years he would rule Europe from Moscow, Berlin, Paris and London; and the British and French would have no one to blame but themselves because they had given Hitler his head, distrusting the Bolsheviks more than the Nazis.

Meanwhile, through his Foreign Minister, Vyacheslav Molotov, he would continue to conduct meaningless negotiations with Hitler. Talks, for instance, about a four-power pact – Russia, Germany, Italy and Japan – which he would torpedo with impossible conditions.

But was it just possible that Hitler was going to launch a premature attack? He was crazy but surely he wasn't that crazy; he wasn't prepared for the Russian winter and it would defeat him just as surely as it had defeated Napoleon. But supposing he reached Moscow next year *before* winter set in?

Frowning, Stalin tossed the papers back on the desk. If only he had one source of information which he could really trust. What a hope when he was besieged by conspirators!

He turned back to the window. He could just see the silhouettes of his guards through the mist; he wished winter would set in, hard and implacable.

Condensation had formed on the window; with one finger he traced the head of a wolf; a drop of water slid from one fang to the bottom of the pane of glass, then the outline dissolved making a ghoul out of the wolf. He stared into the mist, into history, and there was Ivan the Terrible staring back at him.

Stalin poured himself a glass of red Georgian wine.

Where was Viktor?

He peered into the swirling mist. It parted for a moment and in the courtyard below he thought he saw … No, it was an illusion. He closed his eyes and opened them again and there, accompanied by Beria and two men in plain clothes, was his son looking up at the window.

Stalin's glass of wine crashed to the floor. He's come home, he thought.

*

They sat opposite each other across a feast.

And the conversation was as difficult as Hoffman had known

it would be because they were both absorbed with appraisal rather than small talk.

The first thing that had struck him about his father was how much smaller he was than he appeared to be in pictures. That and the expression lurking around those yellowish eyes, benevolent and yet wary.

Stalin was dressed in a grey jacket buttoned up to the neck and black trousers; he seemed to have some sort of infirmity in one arm and when this troubled him he pulled at his shaggy moustaches with his fingers; he ate greedily, drank copiously.

What, Hoffman wondered, do I look like to Stalin on close inspection? Do I come up to expectations? And why was I kept in a glass case for all those years?

Stalin smeared caviar on a slice of black bread and said: 'So what does it feel like to discover that you're the grandson of a cobbler and a washerwoman?' He tossed back a mouthful of vodka and stuffed the bread into his mouth.

Hoffman sipped his vodka. *You don't drink it like that*, he could hear Stalin thinking. He gulped it down and chewed a pickled gherkin, considering a reply to the semi-flippant question.

'I hadn't thought about it,' he said. 'What's important is that I'm the son of the leader of the Soviet Union.'

He had already answered inevitable questions. That he had known for years that he was Stalin's son; that he had overheard a conversation between his foster-parents; that his clandestine knowledge had been confirmed by the privileges he enjoyed.

Why hadn't he done anything about it then?

Surely if the *generalissimo* of Russia wanted the existence of an illegitimate son kept secret than the son would be ill-advised to confront him with it.

Hoffman had phrased these vital replies carefully. By all accounts an indiscreet remark could provoke a murderous rage.

And why had he left Russia?

Hoffman had already decided to tell the truth. Partly to labour the grief accompanying his departure, partly because Stalin probably knew anyway.

He had told Stalin about the mass execution he had witnessed; about his grief that his father could have authorised it.

He had waited for the storm to burst. Instead Stalin had almost pleaded with him. He had been young at the time, hadn't realised that the armed forces were undermined with traitors, that they had to be exterminated 'for the sake of Russia'.

The next inevitable question hung over the table in the sparsely-furnished dining room as they progressed from vodka and hors d'oeuvres to suckling pig and wine. The food, Stalin told him, had been chemically tested; until recently he had employed his own personal taster.

While he talked Hoffman examined his surroundings. It really was a drab seat of power. Apart from a sideboard there weren't any trappings in the room except, of course, for a portrait of Lenin. How many Russians realised that, just before his final stroke, Lenin had been poised to denounce Stalin at the 12th Party Congress? That Stalin had clawed his way to the top at the expense of Trotsky rather than the posthumous patronage of Lenin?

Stalin said abruptly: 'So, why did you return?'

Here it was. 'I couldn't stay away when I heard that my country was threatened,' he said, thinking how glib it sounded.

'Threatened?' Stalin took a swig of wine; when he replaced the glass on the table the benevolent expression had been switched off. 'By whom?'

Hoffman was surprised; he had assumed that Stalin had heard the reports that Hitler was planning to double-cross him. 'By Germany,' he said.

Stalin considered this. Then he said: 'I've heard the rumours. I don't pay much attention to them.'

So it was true: Stalin was blind to any threats which contradicted his own reasoning. He had signed the pact with Germany: if anyone suggested Hitler was going to break it they were implying criticism of him.

Hoffman said: 'The rumours are pretty strong in Lisbon.'

'Do you believe them?'

'I think it would be a mistake to ignore them.'

Stalin pulled at his moustache; head tilted, he stared at Hoffman; it was a long time, Hoffman assumed, since anyone had openly questioned his judgement.

He picked up a slice of suckling pig with his fingers. 'I haven't ignored them,' he said, bad, Georgian-accented Russian worsening, 'I have been considering them. I think they're basically propaganda inspired by the British. After all, the British must be bitterly aware that it was they who forced me to sign the pact with Germany.'

231

Hoffman looked at him questioningly.

'I sought an alliance between Britain, France and the Soviet Union but Chamberlain wasn't having any. Although I must admit,' he said, face full of cunning, 'that at the same time I did ask Merekalov, our ambassador in Berlin, to sound out that bird-brained idiot Ribbentrop about the possibility of a pact with Germany.' He popped the slice of pig into his mouth.

Hoffman drank some wine and said: 'But surely you don't trust Hitler?' *Or anyone for that matter.*

'Of course not. Dictionaries should be rewritten because of him. *Pact* – a fragile bridging gap built to be broken.' Stalin helped himself to some rice. 'Nor does he trust me. But it is to both our advantages to keep shaking hands.'

Hoffman got the impression that Stalin was enjoying confiding in his son so he gave him another cue: 'You have a ... master plan in mind?'

'I think it's fairly obvious,' Stalin said. 'Britain and France and, of course, the United States would like to see Russia and Germany exhaust each other. Hence these mischief-making rumours. Well, my idea is much the same except that I would like to see Britain and Germany exhaust each other – with help from the United States. And, make no mistake, the Americans will come in when their hand is forced by the Japanese. Then *we* will bring the Huns to heel. That's something we have to do; years ago Hitler was referring to the Ukraine and Siberia as part of Germany. Siberia!'

'Supposing,' Hoffman said slowly, 'that Hitler has anticipated such long-term plans. Supposing he has decided to pre-empt them?'

Stalin's eating and drinking slowed down. He rolled a piece of black bread into a pellet. He looked uncertain for the first time.

'He wouldn't be that stupid,' he said after a while.

'If he thought you weren't prepared for an invasion he might. Especially if he attacked in April or May, giving himself time to reach Moscow before our winter set in.'

'*Our*? So you're still a Russian, Viktor?'

'I was never anything else.'

Stalin blinked, eyes moist; Hoffman could scarcely believe it. Stalin said: 'You are right to warn me.' Humility. Astonishing! 'If only I had one single source of information in which I could believe.'

It was then that Hoffman began to guide the conversation towards what he had in mind.

*

Coffee and cognac. The smell of burning tallow from two white candles on the table and Jusuri tobacco smouldering in Stalin's pipe. Snow hovering outside the windows.

All these things made talk come more easily.

'In Lisbon,' said Hoffman who felt replete and just a little drunk, 'I have access to a lot of information.'

'Good information?'

'The best.'

'Red Cross?'

'To an extent.'

'And British?'

'That as well.'

'And German, of course.'

Hoffman realised that Stalin knew his movements; Cross had been right in making sure that he made contact with the *Abwehr*.

'Information comes from all sides in Lisbon,' Hoffman said. 'You have to be discerning. You have to decide which are genuine sources.'

'And you have decided that?'

Hoffman nodded.

Stalin pressed his thumb down on the glowing tobacco in his pipe; it didn't seem to hurt him. 'Tell me something,' he said, splashing cognac into his black coffee. 'Did you make these contacts with the Soviet Union in mind?'

Hoffman said honestly: 'Not at first.'

Ah, said Stalin, he could understand that. But patriotism, the call of Russia, the call, perhaps, of the blood ... had intervened.

Something like that, Hoffman said, and Stalin was satisfied, the tobacco in his pipe glowing brightly, throwing red light on his cheeks while outside the snow fell thicker.

'Gradually,' Hoffman elaborated, 'I began to realise that the facts I was gathering were vital. To Russia. To you.'

The burning tobacco glowed more brightly. Stalin leaned back in his chair, mellow but shrewd nonetheless.

'I always hoped,' Stalin said, 'that one day you and I ... father and son ... might form a partnership. You see, you have to trust someone in this world.' He sounded, Hoffman thought,

233

like an old man recognising God just in time. 'But when you are a leader it's difficult. Everyone has their own cause to promote. Politicians, statesmen, bureaucrats, soldiers ...'

Then, in barely comprehensible Russian, he came out with it: 'I've always wanted to believe one adviser I could trust. And all of a sudden here you are, my son.'

And all Hoffman could answer was: 'That's why I returned to Moscow, to offer my services to you.'

Stalin was silent for a moment; then he thrust his hand across the table and, as Hoffman shook it, said: 'You're my source, you tell me what's going to happen,' and despite everything he had seen and heard Hoffman was deeply moved.

*

Winter settled that night. In the morning Hoffman walked the streets in the centre of the city. Snow was falling heavily; snow-ploughs were out and the air rasped with the sound of *babushkas'* shovels on the pavements. As he strode along beside the Moskva the snow stopped falling for a moment and across the black wound of the river he glimpsed the towers of the Kremlin; the gilded cluster of masonry to which all threads of Soviet intrigue led.

He brushed snow from his eyes and thought: 'And I am the son of the architect of all that intrigue.' What would they say if they knew, the Muscovites around him, burrowing, heads down, through the vanguard of winter as though looking for nests in which to hibernate?

Before going to bed the previous night he and Stalin had discussed his identity. Obviously if he was to keep his Red Cross front he had to remain Josef Hoffman. (Cross would have to sort out the Gestapo.) One day perhaps ... Stalin had gazed fondly at him through the tobacco smoke billowing in the haloes of candlelight.

Of Hoffman's mother he had said very little. Only that she had been a student in Leningrad, that she had been beautiful. But he had told him about the oath he had sworn to her as she lay dying after childbirth. 'Now that you have come to me of your own free will I don't feel bound by it any longer,' he had said.

As the snow began to fall again, a blizzard of it, Hoffman recrossed a bridge over the river. When he reached the gate

234

leading to the Kremlin from Red Square his coat and new sealskin hat with its spaniel-like earflaps were pasted white.

Stalin was waiting for him in his study. His handshake was firm, his eye steady. On his desk was a tray bearing caviar and smoked salmon, bottles of Stolichnaya vodka and Narzan mineral water. Stalin was already drinking. Hoffman wasn't sure that he could face any more liquor; but he supposed it would please his father to see that, like him, his stomach was lined with asbestos.

As snow poured past the window they toasted trust.

Stalin beamed.

Then they discussed practical ways of communicating when Hoffman got back to Lisbon.

Which was when the Judas Code was born.

Chapter Eighteen

Seventy feet below Piccadilly, Churchill slept fitfully.

The cause of his interrupted slumber was twofold.

In the first place he didn't like this dungeon built before the war by the Railway Executive Committee in anticipation of bombing; but Mr. Josiah Wedgwood, M.P., had made such a noise in Parliament about his vulnerability during the Blitz that he had been forced to burrow beneath the West End until the shelter at the Annexe overlooking St. James's Park by Storey's Gate was made stronger. Lying there, feeling London's foundations shudder, he was acutely aware of the plight of the populace taking cover in Anderson shelters, in the new Morrison shelters – metal tables enclosed with steel mesh – in underground railway stations being converted into refuges. *London Can Take It* ran the slogan; soon, Chruchill feared, all the other big cities would have to take it as well. And with all the new weapons devised by Hitler's specialists in terror to keep Britain disciplined until the day (never to be) when Russia was conquered and an Anglo-German deal struck. The latest of these was fire-bombs – on October 15 nearly 500 German bombers had dropped something like 400 tons of high

235

explosives augmented by 70,000 incendiary bombs.

The second cause of his fitful sleep was the dearth of good news.

This, he brooded as he awoke at 3.10 a.m., was only equalled by the surfeit of bad news. In particular losses of British shipping inflicted by U-boats and the Dakar fiasco. The Free French attack on the West African port that had been repulsed by the Vichy French had resurrected the nightmare of Gallipoli, his nemesis in the last world war, because he had given the operation his approval.

He swung himself out of bed and prowled round his wretched subterranean quarters. On a chest of drawers beside the iron bed were his family photographs. His children Diana, Randolph, Sarah and Mary; and, of course, Clementine. It was at times like this when he needed Clemmie, but she was staying at Chartwell which they both preferred to Chequers, their official country residence.

Only she understood these moments of loneliness and, yes, despair. She was the only one allowed to: if the public got to hear about them they, too, would despair. What he must never forget was that he was the lion's roar of the people's will; that was the essence of his function; he wasn't a visionary or a strategist – he was an old predator led out from the back of the cage to snarl defiance through the bars.

Without the war he would have been remembered for … what? Recognition of the tank as a weapon in the last war? The change from coal to oil as a naval fuel? His warnings about the Nazi menace?

He doubted it. Gallipoli would be the submerged rock of any biographies. Around it would foam a few inconsequential waves – his youthful escapades, his novel *Savrola*, the ridiculous Sidney Street Siege, his paintings, his years in the political wilderness … an eccentric of little consequence in times of peace.

Warmonger? No, he wouldn't have that. Warmongers made war; this war has made me. And the ultimate irony is that victory will be my epitaph. Until then I am its snarl and the people must never hear me whimper. After Dunkirk he had gone on record as saying: 'Well, gentlemen, we are alone. For myself I find it extremely exhilarating.' Harrowing more like.

He drank a glass of water. (The public wouldn't approve

of that either.) The walls of his cell trembled. When, he wondered, had his mannerisms become part of himself rather than his image? He had been born truculent; the assumed flamboyance had come much later. Am I just an actor playing the part of Winston Leonard Spencer Churchill?

He picked up the photograph of his wife. Poor Clementine Hozier, what a life I've led you. But I do believe I've made you happy. And you are reality; the arms waiting in the wings as the ham actor comes off the stage.

Who else was there to confide in? A war cabinet of ministers, a detachment of generals, a consultancy of aides? He was close to none of them. His only confidants, he supposed, were Beaverbrook and Jan Smuts, the magnificent old South African who had fought Britain in the Boer War – when I escaped from captivity. And Bracken, of course, who had moved into No. 10 as his parliamanetary private secretary.

Glass of water in hand, Churchill rested his plump frame on the end of the bed. The truth was that he could not share his greatest fears with anyone. Not even Clemmie. Because they concerned the looming possibility of a defeat, no, débâcle, for which only he could be held responsible.

Quite simply, if Mussolini couldn't be persuaded to create a diversion and Hitler launched his invasion of Russia as early as May next year the Germans were quite capable of reaching Moscow before winter clamped down. Then, with the Red Army in frozen, blood-stained tatters outside its capital and Stalin seeking peace, the Führer would turn to England for that tacitly promised pact. If it wasn't forthcoming he would take Britain with one swipe of his panzers.

And by encouraging him I would be responsible for this last body blow to these islands of ours. The end of beleaguered valour, the end of our insular heritage, the end of reason.

How could he explain any of that to even Clemmie? Even if the grand deception still succeeded, he would be responsible for a holocaust. One day, perhaps, he could explain to her that he had tried to avert suffering on an even greater scale; that he had plotted to prevent two bloodthirsty warlords carving up great tracts of the world as they had carved up Poland. But it was impossible to explain such an awesome ploy before it was implemented; no woman in the world would understand such cold-blooded calculation.

Churchill lay back on the uncomfortable bed; he thought he could hear the all-clear above ground. Normally he would either have been up there watching the show from a rooftop or in a deep sleep.

Not tonight.

There was one person in whom he could confide – Sinclair, who had seemd too soft for his job until bereavement had made him pitiless in that deceptive, Anglo-Saxon way that so often baffled foreigners. With Sinclair he could discuss every aspect of the Grand Illusion – except his own fear. Sinclair wouldn't want to know about fear: Sinclair wanted revenge. In that respect Sinclair was the Man in the Street: he wanted the roar not the whimper.

With a sigh not far removed from a whimper Churchill pulled the sheet and blanket up to his chin. For a moment he felt like the new boy at Harrow who knew he must never display loneliness, and never did. And suddenly there was Nanny Everest regarding him sternly, she who had taught him war with lead soldiers in Ireland when his grandfather, the 7th Duke of Marlborough, had been Viceroy, and his parents, Lord Randolph Churchill and his American wife Jenny lived in The Little Lodge in Dublin.

What was Nanny Everest doing here? Those sapling years should surely have been laid to rest. (There had been 1,500 lead soldiers, an infantry division and a cavalry brigade.) But he had been able to talk to Nanny Everest, hardly ever to his brilliant father or vivacious mother. Doubtless the biographers would make something of that; to hell with them – he had been proud of his parents. But he wished they'd played toy soldiers with him.

He closed his eyes. He slept. He dreamed about Knickebein, code-word for the Luftwaffe's system of beam navigation (the British were now bending the radio beams, causing the German bombers to drop their loads off target); he dreamed about his negotiations with Roosevelt – fifty ageing American destroyers in exchange for leases on British bases in the Atlantic; he dreamed about the Italian army advancing towards Egypt; he dreamed about the defence of Malta. When he awoke again he discovered that all these momentous considerations had occupied eight minutes of his life.

His head ached. He considered his intake of liquor the

previous evening. No more than usual. Which wasn't to say it wasn't considerable.

He took a pinch of snuff to blow the headache away.

He slept again and this time he dreamed that German stormtroopers, all made of lead and commanded by Nanny Everest, were storming the gates of the Kremlin.

When he next awoke there on his breakfast tray was good news.

*

What was good news for Churchill was uncommonly bad news for Hitler.

He first heard about the intention of his Italian ally to attack Greece, on October 24.

He had no doubt about Mussolini's motive: jealousy at the glorious victories of the German war machine. When he had heard about the movements of *Wehrmacht* troops in Roumania he had obviously decided it was time Italy stole a little glory.

But Greece! There was only one argument for having the big-mouthed blacksmith's son as an ally and that was keeping the British occupied in the Mediterranean. A military campaign against the tough Greeks could be a disaster which would embroil Germany.

Hitler swore softly as he stared at the snow-covered countryside from the window of his special train taking him to Florence to try and stop his ally from taking on the Greeks. That was one of the troubles with leading a crusade: you encouraged second-rate comrades-in-arms to try and emulate you.

Two hours from Florence he learned that his trip was abortive, that at dawn that day Italian troops had invaded Greece from Albania which they had occupied in 1939.

When he alighted at the platform at Florence the cockahoop *Duce* greeted him with the words: 'Führer, we are on the march ...'

Hitler managed to remain cordial despite the fact that Mussolini might have embarked on an adventure that could have consequences far graver than he could possibly have anticipated: if his troops failed to take Greece swiftly, if the Balkans were set alight by his actions, if the Germans had to go to the Italians' aid, then Barbarossa might have to be postponed.

One month's delay could bring the *Wehrmacht* face to face with the Russian winter. He glanced out of the window of the train taking him north. It was snowing heavily. He shivered.

Part Five

Chapter Nineteen

The door looked innocuous enough. It was painted cream and was located on the fourth floor of the Avenida Palace Hotel in Lisbon. It might have been the door to a linen cupboard or, perhaps, a staff room.

It was neither. It was an exit to the railway station next door and was used by, among others, Antonio Salazar, when he wanted to leave the hotel secretly; that way, sightseers, journalists or more sinister observers could be left waiting on the pavement for hours before they realised that he was long gone.

What helped to make it so deceptive was its altitude. Who would have thought that you could walk off a fourth-floor landing straight into a railway station? But, of course, if the station was built on a hill - and what part of Lisbon isn't? - then it was quite rational.

The existence of the door was made known to Hoffman by Cross while they were sitting near the statue of Peter Pan in London's Kensington Gardens. Even in war-time there were a few nannies wheeling their charges around, but most of those abroad in the park were in uniform. The November day was raw, the silver barrage balloons which had been part of the summer skies suddenly incongruous, like rain-filled clouds that had failed to burst.

'First,' Cross had said as they sat on the park bench, 'we must get the Gestapo off your back. That shouldn't be too difficult.'

'And you,' Hoffman said brusquely, 'can change your attitude. You're aware of what's happened to me since you last saw me?'

Cross nodded.

'Then I'm entitled to a more intelligent approach. I'm not your pawn any more, Cross, I'm your king. Without me nothing. Right?'

Cross glanced at him quizzically. 'Whatever you say. You've done bloody well ...'

After the initial meetings with Stalin Hoffman had spent ten days in Moscow building solidly on the foundation of trust. Then he had sailed for London on a cargo ship from Archangel which, flying the neutral flag of the Soviet Union, was safe from attack by the British or Germans.

Hoffman said: 'It won't be difficult to get the Gestapo off my back? Come off it, Cross – to use an expression of yours – it will be bloody difficult. My skin, not yours.'

Cross, wearing a trench-style raincoat and shoes made of soft black leather – Portuguese probably – and a tan as incongruous as the barrage balloons, looked surprised. 'By God, you've changed,' he said.

'You should know, you changed me.'

'War—'

'—changes everyone.'

Cross shrugged. 'Whatever you say. *You* may have changed, nothing else has. The object of the exercise is still to make sure that Stalin believes Hitler is going to invade Russia before he launches his attack. You're his confidant now and we've got to make sure that you stay good and alive. So we've got to fix the Gestapo. You made their acquaintance, I gather, in Poland?'

'Oh yes,' Hoffman said, 'I did that all right.'

A Wren, black-haired and impudent in her sailor's cap, navy-blue uniform and black stockings, strolled past on the arm of an Australian soldier. Cross smiled at her; she ignored him; he was a civilian.

'One of the prices I have to pay,' Cross said. 'However I can get hold of silk stockings so I'm still in with a chance.' He lit a Three Castles cigarette. 'The point is that we have to get the *Abwehr* on our side.'

'We've already got them. Von Claus ...'

'We have to get them on our side to the extent that, in your case, they wield more power than the Gestapo. Thank Christ, despite Himmler and Heydrich, Canaris still has Hitler's ear. But not for much longer ...'

A rowing boat skimmed past them. The oars were wielded by a muscular young man in an Air Force blue shirt. Opposite him, looking cold but valiantly aware of the play of his muscles, was a blonde nurse. Hoffman envied them. At least the war had liberated love. He thought of Rachel Keyser. What a presumptuous liaison that had been. The clouds began to seep rain.

Hoffman turned up the collar of his black topcoat. 'What you're saying,' he suggested, 'is that we should give the *Abwehr* a coup so that Hitler calls off Himmler's thugs.'

'You're learning,' Cross remarked.

'Simple. We just tell them about some attack planned by the British. A few hundred lives lost. So what? My credibility has been restored.'

Three Spitfires streaked low across the leaking sky.

'You know something?' Cross said. 'Cynicism doesn't suit you. Leave that to me.' He flicked his cigarette end across the path. 'In fact we *have* come up with something in our cynical way.'

'*We?* Who's we? You and Churchill?'

Cross's feeling about Churchill once again surprised Hoffman. When he spoke there was a razor-edge of emotion in his voice. 'Leave any shabby manoeuvres to me. Anything that Churchill does is for the sake of Britain.'

'So it can't be shabby?'

Cross ignored him. 'And for the good of humanity. For peace.'

'On British terms,' Hoffman said. 'For Christ's sake, Cross, don't start trying to sell me Saint Winston. The man's a politician and a warrior. What a combination! He may well win the war but don't tell me he's not capable of pulling a shabby trick.'

Cross struggled to control himself. 'I happen to believe,' he said finally, 'that we are speaking about the greatest man this country has ever produced.'

Skirting the idolatry, Hoffman asked what secret he was going to convey to the *Abwehr*.

'The existence of a new installation on the south coast - near Littlehampton - equipped with beam-bending devices. You know, the Krauts think they're bombing Biggin Hill when in fact they're blowing up a few unfortunate cows in a field. They know we've got this equipment,' Cross said, 'but they don't know where we've got it.'

'And I'm going to tell them, just like that?'

'You,' Cross said, 'are going to tell them where there's a base made of plywood equipped with precisely fuck-all.'

Hoffman digested this, then said: 'But won't their agents over here blow the deception?'

'Almost all of their agents here have been turned. They'll

tell their masters what we want them to tell them. The Luftwaffe will smash the plywood base to smithereens and your rating with the *Abwehr* will go up a couple of notches.'

'But if we go on bending the beams,' Hoffman said, 'they'll smell a rat. Guess that they've bombed a dummy.'

'As it happens,' Cross said, 'they're about to produce a beam that we can't bend; not for the time being anyway. So it will all be academic. Hopefully the *Abwehr* will believe that we're not bending them because, thanks to you, they destroyed our equipment. Canaris will think you're the answer to a spymaster's prayers, call on Himmler and tell him to call off his gangsters. I would like,' Cross said, 'to be present when Bauer gets his instructions.'

An air-raid warden walked past. His arm was in a sling and he was still wearing a steel helmet. He stared at Cross and Hoffman with unseeing eyes.

The rain thickened, the rowing boats headed for the boathouse.

'But it's more than a question of merely saving your skin,' Cross said, taking his last cigarette from a silver case and lighting it with a Dunhill lighter.

'I know – I'm important. I've got to save Russia from the Nazi hordes.'

Cross appraised him. 'Don't you want to?' He blew grey smoke into the rain. 'Did anything happen over there that you haven't told me about?'

'Don't worry,' Hoffman told him, 'nothing's changed.'

'I hope not,' Cross said quietly. A raindrop hissed on his cigarette, extinguishing it. He tried to relight it without success. 'Shit,' he said and tossed it away. 'What I meant was,' he said, 'that it's not merely a question of preserving you to warn Stalin. You will be a double-bladed weapon.'

'The Germans?'

'Yes,' Cross agreed, 'the Germans. You'll be a veritable fount of misinformation.' Hoffman sensed that he had meant much more than that; had been close, or as close as he was ever likely to get, to an indiscretion. Hoffman couldn't imagine what it was. 'And that leaves the Red Cross,' Cross said, diverting the conversation. 'What are we going to do about them? You abandoned your post and since then they've had some disquieting questions asked about you. The last thing they want is their impartiality questioned.'

Hoffman said: 'You'll think of something.'

Fifty yards away a soldier pushed a WAAF against a tree and began to kiss her passionately. They didn't appear to mind the rain.

'Your parents in Czechoslovakia,' Cross said. 'You heard they were in trouble with the Germans. That they had been interrogated, that your father was injured, that he was dying ...'

None of this surprised Hoffman; nothing surprised him any more.

'... you flew to Prague using Red Cross documents. You're very sorry about that,' Cross said, prodding a finger at Hoffman. 'When you got there you found that they'd been taken to a camp in Poland. They're Jewish, of course ...'

'If you say so.'

'You traced them. Helped them to escape. But, apart from travelling on Red Cross papers to begin with, you at no time involved the Red Cross. You are truly penitent and, thank God, your boss in Lisbon is an understanding man. A Jew, I believe.'

'You mean I'll be forgiven?'

'You'll get a bollocking, but, yes, you'll be forgiven.'

'Someone must have a very persuasive tongue if all that's going to be accomplished.'

'Jan Masaryk,' Cross said, 'is an accomplished Czech diplomat even though he's in exile in London.'

Still unsurprised, Hoffman asked: 'So when do I go back to Lisbon?'

'Tomorrow night,' Cross said. 'The following day you have a rendezvous with von Claus – in the railway station. But you don't go directly to the station.'

Which was when Cross told Hoffman about the secret door in the Avenida Palace.

*

That night Cross took Hoffman to clubland.

First to the United Services Club for dinner, then to the underground haunts where the night people danced, drank and dined beneath the falling bombs.

The last club they visited wasn't one of the more distinguished establishments. Its entrance off Baker Street was a sandbagged basement door; admission was £1 each; this entitled you to buy whisky at 2s. a tot and dance to a sextet called The Boys in Blue.

The tiny dance-floor was packed, the men mostly in uniform, bodies barely moving as a blue-suited crooner with a ravaged face sang: 'Some day my happy arms will hold you ...'

Cross pushed his way to the bar, put down a 10s. note and ordered two whiskies. A girl with huge eyes and a powder-white face joined them and said in a Paulette Goddard voice: 'It's been a long time,' and, peering through the cigarette smoke, 'Where did you get that tan?'

'Hollywood,' Cross said. 'What are you having?'

'He knows.' She nodded at the elderly barman. 'Coloured water, what else? But it will cost you.'

Cross placed two half-crowns on the bar and said: 'Sophie, this is Josef. Josef, Sophie.'

Sophie examined Hoffman critically. 'And where,' she asked, 'did you get your pallor?'

'Siberia,' Hoffman said.

'Ha, ha,' she said. 'Joseph as in Stalin?'

'As in Goebbels.'

'My,' she said, 'you are a hoot. Does Tommy Handley know about you?'

Cross said casually, too casually: 'Why don't you two have a dance?' and Hoffman knew that once again he was being set up. For what he couldn't imagine.

She pulled him on to the floor. 'When all the things you are, are mine,' the crooner sang.

'Pale but interesting,' she said, touching his face. She looked up at him. 'Young but lived-in. But a lot of faces are like that these days, aren't they?' He looked down at her and she said: 'But for God's sake don't look at mine too closely.'

He searched for a gallant retort but it eluded him. He couldn't dance but it didn't matter, you just swayed with the bodies. The crooner changed his song. 'Who's taking you home tonight? ...' Beside them a girl dancing with a New Zealand Army lieutenant was crying.

'Who's taking you home tonight?' the girl named Sophie asked Hoffman.

Home? I haven't really got one, he thought. 'No one,' he said. 'I'm staying at the Regent Palace.'

'Why aren't you in unform?' she asked. 'Or is it top secret?'

'Because I'm a pacifist,' he said.

248

'A conchie?'

'Conscientious objector? Put it that way if you like.'

'Then you should be digging spuds.' Her dislike of such people reached him; but still she tried to be pleasant. 'But I suppose you have your ideals,' as though they were something you found on the sole of your shoe.

'If everyone had such ideals there wouldn't be any wars.'

'No,' she said, 'just tyranny.'

'There'll be blue-birds over the white cliffs of Dover,' the crooner sang.

Remembering her role again, she pressed herself close to him. He could feel her small breasts against his chest; her body felt as fragile as a bird's. He assumed she was for sale but couldn't understand how any man could become aroused by her; and was immediately aroused. It was a long time since he had made love to Rachel Keyser; he needed a woman; how ridiculous to remain faithful to a woman who had deceived you; especially in war-time. In war there might never be another opportunity. One bomb on this squalid little cellar ... The Boys in Blue swung into something livelier; in one corner a couple began to jitterbug, the girl's skirt flying high, revealing suspenders and pink panties. He wanted another drink. 'Let's go back to the bar,' he said.

But Cross had gone. 'Said he'd see you at your hotel tomorrow,' the barman said, 'and to tell you that all the drinks are on him and if that's all right with Mr. Cross then it's all right with me.'

Hoffman ordered another tepid whisky and soda and a glass of coloured water for the girl but she said: 'Do you mind if I have a Scotch?' so he changed the order and asked her why.

She sat on a stool, smoothing the skirt of her black dress. 'I don't know,' she said, examining a cheap ring sparkling on her finger. 'I suppose it's because the coloured muck is my professional drink. I don't feel professional at this moment.'

Not so long ago Josef Hoffman would have believed such a remark. No longer.

'You don't believe me, do you?'

'I neither believe nor disbelieve.'

'Sensible old you.'

'Cross put you up to this, didn't he?'

'The funny thing,' she said, 'is that it never occurred to him that you would rumble it. David doesn't know much about people.'

'You're wrong,' Hoffman said. 'Cross knows a lot about people. What he doesn't realize is that they change.' He tossed back the whisky and ordered another on Cross. 'Why?' he asked her.

'I don't know. You don't ask David things like that. Have you got a girl?'

Hoffman said: 'I did have.'

'Was she pretty?'

'Passable.'

'As passable as me?' Paulette Goddard had been abandoned; she was Sophie whatever-her-name-was now.

'You're pretty,' he said. Her shoulders were very white, bones delicate beneath them; the mascara around her big, questing eyes was smudged.

The Boys in Blue changed to a quickstep, a dance that didn't adapt to the small floor. Two men in khaki began to fight but the bouncers moved in effectively and Hoffman wondered why *they* weren't in uniform. It always surprised him how many super-fit athletes weren't fit enough for the Forces.

A Polish Air Force officer lurched up to Sophie and asked for a dance and looked astounded when, politely, she refused. 'I'll pay,' he said.

'Sorry,' said Paulette Goddard. 'I've got a date.'

The Pole looked even more astonished. 'Him?' pointing at Hoffman.

'Me,' Hoffman said.

The Pole said: 'But I said I'll pay.'

'Let's get out of here,' Sophie said to Hoffman. 'I know trouble when I see it.'

The Pole said: 'In the last war they used to give people like this white feathers.'

Hoffman could take the insult aimed at him – the Pole was drunk anyway – but what he couldn't take was the subsequent insult aimed at Sophie in Polish.

The Pole, becoming more theatrically surprised by the moment, said: 'I just don't understand it. She's a whore so why doesn't she want to do a bit of whoring?' looking incredulous as he lay on his back on the floor staring at Hoffman's bunched fist. He felt his jaw and said: 'You speak Polish?'

'Get up,' Hoffman answered in Polish.

The Pole got up swinging slurred punches.

Hoffman ducked and hit him in the solar plexus. The Pole grunted and swore in Polish and Hoffman thought how ridiculous it was to travel from Warsaw to London to fight a Pole.

His arms were pinioned from behind by two arms with concrete muscles; another bouncer got hold of the Pole. Sophie hurled herself at the bouncer holding Hoffman and hit him in the face with her handbag. He pushed her aside and she fell against the bar. The crooner was singing: 'In Room Five Hundred and Four ...'

The bouncer kicked Hoffman's legs from under him and began to drag him towards the door. The Pole, spitting blood, was also being pulled out. The dancers went on dancing.

He and the Pole were hauled up the stone steps leading to the street and left on the pavement. They sat up observed by two steel-helmeted special constables.

The Pole pointed at his uniform and said in Polish: 'You've ruined it.'

'Sorry,' Hoffman said, also in Polish, and one of the constables said: 'They sound like bleeding Jerries to me.'

Sophie ran up the steps and asked breathlessly: 'Are you all right?'

Hoffman said: 'I think we're both all right.'

The Pole stood up, stuck out a hand and said in English: 'I was not a gentleman. And I have lost my cap.'

'And I've lost my job,' Sophie said.

One of the constables said: 'So it's all patched up, is it? Pity they can't solve the war like that. What are you, then, Poles? Been doing a good job by all accounts, shooting Jerry down. But it's quiet tonight,' he said, a tinge of regret in his voice.

And it was. Together they absorbed the eerie quiet. It had stopped raining and the moon was shining through racing clouds. A cat arched its back and crossed the street.

'You can almost hear its footsteps,' Sophie said.

'The Germans have changed tactics,' the Pole said, wiping blood from his tunic. 'They're bombing your provincial cities now.'

'But they'll be back,' said one of the constables as though he couldn't wait for their return. 'Well, we'll be on our way. But don't fight each other, lads, keep your strength for Adolf.'

They walked off, footsteps crisp on the wet, moonlit pavement. The Pole saluted, said: 'My mistake,' and followed them, leaving Hoffman and the girl alone in the street of dignified, Georgian houses just beginning to go to seed.

'Well,' she said, 'you're a bit of an unknown quantity, aren't you? What did he say about me?'

'It doesn't matter.'

'That I was a tart? He wasn't far wrong, Josef; but I'm sure you know that. Still,' beginning to shiver, 'it's nice to be treated like a lady.'

He said: 'I'll get your coat.'

'I wouldn't go back in there if I were you.'

'I'll lob a grenade in,' he said and smiled suddenly so that she said: 'You looked quite different then. Younger. Pre-war.'

He rapped on the door and shouted: 'I want the lady's coat.' The door opened and a cheap coat trimmed with fur was thrown out followed by a gas-mask case. She put the coat on. 'A tart's coat,' she said. And then: 'I'm going home. I only live round the corner ... ' big eyes staring at him.

'I'll see you home.'

They walked past the blacked-out houses and turned into a similar street. A solitary searchlight switched the sky as though washing it.

She stopped outside a door with half a dozen bell buttons beside it and said shyly: 'Would you like to come in and have a cup of coffee?' and he thought: 'You're not a whore at all, not a real one.'

The room was nothing more than a bed-sitter; in one corner a flowered curtain had been strung round a kitchenette; a copy of *Picture Post* and a novel by A. J. Cronin, *The Citadel*, lay on a table beside the single bed.

She put a battered kettle on a gas-ring, took down a bottle of Camp coffee and a packet of powdered milk from a shelf. 'I'm afraid I've used up my sugar ration,' she said. 'I've got a sweet tooth.'

He sat down and lit a broken-toothed gas fire with a match.

She handed him a mug of watery coffee. 'Not very grand, is it?' she said, gesturing round the little room. 'Pitiful, really.' And, laughing; 'Do you know who I sound like? Eeyore, that's who.'

'Eeyore?'

She told him about Winnie the Pooh and when she had finished said: 'Do you want to go to bed with me, Josef?' She

252

sat on the edge of the bed. 'Go to bed ... British under-statement.'

He did, very much.

'Look the other way,' she said, which didn't sound very brazen. He heard the rustle of clothing, the creak of the bed. 'You can look now,' she said. She was sitting up in bed, arms crossed against her small breasts.

Thinking of Rachel Keyser's voluptuous figure, thinking that he didn't owe her any fidelity, Hoffman began to unbutton his shirt. Swinging one arm, he accidentally knocked a photograph of an old lady - presumably Sophie's mother - off the top of the wireless. Behind it was another photograph, a young man in Naval uniform with wavy, studio-bright hair.

Hoffman looked inquiringly at Sophie.

'My husband,' she said.

Hoffman stopped unbuttoning his sleeve. 'Where is he?'

'Tony? He's dead,' she said, luminous eyes still on him. 'A U-boat. In the Atlantic. We'd only been married three weeks,' and she began to cry.

He took off his shoes and switched out the light. He lay down beside her and put his arms round her and he let her cry until she slept and then he too slept.

*

In the morning she made more watery coffee while they listened to the news on the wireless. Coventry had been blitzed by the *Luftwaffe* - the explanation of London's quiet night.

'I'm sorry about last night,' she said switching off the wireless and sitting opposite him at the small table covered with blue oil-cloth.

'I'm not.'

'I always keep the photograph hidden ...'

'I'm clumsy.'

'I'd like to think,' she said, 'that under different circum-stances ...'

He touched her hand. 'The war.' He shrugged. 'The bloody war.'

She smiled at him. 'If it hadn't been for the bloody war I wouldn't have met you.'

'If it hadn't been for Cross.'

'David?' She lit a cigarette, coughed. 'He's a dangerous man. How did you get tangled up with him?'

253

'It doesn't matter. But tell me something. Why the set-up? Were you supposed to rob me, pick my brains ...?'

She inhaled and coughed again; she tapped her chest – 'Lungs, that's why I can't do more for the War Effort. But I do perform a function ... I don't know what David's job is but I've got a bloody good idea. I also know that the set-up as you call it was nothing to do with his job.'

Hoffman looked puzzled.

'That girl you were talking about. Cross fancied her, didn't he? And from what I can make out she fancied him – until you came along.' She smiled at him. 'You know, you really are a dark horse. A blond, dark horse. It's that look of suffering, until you smile ... Anyway, he wanted me to find out about your feelings about this girl. But that was only the half of it, of course. I know our David: he's a born blackmailer. He's one of the ones who finds his vocation in war. In peace-time he'd be a criminal. There's a lot around like that. Killers are the ones who really find they've got it made.'

'Blackmail? I don't understand.'

'Nothing grand. Nothing that Peter Lorre and Sidney Greenstreet would touch with a barge-pole. He just wanted to be able to prove to this girl, whoever she is, that you'd gone with a tart. But it doesn't really matter, does it? You said you *had* a girl. Past tense.'

Hoffman didn't reply. He went to the window. Through the anti-blast netting stuck to the windows he could see men and women hurrying to work. He couldn't believe that Cross could stoop to anything quite so petty.

'Don't believe me, do you? You'd be surprised how jealousy affects some tough guys. So take care, Josef – Cross jealous is doubly dangerous.'

He glanced at his watch and she said: 'I know, I know, you've got to go. But promise me one thing, Josef, don't ever think of me as that tart you picked up, not even a golden-hearted one,' trying to smile, 'because they don't exist, believe me.'

She opened the door leading from the shabby little room. 'Thank you for defending my honour last night.'

He hesitated. 'What will you do?'

'Who knows. Munitions maybe?' She kissed him and he thought how dry her lips were. 'Good luck, Josef, perhaps one day, under different circumstances ...' The door closed firmly.

Cross jealous? The notion cheered him up considerably as he walked briskly in the direction of the Regent Palace. It was like finding a flaw in a suit of armour.

That night he boarded a Lisbon-bound plane. He wrote to Sophie from Portugal but received no reply which wasn't surprising because, although he didn't know it, by that time there was nothing left of the terrace house where she had lived but a heap of rubble. As the special constable had predicted, the *Luftwaffe* had returned to London.

Chapter Twenty

The Gestapo re-established contact with Hoffman in the Praça dos Restauradores.

The agent, a thin-faced Austrian who also worked for the German news agency, D.N.B. (standing, according to the British, for Do Not Believe), took up the trail with extreme caution, being uncomfortably aware that several Gestapo operatives had already died after being assigned to Hoffman. The Austrian rather wished that he hadn't spotted Hoffman walking past the Palácio Foz; on the other hand if, as seemed likely, he was heading for the Avenida Palace, there might be someone there who would report his arrival to Bauer, i.e. his, the Austrian's failure; and it was not advisable to upset Bauer in his present ugly frame of mind.

As he had anticipated, Hoffman entered the Avenida. The agent parked his Citroën across the street. It was 1.18 p.m. Perhaps Hoffman was lunching at the hotel. Or visiting the Jewess. Whatever he was doing, the Austrian calculated that he wouldn't be longer than two and a half hours.

After three hours he was becoming worried, after four frantic. He left the Citroën and approached the hall porter, a Swiss named Riem. Yes, Riem remembered a man answering Hoffman's description enter the hotel; if he wasn't mistaken he had left half an hour later.

Impossible. The Austrian ran up the stairs to the first floor where a handsome, crinkly-haired young Portuguese named

Diamantino Fernandes da Silva ran the switchboard. There had been a call for Hoffman about three and a half hours ago which he had taken at reception. After that ... da Silva shrugged. Was there another exit from the hotel? Another shrug ... that was the business of the management. The Jewess's room number? Jewess? What Jewess? Desperately, the Austrian tried to remember the girl's name. Kaufman ... Koestler ... An author named Koestler, Arthur Koestler, sometimes visited the hotel, the switchboard operator obliged. Keyser, that was it. Her room number? Da Silva said he wasn't permitted to divulge numbers but he could try the room; he plugged in a lead. Together they waited. Finally da Silva said: 'There's no reply from Miss Keyser's room,' and looked pleased about it, damn him.

The Austrian searched the big, chandelier-hung dining room and the salon and the courtyard lined with potted plants and the bar where he had a large brandy. The barman, Domingos, hadn't seen anyone resembling Hoffman. The Austrian consulted his pocket watch. He had been out of contact with Hoffman for nearly five hours. By now another of Bauer's men might have picked him up.

He telephoned the Legation from a call-box outside the hotel.

Bauer was brusque, cutting short the Austrian's timetable of surveillance. 'What you're trying to tell me is you've lost him?'

'He might still be in the hotel.'

'Only if he's taken up residence.' Bauer's voice was a stiletto. 'You realise that Reichsführer Himmler is personally interested in this case?'

The Austrian said he did.

'You can imagine his reaction.'

He could.

'If you haven't found him within an hour I shall have to report your failure to Prinz Albrechtstrasse. You appreciate ...'

He did.

'... There's a plane to Berlin tonight.'

'I haven't the slightest doubt—'

'—Find him!'

The stiletto plunged deep into the Austrian's brain, twisting.

*

In fact Hoffman had spent less than five minutes in the hotel.

256

The porter had been mistaken about him leaving by the main entrance; there had been a phone call – from the Red Cross – which he had taken just before leaving.

From reception he had taken the stairs to the fourth floor and, using the key that Cross had given him, gone through the cream door, emerging in the railway station.

The station wasn't large – only ten platforms – but it was busy enough. One train was just departing, billowing steam that collected under the glass roof, and one had just arrived; the footsteps of the arrivals were sharp on the marble floor, those of friends and relatives who had just said goodbye softer and slower. Through the entrance to the station Hoffman could see sand-coloured buildings and a couple of palm trees.

Von Claus said: 'Restless places stations, aren't they? Sad and exciting.' He took Hoffman's arm. 'Let's sit over there,' pointing at a seat beside a silver-painted pillar.

'So,' he said, 'I gather you're a lucky young man still to be alive.' He was wearing a grey fedora and a black coat cut to minimise the hump on his back; he looked extremely dapper.

Hoffman said: 'You know what I think? I think I should have gone to the Gestapo in the first place. Your people don't seem to have any control over them.'

'We are an intelligence service,' von Claus said, 'not a bunch of bully boys. Which doesn't mean to say we can't be tough … You should have told me you were going to Russia. You were a gifthorse to the Gestapo – Czech consorting with a Jewess, pulling the wool over the eyes of the *Abwehr* and suddenly rushing off to consort with the Bolsheviks.' He paused. 'Why did you go to Russia, Herr Hoffman?'

Hoffman had discussed the answer to this question with Cross. As it stood, the Gestapo had one explanation, the Red Cross another. Cross had decided to let them both stand. To give the *Abwehr* the same story Hoffman had given to the Gestapo (assuming that Adler had lived to repeat it) – he had been heading for Russian-occupied Poland to negotiate the transfer of Poles trapped there. And to persuade the Red Cross in Lisbon, already sympathetic to Hoffman and his fictitious Jewish parents in Poland, to corroborate the story. Hoffman told it to von Claus.

Von Claus wet his lips as though tasting the story. 'But why were you so special, Herr Hoffman? Why did the Red Cross send you halfway across Europe to negotiate the transfer of a few Poles?'

'Not a few. Thousands. And there aren't many employees of the Red Cross who speak all the languages needed. German, Polish, Russian.'

'And were the Poles in the Russian sector really so anxious to return to the Germans, to the SS?'

'To return home, yes.'

'That's very complimentary to the Germans.'

'Not really,' Hoffman said, remembering the place named Katyn, 'they were the lesser of two evils.'

A family of refugees ran past them towards a train that was about to depart. They had probably abandoned hope of leaving Lisbon and were going to settle in the country; they ran as if they were pursued; perhaps they were.

Von Claus said: 'But why Moscow, Herr Hoffman?'

'A precaution. The Red Cross thought I would probably have to go there to complete the negotiations. A necessary precaution as it happened.'

'And these poor Poles, have they been repatriated?'

'We've done everything we can; it's up to the Russians now. They have promised ...'

Von Claus grunted his view of Soviet promises. 'I should have thought,' he said in his precise voice, 'that there were far more worthy causes. However I accept your story – for the time being. Now perhaps we can put your Russian odyssey to some better use. What do the Russians think of Germany?'

'They're not happy with the German incursions into Finland and Roumania, if that's what you mean.'

'I think Molotov made that perfectly clear in Berlin,' von Claus said. He smiled. 'With a little help from Churchill. I believe he laid on an air-raid so that Ribbentrop and Molotov had to take to the shelter during their discussions. When Ribbentrop assured Molotov that Britain was finished Molotov said: "If that is so, why are we in this shelter and whose are those bombs which fall?" ' Von Claus shrugged. 'So the story goes. What I really meant was: do they think the pact will hold?'

'Between Germany and Russia? They think it will hold, yes. Not for ever. For another couple of years perhaps.'

'Your sources are good?'

'Modest, but reliable.' If you only knew, Hoffman thought.

Von Claus seemed to accept what he had said; it probably concurred with his own intelligence from Moscow. 'And what about England?' he asked. 'You really do get around, don't you.'

The refugees had just made the moving train but, as he swung himself into a compartment, a little boy dropped a suitcase on the platform. A whistle blew. The train stopped. The boy retrieved the suitcase, the train set off again. The incident gave Hoffman as much pleasure as the knowledge that Cross was jealous and therefore vulnerable had given him.

He told von Claus: 'I have good information from England but it will cost you.'

'Allow me to evaluate it,' von Claus said.

'Five hundred American dollars – in dollars, they buy more.'

'Nothing you can tell me is worth five hundred American dollars.'

'If I told you how the Luftwaffe can stop dropping bombs on fields instead of cities?'

Von Claus looked at him quizzically. 'I presume you're referring to the British method of bending radio beams to divert bombers from their targets?'

'If I told you where it was being done would that be worth 500 dollars?'

Von Claus tried to straighten his body; his back seemed to be paining him. 'It might,' he said eventually. 'But I'd have to have proof before paying out.'

'Two-fifty now, two-fifty when I've proved it.'

'Mercenary, aren't we.' He tapped his pockets with thin fingers. 'I haven't got 250 US dollars with me.'

'In one hour's time,' Hoffman said. 'I'll wait here.'

Von Claus considered the proposition, then said: 'Very well, but if the information is false I'll hand you over to Bauer.'

When he had gone Hoffman strolled around the station. He enjoyed the atmosphere even if it did smell slightly of fish. He bought himself a coffee and a copy of *Diario de Lisboa*. Birmingham had been bombed, so the beam-benders hadn't been of much use that night.

Von Claus returned one hour later with the money inside a copy of *Signal*. Hoffman told him where the plywood installation was on the south coast of England.

Von Claus made a note and said: 'I suppose this isn't an elaborate ploy to save your skin from Himmler's assassins?' He thought about his own words. 'But why then should your skin be so important to the British?' He frowned.

'The question,' Hoffman reassured him, 'doesn't arise because there isn't any ploy.'

'But it does seem odd that a Red Cross official should be privy to such secrets as this,' tapping his coat pocket containing the location of the dummy base.

'You forget that people trust the Red Cross with their secrets. They're not even aware that they're letting them out of the bag.'

'I suppose so.' Von Claus didn't seem wholly convinced. 'Careless Talk Costs Lives. I believe they have posters to that effect in Britain.'

'But people don't take too much notice,' Hoffman said.

Von Claus stood up. 'Just out of interest,' he said, 'what are you going to do with all that money?'

'Count it,' Hoffman said.

*

The hour was almost up. Two more minutes before he was due to telephone Bauer. Hoffman almost certainly wasn't in the hotel and he wasn't in his lodgings because the landlady hadn't been lying – the thin-faced Austrian was adept at picking up the ring of truth.

Fearfully he made his way to the callbox in the Largo do Carmo. He had no doubt what fate awaited him in Berlin; the question was whether to make a break for it before he reached Sintra airport.

One more minute.

No sign of Hoffman.

He dialled the Legation number.

Bauer said: 'Where is he?'

The thin-faced Austrian said: 'He's just rounded the corner of the Largo do Carmo and is heading towards his lodgings.' And so joyful was he that he essayed a little joke: 'And do you know something? He's really on our side – he's carrying a copy of *Signal*.'

*

On November 22, 1940, the day the Greeks inflicted a shattering defeat on the Italians at Koritsa, a German reconnaissance aircraft was spotted high over the south coast of Britain.

260

Two days later three Ju 88 bombers escorted by Messerschmitt 109 fighters dropped 15,000 pounds of bombs on and around a camouflaged installation two miles inland from the seaside resort of Littlehampton. The installation was destroyed and for weeks afterwards householders in the area were able to supplement their allocations of coal with pieces of shattered plywood.

In the New Year, transmitting information gathered by Britain's Ultra cryptanalysts, Hoffman was able to convince Stalin that, through contacts in Lisbon, he had penetrated the inner sanctums of the Reich Chancellery. Using the Judas Code, he anticipated among other things the despatch of Luftwaffe aircraft to Italy and the appointment of a new German Army commander in North Africa. The commander's name was Erwin Rommel.

Chapter Twenty-one

'But why *Judas* Code?' Rachel Keyser asked.

About time, Hoffman thought. It was now February and he had been waiting for three months for her to start probing for details of his method of communicating with Stalin.

'Why not?'

He tapped out Victory V – three dots and a dash – on the transmitter on which, under Rachel's supervision, he was practising morse in the apartment she had acquired overlooking the Parque Eduardo VII. Rain sweeping across the deserted park and spattering against the window added its own tattoo to the morse.

'I don't know. It's just that it sounds so Biblical.'

'Judas ... treachery ... we're in a treacherous business, you and I.'

'That's not the whole reason, is it?'

So she could impale the small untruths he uttered; even though there was no longer any physical love between them there was still understanding; and humour, probably, if it was given a chance. What if she perceived the greater untruths that he might have to perpetrate?

She got up from the window-seat and wandered around the small apartment. It was old and, despite the new paint, a little musty; she hadn't tried to rejuvenate it; instead she had installed green plants, a couple of mottled mirrors and a chaise-longue with moss-coloured scatter cushions. 'Never fight age,' she had said, 'just adapt.'

But here we are, he thought, not even bothering with youth.

'Would you like some tea?'

He shook his head, varying his touch with the transmitter as she had taught him so that he couldn't be identified by experts. 'Your touch can be as distinctive as a pianist's,' she had told him.

Why had she left it so long to sound him out? He was still being used – he had no illusions about that – and he would have thought she would have made it her business to discover how he spoke to Stalin in case anything went wrong.

Once, of course, she would have found out in bed. But that was before Sintra. Before she had revealed that the whole beautiful romance had been engineered.

She went into the kitchen and, beneath a ceiling hung with dried herbs, made tea. Her voice issued through the serving hatch: 'You say we're engaged in treachery; I don't agree. If we're betraying anyone it's the enemy.'

And ourselves?

He abandoned the transmitter and sat on the cushion she had vacated. A lone man and his dog walked through the patterns of midget hedges sweeping down to the statue of the Marques de Pombal, their figures distorted by the raindrops on the window.

Day after day Hoffman had been confined to this room with her, learning his new craft, what they euphemistically called communications. And they had barely touched hands. It was ridiculous, naive, unnatural; it was also a strength.

Supposing she wasn't still deceiving him?

'So why Judas?' she asked again. Cup and saucer rattled; he smelled tea above the aroma of the herbs. 'There's no secret about it, is there?'

Oh yes, there was a secret. Such a secret! And only two people knew it: Stalin and himself. It was the twist, the ultimate safeguard. Perhaps he should leak a little of it to her, assuage her with everything except the ultimate irony.

When he didn't reply she said, more loudly (perhaps Cross

had been getting at her): 'I mean we're supposed to be in this together. And I have taught you everything you know ...'

True. He could encode and decode with the best of them. He could use a one-time pad – transmit a code that was virtually unbreakable. Relatively simple when you knew how: you just used a page from a pad containing a sequence of, say, five-digit numbers representing the letters of the alphabet and added a previously-arranged number of the alphabet – 27, perhaps, for A descending to plain 2 for Z. As the original numbers had no pattern the result was well-nigh indecipherable to a code-breaker. After each message had been sent and received you destroyed that leaf of the pad and there on the next page was another virgin sequence of random figures available only to you and the recipient of the message. She had even told him about the Voynich Manuscript, an apparently coded volume 204 pages long that, since its discovery in Italy in 1912 by an American, William Voynich, had defied analysis.

Yes, she had taught him a lot. Love and deception included.

As for his method of communication with the Kremlin, well, she wouldn't be all that impressed. It was one of the oldest known methods of sending coded information: all you needed was the key. But until you had that key it could give you migraine.

The key was a book. They had agreed that in the Kremlin, he and Stalin. The Bible was the first book that Hoffman had thought of – it had been his benefactor once before! – but he had rejected it because it would probably occur immediately to a cryptanalyst and because he didn't think Stalin would appreciate it.

They had agreed upon *War and Peace*. It was singularly appropriate. And from a specialist at the NKVD's Moscow Centre he had learned how to tally numbers with letters and to vary references to confuse hostile cipher experts if the key was discovered.

If it was discovered. It was quite probable that it already had been, all 1,315 pages of it – hidden with the transmitter he used to contact Moscow in the room he had rented in the Alfama. Without a doubt he was under surveillance; perhaps, even as she made the tea, Rachel knew about *War and Peace*.

But when the time came he could change the key. And she didn't know the ultimate secret of the Judas Code ...

The dog jumped over one of the dwarf hedges; it seemed to

be enjoying the rain which was more than its owner was; but he was enjoying the dog.

Cup and saucer in hand, Rachel came back into the room, dressed in a navy costume, black hair longer than when they had first met; a couple of spider-web creases at the corners of her eyes that hadn't been there in those days.

She sat opposite him, sipping her tea. 'The Bible?'

'Judas? No. It's a personal thing. Stalin doesn't even know I've called it that.'

'It's not your code-name?'

He shook his head. His code-name was Dove. But why make Cross's job easier? Then again why should Cross and Rachel want to deceive him? But they had done so once before …

'I wouldn't mind betting,' she said, nibbling a chocolate biscuit, 'that because you're a man of peace you've chosen a code-name like Dove. Something like that.'

'*Was* a man of peace,' he said. 'You can call me Judas. You and Cross. And Churchill.'

'You didn't tell me everything that happened in Poland, did you?'

'I told Cross. That was enough, wasn't it?'

A clock on the mantelpeice chimed; the day felt like a Sunday but it was Wednesday.

She said sadly: 'We should have told you everything right from the beginning. Cross will pick his own pockets one of these days. Double-Cross, very funny, very true …'

But does he still make love to you? He hadn't displayed any symptoms of jealousy. He wouldn't, would he, when he was a satisfied lover?

She said: 'Cross told me all about that girl in London.'

'She was a poor little thing.'

'I'll bet.'

If he hadn't known her better he could have sworn that there was a hint of jealousy in her voice.

'You were so different,' she said, 'when you came back.'

'I hadn't killed anyone before I went away.'

'Not just tougher,' she said. 'More … insular …'

'Secretive?'

'Self-contained. Living within yourself. And older,' she added.

'Then I've just got to adapt, haven't I,' he said.

264

... *Just got to adapt,* he tapped out, returning to the transmitter.

'All right,' she said, voice brisk again, 'now the second part of the lesson. Transmitting *and* receiving. I'm going over to the Embassy. Wait here, I'll start transmitting in fifteen minutes.'

From the window he watched her cross the street five storeys below. The dog had disappeared and the man was standing in the rain looking for it as though he had lost a partner.

*

'Are you receiving me?'

'Loud and clear,' he tapped back.

'Anything to report?'

'I had a visitor this afternoon.'

'Friend or bandit?'

'I wish I knew.'

'Not bad. You could speed it up a bit.'

He speeded it up. 'I recognise your touch. Vary your touch – like you taught me to.'

'Are you taking down the messages?'

'Of course. Object of exercise.'

'Try this.' Tap, tap, tap ...

He looked at what he had written.

He replied: 'Please repeat message.'

A pause. 'Is it so terrible?'

'Please repeat.'

'I ... LOVE ... YOU.'

'Report back to base,' he tapped out.

It was the fastest response he had ever transmitted.

*

So the cliché was true. First contact, after a long long time, *was* like electricity.

No, she had said when she had returned, no preliminaries; and they had taken off their clothes and laid on the bed in her small, blue-papered bedroom and the electricity had darted between them, melded them; and she had pulled him down on to her, into her.

Then because he was still inside her and, for the moment at least, he was hers, and because she had begun to lose hope, and because he was so thin and proud, she had wanted to weep; but instead she had smiled at him and said: 'There.'

'I had forgotten,' he said.

'I hadn't forgotten. I had begun to despair. But it will be all right now,' she said, wanting him to say: 'Yes,' because that was something even if she knew it wasn't true because of what she had to do. But in war all that mattered was now.

'Yes,' he said, 'it will be all right now.'

But the wariness was still there.

'I don't want it ever to happen again,' she said. 'That terrible thing that came between us.'

'Don't worry,' he said. He raised himself on one elbow, stroked her hair, her breasts. 'Don't worry.'

'I should have told you ...'

'It wasn't your fault.' He kissed her breasts. 'But now ... You wouldn't deceive me again, would you?'

'If I was going to deceive you I would still say no so my answer can't bring you any satisfaction.'

She noticed that it had stopped raining and the raindrops on the window were sparkling in pale sunshine.

'That's a very complicated answer,' he said without surprise. 'Just say no – if that's your answer.'

'What I want to say is even more complicated. I want to say that you must trust me whatever happens. I want to say that, because of this terrible bloody war, a person's actions may be misunderstood. I want to say that no I won't deceive you but if circumstances change ...'

'Then you will?'

'I won't.' What else could she say? If she told him the truth she would lose him. What if she told him that she had refused to bargain for his life when he was in Poland?

He lay back on the blue-and-white coverlet and when he spoke the wariness was still there.

'Aren't you going to ask me about the Judas Code again?'

'To hell with the Judas Code. Will you take me out to dinner?'

'You were very interested in it just now.'

'Just its name, that's all. It sounds very ... ominous. Or shall I take you to dinner?'

'I'll take you. The Germans are paying anyway. But shouldn't you know more details?'

She ran her hand down his body; it was thin but it was muscular, too. Muscles sheathing the sides of his ribs moved

266

when he shifted his arms. She rested her hand in the blond, curly hair at his crotch.

'Why should I? You send the messages.'

'Supposing something happened to me?'

We made a mistake there, she thought; at least Cross did. I should have got the details as soon as he got back; now his suspicion has germinated. If I'm not careful he will realise that we know about the room in the Alfama, about *War and Peace*, about the elementary method of encoding he was employing, about the transmitter. And he will know that even now I am deceiving him.

She kissed him and said: 'You're right, of course.'

'But only if something happened to me.'

'I don't understand.'

'I've left the details of the Judas Code in a sealed envelope with a lawyer named Eduardo Alves who has an office on the Avenida da Liberdade. He has instructions to deliver it to you in the event of my death.'

'You don't really trust me, do you?'

'I want to,' he said.

He turned and kissed her eyes, mouth, breasts; the electricity was regenerated; she moved above him and sank on to him; and this time they were lost together for much, much longer.

And it wasn't until they were eating lobster and drinking white wine in a little restaurant in the Alfama that she again thought about his code. It was so basic. Could there be more to it than was apparent?

Why Judas?

*

Rachel Keyser had another presentiment of danger later that night.

When she got back to her apartment Cross was there; the gramophone was playing and he was looking for hidden microphones.

'It seems to be clean,' he said after a while. 'But just in case ...' He turned up the volume of the gramophone. Bing Crosby singing 'Pennies from Heaven'.

'Do you have to come as late as this?' She sat in an armchair and crossed her legs; she was tired and all she wanted was to lie down and re-live the evening.

267

'Why, are you expecting lover-boy?' He pointed through the open bedroom door at the rumpled coverlet. 'Is he insatiable?'

She realised for the first time that Cross was jealous. There could be nothing more perilous to a delicate espionage operation than a jealous partner.

She said: 'It's what you wanted, isn't it?'

'It's obviously what you wanted.' He had been drinking but he wasn't drunk. 'What made him succumb again after all these months?'

Love, she wanted to say, but 'My natural charms' were the words which emerged. 'What do you want?'

'Have you got a drink?'

'One,' she said, 'then out. The whisky's in the kitchen.'

When he returned he had a glass of whisky in one hand and a photograph of a document in the other.

'Do you know what this is?' waving the photograph.

How could she possibly know?

'It's Directive 21, the brainchild of Adolf Hitler, dated December 18, 1940. It's called Barbarossa and it's the blueprint for the invasion of Russia.'

'When?' interest revived.

'May 15. But thanks to Mussolini he will probably have to postpone it for a few weeks. Listen to this.' He read from the foot of the photograph. *The German armed forces must be prepared, even before the conclusion of the war against England, to crush Soviet Russia in a rapid campaign.* Dynamite, eh?'

'But not if it falls into Stalin's hands. It would finish everything we've been working for. Two great armies facing each other? Stalemate. Worse, another alliance with Germany *and* Russia lined up against us.'

'Don't worry,' Cross said, 'I got this from an exclusive source. He assured me there aren't any other copies flying around and I believe him.' He gulped his whisky, went into the kitchen and refilled his glass and she thought: 'Bastard, you know I'm not going to throw you out until you've told me what this is all about.'

'So what we have to do,' Cross said, chinking ice in his glass, 'is make sure that lover-boy feeds Stalin enough information about the German Army's movements to maintain his credibility. The information must be good but it mustn't alarm Uncle Joe too much. The actual figures,' he said, 'are staggering.'

'Stagger me,' she said.

268

'Apparently Hitler intends to move 3,400,000 men, 600,000 horses and 600,000 vehicles up to a line stretching from the Baltic in the north to the Black Sea in the south.'

'You've staggered me,' she said.

'But what matters is the present deployment. As far as we know he's so far managed to move twenty-five divisions into position.' Cross took a typewritten sheet of paper from his pocket. 'This is what I want lover-boy to transmit.'

Rachel took the sheet of paper and read: *'Understand considerable German troop movements in easterly direction. These easily explained by Nazi concern with Bulgaria, Roumania, Hungary and Yugoslavia and her designs on Greece.'*

Cross said: 'That should allay Uncle Joe's fears for a while.' He finished his whisky. 'You don't really give a damn for lover-boy, do you?'

His jealousy surprised her: it was the last emotion she had associated with him. She had known him for so long; it was he who had awoken her; perhaps she had been so absorbed with that awakening and the subsequent pleasures that he had brought her that she had never noticed other characteristics.

She wished Hoffman had been the first, the only one. No, that was ridiculous, schoolgirl talk.

'Well, do you?'

'Yes,' she said, quietly, 'I do.'

'You stupid bitch. You could jeopardise the whole thing, letting your emotions take over like that.'

'Don't worry,' she said, 'I won't do that, I promise.' It was all so hopeless.

'Is he good?'

'Good?' She frowned.

'In bed.'

'It's none of your business. Now for God's sake get out.' She stood up. 'You've had too much to drink ...'

'I should think he's very good. Since he met you, that is, because you must be a very good tutor. It's important to have a good tutor. You did. That little tart in London must have had a pleasant surprise with lover-boy.'

He grabbed her jacket. Silver buttons flew across the room. Then her blouse. The silk ripped easily but, oddly, what she feared most was the thought of him kissing her. The prospect made her feel sick.

He said thickly: 'Come on, you bitch, don't pretend you don't like it rough,' which was when she hit him with the back of her hand, hard across the face, the amethyst ring on her finger drawing blood.

She backed towards the serving hatch and picked up a kitchen knife. 'Touch me again,' she said, 'and you get this.' She felt quite calm.

He touched his cheek. The sight of blood on his fingers seemed to surprise him. He took a handkerchief from his pocket to stanch it.

He managed a smile. 'God help the Arabs if you ever get to Palestine,' he said. He opened the door and walked into the corridor.

*

At the same time that Cross was leaving Rachel Keyser's apartment his 'exclusive source' was lying in bed elsewhere in the city torturing himself with doubt.

Had he done the right thing by handing over details of Barbarossa?

Although the window was closed he could hear the plaintive notes of the *fado*; that didn't help. He shivered and with his feet searched for the hot-water bottle, but it was almost cold. Switching on the bedside lamp, Admiral Canaris got out of bed and fetched another blanket from a cupboard.

That wouldn't make much difference; if you were born cold there wasn't much you could do about it; and doubt and fear brought their own special, inner cold.

He put on his thick grey dressing-gown, sat on the edge of the bed and from his briefcase took his own copy of Hitler's Directive No. 21. The British would almost certainly pass details on to Stalin. What if the Red Army made a pre-emptive strike and smashed its way through Eastern Europe?

Canaris ran his hand through his grey hair and studied the details of the Führer's precocious brainchild. He intended to marshal three great armies. The Southern group would plunge across the Ukraine to Kiev; the Northern would strike from East Prussia towards Leningrad. But the main attack would be launched by the Central Group towards Smolensk and Minsk with the object of cutting off vast portions of the Red Army.

In addition Hitler intended to send a detachment from Finland to take Murmansk, the all-season Arctic port.

270

Some German generals were against the whole concept. Notably Guderian, King of the Panzers. Others, such as von Brauchitsch, Paulus and Halder, disagreed about strategy after the initial attack: Hitler wanted to mop up industrial and agricultural areas and the Baltic States before taking Moscow: the three generals wanted to seize the Soviet capital as soon as possible and deprive the Russians of their communications and administrative centre.

Canaris had no doubt whose view would prevail. Although they were often appalled by his unconventional strategies – disgusted (like Canaris) by his Aryan policies – the generals couldn't deny Hitler's flair, his predatory instincts.

No, Hitler would brook no argument. He was convinced his armies would reach a line east of Moscow stretching from Archangel in the north to the Caspian Sea in the south by October 15. Five months in which to smash the resistance of the biggest country in the world.

Not if I have my way, Canaris thought, putting the directive back in his briefcase and climbing back under the blankets, because Barbarossa is the ultimate act of madness. A war fought on two fronts (if the British broke their word) and a campaign that could freeze the *Wehrmacht* to death in the Russian winter.

He switched off the light.

Am I really a traitor? he wondered. All I want to do is save German lives, hundreds of thousands of them. But, armed with Directive 21, would Stalin strike first?

I wouldn't if I were him, Canaris comforted himself. Not with my army catastrophically purged, not with my obsolete guns and prehistoric aircraft. Not if my Army couldn't even thrash the Finns convincingly. No, I would merely move my divisions up to the border to show the Führer that I was ready for him.

Not even Hitler would then risk a drawn-out engagement with the endless ranks of Soviet troops – Stalin had no shortage of available bodies. Another pact would be sealed and the two warlords would start exchanging birthday greetings once again.

Of course that's what would happen. Saviour not traitor.

And what would happen if anyone discovered that he had handed over Directive 21 to a British agent? Simple: he would be liquidated.

The fresh blanket had, if anything, made him colder.

Chapter Twenty-two

The Grand Deception, Churchill thought, pressing a brick into its bed of cement, was reaching its climax.

By mid-summer he would know if he had succeeded in tricking the two arch enemies of democracy into a wasting war.

And success or failure would be determined this month, March.

'This is the vital month,' he said to Brendan Bracken who was watching him build a garden wall at Chartwell.

'In what respect, Winston?'

It was always refreshing to hear Bracken asking a question because he was usually occupied in spouting facts. But there was one subject about which he knew nothing: Judas and his mission. Nor did Churchill's deputy, Clement Attlee, nor did Eden, nor did Beaverbrook, nor did Clemmie.

He answered Bracken in general terms. 'This is the month when Hitler will have to decide whether he's going to get Mussolini off the Grecian hook. If he does he will have to postpone Barbarossa – and that could bring him face to face with the Russian winter.' With his trowel Churchill removed a wad of cement squeezed from under the brick.

'And we both know the deciding factor in that context,' said Bracken, getting into his stride. 'Germany, or Austria if you prefer it, is separated from Greece by four countries – Hungary, Roumania, Bulgaria and Yugoslavia. The first three have all succumbed: Yugoslavia is still holding out. To march on Greece, Hitler needs Yugoslavia's co-operation ...'

Churchill handed Bracken the trowel. 'Here, let's see if you know everything there is to know about brick-laying.'

He stood back and watched his ginger-haired parliamentary private secretary, incongruously dressed in a charcoal grey suit and stiff white collar, pick up a brick.

He frowned. Something Bracken had said had alerted an instinct; he knew the feeling well; a brilliancy or an idiocy was about to surface.

Bracken pushed the brick home and sliced off errant cement. He picked up another brick. By the time he got back to

Westminster he would be the world's greatest authority on brick-laying.

Churchill wandered a few yards away and stared across the garden. It was bathed in delicate sunshine; daffodils and narcissi trembled in a breeze that smelled of rain-to-come. For twenty years Chartwell had been his haven; soon he would have to leave it and make do with Chequers because it was going to be used as Government offices. But he would return when the war was won.

When ... Yugoslavia. What had Bracken said? *To march on Greece Hitler needs Yugoslavia's co-operation.* Not a particularly profound observation. But what, Churchill speculated, if Yugoslavia was persuaded *not* to co-operate? What, his enthusiasm rising, if they were persuaded to resist?

Then Hitler would have to divert more divisions to the south. And Barbarossa would have to be delayed for even longer.

Excitedly, he returned to Brendan Bracken, brick-layer. He pointed at the Irishman's handiwork. 'Crooked,' he said. 'Terrible. Don't bother to apply for membership to the Union, I won't give you a reference.'

He took Bracken by the arm and led him towards the house. 'Are you staying the night? Good,' before Bracken could reply. 'I've got to pay someone a visit. Clemmie will look after you while I'm gone.'

'But you said—'

'That we'd have a long talk. So we shall, Brendan, so we shall. But something's come up.''

'While I was laying those bricks?'

'Yes,' Churchill said, 'while you were laying them crookedly.'

'Am I permitted to know who you're going to see?'

'No,' Churchill said, giving his arm a squeeze, 'you're not. But I've been thinking, Brendan. You know so much about so many things. What if I were to make you Minister of Information?'

He winked at the astonished Irishman and summoned his driver to take him to the only man in whom he could confide his own plans for Barbarossa, Robert Sinclair.

*

It was dusk when he arrived at the house in Berkshire.

Sinclair was just about to take his dog for a walk. Churchill asked if he could join them and Sinclair said yes, why not. But, as they strolled through the thick, overgrown woods, Churchill felt like an intruder; this was the time which Sinclair put aside to commune with his son who had been dead for nine months. But Sinclair listened just the same, making brief and astute responses when they were needed.

Churchill approached the reason for his visit through an assessment of the war – felt his way to see if he had strayed along any false trails.

'One of our greatest victories,' he said, 'was last November.'

'Roosevelt?'

'When he was re-elected we were no longer alone. Roosevelt said the United States would be "the arsenal of democracy". A nice phrase – I wish I'd thought of it. And, by God, Sinclair, that's just what it has become. Lend-lease – America's intervened without intervention. But soon, of course, the Japanese will fall upon them and then, thank God, we'll all be in it together. Until then ...'

'Barbarossa.' Sinclair threw a stick for the red setter; the dog scampered away barking but the barks were lost among the rotting silver birches and the cushions of leaf mould. 'Which, I presume, is why you've come to see me.'

'An off-shoot,' Churchill said. 'Yugoslavia.'

'The back-door to Greece.'

'To Greece and Albania and Mussolini's beleaguered army. You know something, Sinclair, we're almost as lucky in the Führer's choice of allies as we are in our own. At least the little corporal seems to be behaving honourably to his unfortunate comrade-in-arms.'

'He doesn't have much choice,' Sinclair remarked. 'He can't allow Mussolini to lose his footing in Greece. It wouldn't do to let Britain have bases there, would it? Or Crete for that matter.'

The dog brought the stick back and waited for it to be thrown again, tongue hanging from laughing jaws.

Churchill said: 'You know what I'm getting at?'

'I think so.'

'I wouldn't describe you as expansive, Sinclair.'

Sinclair said: 'With respect, it's fairly obvious. Yugoslavia is on the point of doing a deal with Hitler. When that happens the *Wehrmacht* will swoop on the Greeks and polish them off; Hitler will then be ready to finish his build-up for Barbarossa.

274

We don't want that just yet ...' His voice faded away; Churchill sensed that these days he had to concentrate to sustain his interest.

Churchill swung at a clump of dead bracken with his stick. 'What we want is at least a month's grace.'

'So an anti-German coup in Belgrade would do the trick?'

'I had been thinking along those lines,' Churchill said as the dog returned yet again with the stick.

'It's already in hand,' Sinclair said. 'I was going to be in touch this evening – for your final approval.'

For once Churchill was speechless. Finally he said in an aggrieved tone: 'Very well, you've got my approval.'

'That's all right then. Shall we return to the house?'

They walked back in silence.

*

Churchill was sitting alone in the underground War Cabinet Room under Horse Guards Parade on March 24 when he heard that the Regent of Yugoslavia, Prince Paul, and the Prime Minister, Dragisa Cvetković, intended to do a deal with Hitler.

For a moment he sat tapping his fingers on the red dispatch box beside him. Then he lit a cigar and picked up one of the tags he attached to his memos according to their urgency. This one said ACTION THIS DAY. 'Today that applies to me,' he thought.

He hurried down the yellow-painted corridor to Room 63, his private telephone cubicle, fitted with a door to which was attached a VACANT and ENGAGED lavatory lock.

He slipped the bolt and telephoned Eden who had moved from the Ministry of War to become Foreign Secretary.

Later that day Eden sent a cable to the British Ambassador in Belgrade:

'You are authorised now to proceed at your discretion by any means at your disposal to move leaders and public opinion to understanding of realities and to action to meet the situation. You have my full authority for any measures that you may think it right to take to further change of Goverment or régime even by *coup d'état*.'

Churchill also telephoned Sinclair. 'You've heard about Yugoslavia?'

Sinclair said he had.

'Are your men ready?'

Sinclair said they were.

*

On March 25 Hoffman was given a scoop to convey to Stalin. It was so good that he wasn't sure whether he could believe it.

Before taking it to the room in the Alfama to encode and transmit he said to Rachel Keyser: 'How the hell would the British get to know something like this?'

'Ours not to reason why,' she told him.

'It had better be right,' he said. 'If it isn't we're endangering the whole project. One piece of false information and we lose credibility.'

'It's right,' she said.

The message he transmitted said simply: 'Anti-Nazi coup expected in Belgrade tomorrow night March twenty-five stroke twenty-six.'

*

Hitler didn't hear about the coup until March 27. The news threw him into a fury.

Apparently a Yugoslav air force general, Bora Mirković, had overthrown the government in the name of the young heir to the throne, Peter II. Crowds were celebrating in the streets and the German Minister's car had been spat upon.

So there was no doubt about the mood of the people. They had turned on their saviour – What greater honour than being invited to join the Axis powers? – and they would have to be punished.

Immediately he called a council of war in the Chancellery. So passionate was his rage that he didn't wait for von Ribbentrop or the Commander-in-Chief of the Army, von Brauchitsch, or the Chief of the Army General Staff, Franz Halder, to arrive before launching into a diatribe.

Yugoslavia, he said, would have to be crushed with 'unmerciful harshness'. To Hermann Goering he said: 'You must destroy Belgrade in attacks by waves.'

Then he issued Directive 25 authorising an immediate attack on Yugoslavia. The Directive stated: 'It is my intention to force my way into Yugoslavia ... to annihilate the Yugoslav Army ...'

He ordered his generals to draw up invasion plans that evening.

He went to bed in the early hours of the 28th after cabling a letter to Mussolini in Rome setting out his intentions.

But it was a long time before he slept. Every time he closed his eyes he was awoken by his own words ringing out to his generals and ministers in the Chancellery:

'The beginning of the Barbarossa operation will have to be postponed for up to four weeks.'

For the first time since his armies had rolled across Europe he wondered if he had made a mistake. But surely it was only fatigue and emotion that had opened the gates of doubt. He did not make mistakes.

Finally he slept – and dreamed of a German army frozen in blood-stained snow. At their head on a white horse sat Napoleon. He, too, was frozen.

*

Churchill's reaction to the Belgrade *coup d'état* was less dramatic than Hitler's. He ordered a bottle of slivovitz, the national drink of Yugoslavia, and sent it to Sinclair by special messenger.

*

While Hitler mustered his tanks to crush Yugoslavia and Greece, Josef Hoffman bought a bicycle.

It was by far the best way to shake off surveillance. Gestapo, *Abwehr,* NKVD or MI6. If you were on a bicycle they couldn't follow you on foot and when you dived into one of the narrow, hillside lanes of Lisbon they couldn't follow you by car. So they, too, had to take to bicycles and there was no way you could conceal yourself hurtling through a precipitous maze on two wheels.

Hoffman also enjoyed cycling. He could pedal at a leisurely pace through the city and admire its landmarks: the Belém Tower on the Tagus waterfront, the eleven mile-long aqueduct of Aguas Livres, the palaces and parks ... then suddenly launch himself down a lane as steep as a shute.

The bicycle was a Raleigh, austerity-built and painted entirely in black to avoid reflections in the black-out in Britain. Hoffman guessed that a British seaman had traded it in the

Alfama for a crate of local brandy or a girl. It had three gears which helped him up the hills and whooshed him down them.

On April 1, April Fool's Day in Britain, the devil got into him.

Who was on duty? He accelerated along the Rua Aurea, the Street of Gold so named because of its jewellery shops, and glanced behind. A bicycle had also accelerated. Seated on it was the thin-faced Austrian. Gestapo. Hoffman was glad. He enjoyed confounding Himmler's secret police force more than the others.

In his pocket he had details about German troop movements in the region of Yugoslavia. But there was no hurry to transmit them. The attack there wasn't due to be launched until April 6, according to British sources; and they, it seemed, were always right.

He stopped outside a cinema bearing an old legend *animbio-grafo* which was showing a German propaganda film and went inside. The thin-faced Austrian, he felt, would be embarrassed by the experience because although the Portuguese showed such movies to appease the Nazis they treated them derisively. They didn't let him down. The film was about the French, Belgians and Dutch welcoming blond Germans dedicated to wiping out corruption in their cities; there were a few saboteurs but they were all Jews; the Germans were catcalled by the audience, the saboteurs cheered.

Hoffman departed by the rear exit. Behind him he heard a commotion as the Austrian who had just sat down got up again to leave. Hoffman mounted his bicycle which he had chained to a lamppost and headed for the Praça do Comércio.

There he wheeled his bicycle on to an orange ferry bound for the opposite bank of the Tagus. The Austrian just made it; he stood in the stern of the ferry while Hoffman rode in the bows. There was a lot of activity among the ships lying at anchor; the previous afternoon a German U-boat had surfaced a mile down river and loosed off a couple of shots at a British cargo boat before submerging again; there had been an official protest and the Portuguese Navy was making a show of looking for the U-boat which was probably half-way across the Atlantic by now.

The ferry butted its way between looming hulls and Phoenician-rigged fishing boats. Sunlight danced on the water.

When they reached the far bank he waited. The Austrian

hesitated; plainly it was ludicrous for just the two of them to stay on board; head bowed, he wheeled his bike down the gangway; Hoffman stayed behind. Just as the ferry was about to return the Austrian hurled himself on board. He was sweating and he looked worried; if he hadn't been Gestapo, Hoffman would have felt sorry for him.

Back on the city shoreline, Hoffman mounted the Raleigh and pedalled along the waterfront. He rounded a corner; ahead stood a group of muscular women wearing headscarves carrying wooden boxes of sardines as bright as quicksilver. The Austrian, Hoffman guessed, would accelerate, fearing he had lost him; he slowed down; the surface beneath the wheels of the bicycle was slippery with fish-scales; as the Austrian rounded the corner Hoffman took off, fast, passing the group of shouting women. The Austrian didn't pass them; he plunged into them like a shark hitting a shoal of fish.

The shouting and swearing that ensued was an education.

Hoffman cycled slowly towards the English Bar. It was an old-fashioned place with shelves of dusty bottles, ceiling fans and hunting prints on the walls. As its name suggested, it was frequented by the British.

Next door stood the British Bar. It had a black marble bar and a similar atmosphere to the English Bar. Except that, contrary to its name, it was frequented by Germans.

Across the street stood the Bar Americano; that, too, was similar to the English Bar except that it had a stag's head on the wall.

Hoffman drank first in the English Bar, then moved swiftly to the British Bar, catching a glimpse of the Austrian staring into a tobacconist's, before crossing the street to the Bar Americano where a fight was taking place.

The contestants were United States sailors and they were systematically wrecking the place. Hoffman ducked into a corner and ordered a beer from a phlegmatic barman.

'Soon,' the barman confided in English, 'the stag's head will go.'

'How do you know?'

'Because it always does. The Americans seem to like swinging from stags' heads. I think they see too many films. You know, in the fights one of them is always swinging from a chandelier. Well, we haven't got a chandelier, we've got a stag's head.'

As he spoke a sailor leaped for the stag's muzzle and the head came away from the wall.

'We don't screw it in too tight,' the barman explained. 'There is no point, is there?'

The sailor picked up the stag's head and charged two brawling comrades, drawing blood with the horns.

The barman said: 'Always they do that. One day someone will die.'

Hoffman ordered another beer. He glanced at what remained of a clock on the wall. He had been in the bar ten minutes. Any minute now the Austrian would come in, fearing that he had left through a rear exit.

One minute later the Austrian sidled through the door and was hit on the head with a bar stool by a sailor attacking the stag's head. He fell to the floor unconscious.

Hoffman stepped jauntily over his body into the street. As he mounted his bike a clock struck midday: in Britain it was time to stop all April Fool's tricks.

In Portugal, too, he thought as, grinning, he pedalled away in the spring sunshine.

*

He left the bicycle padlocked to some railings in the centre of the city. From there he took a yellow tram up the hill to the castle.

The metal thighs of the tramcar brushed against pedestrians and the rails glistened behind it like thread spun by a spider. On either side balconies dripped with pink and red geraniums.

Hoffman alighted three hundred yards from the castle walls.

He looked up and down. The city was lazy in the midday warmth; like a cat stretching out in the sun, except that its voice still had a vigour alien to sleep.

He couldn't see any pursuers.

It wasn't far from here, he remembered, that it had all begun; that a man had pretended to try and kill him; that he had been rescued by men whose last consideration had been rescue. Nothing was as it seemed and he shouldn't be deceived by a street that looked innocuous.

He turned into an alley. Then he ran, twice doubling back on his tracks.

Finally he dodged into a patio in which blue and white *azulejos*, tiles, were for sale. The proprietor smiled lazily at him. Why should he worry if a crazy refugee chose to pay him good money, dollars, for a room he didn't occupy?

Hoffman went through the patio into a second courtyard stacked high with tiles. In the centre stood a dusty statue of a saint and, in one corner, a small Judas tree vivid with pinky-mauve blossom. What else?

He waited. There was no following movement. From his trouser pocket he took a key and inserted it into the lock of an old door studded with nails.

The door swung open. Hoffman backed inside, still watching. Farcical, perhaps, but in the past few months he had learned.

He closed the door and switched on the light. A gecko took to the shadows.

He sat on the earthenware tiles of the floor, listening. Nothing. He levered four tiles from a corner of the room watched by the gecko.

Carefully he removed *War and Peace* from the cavity, then the transmitter.

It took him half an hour to encode the message in Russian.

He consulted his watch. It was time. He plugged the lead into a primitive connection in the white-washed wall.

He made contact immediately. 'Dove here.'

'Come in, Dove. Receiving you loud and clear.'

He began to transmit. *Operation Marita* (the original German plan to take Greece) *revised as follows ... Luftflotte IV commanded by Colonel-General Alexander Löhr to raze Belgrade ... Panzergruppe Kleist to mount assault ... 32 divisions of which ten are armoured and four motorised ...*

So it went on.

British information was incredible.

As far as he could make out Yugoslavia was doomed. It was indescribably sad but now it was inevitable. What *did* matter was that Stalin should receive information that he believed.

As he transmitted he wondered if anyone had previously managed to follow him to this room in the Alfama. The British for instance. What was so hilariously funny, if it wasn't so tragic, was that it didn't really matter.

From Moscow: 'Received and understood. Is that it?'

That was almost it. Watched by the gecko, he sent the final five words: 'In this instance disregard Judas.'

'Understood.' He could almost see the uncomprehending frown on the forehead of the receiver at the Moscow Centre.

'Over and out,' Hoffman sent, signing off: 'Dove.'

* * *

A week later Hoffman managed to find berths for a family of five Czechs on a Liberian cargo ship bound for New York. The Red Cross were surprised at his success because the captain had been demanding a bribe on top of the fares that they weren't prepared to pay. Hoffman paid him with money saved from von Claus's payments. The deal gave him as much satisfaction as any he had concluded: Germans unwittingly paying for the escape of their victims.

With the balance of his savings he bought a tuxedo and that night he took Rachel Keyser to Estoril. They travelled on the little train that skirted the coastline from Lisbon and arrived just as the sun was setting. But the air was warm and scented from flowers in the gardens sweeping up from the railway station to the casino.

They strolled under the palms to the Palácio. Beyond it stood the Hotel do Parque. 'Favoured by off-duty German spies,' Rachel told him. 'The British and Americans stay at the Palácio. It's all very insular – until they start spying, of course.'

They had a drink in the bar at the Palácio. 'Where we met,' he said. 'I felt very gauche.'

'You certainly don't look it now,' she said. 'More like a Hollywood croupier, except that they're always dark.' They sat at a table; the bar hadn't filled up yet and the pianist was playing and singing 'Tea For Two.'

Rachel said: 'When it's all over, when we're living ... wher-ever we are living ... we'll have to return here.'

Hoffman sipped his Scotch. Rachel looked glossily beautiful in shimmering green, her favourite colour, with amber beads at her neck. He wanted her always at his side; without her he was incomplete; life was meant to be shared. He wanted to tell her this but he had acquired other instincts since they first met. Caution. Be honest with yourself, Viktor Golovin – suspicion.

'I wonder,' he said, 'how many couples are sitting together at this moment wondering where they'll be when it's all over.'

'Palestine? Would you like to visit Palestine, Josef?'

'Would you like to visit Moscow?'

'With you, yes. If ...'

She closed her eyes for a moment.

So many unfinished sentences, he thought.

An urbane-looking man wearing a white tuxedo entered the bar with a pretty blonde. Catching sight of Rachel he smiled and bowed slightly. The couple sat at the next table; Hoffman could hear him speaking English with a slight stammer.

As they walked through the gardens towards the casino he asked Rachel who the man was.

'Kim Philby,' she told him. 'A useful contact,' she added but didn't elaborate.

The casino hadn't filled up and the only games being played were roulette, baccarat and French Bank.

Hoffman bought twenty dollars' worth of chips which they lost in style. Before buying any more they watched the roulette.

Hoffman stood behind Rachel, hands around her waist. He could feel her warmth, smell her perfume. She leaned against him.

'I never thought I'd be a gambler,' he said.

'Twenty dollars, you call that gambling?'

'I wasn't thinking about roulette, I was thinking about us. We're gambling, aren't we?'

She didn't deny it. 'If it wasn't for the war we wouldn't be.'

'If it wasn't for the war we wouldn't have met.'

'This gamble you're talking about ... do you think you're going to win?'

'I think you know,' he said. He felt her move fractionally away from him. 'Don't you?'

'Why don't you buy some more chips?' she said.

He returned with ten dollars' worth. 'Odds or evens?'

'Blow the lot. All ten dollars on one throw. Wow!'

'On us?' He didn't know why he was doing it. Perversity. Hope?

'If you wish.'

'Red or black,' he said. He kissed the back of her neck. 'Red says you're not setting me up for anything I don't know about.' He placed the chips on *rouge*.

The wheel spun. The ball bounced, danced. He could feel she was holding her breath. The wheel slowed. The ball dropped into a red pocket; then with a last exhausted jump made it into a black.

As she fled a man standing beside Hoffman exclaimed: 'She must have lost a fortune.'

'More than that,' Hoffman said, thrusting aside a fat man who was pushing himself into the space she had left.

He glanced around but she had disappeared. He ran to the exit. A security guard in evening dress stopped him, asking him in Portuguese, what the hurry was.

'A girl in green. Did you see her run out just now?'

'What if I did? If she wants to get away from you that's her business. May I suggest you go to the bar and calm down?'

She could have done one of two things, Hoffman decided. Gone to the ladies or fled from the casino. He decided she had fled.

He broke free from the guard's grasp and raced to the exit. The moon was riding high and chauffeur-driven limousines were lining up to deposit their passengers.

Where would I go if I were her? Towards the sea. He set off across the gardens. To his left he thought he caught a glimpse of flying skirt but he couldn't be sure.

The sea was a gleam of silver ahead of him.

Why the hell had he made the stupid gamble? he wondered as he ran. In war you hold on to what you've got until it's taken away from you.

When he reached the road he ran straight in front of a Rolls Royce. The driver swerved, hooted, shouted. Hoffman ran on. When he reached the beach he stood listening; but all he could hear was the lick of small waves and the creak of rope on wood.

He began to walk, between the waves and a line of pink, candy-striped tents, towards the mock castle at the end of the deserted beach. He searched for footprints but the sand had been scuffed during the day.

If he had lost her then it was his fault. The possibility scared him.

He found her in the last tent sitting inside the open flap staring across the Atlantic.

He sat beside her and put his arm round her. She felt cold.

'I'm sorry,' he said.

She didn't answer.

'It was a stupid thing to do.'

Still she didn't answer. A ship hooted and the moonlight was cold on the sea.

He kissed her cheek. 'Let's keep whatever we have,' he said. 'While we can.'

And at last she turned to him and rested her head on his shoulder.

*

Rachel Keyser had always shrunk from asking how the final deception would be accomplished. All she knew was that when Hitler was poised to attack Russia a message to the contrary would be transmitted to Stalin.

The time when that message would be sent was drawing close and the day after her visit to Estoril she confronted Cross.

She met him at a pavement table outside the Nicola Café on the Rossio. It was a fine day, sunlight dancing in the fountains in the square and opening the buds of the flower-seller's wares.

Cross threw a newspaper on the table. 'On the ball again,' he said. 'Hitler attacked Yugoslavia on the sixth. Belgrade's being razed by the Luftwaffe and the Panzers are moving in for the kill. I don't give the Jugs much longer than a fortnight.'

'So our operation can't be far off?'

Cross sat down and ordered a beer. 'Well, Hitler's got to beat the Greeks first. They'll be a tougher nut to crack: they've sharpened their teeth on the Italians. But they can't last all that long, not even with British help. Then the Krauts will have a go at us on Crete. That'll be a hell of a battle but they'll win it. Then ...'

'I've got to talk to you,' Rachel said.

'Go ahead.' He drank some beer.

'It's too risky here.'

'Okay. When I've finished my beer we'll walk. I can guess what it's about,' he added.

He paid the bill and they walked round the Rossio and down the Rua Augusta towards the river, catching up with a funeral procession. The horse-drawn hearse looked like a coronation coach, decorated with wooden gold-painted garlands and surmounted with a crown. The sides of the coach were made of glass and you could see the coffin inside; the coffin was also glass and the corpse, a benign old man with a grey beard, rolled with the motion of the carriage.

'The information Hoffman gave Stalin about the coup in Yugoslavia,' Rachel said. 'Was that Ultra?'

'That and the details about the German attack. Churchill's "most secret source" ... Stalin must be very impressed with his son.'

'So we'll know as soon as Hitler is about to attack Russia?'

'We virtually know now. Round about June 20. It depends on Greece, Crete, British resistance ... But Hitler hasn't put a foot wrong so far. Let's hope Barbarossa is his first mistake. I

285

think it will be: Churchill, with his limited resources, hasn't put a foot wrong either. Isn't it fantastic to think that he's relying on you and me?'

'And Hoffman.'

The bearded old man rolled to one side; he seemed to be smiling at Rachel.

'Without him there would have been another plan. Winston is nothing if not ingenious.'

'I don't happen to share your hero-worship.'

She walked faster but the horses seemed determined to keep pace with her.

'So,' Cross said, 'what did you want to talk to me about? How we're going to stage-manage the finale?'

'Well, how?'

'You know the basics, that Stalin has got to be persuaded that Hitler doesn't intend to attack ...'

'The basics,' Rachel said, 'aren't enough. If I'm going to co-operate I've got to know how. I presume,' and she had presumed all along without facing up to reality, 'that you're not going to allow Hoffman to transmit any message.'

'You presume correctly.' Cross looked surprised.

'So how are you going to manage that?'

'Leave that to me,' Cross said.

The old man rolled to the other side; Rachel noticed that although his beard had been neatly trimmed the hair at the nape of his neck was unkempt. She thought he must have been a nice old man.

'I want to know,' she told Cross, 'and you're going to tell me because if you don't I'll blow the whole thing.'

'Really? What about those poor Jewish children in the streets of Berlin? What about the holocaust? Would you really abandon your cause because of one man?'

'I want to know,' she said.

He was silent, weighing up her determination. Evidently he decided that there was no point in risking her perversity. 'Very well,' he said, 'he will have to be ... overcome.'

'How?'

'It won't be difficult.' Nothing according to Cross was difficult. 'We'll receive the coded message from London at the Embassy. Hoffman needn't even know that it's arrived so he won't be on the alert.'

'And?'

'We put him out for a while. Drugs probably. We go to this room of his in the Alfama and send the message to Moscow on his behalf. HITLER HAS NO REPEAT NO INTENTION OF LAUNCHING ATTACK. Stalin will rejoice that his own son has confirmed his own views and relax. The Red Army won't be put on alert and, wham! Hitler will wade into the Soviet Union. But Hitler, thank God, hasn't any idea of the reserves of Soviet manpower, of the magnitude of the terrain. He's a victim of his own successes. And so, thanks to the delay over Mussolini and Yugoslavia – thanks, I suspect, to some skullduggery of Winston's – he marches straight into the Russian winter.'

Rachel considered this. She slowed her pace but the horses slowed theirs and the old gentleman was still beside her.

'If,' she said after a while, 'Hoffman doesn't know the message has arrived from London why does he have to be overcome?'

'Because he might catch us transmitting the message in the Alfama. That's obvious, I should have thought.'

It was. She tried again. 'Haven't you overlooked something? The message will have to be transmitted in Russian.'

'Which is why,' Cross said smiling at her, 'an interpreter from the Foreign Office who is fluent in Russian arrived in Lisbon by plane this morning. He will assist you because, of course, you will be transmitting the message.'

Touch, that was it. Whoever was receiving the message in Moscow would recognise that it was not Hoffman transmitting. She told Cross.

'And so,' he said, 'you will be even more valuable than we ever dreamed. You've trained Hoffman – in more ways than one – and you know his touch. You can simulate it, his speed, everything ...'

The funeral procession turned down a side street. As it turned the old man rolled towards her for the last time. But his lips had opened and the smile had been replaced by a look of horror: he hadn't wanted to die.

Cross said: 'Meanwhile everything is proceeding according to plan. Every other agent that Stalin treats seriously has been fed misinformation to discredit them. This man Philby has been a godsend; apparently they think very well of him in

Dzerzhinsky Square. First of all we arranged for him to tell the Kremlin that Hitler did not intend to attack – to gain credibility. Since then he's been fed two stories which we knew bloody well he'd communicate to Moscow: both of them were bullshit. Even if he – or any of the others – gets wind of the date for Barbarossa he'll be ignored. Odd to think that if he's ever blown as a Soviet agent the public will say British intelligence was criminally naive when the reverse is true.'

They reached the Terreiro do Paço; it was from here, Rachel recalled, that she had set out by boat with Hoffman the day when she had discovered that a pacifist can be brave.

A stiff breeze blew in from the river, flattening their clothes against them. She said suddenly: 'How would you drug him?'

'Me? No, my dear. You would do that. After all, you're closer to him than I am.'

She sensed that his answer wasn't spontaneous; that if she had been chosen to drug Hoffman she would have been prepared already for the task.

Suddenly she understood. How could she have been so stupid? It was quite simple. Cross intended to kill Hoffman.

Chapter Twenty-three

Nine thousand miles away in Tokyo a man with scarred legs and a prematurely-lined face was being bathed by a young girl whose name meant Camellia.

But for once her hands, now strong, now gentle, brought him no relief from the worry with which he lived these days.

There had always been worry – you could hardly be a spy without it – but recently the worry visiting Richard Sorge had become erosive.

Twice now, information he had passed to Moscow Centre had been incorrect. He couldn't understand it: he had the best contacts in Japan. And so he should: it had taken long enough to perfect his front.

Sorge, aged forty-five, son of a Russian mother and a

288

German father, had lived in Berlin before joining the German army in the previous war. His legs were savaged by shrapnel and, having witnessed the futile carnage of two capitalist countries embroiled in battle, he had become a pacifist and a communist.

In 1925 he went to live in Russia where he learned Russian, French and English. He also added espionage to his qualifications. He visited Los Angeles, Stockholm and London and spent three years in China spying for the Russians.

Then he returned to Germany to re-establish his patriotism. He met many of the top Nazis and in 1934 went to Tokyo as a journalist representing the *Frankfurter Zeitung*.

Almost immediately he penetrated German diplomatic circles through an assistant military attaché named Eugen Ott. When Ott became German Ambassador he made Sorge his press attaché.

With this status Sorge promptly moved into Japanese diplomatic circles. Moscow was euphoric. Through fifteen years' application they had established one man with access to their two potential enemies, Germany and Japan.

And Sorge didn't disappoint the Kremlin. He advised them about the pact between Germany, Italy and Japan; he forecast Germany's attack on Poland on September 1, 1939.

Then things started to go wrong.

Information obtained from Ozaki Hozumi, a Japanese journalist with contacts among British espionage agents, had proved to be a disaster. Sorge had assured Moscow that the British had no intention of counter-attacking in the Western Desert. What had happened? Operation Compass was what had happened and Wavell's tiny army had decimated the Italians.

The girl named Camellia massaged his neck and shoulder muscles with strong fingers. He closed his eyes. The oil she used smelled of lemons. 'Is that good?' she asked him anxiously because it was her duty to please him.

'That's fine.' He patted one of her hands, smiling at her through the steam. But it wasn't fine at all; the worry had spread to his muscles and they ached with it.

The fact that he had misled Moscow about Operation Compass wasn't in itself such a calamity. What was disastrous was that it began to throw doubt on his credibility. When he got the big one he wouldn't be so readily believed. And he was convinced that there was a big one in the pipeline.

Then Ott of all people had misled him. Ott, his mentor, his prime contact. Ott told him that reliable Japanese agents in Hong Kong had heard from 'an unimpeachable source' that on April 9 this year Britain was going to seek peace with Hitler through a Swedish intermediary. What had happened on April 9? The RAF had bombed Berlin, that's what.

And made an idiot of Richard Sorge.

Which again wasn't catastrophic but it was another sizeable bite out of his plausibility.

Sorge heard the gunfire in France in the 1914-18 war, felt the shrapnel tear into his legs. That was when his role in life had been determined. Peacemaker. But to work for peace through espionage you had to be plausible.

He said to the girl: 'Let's go over to the couch.' From beside the bath he picked up the waterproof pouch containing a message to be passed on to a GRU agent in Tokyo and slipped it under the pillow.

It wasn't a couch really, it was a massage table. Sorge lay on his stomach while Camellia applied herself to his naked body.

What principally concerned the Kremlin was Japan's attitude towards Russia; whether, that was, she planned an attack. Sorge suspected that soon he would have news of a more imminent peril: Germany's intention to attack Russia.

The girl's hands dug into his buttocks, then began to work their way up his spine; at last he felt himself beginning to relax.

The message in the pouch wasn't that important strategically, but it was important as far as the reputation of Richard Sorge was concerned. One more fiasco and he would be blown as far as the Kremlin was concerned. One more item of good, accurate intelligence and his star would be in the ascendant again.

Her hands were at the base of his neck. Strong and gentle, commanding, coaxing, reaching nerves through muscles ... he closed his eyes.

'Am I pleasing you?' she asked.

'Mmm ... '

Staring down at his body the girl named Camellia smiled but it wasn't a smile of professional pride; there was a touch of contempt about it.

There was, Sorge thought as he hovered on the brink of sleep, a common denominator to both items of inaccurate information that he had sent. The British. Hozumi's contact had been British, so, he had discovered, had Ott's 'unimpeachable source'.

And the item in the waterproof pouch? There couldn't be much doubt about this one. Again it came from Ott, but this time the source was Berlin. The Führer intended to invade Crete on or about May 20.

If he was proved to be right about that date ... her hands were coaxing him into unconsciousness, blurring his judgement ... if he was proved right then the next message he sent ... he was awake and yet he was asleep and it was beautiful ... then the next message ... the date of Barbarossa ... the big one ... would be believed ...

When his breathing was shallow and regular the girl reached beneath the pillow with one hand, maintaining the massage with the other. With slim, strong fingers she opened the pouch and removed the manilla envelope; from the folds of her kimono she produced an identical envelope, substituted it and replaced the pouch under the pillow.

Then she dug deeply into Sorge's shoulder muscles with the balls of her thumb, so powerfully that he awoke with a gasp. One hand delved below the pillow. Satisfied, he turned on his back.

What a mixture his face was, she thought. Old before its time, idealistic yet cunning.

'All right,' he said, 'that's enough. You did well, I'll be back tomorrow,' swinging himself off the massage table, draping a white towel round his belly. Later outside the bathhouse he handed the envelope to the GRU courier bound for Moscow.

Half an hour later another patron claimed the attentions of Camellia. He said he was an American but Camellia thought he was British.

He was direct to the point of rudeness but there was a certain masterfulness about him that appealed.

'Well,' he said, 'did you do it?' Apparently he wasn't even going to bother with a bath or a massage which was a pity.

'Of course. As I told you, he never leaves anything important with his clothes.'

'You have the original?'

She took the envelope from her kimono and handed it to him. He ripped it open and read the contents. He seemed satisfied.

He handed her a wad of yen. 'Go and buy yourself a bathhouse,' he said and was gone.

*

The following day a GRU cryptanalyst decoded the message brought by courier from Tokyo. UNDERSTAND HITLER HAS ABANDONED PLAN TO CAPTURE CRETE RICHARD SORGE.

The message was relayed to the NKVD and taken to Molotov and Stalin who were conferring at the Generalissimo's home in the Kremlin.

Stalin said: 'This will make or break Sorge.'

Molotov, as inscrutable as ever, said: 'We shall see.'

Stalin, cup of lemon tea in hand, went to the window and stared into the melting day. Not that it matters, he thought, I have my own source.

*

Eleven hundred miles north-east of Lisbon, in Lucerne, a slight, shabbily-dressed man with sad eyes behind spectacles that seemed too big for him fought two battles. One with his black chess pieces, the other with his conscience.

His name was Rudolf Roessler. He was forty-five years old, although he looked older, and he was a German publisher who had come to live in Switzerland in 1934. He was also a spy.

His opponent at chess was a British businessman from Berne named Richard Cockburn, pronounced, he had told Roessler, *Coburn* 'like the port'. Cockburn was a flashy-looking man with longish silver hair and a fierce moustache that he frequently stroked with thumb and forefinger.

Roessler didn't like him. What he was saying made sense but Roessler knew a bully when he saw one, even if he was disguised in a Savile Row suit, and he had resisted them all his life.

'Well?' Cockburn said, 'will you do it?'

'It's your move,' Roessler said. He wished he was playing white; bullies didn't like playing black.

Cockburn studied the board.

Roessler said: 'If this is going to take a long time do you mind if I make some coffee?' He lived on the stuff; it was his only indulgence.

'Make some by all means,' said Cockburn, clearly grateful

292

for the extra time. Like a bully, he had attacked too precipitously on the board and over-extended himself.

Roessler went into the kitchen of the small apartment in which he lived with his wife, Olga, in Wesemlin, a suburb of Lucerne some three miles from his publishing house, Vita Nova Verlag, at 36, Fluhmattstrasse.

It was from Fluhmattstrasse that Roessler poured out his hatred of one particular breed of bullies: the Nazis.

Like Richard Sorge, Roessler had fought in the trenches in the last war. Like Sorge he had emerged a pacifist and propounded his views through writing and lecturing. He was still a patriot but when, in 1933, the bullies came to power he knew that decent patriotism had, for the time being, been buried.

When he came to Switzerland, however, he brought with him more than just memories: he brought contacts with leaders of the German armed forces who secretly abhorred Hitler's racist policies. Among them Admiral Wilhelm Canaris.

Already he had given Bureau Ha, the Swiss intelligence organisation in Lucerne, the correct dates for the German invasions of Poland, Belgium, Holland and Denmark.

He had also made sure that the information reached the British – but they had ignored it. Which was why he had joined a Soviet spy ring headed by a jovial Hungarian named Alexander Rado. Roessler was code-named Lucy (Lucerne) and the agency was known as The Lucy Ring.

Now suddenly, impudently, the British wanted his help.

Roessler filled his cup from the percolator. As he picked it up he was overcome with a fit of coughing. An attack of asthma was something he could do without while pitting his wits against the Englishman.

He fought the attack, regained control of his breathing and, cup and saucer in hand, returned to the dining room.

Cockburn looked up, a complacent smile on his face. So, Roessler thought, he thinks he's outmanoeuvred me. He sat down and studied the board: he hadn't. Cockburn was so obvious. He reminded Roessler of a confidence trickster who preys on widows.

Obvious or not, the widows often succumbed. Will I succumb in the battle with my conscience?

The trouble was that Cockburn's arguments were logical.

'It's very simple,' Cockburn said – he preferred to talk when

293

Roessler was concentrating on the board – 'just two phoney items, that's all we need.'

'But that will destroy my credibility.'

'Not for long. When Moscow realises that you've given them the right date for Barbarossa you'll be right back in favour again.'

'I suppose you're right.' Roessler moved a pawn; Cockburn underestimated pawns. 'A pity your people didn't pay more attention to my earlier reports.'

'We've realised our mistake. I've apologised on behalf of the British Government. Now let's put the record straight. You've seen the evidence,' gesturing at the documents on the dining table.

Roessler didn't warm to Cockburn's candour, but the documents seemed genuine enough. What shall I do? Roessler wondered, waiting for Cockburn to move his bishop.

He looked around the dining room. Cheap furniture, moulting carpet, family portraits on the mantelpiece and a couple of paintings of lush Bavarian scenery on the walls. Not much to show for a publisher who had once been a member of the Herrenklub in Berlin.

But I still have my ideals ...

Cockburn moved his bishop.

... which are more precious than material possessions ...

Cockburn sat back, pleased with his move and himself.

... although now they are under attack ...

'Your move,' Cockburn said.

... and have to be defended ...

Roessler moved his knight and picked up the documents again.

What Cockburn was suggesting was incredibly devious. *Ironic how my ideals have always had to be maintained by double-dealing.* Cockburn was saying that if Stalin believed Hitler was going to attack he would shore up his defences.

Obviously.

Then there would be no Russo-German war.

Right.

Which would leave Germany just as brutally strong as she was now.

Wrong. I don't want the Nazis strong, Roessler had thought.

He remembered the first intelligence he had transmitted

294

from Switzerland. Details of a policy statement drawn up by Reinhard Heydrich, Himmler's deputy:

'The Third Reich will not rebuild Poland. As soon as the conquest has been completed, the aristocracy and the clergy must be exterminated. The people must be kept at a very low standard of living. They will thus provide cheap slaves. The Jews will be grouped into towns where they will remain easily accessible. The final solution will take some time to be worked out and must be kept strictly secret.'

The final solution. Roessler had no doubt what the infamous phrase implied.

No, the Germans – 'my people' – must not be left in a strong position.

And it was at this point that Cockburn had made the point that neither should the Russians. And produced the documents collected by British Intelligence that Russian atrocities in Poland were just as bad as those perpetrated by the Nazis.

'So what we have to do,' Cockburn had said, 'is to make sure that the Soviet Union is not prepared for a German attack. That way the Germans will be enticed into the wastes of Russia; that way two tyrannies will cripple each other.'

'So where do I come in?' Roessler had asked.

'Simple. You will get advance warning of the date when Hitler intends to attack.'

'So?'

'Your information has hitherto been so good that Stalin will believe you.' Cockburn spoke good German, Berlin-accented; but so would any competent confidence trickster dealing with a German.

'So what do you want me to do?' Roessler had asked. 'Send him the wrong date?'

'On the contrary. I … we … want you to dispatch two incorrect items of information. Then when Stalin gets the true date of Barbarossa from you he won't believe it.'

Cockburn castled. Into trouble, in Roessler's opinion.

'So what have you decided?' Cockburn asked, pulling at the wings of his silver moustache.

'I haven't decided anything.'

'You left Germany because of what they were doing to the Jews, the gypsies, the mentally-deficient … Stalin will do the same, worse … You are in a position to prevent this.'

'Me alone?'

'Not completely,' Cockburn admitted.

An uncharacteristic display of honesty.

Roessler slid a bishop in behind his queen.

Cockburn saw the danger and covered his king's knight's pawn with a knight; but that's not enough, Mr. Cockburn ... sorry, *Coburn*.

Roessler sipped the last of his coffee, went to the kitchen to get some more. The doctors had said he should lay off the coffee. What would that leave him, for God's sake? He coughed; when the bout had spent itself he could hear his breathing whistling and singing in his lungs.

One thing was certain: he would get the date – and time – of Barbarossa before anyone else, with the possible exception of Richard Sorge in Tokyo. With his contacts he couldn't fail to do so. For decades historians would wonder who those contacts were. Would they ever believe that the head of the *Abwehr* was among them?

Returning to the dining room, he swept a rook across the board. The sort of move that Cockburn would have enjoyed – if he'd had the wit to move with more caution in the first place.

Cockburn looked nonplussed. He abandoned his moustache and stroked his hair. He must have been hellishly handsome as a young man, still was in a theatrical sort of way.

Roessler said to the frowning Cockburn: 'What are these false items you want me to send?'

'Nothing devastating. Details of a commando raid that never takes place ... British moves against Iraq ... none of it matters as long as it's wrong, wrong, wrong ...'

Cockburn touched the queen, then withdrew his finger; he was now obliged to move the queen; instead he moved a pawn; Roessler could have made him move the queen but he didn't bother. Why should he? Cockburn was doomed.

Roessler moved in for the kill with his knight. 'Check.' One move later Cockburn resigned with bad grace; he should have quit three or four moves before.

So, one battle won. 'All right,' Roessler said, 'I agree.' The other battle lost. Or won? Who was to say?

*

Three hundred miles from Lucerne, in a luxurious apartment overlooking the Bois de Boulogne in Paris, two homosexuals were having an impassioned argument.

One, Pierre Roux, the dominant partner, was in his early thirties, a physical fitness fanatic who had left the army after the 1940 débâcle and returned to the Parisian underworld; he managed a night club near the Place Pigalle which featured a transvestite cabaret and was popular with certain elements of the German army of occupation.

The other, Jean Capron, one of the transvestite dancers, was as willowy as Roux was muscular. He was wearing a black silk dressing gown embroidered with gold dragons, and a little make-up although his mascara had been smudged with tears of rage.

Roux, in addition to running the club, worked for the French Resistance and kept a radio transmitter under the floorboards of the club – under the feet of the Germans who came to see his young (and not so young) men waggle their hips and raise their skirts.

Capron, in addition to being on of the stars of the show, acted as an informant for the Soviet spy ring known as the Red Orchestra, masterminded in Paris by a Pole named Leopold Trepper who carried a forged Canadian passport bearing the name Adam Mikler.

The row had begun at midday when they tumbled out of bed. It had now consumed one hour of time, half a bottle of Ricard and, in Capron's case, ten Gauloise cigarettes.

'I won't do it,' Capron said. 'I just won't and that's the end of it.' He walked across the white carpet and examined his face in a gold-framed mirror, brushing ineffectually at the smudged mascara with one finger.

'You'll do what I say,' said Roux calmly. He felt his biceps under his sweat shirt, a habit of his. 'Otherwise—'

'You mustn't threaten me. You know what the doctor said—'

'That you're neurotic? I didn't need a doctor to tell me that.' Roux stared into his cloudy drink; he had drunk too much and would have to run in the Bois de Boulogne later to sweat it out. Who knows, he might meet some attractive young German soldier giving rein to his homosexuality suppressed (overtly anyway) in Germany by the Nazis. 'So be a good girl.' He yawned; the quarrel was becoming a bore.

'I won't,' Capron repeated. 'It's deceitful.'

'Since when did that bother you?'

'I don't know why you're so terrible to me.'

'Look,' Roux decided to try one last appeal to reason. 'All I'm asking you to do is to feed your Red Orchestra with a couple of false leads. The reason needn't concern you; I'm not sure that I understand it but I trust my sources.'

'On the radio?'

Yes, Roux agreed, on the radio; in fact he had met a British agent dropped by parachute near Melun.

'But everything I've told them so far has been true.'

'Of course. The information you get at the club is good. Germans are warned about not divulging secret material to girls: no one's ever warned them about keeping their mouths shut in the presence of the queens of Paris.'

'So what will happen if the Orchestra suddenly discovers that my information is unreliable?'

'They'll slap your wrists,' Roux said. He took one last sip of his Ricard. 'It might hurt a bit but you won't mind that, will you?'

Capron lit another Gauloise. 'And what will you do,' he asked, blowing a pout of smoke towards the ceiling, 'if I refuse?'

'First of all throw you out of the club.'

'I can find a job somewhere else. I'm very popular, you know.'

'And denounce you to the Krauts.'

'Two can play at that sort of game.'

'And maybe kill you.'

Capron sat down. The hand holding the cigarette was shaking, sending the stem of smoke into lacy patterns. 'You're joking, of course?'

'I was never more serious.'

'But I thought you cared ...'

'I don't give a fuck for anyone who doesn't do what I tell them.'

'You're a brute.'

'So?'

'I still won't do it.' Capron managed to look frightened and coquettish at the same time.

With a sigh, Roux stood up. He rolled one fist in the palm of the other. 'I had to discipline you once before, remember?'

'But that was before we lived together.'

'I've been too lenient with you ... Are you going to do what I've told you?'

'I can't betray people. I have my standards ...'

'Standards? Don't give me shit. What standards did an old Pigalle queen ever have?'

'Not so old,' Capron said.

'Yes or no?'

'You don't scare me.'

'We'll see,' said Roux as he hit Capron around the side of the face with the flat of his hand, knocking him out of the chair. He picked him up by the lapels of the dressing gown and hit him again on the other side of the face. 'We'll see,' letting him fall again.

Capron stared up at him, breathing hard, blood trickling from the corner of his mouth. 'Do what you like to me,' he said, a note of excitement in his voice, 'I don't care.'

'Very well.' Roux picked him up again. 'This time I'm really going to hurt you. You know, with a razor ...'

Capron began to sob. 'I thought you cared ...'

'You'll do it?'

'Yes, yes ... What do I have to do? You're so cruel ...'

Roux threw him in the chair. All he had to do, he told him, was convey two items of information about German troop movements to the Red Orchestra. There was one proviso about them: they both had to be wrong.

'Do you agree?' he asked Capron.

'On one condition.' Capron swallowed the rest of his glass of Ricard.

'Condition? You're in no position to lay down conditions, my dear.'

'That we stay together.'

'But of course, I wouldn't want it any other way.' Roux pointed to the bedroom. 'Come let's seal the bargain.'

How much longer, he wondered, would the British insist on him consorting with this tiresome creature. Really, war was hell.

Chapter Twenty-four

Two factors persuaded Josef Hoffman that it was time to change the location of his code-book and second radio transmitter. One was the inexorable build-up of the German Army and Luftwaffe on the Baltic-Black Sea line dividing them from the Russians; two, the discovery that a Russian linguist had been imported into the British Embassy.

The conclusion was obvious: one way or the other his mission was reaching its climax: either he was going to send the ultimate message to Stalin his own way or the British were going to meddle.

He had discovered about the Russian one fine morning at the beginning of May when he visited the British Embassy on Red Cross business.

Summer heat was beginning to settle on the city but it was fanned by a breeze coming in from the Atlantic and the Union Jack fluttered defiantly above the low, rather shabby building on the Rua S. Domingos a Lapa, a genteel but poor place compared with the German diplomatic HQ.

With Hoffman were two refugees who had fled from the Russians rather than from the Germans, which made a change. They were Ukrainians; they claimed they were influential and they wanted to see the British Ambassador to pass on details of Ukrainian underground movements. Deputies had been suggested and rejected, only the Ambassador would suffice.

The three of them were waiting in the entrance hall. With its cracked, black and pink floor tiles and worn carpet covering baronial stairs it reminded Hoffman of an exclusive men's club in London; any moment now a bandy octogenarian with a yellowing boiled shirt would lead them to the ambassadorial presence.

But His Excellency was obviously busy: he couldn't be anything else in war-time Lisbon. The minutes dragged into half an hour. The Ukrainians began to talk angrily to each other in a heavy, regional dialect that Hoffman had difficulty in understanding. Not so the wispy-haired, bespectacled man who emerged from an office.

'What's the trouble?' he asked, using the same dialect.

One of the two men, both sturdy, bleak-faced and neckless, exuding importance, told him.

The stranger said: 'You should be used to waiting if you come from the Soviet Union.'

Hoffman who understood him better than the two Ukrainians said in Muscovite Russian: 'I didn't know there were any Russians in the British Embassy.'

The wispy-haired man looked at him with surprise. 'I'm not, I'm what they call a Russian expert. In other words I can speak Russian; not many people in Britain can do that, you know. And you?'

'Czech,' Hoffman said. 'But I have a way with languages.'

'Me too. People mistake it for brains.' He smiled brightly.

Hoffman asked: 'How long have you been at the Embassy?'

'A couple of weeks, that's all. There doesn't seem to be very much for me to do. But I gather they've got an important job coming up.'

I bet they have, Hoffman thought, and said: 'Communications?'

'I liaise with them, yes …' He frowned. 'Well, I must be on my way,' as though he had just remembered that he had been told to keep his mouth shut.

He gave them another bright smile and walked hurriedly away as if pursued.

That evening Hoffman sent an encoded message from the old room in the Alfama.

ONE HUNDRED FORTY FIVE GERMANS DIVISIONS MOVING TOWARDS SOVIET CONTROLLED FRONTIER STOP AN ESTIMATED THREE MILLION SOLDIERS SUPPORTED BY PANZERS COMPRISING 2,400 TANKS COMMA MOTORISED INFANTRY ETCETERA STOP ALSO UNDERSTAND FINNISH AND ROUMANIAN UNITS ASSEMBLING STOP LUFTWAFFE SUPPORT PLANES IN REGION OF 2,000 ALSO BELIEVED TO BE STANDING BY THROUGHOUT EASTERN EUROPE STOP.

Before signing off he again added a rider: DISREGARD JUDAS.

Then he waited for the acknowledgement.

After a couple of minutes the receiver stuttered into life: RECEIVED STOP HERE IS ONE FOR YOU.

After the operator in the Centre had finished transmitting it took Hoffman half an hour to decode it using *War and Peace.*

The message signed Hawk – Stalin's confidential code-name – sought elaboration of previous messages that Hoffman had sent. Was it possible that the military build-up was a diversion from Hitler's true purpose, the invasion of Britain?

Three million men a diversion? Jesus Christ!

And did Hoffman have a date for any supposed attack on Russia? Supposed! Was the man blind?

During his conversations in Moscow Hoffman had to an extent understood his father's reasoning. He didn't want to provoke Hitler in any way – a Soviet build-up would be just such a provocation – so that he could buy more time to re-arm. And he didn't believe that Hitler was crazy enough to make the same mistake as Napoleon.

But that was before three-quarters of the *Wehrmacht* had started rumbling towards the border!

Hoffman sent a formal acknowledgement. No, he hadn't any date and yes, he would investigate Lisbon's assessments of Hitler's motives.

What, he wondered, would happen if and when he did get a date? *If* because he suspected that Cross wouldn't pass it on to him. The wispy-haired linguist must have been brought out to translate a message into Russian which could then be encoded by …

Rachel. Who else? He covered his face with his hands.

When because he had every intention of getting the date from the British.

He packed up the transmitter, Tolstoy's bulky masterpeice, pads and references. But this time he didn't replace them beneath the floor. Instead he removed six *azulejos* from a portrait of St. Anthony of Lisbon; the saint regarded him balefully through his one remaining eye; but he had been a defender of human rights so he ought to understand.

Hoffman passed the black suitcase containing the tools of his trade through the opening into the tunnel that lay beyond. Then he replaced the tiles.

Dusting himself down, he emerged into the patio and walked into the street. It was full of noise and people and heat that had built up during the day but Hoffman knew that he could pick out any shadow easily enough – he was experienced in such matters these days. He wasn't disappointed.

302

He strolled down the Beco do Mexias, past the inner patio where the housewives did the washing in a fountain; under balconies blooming with geraniums and dripping with laundry, through a ring of dancing children, past pigmy shops selling spices and nuts and fishing tackle and into the black mouth of a bar where everything except the customers' tongues was suspended in the gloom.

He ordered a glass of port. The barman, as listless as an over-fed dog, poured the ruby liquid, Portugal's blood, and returned to his stool while his customers continued to argue heatedly about bull-fighting and fishing and women.

Hoffman, sitting beneath a photograph of Salazar, watched the doorway. Soon his pursuer would peer in with studied nonchalance.

Five minutes passed. He ordered another glass of port. As he began to sip it a swarthy, middle-aged man with a sad moustache and a burgeoning belly peered in. Then he went on his way. Hoffman sipped and waited. The swarthy man – Portuguese by the look of him – returned. Hoffman assumed that, tonight, he was the only watchdog. Employed by whom?

Hoffman finished his port, paid the barman and strode into the cramped street. Then he lengthened his stride; below, he could see lights glittering in the streets, pulled into water-colours on the river.

He made a series of quick turns. Wherever he went the lament of the *fado* followed him. So at a distance did the man with the sad moustache.

Hoffman glanced at his watch. It was nearly midnight. He turned, passing his pursuer, and ran to the railway where he had chained his bicycle. He unlocked it and set off down the hill. The man with the moustache ran behind him.

At the bottom of the hill Hoffman changed gear and pedalled furiously across the Baixa. He dismounted near the elevator and chained the bike to a lamppost. Then he joined the queue.

What would I do if I were the pursuer? he wondered. I would race the elevator, he decided, and wait at the point where the overhead bridge joined the street.

The elevator rose slowly, occupants staring everywhere except at each other. When it reached the platform at the top Hoffman emerged, then doubled back round the observation platform, clambering over a wooden barrier marked DANG-ER in English, German and Portuguese.

He waited.

The elevator descended with a sigh.

He could hear the traffic far below, an aircraft droning across the starlit sky, the farewell siren of a departing ship. Footsteps approaching across the bridge.

He shrank back. To his left was the reason for the danger sign: the metal fencing around the platform had only been partly repaired.

He pushed himself against the inner wall.

First a hand rounding the corner. Then a foot. A pause. Then the belly. Then the face with the drooping moustache. Like a Mexican bandit's, Hoffman thought.

As he rounded the corner Hoffman kicked his legs from under him and, as he fell forward, clubbed him over the back of the neck with the blade of his hand.

Grunting, the man tried to stand up. Going for a knife at the same time. Hoffman brought up his knee into his groin.

The man doubled up, and vomited; the knife fell from his grasp, bounced on the platform and fell into space, glinting like a silver fish.

'Who sent you?' Hoffman asked the man lying at his feet.

He could hear the elevator starting up again below.

'PIDE.'

'Portuguese secret service? Why should they be interested in me?' He put his foot on the man's throat. 'Who sent you?'

The man grabbed his foot. Hoffman lost his balance. And the man was on top of him. They rolled to one side. The metal fencing broke and swung open like a gate.

Hoffman's head was over the brink of the platform. Far below he could see the lights of street lamps and traffic. A fist crashed into the side of his face.

He rolled away from the edge.

The platform shuddered as the lift began its ascent.

A breeze suddenly sprang up; it caught the swinging flap of metal and slammed it shut. The flap hit the man on the side of the head. He loosened his grip.

Hoffman broke loose. He grabbed the man by the neck as he tried to sit up. 'Who sent you?'

The man stared at him.

Hoffman pushed him forward. The flap swung open again.

The man's head was suspended over space. 'Who?'

'The British.' Even though he had half-expected the reply it sickened him – the Russian at the Embassy, Rachel knowing ... he thrust the man's body further over the edge of the platform hearing, without comprehending, his scream.

The two men who hauled them back were Americans. 'Christ,' one of them said, 'what the hell was all that about?' He was elderly, shuddering from the exertion.

Hoffman stood up and leaned against the wall. I was going to kill him, he thought. Who am I to pass judgement on men of violence?

He stumbled away. One of the Americans shouted: 'Hey, you, stop,' but he broke into a run, through the gaping crowds, across the bridge, into the Largo do Carmo, up the street, through the door of his lodging house, up the stairs and on to his bed where he lay as though dead.

Ten minuts later he got up. He went to the bathroom, stripped and poured a jug of cold water over himself. He felt as though he had surfaced from tranquil depths and, through a periscope, glimpsed insanity.

He dried himself, returned to his bedroom, put on flannel trousers and shirt and went out again into the night. He walked downhill to the Baixa where he unlocked his bicycle. Swiftly he pedalled back to the Alfama, up through the still-crowded alleys to a basement beside the ramparts of the castle.

With an iron key he opened the heavy, studded door. It opened with a groan. He locked it behind him and lit a candle. At the rear of the basement was a flight of stone steps leading down to a cellar. A tunnel led from the cellar to the back of the tiled portrait of St. Anthony in the room where Hoffman had been transmitting. When he had discovered the existence of the tunnel he had promptly rented the basement.

He crawled along the tunnel. There at the end was the suitcase. He hauled it into the cellar and placed it in a cavity he had prepared beneath a flagstone.

He left the cellar by another flight of steps, emerging in the grounds of the castle where Romans, Visigoths and Moors had once ruled. Now it was neutral just as the world should be, thought Hoffman as he breathed deeply of the cool night air.

*

He didn't return to the lodging house that night. Instead he went to Rachel Keyser's apartment where he made love to her with an abandonment that frightened both of them.

When she finally slept he thought: 'What has happened to you, Viktor Golovin?' *War changes everyone* ... but what if there had been no war?

And what is true character? In my case it needed only a catalyst to change it. How many murderers had been quiet, unprepossessing men until a slumbering passion was aroused?

And it wasn't until he accepted the explanation that true character needs a test before it is established – that the old Viktor Golovin had been an innocent impostor – that he slept.

In the morning realism settled coldly upon him. After breakfast he went out and purchased a gun.

He bought it from a Polish refugee who had made it known that he had one for sale. It was Russian – a TT 1930 modelled, according to the refugee, on a Colt M 1911, which meant nothing to Hoffman. But obviously he had to learn how to use it.

He crossed the river by ferry and boarded a bus for the port of Setúbal. He alighted halfway there and, carrying gun and ammunition in a canvas bag, headed across fields of maize and wheat. When he reached a clump of eucalyptus he stopped and gazed around; the green countryside stretched to the horizon, shimmering in the midday heat; there was no one to be seen.

He had brought with him a book about handguns borrowed from the British Library. Consulting it, he managed to load the gun, an automatic.

With a stick of chalk he drew a target on the trunk of a eucalyptus. He walked back ten yards and took aim; he was surprised how calm he felt; he fired; the bullet whined viciously off a boulder beside the tree.

He fired again; a chip of bark flew off the trunk a foot from the target. He held his breath, took aim again, fired. A little nearer. He was enjoying it. When a bullet smacked into the outer circle he grinned fiercely.

He sat down and took a bottle of cheap red wine from the canvas bag. He took a swig of it, wiping his mouth with the back of his hand. Then he reloaded the gun.

Slowly he raised it, keeping his arm stiff and straight. He lined up the sights with the target. He saw the face of the man on the platform of the elevator, he saw Cross, the two Gestapo officers in Poland ...

The bullet dug a hole dead centre of the target.

Hoffman licked his lips. Fired again. Another bull. He drank some more wine. A celebration. A few more shots. No more bulls but most of the shots were on target.

He laid down the smoking gun with its grooved butt bearing the letters CCCP and took bread, goat's cheese and olives from his bag and ate them, washed down with the rest of the wine.

Then he lay down beneath the whispering fronds of the wounded eucalyptus and slept.

He was awoken by a dog sniffing him. He sat up and saw a shepherd with a flock of sheep regarding him. The shepherd, toothless and shrivelled, pointed at the trunk of the tree. 'Why shoot a tree?' he asked.

'It won't hurt it,' Hoffman said, but he felt ashamed.

'It might kill it.'

'No. Eucalyptus look beautiful but they are also tough.'

'It will do it no good.'

Hoffman picked up his bag. 'I am sorry for what I have done to the tree.'

'But why shoot it?'

Hoffman left him staring at the bullet holes and began to walk back towards the road. It was very hot and he felt drowsy with wine.

When he reached the road he thumbed down an old Citroën driven by an oyster-farmer from Setúbal. What, he wondered, would the farmer say if he knew his passenger carried a gun in his bag?

He would probably sigh: *'Se Deus quizer,'* if God wills, which reflected the Portuguese philosophy; fatalistic and easy-going with an appreciation of all things melancholy which could erupt into spontaneous gaiety.

Hoffman thought he would have liked to have been born Portuguese. Instead, so it seemed, his veins ran with Tartar blood.

The farmer dropped him in the centre of Lisbon.

Hoffman took his gun to his lodgings and locked it in the tin chest. Then he cycled to Rachel's apartment.

'What have you been doing?' she asked.

'Completing my education,' he said.

*

In the thick forest near Rastenburg in East Prussia it was raining hard.

307

'What do you think?' Hitler asked, gesturing around the dark green, dripping pine trees.

Canaris shivered; the place depressed him; but as an HQ for the invasion of Russia it was, he supposed, fair enough.

It was ideal, he told the Führer, wishing that they could get the hell out of the place. Hitler, who was wearing a black leather coat, didn't seem to mind the rain plastering the lick of dark hair across his forehead and streaming down his face; Canaris minded it very much indeed and thought it might germinate a cold or even pneumonia. Spaced out around the glade among the trees were half a dozen soaking wet SS bodyguards.

Hitler said: 'It will have everything a command post should have. And every comfort, even central heating. Do you know what I intend to call it?'

Canaris brushed rainwater from his grey hair and thought about it. The forests in this part of Prussia were thick with legends about witches. 'The Cauldron?' he suggested.

'Not bad. But I've thought of something a little more war-like. I intend to call it the Wolf's Lair.'

'Very good, *mein Führer.*' And now, pray God, they could climb into the Mercedes-Benz and drive to the nearest village to dry out their bodies in front of the flames from a roaring log fire.

But Hitler was still in his lair. He pointed to the east. 'Soon we will possess the ultimate living space – the heartland of the Soviet Union. Their agriculture will feed us, their industry will fuel us, their Aryan masters.'

Canaris who thought Hitler looked about as Aryan as Himmler or, for that matter, Goebbels – what a gang! – said: 'It is a marvellous concept.'

If the British had passed on details of Barbarossa why for pity's sake hadn't Stalin taken any steps to shore up his defences? Has my act of betrayal been for nothing?

Hitler said: 'I'm glad you think so. As an admiral you have more military sense than some of my generals.'

Canaris thought: 'If Barbarossa succeeds then one day Hitler will find out from the British what I did. Unless I can liquidate everyone involved in the leak.'

Hitler was striding around the glade, already directing operations, poring over maps on which the cartographer's arrows swept through Lithuania, Belorussia, the Ukraine ...

The first move, Canaris thought, would have to be made in Portugal. Eliminate the Lisbon connection. A man named Hoffman, according to von Claus, who sold information to the *Abwehr*. Von Claus's radio sleuths had recently picked up transmissions to Moscow sent from an address rented by Hoffman.

Hitler stood, hands on hips, staring through the rain at Moscow. Taking the salute in Red Square, having removed Lenin's mummified corpse from the mausoleum.

But before eliminating Hoffman and the other conspirators, Canaris decided, I will make one last bid to convince the British, and thus the Russians, about Hitler's intentions. Give them the exact date of Barbarossa.

If that fails then the liquidations will start. First Hoffman. To dispose of the prime witness to my treachery *and* to prove to Hitler that I was more on the ball than Himmler.

Poor, doomed Hoffman. Everyone would want to kill him. The inevitable price a spy had to pay. The price I will have to pay if I don't out-smart Himmler and Heydrich ...

But at least I still have the ear of Hitler, he consoled himself, as the Führer clapped him on the shoulder and led him towards the waiting limousine.

The driver jumped out and opened the door. Hitler and Canaris climbed in, dripping water over the leather upholstery.

Motorcycle outriders gunned their machines. Wheels splashing wings of water, the Mercedes-Benz took off along a lane leading to a highway. Rain poured from a low sky, splashing on the glistening surface.

Hitler mopped his face with a white silk handkerchief. 'We will be remembered you and I' - he had this knack of embracing you in his future - 'for restoring Germany's greatness. For establishing the Third Reich in its rightful place at the helm of Europe, of the world ...'

It was at times like this that Canaris doubted terribly what he was doing. If he dropped the whole thing Stalin would probably continue to ignore the warnings and Germany *would* assume her place at the helm where she belonged ...

'And,' said Hitler, patting his still-damp forelock, 'we will be served by a vast army of slaves. Slavs, peasants, even a few Jews perhaps ... But first, of course, we shall have to assert ourselves far beyond the normal military requirements.'

'I'm afraid I don't understand,' Canaris said.

'Come now, my good admiral, we can't have political subversion after we've brought the Russians to heel, can we? I'm about to issue two decrees. But you probably know about them already.' Canaris didn't. 'First, political commissars in the Russian armed forces will not be treated as prisoners of war. No Geneva Convention, nothing like that.'

'Executed?'

Hitler nodded vigorously. 'Liquidated. And so that there shall be no doubt about this among our troops I'm issuing the second decree.'

Numbed, Canaris waited for it.

'There will be no retribution against any member of the *Wehrmacht* who kills or in any way maltreats any member of the Bolshevik civilian population.'

Canaris was grateful to Hitler: he had restored his faith in his own betrayal.

Ahead of them a crow rose from the road and flapped heavily into the pine trees.

'That reminds me,' Hitler remarked, 'I want to issue a local order. No hunting in the forest; I want all game, all birds, preserved,' and Canaris thought: 'You're stark, staring, raving mad, *mein Führer.*'

Aloud, he said: 'The final date for Barbarossa ...'

'You mean you don't know?'

Hurriedly, Canaris said: 'I understand you made your decision about the date on April 30 ...'

'You had me worried for a moment, Herr Admiral. The head of military intelligence should surely know in advance the plans of the Supreme Commander of the Armed Forces ...'

'I was merely seeking confirmation.'

Hitler nodded approvingly. 'Check your facts. You really are a fine example to some of my more irresponsible lieutenants,' without actually naming Goering. 'Very well, we attack on the shortest night of the summer – June 22.'

Canaris did a rapid calculation. Today was May 9. Unless he was able to forestall it, there were forty-four days until the beginning of the end.

Part Six

Chapter Twenty-five

Nervously, the pilot of the Messerschmitt 110 scanned the evening sky for British fighters. It wasn't merely his own skin that concerned him: he was frightened that his sacred mission might never be completed.

Below him lay the North Sea as calm as sheet metal. Ahead the coastline of Scotland. He didn't doubt that his aircraft would be picked up by radar; but he didn't think the British would bother to launch a full-scale attack on a solitary aircraft.

He consulted the instrument panel. He had taken off from Augsburg at 1745 hours. Destination: Dungavel. As far as he could make out he was on course, on schedule. As anticipated, fuel was running out.

It was the fuel factor that should confuse the British. Why would a Messerschmitt 110 be flying over Scotland when it couldn't possibly have enough fuel to get it back to base?

Well, they would find out soon enough.

He was over Scotland now, the end of his 900-mile flight almost in sight. He began his descent, grateful for the training Willi Messerschmitt had given him.

The pilot, forty-six, with a face that was third saint, third fanatic and third brute, checked in his flying suit to make sure that he had the photographs that would identify him; he was slipping them back when the fuel ran out.

He did what he had known he would have to do: he baled out. When he hit the ground he felt a bone in his leg snap; but he managed to roll up his parachute and limp to a cottage.

The door was opened by a farm labourer. The pilot told him that his name was Horn of which only the H was correct: his real name was Rudolf Hess and he was Adolf Hitler's deputy.

*

Hess had worshipped Hitler for more than twenty years. As a young man he had taken part in the Munich *putsch* and been

313

jailed with Hitler at Landsberg where he had helped him to write *Mein Kampf.* He had become third in the line of succession to Hitler – Goering was second – in 1939.

But recently, as Hitler became more absorbed with military strategy than with politics, he had been forced into the background by men of war. There was only one answer – prove himself once more to his God, who had rebuilt Germany from the ashes of humiliation.

So far, one task had eluded Hitler: he had been unable to persuade the British, whom he admired, to seek peace. So Hess had decided he would do it, to remind Hitler of his devotion and his genius. As it happened he had the contacts, in particular the Duke of Hamilton, a friend of the son of his own political adviser, Karl Haushofer.

The Duke was also Lord Steward. A confidant of the King and, no doubt, of Winston Churchill. So Hess determined to fly to the Duke and tell him that Hitler merely sought friendship from the British – on the Führer's terms, of course.

He had been a little perturbed when Canaris had approached him just before he took off from Augsburg. If the wily admiral knew what he was up to, how many other members of the wolfpack surrounding Hitler knew? But Canaris had reassured him: 'It is my job to know about such matters but I haven't confided in anyone else.'

In fact Canaris had merely elaborated on Hess's mission. Why not show Churchill how Hitler planned to crush the Soviet Union – with dates and details? Anyone could see from the plans that it would be a swift and devastating victory. Then Hitler would turn on Britain. Unless …

'… Churchill agrees to do a deal,' Canaris had said. 'In other words pressurise him a little. With Russia in flames on one flank, the Führer can't fail to crush Britain on the other. Even Churchill must appreciate that.'

And Canaris had given him the details of Barbarossa complete with date, June 22. Details that I should have known about, Hess had thought bitterly. Canaris's last words had been: 'But don't mention my name.'

*

Churchill was told about Hess's arrival while he was watching a Marx Brothers film. He told Eden to arrange for Hess to be interrogated.

314

It was the results of the interrogation that absorbed him as he stood in the ruins of the House of Commons, hit by a bomb the night Hess arrived. It had been a barbarous night, that Saturday. Two thousand fires had been started and, with the Thames at low tide and 150 water mains smashed by bombs, the fire-fighters hadn't been able to cope. Three thousand people had been killed or injured, nearly every main railway terminus blocked, five docks and scores of factories hit ...

In a way it made what he was perpetrating easier to contemplate. The wreckage around him proved that the Germans had no compunction about bombing civilian targets; nor would the Russians – less, probably; so the only way was to manipulate the two enemies of common decency into a war of attrition.

But why did he have to keep reassuring himself?

Stick in hand, hunched in his topcoat, he glowered for the photographers.

Would anyone understand when the deaths of, say, twenty million people were attributed to him? *Warmonger* ... the taunt rose from the shattered masonry at his feet. But they wouldn't be content with that if they knew the truth. Mass murderer. More. As it was they would no doubt throw him out when the war was won. He had been born for war just as Chamberlain, whose death he had mourned seven months ago, had been born for peace.

Loneliness visited him sharply and once more the photographers' cameras clicked.

One day, perhaps, people would understand that he had saved their children from monstrous oppression. They would still remember what the Nazis had done to the Jews, they would still be witnessing what the Russians were doing to neighbouring minorities. Forty years ... that was about the time it would take; four decades had a middle-aged ring of responsibility about them. Perhaps young Hoffman who would then be in his sixties would tell the story. (I must give him the authority.) Or perhaps some journalist trying to puzzle out one of the enigmas of the war – and, by God, there were enough secrets – would stumble upon the truth.

Churchill picked his way through the rubble past the spot where, some forty years earlier, he had made his maiden speech. How many of those listening that day had realised how nervous he was? But he had acted his way through the ordeal;

315

acted his way through the rest of his public life; given a vast audience the act they wanted.

He reached the car and told the driver to take an indirect route back to No. 10. He wanted to think. The car moved away; he gave a V sign to the crowds, then settled back in the cushions.

Ironic how closely Hess's idea corresponded with what he had proposed to Hitler through clandestine channels to make him call off the invasion of Britain and attack Russia. Hess, of course, hadn't known anything about the tacit agreement – a swift victory over the Bolsheviks then a negotiated peace with Britain.

Some hope! Churchill grinned and lit a cigar.

They were close to Victoria Station. He glanced out of the window at the sand-bagged scene. *Black Vanities* was playing at the Victoria Palace, *The Philadelphia Story* at the New Victoria cinema. On the theatre wall was a poster LET US GO FORWARD TOGETHER complete with a photograph of the star of *that* show, Winston Churchill.

The car turned into Downing Street. June 22 – that was the date Hess had given for Barbarossa. That corresponded with other reports Sinclair had received. But the date would not be given to Lisbon until June 18; Stalin had to be kept on as tight a rein as possible; if he was allowed time to brood over his son's message – that Hitler did not intend to attack – then he might still put the Red Army in a state of readiness.

June 18-22. Four days in which the future of the world would be decided. He climbed out of the car and strode purposefully into No. 10.

*

June 17.

In his country residence at Kuntsevo Joseph Stalin agonized over the evidence of Hitler's intentions.

He moved from one of the three main rooms – each furnished with a long table and a sofa – to another, and stood in a shaft of dusty sunlight trembling on the floor. Despite the warmth, log fires burned – to keep the wolves of doubt at bay.

He still believed that Hitler was bluffing. That the army massing on the border was a feint to conceal his intent to invade Britain. That in any case Hitler would deliver an ultimatum before making a move against the Soviet Union.

That he, Stalin, would then be able to make a few concessions while he re-armed the Red Army. That Hitler would be stark raving mad to take on the Russian winter ...

The trouble, Stalin brooded, was that no one agreed with him and the only informant he could trust, his son in Lisbon, had been out of touch for days. If Viktor didn't make contact tomorrow he would have to re-inforce the border. And provoke Hitler into attacking?

Head aching, he sat down at a table and reviewed the warnings he had received.

The United States. Three months ago the American Secretary of State, Cordell Hull, had handed over a copy of what was alleged to be a copy of Barbarossa to the Russian Ambassador in Washington, Konstantin Oumansky. It was said to have been obtained by the U.S. commercial attaché in Berlin, Sam Woods.

Stalin had totally disregarded that one. It was in the interests of America, Britain's undeclared ally, to persuade Russia to take military steps that *would* provoke Hitler. Vicious mischief-making pure and simple.

Britain. In April Churchill had cabled a warning through his Ambassador in Moscow, Stafford Cripps. What else would you expect from an anti-Bolshevik capitalist warmonger?

Richard Sorge. On May 19 this once-trusted spy – why anyone should trust a spy Stalin couldn't imagine – had sent details of the German military build-up on the border; on June 1 he had outlined the tactics the Nazis would use; two days ago he had given June 22 as the date for the invasion.

But Sorge had got Operation Compass wrong and a lot more besides. His final *coup* had been a message that Hitler didn't intend to take Crete. On May 20 Hitler had attacked Crete!

So much for Richard Sorge.

The Lucy Ring. According to Marshal Golikov, head of Military Intelligence, the information provided by this agency had been the best in Europe. Until recently. Suddenly the intelligence supplied by a master agent named Rudolf Roessler had become suspect. A British commando raid that never took place, British policy in Iraq totally wrong ...

The Red Orchestra. Another spy ring that was supposedly milking the Third Reich of its secrets. They, too, had botched up their last two messages.

Stalin sat up abruplty.

317

Why should I take any notice of any such sources?

He felt better. He lit his pipe and blew coils of smoke into the shaft of sunlight. From the wall Lenin smiled at him approvingly.

There was still the evidence seen through Red Army field-glasses: a vast army *was* concealed in the pine forests, marshes, hills, stretching from the Baltic to the Black Sea.

But a bully has to flex his muscles.

No, Hitler won't attack. Stalin poured himself some vodka, drank it and munched black bread and pickled gherkins.

Or will he?

The headache returned.

Speak to me, Judas. Speak to me, Viktor.

*

Three weeks after leaking details of Barbarossa to Hess, Canaris had visited Hitler at Obersalzberg.

Martin Bormann, who was taking over from Hess, had been there together with Frau Bormann and Eva Braun and her mother and sister. Canaris could never understand Hitler's liaison with the dumb little shop girl. Perhaps she was an accomplished performer in bed; but then again it was by no means sure that Hitler had sex with her – Canaris's intelligence stopped at the bedroom door.

More likely she was a good listener as everyone close to the Führer had to be. Including the brutal, balding Bormann who when Canaris arrived at the Berghof was stomping around the grounds pointing out to the Brauns his achievements in reconstructing the whole Obersalzberg area.

While Bormann continued to show off Canaris took the opportunity to speak to Hitler in his study on the first floor. At Hitler's feet lay his Alsatian, Blondi. From time to time Hitler stroked the dog and tickled it behind its ears.

Canaris, who assumed that Hess must by now have passed on details of Barbarossa to the British, told Hitler that he feared a British agent in Lisbon was poised to pass on details to the Kremlin. Why hadn't he been liquidated? Because, Canaris said, the Gestapo had botched surveillance and alerted the agent.

Hitler gave Blondi a final pat and straightened up. 'So you consider this man to be a real danger to Barbarossa, Herr Admiral?'

318

Canaris said he did.

A rasp of hysteria edged Hitler's voice. Barbarossa forestalled by one British agent ... by Gestapo bungling ... He said: 'Then you will stop him, admiral. I hold you personally responsible ...'

'In that case,' Canaris said, 'perhaps you would be good enough, *mein Führer*, to give me written authority ...'

From a drawer in his desk Hitler snatched a sheet of personally-embossed notepaper and an envelope. He scrawled rapidly across the paper. His breathing was rapid, pale eyes wild.

He folded the paper, thrust it into the envelope and threw it across the polished surface of the desk to Canaris, who picked it up and put it in his pocket without reading it – that would have been a mistake.

Hitler swung round and stared through the tall, lace-curtained windows. His voice cracked with emotion as Canaris had heard it crack during speeches in the early, euphoric days. 'If I have ever made one mistake it is to deploy police power. You ... Himmler ... Heydrich ... You should work together not against one another ...'

But they would continue to work against one another and Canaris had no illusions about who would win in the end. The racists, the brutalised fascists, those who asserted power through mass terror. But until then he had this one chance of saving ordinary German soldiers from being massacred by the icy armoury of the Russian winter.

Canaris stood up, clicked his heels, gave the Nazi salute. 'Have no fear, there will be no leak from the British agent in Lisbon.' He stood up, turned and walked briskly away. Escaped.

So at least he had reported the Lisbon conspiracy. A point in his favour. If things went wrong and the true source of the Barbarossa leaks – me! – was suspected he could point out that he had reported the matter to Hitler. Hardly the behaviour of a traitor.

What's more he had obtained Hitler's authority to eliminate the leak. A traitor didn't seek permission to destroy his own channels of communication. And, he congratulated himself, he had also managed to lay the blame for the negligence at the door of the Gestapo.

He decided the British would wait until about June 18

before warning Stalin. That's what I would do if I were in Churchill's place. Let the devious little Georgian stew in his own sweat, then give him four days, just enough time, to rush reinforcements to the border – and prevent a holocaust.

He ignored Bormann's friendly wave and climbed into the back of his Maybach. As the tourer glided through the green valley he felt his pulse; fast; he told the driver to stop at an inn where he swallowed a pink tablet with a glass of water.

When he got back to his office in the Tirpitzufer he sent a cable to von Claus in Lisbon. Josef Hoffman had to be liquidated on June 18. And Cross, of course. And Rachel Keyser.

*

Von Claus was in command and he was enjoying it.

On his desk separating him from Bauer lay the written authorisation from Hitler. You would have thought it was primed to explode the way Bauer was looking at it.

'So I am taking complete control of the Hoffman case,' he told Bauer. 'As from now there will be no Gestapo interference whatsoever.'

Bauer tugged furiously at one of his little ears. 'Of course, if that is the Führer's wish.'

'No more agents being hit on the head with bar stools,' von Claus remarked. His back had been aching earlier that morning, but this exchange was so stimulating that the pain had disappeared.

'An unfortunate accident,' Bauer said. 'The agent concerned has been dealt with. He has been sent back to Berlin.'

'So you'll be meeting him there?'

Bauer leaned forward over the desk; he was sweating profusely. 'What do you mean by that?'

'The Führer was far from pleased by what's happened over here.'

'But nothing has happened,' Bauer said.

'Precisely. In fact so little has happened that I understand you may be recalled to Berlin to explain this dearth of activity. Himmler and Heydrich like action, I understand.'

'But you've done even less!'

'On the contrary,' von Claus said. 'We picked up certain radio transmissions.'

'What radio transmissions?'

320

'That needn't concern you.' The conversation really was the best fillip he had enjoyed for years. Not that his cryptanalyst had been able to decode Hoffman's messages. But the British-Soviet connection ... it had to be Barbarossa.

Bauer lit one of his filthy black cigars. 'Is there to be a ... liquidation?'

'That needn't concern you either.'

'If it is then my men can—'

'No help,' von Claus snapped.

'May I ask when?'

Von Claus shook his head happily. 'By the way,' he said, 'I just spoke to Canaris on the telephone. He said Himmler was in a filthy temper. I can't think why, can you?'

By the expression on his face Bauer could.

Von Claus stood up to indicate the interview was over. 'By the way,' he said, 'I thought this might be of some use to you.' He handed Bauer a timetable listing aeroplane connections to Berlin.

Chapter Twenty-six

Judging by the German military build-up Barbarossa was imminent.

So why hadn't any information reached him from London?

On Wednesday, June 18, Hoffman decided to contact Moscow to see if Stalin had reacted to the deployment of Nazi troops.

He wheeled his cycle from the hallway of his lodgings at eight a.m. and set out across the city. It was going to be a lovely day; mist from the Tagus lay in pools at the foot of Lisbon's hills but soon the sun would burn it away.

The air smelled of coffee and hot bread; newspaper-vendors were shuffling their morning editions, flower-sellers arranging bunches of carnations and bird of paradise blooms in green buckets. Weaving in and out of the trams and taxis, Hoffman made his way to the Alfama and padlocked his cycle to some railings.

He paused for a moment, then darted into the mist. A few phantoms loomed up, briefly gaining substance before vanishing again. He was satisfied that he had shaken off any pursuers. Thank God for the mist.

He made his way towards his new HQ, unlocked the heavy door, removed the transmitter from below the flagstones and got through to Moscow.

The response came back as though the operator at the Centre had been poised waiting for him. It was brief and he decoded it while keeping contact.

SOURCES HERE ASSERT GERMANS PLANNING ATTACK JUNE TWENTY-SECOND STOP PLEASE CONFIRM OR DENY URGENTEST REPEAT URGENTEST HAWK

Hoffman sent back WILL DO DOVE and cut the connection.

He sat for a moment. If Moscow had a date – provided, of course, that it was the right one – why didn't London? Strange, because the British had incomparable sources of information.

Thoughtfully, he replaced the transmitter under the flagstone, locked the door and made his way back to his bicycle. The mist had cleared and the Alfama was as busy as a street market once more.

As he pedalled round the Rossio he thought: 'Perhaps the British *do* have a date.' And then: 'But what reason could they have for withholding it from me?'

Rachel's apartment was locked but he had a key. On the table was a note GONE TO BUY BREAD, BACK IN FIFTEEN MINUTES.

So she wasn't going to the Embassy this morning.

Hoffman stared through the window at the sunlit park.

When she came back he would ask her about June 22. But would she tell him the truth?

There had to be another way to find out and, of course, there was. He fetched the other transmitter from her bedroom. He knew her call-sign, he knew her touch ... What he didn't know was how long she had been away from the apartment.

He placed the transmitter on the dining-room table and made contact with the British Embassy. The old Josef Hoffman would have asked naively: DO YOU HAVE A DATE FOR BARBAROSSA?

Not the devious replacement. Using her call-sign RAVEN and her touch he asked:

CANST CONFIRM BARBAROSSA DATE JUNE 22
NOT 21 RAVEN

A pause. Outside he thought he heard the lift.

Come on, he entreated the silent machine.

The clang of the lift door shutting. Footsteps.

The machine came to life.

The footsteps stopped.

Letter by letter he wrote down the message.

C...O...N...F...I...R...M...E...D ... There had never been a slower operator.

A key in the door.

T...W...E...N...T...Y...S...E...C...O...N...D...

The door opened and he said: 'Hello, Rachel, I was just practising,' and Cross said: 'In that case you won't mind showing me what you've written on the pad.'

Hoffman said: 'It's none of your—' and looked into the barrel of an automatic.

Cross waved the barrel impatiently. 'Hand it over.'

'Come and get it,' Hoffman said, one hand on the pad.

'Don't be under any illusions, my dear Judas, I will have no compunction about killing you.'

'And then who will send your message to Moscow?'

As he spoke he knew. Rachel. How could he have been so stupid?

Cross said: 'Pass it over very slowly, no sudden movements.'

Hoffman handed Cross the pad. What they didn't know was the new location of the second transmitter. But they didn't have to, did they? They could transmit from here; Rachel could do the job quite adequately. Call-sign, touch ... and, of course, they had details of the code from his first HQ.

Russian? No problem: they had the wispy-haired interpreter from the Embassy.

If only Rachel ... a controlled rage possessed him: he wasn't going to allow them to get away with it: they had to learn that he wasn't that gullible.

And he wasn't! He had one card left – the refinement of which they knew nothing, the Judas Code. But if the card wasn't played correctly it could destroy everything.

Cross said: 'So you've got the date.'

'Weren't you going to tell me?'

'Tell you, lover-boy? Why should I? You'd warn Uncle Joe and then what would happen? He'd rush his troops up to the

Border. Stalemate. The two warlords left evenly balanced ...
Don't you understand, we want them to destroy each other.'

'But I understood—'

'That we wanted to save the Bolsheviks? How can you have
been so naïve? I was scared at one time you'd rumble it. But
no, not you. You were too prick-happy. Rachel played her part
very well, didn't she?'

Superbly well, Hoffman thought. Surely Cross wouldn't risk
shooting him here.

Cross prodded the automatic towards him. 'Stand up and
turn round, hands behind your head.'

The scrape of the chair as he stood up synchronised with the
key turning in the lock of the door.

From the doorway Rachel, two loaves of bread under her
arm, shouted: 'No!'

Without taking his eyes off Hoffman, Cross snapped: 'Keep
away,' fingers tightening on the butt of the automatic.

'No,' she shouted again and threw herself at Cross. As he
staggered back she grabbed his wrist, pushing it down. Cross
thrust her aside as Hoffman came at him. The gun went off as
they grappled, the bullet smashing the window. Cross tore his
wrist from Rachel's hand and clubbed her on the head with the
gun.

As she fell Cross broke free from Hoffman and aimed the
automatic at his chest. From the floor Rachel hooked a foot
round one of his legs; as he staggered Hoffman hurled the transmitter at him. It hit him on the side of the head and he collapsed.

Hoffman knelt beside Rachel. Her face was terribly pale but
she said: 'I'll live ... you must get away.'

On the other side of the room Cross was trying to get to his
feet.

As he slammed the door behind him Hoffman heard Rachel
call out but he couldn't make out the words. He thought he
heard the word LOVE but he wasn't sure.

The lift was engaged.

And it wasn't until he was running down the stairs that he
remembered that his recent purchase, the Russian automatic,
was stuck in the belt of his trousers.

*

The man chosen by von Claus to kill Hoffman – then Cross
and Rachel Keyser – was an albino.

324

But although his eyes had a pinkish tinge to them his sight was perfect, the eyesight of a marskman.

Seated at the wheel of a BMW 326, he was taken by surprise at the speed of Hoffman's exit from the apartment block. He came out on a bicycle, would you believe, which he must have left in the hallway.

Shit! The albino had heard about this bike. Difficult to follow on foot, equally difficult by car in the narrow lanes of the old town. But here there shouldn't be any difficulty; especially if Hoffman decided to cycle down the Avenida da Liberdade with its broad lanes of traffic and island gardens. It was a mile long and if he couldn't pick him off in that distance he didn't deserve his job. From a shoulder-holster he took a Luger pistol.

He let in the clutch and took off after the black bicycle. A bicycle! Different.

The only drawbacks were the trams and the police on duty at the intersections. Hoffman didn't seem to pay much attention to either.

The BMW with the rakish bonnet and flaring mudguards was capable of 80 mph. As Hoffman rounded a tramcar picking up passengers, the albino put his foot down. But to his consternation Hoffman swerved to the left, ignoring a police-man's outstretched hand. Should he follow suit and risk a bullet in one of his tyres – or in the back of his head?

Swearing, the albino slowed down. The policeman waved him on, glaring at him as he lifted one foot off the clutch abruptly and rammed the other on the accelerator.

Through his pink eyes he saw Hoffman turn right. Soon he would be approaching the old quarter, the Alfama. If I don't get him before that I'll have to chase him on foot. *Himmel Sakrament!*

50 mph … 55 …60 …

Hoffman, bowed over the handlebars, was a hundred yards in front. 70 mph … The albino leaned out of the window and aimed the Luger.

Which was when he became aware that a green MG was about to overtake him.

*

That morning Stalin, back in his gloomy apartment in the Kremlin, received another warning about Hitler's intentions. It came from a Soviet spy in Switzerland named Alexander Foote, a British member of the Lucy Ring.

The punchline of the message read: 'General attack on territories occupied by Russians dawn of Sunday 22 June 3.15 a.m.'

So now they weren't just giving dates, they were giving times.

Stalin glanced at the wall-clock. It was midday, the time he had intended, against his better judgement, to put the Red Army on full alert even if such an action did provoke Hitler.

But since then he had received word from his son. Three words, to be precise. WILL DO DOVE. In other words Viktor was checking these rumours, surely nothing more, about June 22.

Stalin decided to give him another hour.

*

Hoffman, speeding down a hill behind a yellow tramcar, glanced behind him.

He saw a grey saloon. A very blond man with a gun in his hand was leaning from the window. He was just about to be overtaken by Cross in his MG.

Hoffman ducked. Nothing happened.

He glanced back again. The MG had drawn level with the grey car. It was lower than the saloon but, as Hoffman watched, its windscreen struck the arm of the blond man holding the gun.

Then Cross's MG was in between the saloon and his bicycle.

So now there were two assassins trying to kill him.

What chance did he stand on a bicycle? Unless he could plunge into an alleyway.

He noticed a narrow road to his left. He tried to turn and found that he couldn't. He wrenched the handlebars but nothing happened; he continued to speed straight ahead behind the tramcar with the two cars in pursuit.

He tried to turn the other way. Nothing. He peered down and realised that the wheels of the bicycle were trapped in the tram-lines.

He stood up and pedalled furiously, aware that he was presenting a better target. But he was gaining on the tram. Passengers stared at him curiously.

He glanced round again.

Cross was aiming his gun at him.

Hoffman was ten yards from the tram. He swung one leg over the saddle so that he was balanced on one pedal.

He heard the crack of the gunshot as he jumped. The cycle continued, riderless, along the tramline.

And he was running faster than he had ever imagined he could, the impetus of hitting the ground bowling his legs along.

He reached the running board of the tram as another shot cracked out. He grabbed the rail. It felt as though his arm was being pulled from its socket. Hands reached him and pulled him in and he shouted to the passengers: 'Duck, for God's sake, duck,' as another shot rang out.

He peered over the window of the platform. The driver of the grey saloon was trying to push the MG off the road. Just ahead of the two cars, still speeding along the tramline, was his bicycle.

Cross fired again.

The bullet shattered the window above him, ricocheted above the heads of the crouching passengers and hit the driver in the chest. As he slumped to one side the tramcar gathered momentum.

He saw the MG hit the bicycle and knock it to one side. The saloon crunched over it.

The tramcar gathered speed.

Another bullet shattered a window; Hoffman couldn't tell who had fired it. Passengers were screaming, the two cars, side by side, were gaining.

Hoffman lay on the floor of the driverless tram and peered round the side. The driver of the saloon was aiming his gun not at the tram but at Cross. He must have missed because the MG didn't waver.

The tramcar breasted a slight rise in the street and plunged down a steep hill, swaying wildly. Beside Hoffman a small boy was sucking a lollipop with evident enjoyment. His mother was screaming.

At the bottom of the hill, Hoffman remembered, stood a street market specialising in second-hand goods – clothes, electrical goods, cracked china, books …

As the tramcar left the rails and charged the stalls, Hoffman jumped. He hit his head on the ground and spun sideways.

Stunned, he saw the tramcar toss aside a couple of stalls like a charging bull and smash into a wall.

Where were the gunmen?

He crawled behind an upturned bookstall, listening to the cries of the wounded. He peered round a heap of books and saw the saloon and the MG abandoned a hundred yards away. Of Cross and the other assassin there was no sign.

Gripping his automatic in one hand, Hoffman wormed his way through the debris. When he reached the end of the stricken market he straightened up and ran.

Cross came at him from one side, the blond man from the other.

As he ran he aimed the gun at Cross and pulled the trigger. The gun jerked but Cross kept running.

He reached a small dusty square. He heard gunshots. People scattered until there were just the three of them, assassins converging on their quarry.

He fired again at Hoffman, then at the blond man.

He saw Cross stop and take careful aim, gun balanced on his forearm. He dived into the dust beside a mangy dog as Cross fired. On the other side of the square the albino screamed, reared up and fell to the ground, blood pumping from his chest.

*

Rachel managed to reach the telephone, blood seeping from the wound on her temple. She called the British Embassy and told the telephonist that she was injured.

Not that she really cared what happened to her. She had betrayed the one man she had ever loved and, provided he escaped, the plan to save the world from tyranny had failed.

She saw him before the horns of a bull ... she saw the passion on his face as he made love to her beneath the chandelier in her hotel bedroom ... she saw the realisation in his eyes that she had lied to him ...

She sat down and wept.

*

Gun in hand, Hoffman ran through the Alfama towards the ramparts of the castle. The crowds scattered before him. A policeman drew his gun but Hoffman dodged through a patio hung with laundry into another alley.

Behind him came Cross.

Hoffman ran past bars, shops, stalls, churches. Church bells chimed; the *fado* mourned lost ideals, trust.

He was staggering now but so was Cross. He put on a last spurt, reached the door of his new HQ, slid the key in the lock and fell into the cool darkness.

Behind him he could hear laboured breathing.

He switched on the lights and ran down the stone steps into the cellar, then backed into the mouth of the tunnel aiming the gun at the head of the steps.

Cross stood there, swaying. 'Josef,' he shouted, 'you've got to listen. You don't understand.'

'Oh, but I do,' Hoffman said, and shot him in the head.

*

From beneath the flagstone he took the transmitter. He was through to Moscow within a couple of minutes. With trembling fingers he sent his message:

CONFIRM GERMANS DO PLAN TO ATTACK ON TWENTY-SECOND STOP REPEAT DO PLAN TO ATTACK ... DO PLAN TO ATTACK.

Decoding

'But I don't understand,' I protested to Judas. 'You warned Stalin that Hitler *was* going to attack but he still didn't take any notice.'

As the world knows, the Germans had attacked on June 22; four months later they had been poised to take Moscow; then they had encountered the Soviet winter, the indomitable will of Mother Russia and her inexhaustible supplies of manpower. Germans had continued to fight Russians for another three and a half years ...

Josef Hoffman, or Viktor Golovin or whatever he called himself these days, gave a small conspiratorial smile. 'But you don't understand the Judas Code.' He had guarded the secret for more than forty years and was reluctant to part with it.

Three days had elapsed since we met in Madame Tussaud's. We were sitting on a bench beneath the chestnut trees in the Broad Walk of Regent's Park. Hoffman was talking into a microphone plugged into a small tape-recorder as he had talked for hour after riveting hour. I hadn't been home since that first meeting, staying instead in a small hotel in Baker Street.

The air smelled of the shower that had just spent itself and spring blossom; lovers strolled past arm in arm; children played on the grass.

I waited but the slim, contented-looking man in his mid-sixties, fair hair only just beginning to turn grey, wasn't going to put me out of my agony. Not yet anyway.

I approached from another direction: the story had made me devious. 'So what happened in Lisbon after you sent the message?'

'Oh, I cleared out: I was tired of being used as a target.' The sun was warming up; he unbuttoned his raincoat; beneath it he wore a Harris tweed sports jacket and sharply-creased grey flannels. 'I assumed yet another identity. The one I use now.' He didn't elaborate.

'There must have been an almighty hue and cry.'

'There was. But in Lisbon in those days almost anything could be covered up. Some maniac had loosed off a gun at a

333

tram – miraculously no one was badly hurt in the crash – and he was caught in the Alfama after a chase. Cross recovered from the bullet wound' – a note of regret there? – 'and came back to England. He's still very much alive.'

'And Rachel Keyser?'

He didn't reply to that one. Instead he said: 'But once I had sent the message anything that happened in Lisbon was of trivial importance.'

Very well. 'So what about the other protagonists?'

Hoffman named them one by one, according each a terse obituary.

Stalin. Died at Kuntsevo on March 5, 1953, following a cerebral haemorrhage.

'Did you ever see him again?'

Hoffman seemed surprised. 'Good God, no. He would have had me hanged, drawn and quartered.' The surprise brought out a few mid-European accents in his almost perfect English.

'Did he ever realise what had happened?' I asked hopefully.

But Hoffman wasn't to be drawn.

Hitler. Committed suicide with Eva Braun in the *Führenbunker* beneath the ruins of Berlin on April 30, 1945.

Hoffman stared into the distance, into time. 'The British were quite right, of course. The Germans were routed and the Russians lost so many lives that they couldn't sweep through the rest of Europe as they would have done if they had been stronger.'

There was something about his intonation that alerted me to an unintentional clue: he sounded as though he had known about the British conspiracy *before* it was carried out.

I asked him. His reply was his most unsatisfactory so far. 'Not really.' What was I supposed to make of that?

His voice became suddenly harsh. 'The Russians lost twenty million lives, Mr. Lamont. Can you imagine what it's been like to live all these years with the knowledge that you were responsible for all those deaths?'

Certainly the magnitude of such guilt was beyond comprehension if he *had* been responsible. But he had warned Stalin that Hitler *was* going to attack ...

Canaris. Hanged, naked, on April 9, 1945, for alleged complicity in the abortive plot in July 1944 to assassinate Hitler with a bomb.

Sinclair. Died of natural causes on May 18, 1960. After the war he had opened a home for underprivileged children. He died, said Hoffman, with a photograph of his son, Robin, at his bedside.

And finally:

Churchill. Died on January 24, 1965, aged ninety, from a stroke after lying in a coma for fourteen days.

'Did he suffer the same guilt as you?' I asked.

Hoffman shook his head firmly. 'Churchill was convinced that he had acted for the good of humanity. And he had, hadn't he?' gesturing around the placid park. 'You and I wouldn't be sitting here free to move and think and do as we please if it hadn't been for his Grand Deception. All he did was match against each other two massive armies intent upon aggrandisement. That's terrible enough to contemplate. Can you imagine what would have happened if they had combined? If Stalin had been prepared to repel a German attack? If, realising this, Hitler had done a deal? Britain today could well have been a colony of Germany or Russia or both ... In any case I didn't say I suffered guilt. Responsibility is a different quality altogether.'

He seemed to lose some of his purpose; he had, after all, been talking for something like twenty-four hours. I glanced at him: he was staring down the Broad Walk at a figure approaching about a hundred yards away.

'Did Churchill authorise you to tell the full story?'

'Written authorisation. I have it here.' He took a yellowing envelope from his pocket and handed it to me. 'I got it from the solicitors this morning. You can open it if you like.'

Inside was a brief letter written on faded notepaper bearing the address 28, Hyde Park Gate and signed by Churchill. It stated that he gave Josef Hoffman 'or Viktor Golovin or whatever identity he chooses to adopt' permission to publish the full story relating to the German invasion of Russia not less than forty years after June 22, 1941.

Hoffman told me to keep the letter – 'you may need it.'

'Why 1945?' I asked, glancing at the date on the letter.

'Because he had just lost the election. He expected to but just the same he felt a sense of betrayal. He felt that one day, when he was dead and passions were less likely to be aroused by such revelations, those who had voted against him should know that his achievements were far greater than they had ever dreamed they were.'

335

'What kept you?' I asked. 'It's 1983 now.'

'I didn't really know if the truth should ever be told even though Churchill wanted it to be. Then you inserted that advertisement in *The Times* ... It was as though Churchill was nudging me. Reminding me that I was reneging on a promise.'

I was debating how to ask him again about Rachel Keyser – how could I write the story without knowing what had happened to her? – when the figure Hoffman had been gazing at stopped in front of us.

'Rachel,' he said to the woman smiling down at him, 'I want you to meet Mr Lamont. Mr. Lamont, my wife.'

She was an elegant woman dressed in grey with a healthy complexion and silver hair who had grown gracefully into her sixties. As I stood up I peeled back the years and there she lay wounded in her apartment in Lisbon, raven-haired and voluptuous, calling out to the man she thought she had lost. And the one word he had thought he heard was LOVE and that's what it must have been.

Hoffman switched off the recorder, disconnected the microphone and put them both in a black case. Then he, too, stood up. 'Let's take a stroll,' he said and she tucked her arm in his.

'So Josef has told you everything?' she asked as we passed a young couple, absorbed with each other, with many years ahead of them.

'Not quite all.'

'Ah, the Judas Code. I'm not at all sure that he will. He's had it locked away for a long time.'

But he did.

When he had finished he stopped walking. He handed me the case containing the tape-recorder and shook my hand. 'And that's the end. Tell it well.'

'But there might be a few more queries ... The young man in the zoo, your son?'

Rachel Keyser smiled a mother's smile. 'He works for the United Nations.'

'And Palestine,' I said desperately. 'Did you ever go there?'

'For a while,' her husband said. 'Happy years. And now we really must go. If you have any more problems you will have to solve them yourself. You don't know our present name and you never will. We are now returning to obscurity.'

'And happiness,' said Rachel Keyser, kissing him on the cheek.

Another shower had blown up and I was glad because I wasn't sure whether there were tears on my cheeks.

Together, they walked across the grass past the children and the young people and the parents and the grandparents whom they had saved from oppression.

*

When I got back to my flat I found Chambers, the man who had warned me not to pursue Judas, sitting in my armchair. He reminded me once again of a City businessman with the reservation that City businessmen don't usually aim pistols at your head.

'Mr Cross,' I said, 'you might as well put that thing away – there are two policemen waiting outside,' I lied.

He considered this. 'Cross ... So you didn't heed my warning?'

'On the contrary, it inspired me.'

'How very stupid of you. I don't believe there are two policemen outside and now I have no alternative but to kill you. This gun,' he said conversationally, 'is quite capable of blowing your head off.'

'Whereas Hoffman's bullet only grazed your cheek ...'

His free hand went to the scar. 'You've seen Hoffman?'

'He sends his regards. I presume you're protecting the good name of Winston Churchill?'

I sat down opposite him and stared into the barrel of the gun; it was larger than the Browning he had previously wielded, a Magnum, quite capable of blowing my head off.

'How very perceptive of you.' His voice grew harsher. 'He was the greatest Englishman who has ever lived. The greatest man the world has ever known ...'

'And you're determined to stop anyone telling the truth about his part in Barbarossa?'

'Correct, even if it means killing them. Why should the public be given a chance to misunderstand him, revile him ...'

'I shall write it so that they don't, so that they understand the contribution he made to humanity ...'

'Except that you won't be writing the book,' finger tightening on the trigger of the Magnum.

'Someone will. The tape on which Hoffman recorded the story is in a safe deposit box.' That at least was the truth – it was at Harrods.

337

That stopped him, but the madness didn't leave his face. 'Give me the key.'

'I haven't got it with me.' Again the truth – I had put it in a registered letter and posted it to myself. While he considered this I followed up with: 'But I do have a letter.'

'Letter?' He frowned. 'Who from?'

'Winston Churchill,' I said.

That sank home. 'Are you crazy?'

'Supposing I were to tell you that Churchill wanted the book written?'

'Then I would say you were certifiable.'

'The letter's in the inside pocket of my jacket.'

'That, if I may say so, is pretty corny. What sort of gun have you got in there? A Derringer?'

'Come and find out.'

'No,' he said, 'I have a better idea. Stand up and take your jacket off and throw it on the floor in front of me. Not in my face, that way I blow your head off and put a hole through that nice jacket as well.'

I stood up and, very slowly, removed the jacket of my blue suit. I threw it on the floor, and, still keeping the gun levelled at my head, he withdrew the envelope from the inside pocket. I sat down.

He read the letter. I watched his eyes. He read it again. And again.

When he looked up his face was washed of emotion. He looked tired and ashen-faced, as though he needed some sun on the beach at Estoril.

He said what I had expected him to say: 'How do I know this isn't a forgery?'

'You don't. You'll just have to believe me until you get the signature checked by a handwriting expert.'

He considered this. He looked much older than he had a few minutes earlier.

Finally he said: 'Very well, I'll take your word for it – for the time being,' and put the gun back into the shoulder-holster beneath his jacket.

I slumped back in my chair. Then I asked him: 'Would you like a drink?' He didn't reply but I poured him a large Scotch and soda just the same, and an even larger one for myself.

When he had drunk the whisky he said: 'You know, one thing has always puzzled me. If Hoffman warned Stalin that

338

Hitler was going to attack why didn't Stalin do anything about it?'

'The Judas Code, of course.'

'I never fully understood what that was. I suppose Hoffman was smarter than I imagined,' he admitted. 'Did he tell you?'

It was too good to be true. 'No,' I said and grinned at him because now he would never know and the question would haunt him to his grave.

*

The Judas Code, Hoffman had told me as he and his wife walked with me in Regent's Park, was really invented by a Mafia gangster named Frank Costello. Realising that all his mail was scrutinised by the FBI he used the very simplest of codes: he told all his confidants that they were to infer the opposite of what he wrote.

If he wrote that he would *not* be dining at a particular restaurant on Lexington Avenue in New York at eight p.m. he meant that he would be there all right. The FBI never cracked this crudest of codes, possibly because it was too obvious.

Hoffman had heard about the ploy in Lisbon from an Austrian refugee who had once laundered Mafia money. He had suggested it to Stalin as their ultimate safeguard to be applied only to Barbarossa; Stalin had been delighted with the idea.

For CONFIRM GERMANS *DO* PLAN TO ATTACK ON TWENTY-SECOND read CONFIRM GERMANS DO *NOT* PLAN etcetera.

'One last question,' I had said to Hoffman.

'Why in my own way did I go along with the British? Why, in other words, did I send the affirmative message?'

I nodded. It was the crux of the whole story.

'It's very simple: I went to Poland. I saw the horrors perpetrated by the Germans. Then I went to Katyn. It was then that I realised that my own people were capable of committing atrocities just as terrible as those perpetrated by the Germans.'

'And you knew all along what Cross and Rachel ... your wife ... were planning to do?'

Hoffman said that he only suspected that he was going to be double-crossed; that he had always hoped Rachel would tell him the truth. But whatever they intended to do was irrelevant.

'After Katyn I had decided to mislead Stalin. As it happened, Churchill and myself chanced on the same idea.'

'A horrendous decision for a man of peace to make ...'

'But I wasn't a man of peace any more. War changes everyone. I don't know whether or not you find your true character. But I do know this: you learn to understand yourself.' He paused. 'Perhaps, Mr. Lamont, you are too tactful to ask why I married the woman who had betrayed me?'

I had been leaving the question to last. 'Why?'

Hoffman said: 'Because I understood her. War had done that for me. I understood that, even though she loved me, what she had to do was more important. And, of course, in the end we were both trying to achieve the same ends.'

'I wonder what happened to those children in Berlin,' his wife said. 'It was their eyes. Every time I wanted to confide in Josef I saw them looking at me. Pleading.'

'And do you know why I called it the Judas Code?' He answered his question himself. 'Because it was the ultimate act of betrayal, that's why.'

*

On the landing outside my flat Cross and I stood waiting for the ancient lift to haul itself up from the ground floor.

As it made its laborious approach Cross said: 'You know something? I think you do know the secret of the Judas Code.'

I smiled in a self-satified way.

'I said just now,' Cross went on, 'that I never *fully* understood it. But I have my theories. That Hoffman and Stalin agreed that the opposite of what Hoffman transmitted would be the truth. How does that strike you?'

I tried to maintain the smile as the lift shuddered to a halt. Cross opened the doors and stepped in. 'You've enjoyed your little triumph,' he said. 'Now it's my turn.'

I could feel my smile fading.

'Just supposing,' he said, 'that Hoffman still employs the Judas Code. Just suppose that the opposite of what he's been telling you for the past three days is the truth. In other words that it's a pack of lies.'

He pushed the ground-floor button and disappeared from sight.